Greg Barron has qualifications in education and science, and has studied terrorism at Scotland's prestigious St Andrew's University. He has lived in both North America and Australia, and has travelled widely, combining his interests in politics and current events with a passion for new horizons. His favourite places include the African savannah, the Canadian Rockies and Australia's Top End. Along with abseiling, offshore boating, skindiving and canoeing, his greatest adventure was a three-hundred-kilometre trek through the wild East Alligator region of Arnhem Land.

Greg lives on the North Coast of New South Wales with his wife and two sons. *Savage Tide* is his second novel. For more information about the author, visit gregbarron.com

 GregBarronAuthor

 @gregorybarron

See more at
gregbarron.com

Also by Greg Barron
Rotten Gods

GREG BARRON

SAVAGE TIDE

HarperCollins*Publishers*

HarperCollins*Publishers*

First published in Australia in 2013
by HarperCollins*Publishers* Australia Pty Limited
ABN 36 009 913 517
harpercollins.com.au

Copyright © Greg Barron 2013

The right of Greg Barron to be identified as the author of this work
has been asserted by him in accordance with the *Copyright Amendment
(Moral Rights) Act 2000*.

HarperCollins*Publishers*
Level 13, 201 Elizabeth Street, Sydney NSW 2000, Australia
31 View Road, Glenfield, Auckland 0627, New Zealand
A 53, Sector 57, Noida, UP, India
77–85 Fulham Palace Road, London W6 8JB, United Kingdom
2 Bloor Street East, 20th floor, Toronto, Ontario M4W 1A8, Canada
10 East 53rd Street, New York, NY 10022, USA

National Library of Australia Cataloguing-in-Publication data:

Barron, Greg.
  Savage Tide.
  978 0 7322 9436 6 (pbk.)
  978 0 7304 9862 9 (ebook)
A823.3

Cover design by Matt Stanton, HarperCollins Design Studio
Cover images: Figure by Jon Spaihts; all other images by shutterstock.com
Author image by Cliff Kent
All maps by Laurie Whiddon
Typeset in 11/15 ITC Garamond Std by Kirby Jones

for Catriona

PROLOGUE

Istikaan found the technician hanging from a beam; face blue, tongue distended, and eyes misted with dried blood from burst capillaries.

On the concrete floor nearby sat a pair of government-issue patent leather shoes, laces untied, and a folded square of notepaper. On the top fold was written the salutation *To the Living from the Dead* in beautifully scripted Arabic. Words, it seemed, from beyond the grave. Istikaan slipped the note into his pocket, promising himself that he would read it later.

Later, however, there was no time. While a squad of engineers laid their charges at the bunker entrance, unravelling a coil of wire far out over the bare desert, Istikaan walked the rubber mats of the facility for the last time. Sealed the last seals. Locked the last doors. The unread note had upset his equilibrium, already strained at being forced to abandon his work.

The captain waited for him outside, a cigarette pinched between lips as pale as scar tissue. Blood, Istikaan saw, had splattered just below the breast pocket of his blue serge jacket — the uniform of Amn al-Khas — the Special Programs Unit of the Mukhabarat, the secret police.

From deep underground rose the clamour of the hundreds they had left in the holding cells to die. Istikaan could picture them clawing at the walls with their nails like animals. Women's shrieks, crying children, and the angry, helpless shouts of men.

Animals indeed, thought Istikaan, his lip curled in disgust. *They are nothings. Sub-humans. Kurds, criminals and marsh people.*

Finally, flanked by his most senior assistants, and escorted by the captain of Amn al-Khas, Istikaan boarded a steel-grey Polish-built Mi-2 chopper. The side doors closed behind him, and he settled into the rear seat. The Mi-2 rose five hundred gut-wrenching feet in the air, then hovered while the engineers on the ground did their work.

The explosion was designed not to destroy, but to throw earth and stone over the entrance. The blast showed through the canopy as a puff of dust against the stony desert hillside.

The chopper gathered speed, taking Istikaan back towards the capital.

A terrible secret lay hidden. War came and went, leaving the country a wasteland, a million refugees on the march. Then a decade of internecine warfare. Yet it was never forgotten. Not by those who knew.

The seeds of murder lay unsown beneath the earth.

BOOK ONE

'I knew that its police force was searching for psychopathic killers and sadistic serial murderers, not in order to arrest them but to employ them. I knew that its vast patrimony of oil wealth, far from being "nationalized," had been privatized for the use of one family, and was being squandered on hideous ostentation at home and militarism abroad.

'I had seen with my own eyes the evidence of a serious breach of the Genocide Convention on Iraqi soil, and I had also seen with my own eyes the evidence that it had been carried out in part with the use of weapons of mass destruction. I was, if you like, the prisoner of this knowledge. I certainly did not have the option of un-knowing it.'

Christopher Hitchens, *Hitch-22: A Memoir*

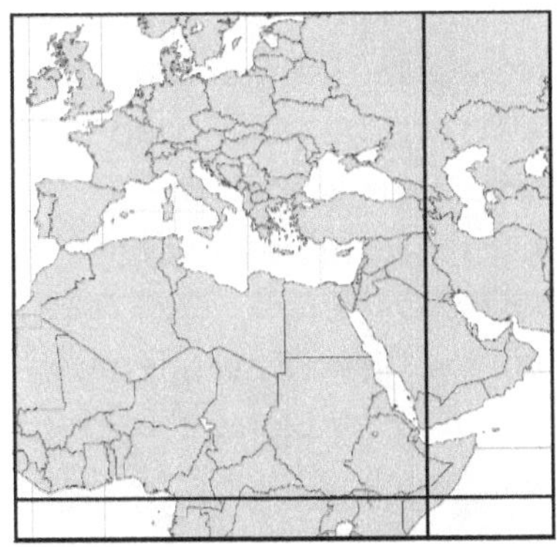

1 SOMALIA

Chakula Refugee Camp

Fourteen kilometres from the white tents and makeshift tukuls of the camp, just past the rutted, muddy crossing place they call *buundo*, Khadija Onyango emerges from the yellow school bus into the open air, slow with her pregnancy and a languor brought on by the warmth of the day. Forty-seven children aged from five years to twelve mill around the bus, their teachers nagging and haranguing them into lines.

The sky is clear and razor sharp. The broad Jubba River winds through desiccated plains and stone ridges. The scent of mud and hippopotamus dung mingles with that of fragrant yellow and white iris flowers, scattered on the high ground among the dry stubble.

This is a perfect day, Khadija thinks, hugging her shoulders in anticipation, for dragonflies, birds, and children singing on the bus. A day for holding hands, childish secrets, and first kisses. A day to forget the realities of the camp, if just for a few hours.

While the children dance and chase, the driver distributes the provisions that had been carefully hoarded for the picnic. Teachers direct the children into a rough line and set off. Khadija follows, carrying a box of oranges over her swollen belly. Workers from the camp who have elected to join the excursion walk nearby, one American, one French, and it is good to hear their banter — doctors from Médecins Sans Frontières.

Looking ahead at the laughing children, Khadija lifts a fold of her yellow kikoi. Dabs first at one eye, then at the other. Soon she will be leaving them. This afternoon she will catch the World Food Program delivery plane, the Antonov 32, to Nairobi, Kenya for the last four weeks of her pregnancy. Travelling such a distance is a frightening thought, but there are complications to her pregnancy. A Type 1 diabetic, she is now showing signs of pre-eclampsia.

Matthew Doni, another helper at the school, catches up to her on the beaten earth of the track, clicks his tongue, and takes the oranges from her hands. He is a big Tanzanian, broad across the shoulders. A brass disc hangs from a chain around his neck, nestling just below the muscular notch of his collarbone.

'I can manage it,' Khadija says, hands flying to her hips, mock-offended. 'I'm pregnant, not crippled.'

'I said nothing.' Matthew smiles at her, his voice deep and honey-sweet to her ears. 'But why should you carry so much when I have so little?'

The gentle Tanzanian is in love with her, she knows that. Seems not to care that he isn't the child's father. Yet she does not love him. When Anyap, her husband, was killed in inter-clan fighting in the camp, she vowed never to love again. Now she is not so sure — but she knows that Matthew is not the one.

Khadija smiles at how the children leave their lines and dance around the adults, unable to control their excitement as they move over a crest and towards the rounded glade, grassy and fertile alongside the dense scrub that hides the river.

Originally Khadija came to Chakula Camp with Anyap after gunmen from the Islamist group al-Muwahhidun had terrorised the farming district where they scraped together a living. After Anyap's death she was able to get a job helping at one of the

UNICEF-run schools. Khadija can read and write, in English and Somali. These skills are prized by the foreign aid workers running the schools.

Finally reaching the glade, with glimpses of the brown flowing river through the crouton bush and ficus trees, Khadija watches Matthew throw the picnic blankets, sunshine slanting through from the trees. She laughs, hands crossed over her middle, aware that this is one of those moments that she would like to freeze and keep in her heart. Hibo, one of the boys, exhorts her to sit on the folding chair he carried for her from the bus.

'I love you, Miss Khadija,' he says, bringing her a sandwich and packaged fruit juice, white teeth showing as he smiles.

'I love you too, Mister Hibo.'

'If Farsameeye Matthew does not marry you,' he declares, 'then I will.'

Khadija smiles and pats her belly. 'First I have to go and have my baby.'

Hibo's forehead creases with worry. 'Why must you go?'

Khadija stares, trying not to let him see that she, too, is afraid. The outside world is a complicated and threatening place. In Somalia women give birth in their own homes, with the local midwife brewing her potions and drawing new life with practised hands. There is no mystery to it. 'Because the shisheeye in Nairobi,' she says at last, 'have engaged for me a favoured dhaliye — a midwife who is very skilled.'

Hibo appears to take this information in. 'You have your baby, Miss Khadija, then bring him back here. I will be a father to him. I will teach him everything I know. I will ...'

The boy is still talking when one of the little ones comes to sit on Khadija's lap. The young woman runs one hand through wiry hair, then kisses the little girl's scalp, loving the firesmoke smell of her.

'How are you, my precious one?'

'Well, thank you, Miss Khadija.'

'Have you had something to eat?'

'Yes, Miss Khadija.' Her head tilts back and eyes as dark as eclipsed moons stare up at her. 'You will not stay away for a long time, will you?'

'No, child, I won't.'

'You will not forget us?'

'How could I forget you? Now, hop off and Farsameeye Matthew will give you an orange.'

The promise of fruit is enough, and the child slips off Khadija's knee to the ground, joining the line of clamouring kids. Khadija watches the desperate pace at which they eat, sucking the fruit dry, chewing the pith, dropping the peels on the ground. Their bodies are desperate for nutrition; calories. She thinks of the new life inside her. Wonders how she will feed and clothe a child.

Looking up at the sky, she sees a lone cloud, puffy with changing animal shapes, and highlights of white and cream. No hope of moisture in it, not yet, still a month from the short rains, but it is beautiful, nonetheless, and Khadija watches it for a moment before turning her attention back to the child on her lap and the others scattered across the river glade.

Matthew has brought a football, and the older children take charge, marking out a field and goals with sticks dragged in the dirt.

Hibo is striker for the knotted-shirt team, long legged and athletic with his T-shirt tied at the front. 'Miss Khadija,' he shouts. 'I will score a goal for you.'

The cloud passes in front of the sun. Khadija clasps her hands under her chin, fingers interlocking as if about to say a prayer. 'Good boy. I will be watching.'

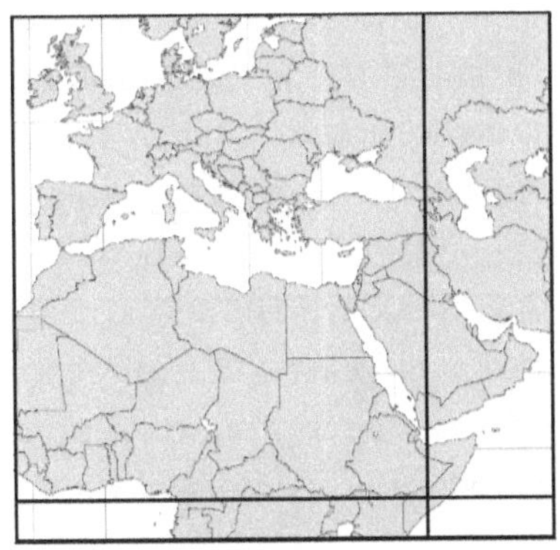

2 SOMALIA

Chakula Refugee Camp

Pulling the brim of her cap lower over her eyes, Marika Hartmann turns into the morning sun, weapon slung over her right shoulder, moving briskly towards the cluster of transportable buildings that make up the garrison admin centre.

The message she had just received was flagged as urgent, sent by the young Kenyan Defence Force officer assigned as her aide. There is a hint of worry in the crease of her eyes.

Chakula is the third major refugee camp Marika Hartmann has visited in five weeks. The last was the even larger, and much older, Dadaab. Before that, the new Setareh camp on the Iran–Iraq border, where millions of Iranians fled, first from coastal flooding, then war with Israel and the West.

Improving procedures for the garrison here has proved difficult but rewarding. They are good soldiers, here under the banner of AMISOM — the African Union's ongoing mission in Somalia, drawn mainly from Kenya, Burundi and Uganda. Marika's role includes site assessments, training courses and active patrols in the camp itself.

A veteran of the Dubai hostage crisis of a year earlier, and with five years' service as a field agent at Britain's DRFS — Directorate of Resource and Future Security — Marika was a natural choice for the program. She has always been most comfortable in khaki, and the company of hardened soldiers suits her just fine.

The administration area occupies a low, central hill, with views over the camp for kilometres in either direction. A high cyclone fence topped with razor wire surrounds it on all sides. The path winds up through a garden, maintained by a dozen busy camp dwellers, towards the door of the barracks. Two guards at the doorway recline on white plastic chairs, AK47s resting on their laps, swiping away flies, playing with old Nokia phones. They scarcely look up as she walks through.

Kifimbo meets her in the corridor, wringing his hands; highly agitated. He is slender but wiry, with heavy brows and deep-set eyes. He wears no watch or jewellery apart from a broad copper ring with embossed designs traced with verdigris.

'Tajiri,' he says, using the Swahili word for *boss*, 'we've had a report of armed men moving down the river bank near the village of Kafee.'

Marika feels a chill, knowing that a busload of kids and aid workers had set off for a picnic in the area that morning. 'Where?'

'Come in, come in. I'll show you on the map.'

She walks behind him into the briefing room. Louvred windows, lino tiles and steel-framed furniture. Empty Pepsi cans and stale cigarette smoke. Rifles lean against walls. Uniformed men slouch in chairs, drinking coffee from polystyrene cups.

The wall has two large-scale maps. One of the region: the Lower Juba district of Southern Somalia. The other is of Chakula Camp. Fifty square kilometres. Six hundred thousand people.

Kifimbo jabs a forefinger at a bend of the Jubba River on the district map. 'The gunmen were seen here.'

'And where are the children?'

He looks at her uneasily, then slides the finger down two grid squares along the river. Two kilometres. 'Here.'

Marika becomes intensely aware of her own heartbeat, her lips suddenly dry. 'Mobilise the duty Ranger platoon. We'll assemble at the helipad in five minutes in full battle rig.'

Kifimbo says something, but she doesn't hear, already out the door and running towards the barracks.

While the children play, Matthew unfolds another chair next to Khadija. They watch the game together. Cheering, talking and arguing over the rules and their interpretation.

Matthew says, 'I have been thinking about your … situation.'

Smiling, Khadija says, 'Thank you, but please don't worry. You know I'll be fine.'

'Yes, but you will return here with a child.'

'That's true.'

Hibo dances in front of the midfielders. He has real talent, Khadija realises, and if he were in London or Madrid, instead of Somalia, the talent scouts might have already knocked on the door to speak to his parents. Watching him dribble the ball through two defenders like a conjuror, she wonders how she could help get him somewhere where these skills might change his life …

Matthew is still talking. 'Your baby will need a father.'

Khadija does not turn now, aware of where he is heading. She has been expecting and dreading this.

'I don't want to pressure you. It must be your decision alone,' he goes on, so nervous that Khadija feels a surge of tenderness for him, a desire to spare him further embarrassment.

Hibo passes to Sameh, hustles forward then accepts a return pass, feet skidding on the earth, raising a little puff of dust. He stands poised for the goal attempt. Khadija feels herself tense. Hibo balances his weight on his left foot, using his right to jab at the ball.

Just as he does so, movement in the riverside foliage catches Khadija's eye. At first she thinks it must be a couple of straying children, but then she sees the headgear, the para-military clothing. Most of all she sees the guns.

The first shot sounds like a thunderclap followed by a wailing demon. A shout of fear and warning comes to her lips, blending with the storm of gunfire that follows.

Marika clicks the webbing belt into place around her waist as the Blackhawk rocks, sweeping over the camp. From the chopper she can see people squatting around tukul shelters, cooking on dung-and-charcoal fires, staring up as they pass overhead. She checks the load on the Heckler & Koch UMP, dropping the black curved magazine, heavy with 9mm rounds. Slams it back home, the mingled scents of gun oil and avgas filling her senses.

The growing Almohad organisation roams outside the accepted moral sphere of any functioning society. She has seen a translation of one of their signs posted in a village square. The playing of secular music or dancing — banned. Alcohol — banned. The playing or watching of football — banned. Accepting foreign aid — banned. Like the Taliban, who once shot a schoolgirl who criticised Islamists on her blog, who have murdered people for singing and dancing, these men have guns and will use them on those who do not obey.

'How far out are we?' she shouts to the pilot.

'Ten minutes if we can get under this breeze.'

Marika swears under her breath. *Too long.*

This is 4GW — fourth-generation warfare. Asymmetrical chaos. Where nothing is simple. No easy gains.

The Blackhawk has threadbare upholstery that scarcely covers the metal frame underneath. There are rattles that begin somewhere above, ending aft of the rear seats. This is one of a number of machines supplied by the US in a $30 million deal that involved both Djibouti and Kenya some years earlier.

The Blackhawks have been used hard in Kenya's border skirmishes and incursions. Each carries XM-214 Microguns on either side, and ten men with AK47s, all members of the elite Kenyan Ranger strike force. Marika has come to know these men. They are well trained, and share an easy camaraderie. All have that inner confidence common to Special Forces troops all over the world.

Marika hands her weapon to the man next to her, then slips her arms through the Kevlar vest, fastening the velcro straps around her abdomen. She takes her gun back and sits up higher, feeling that raised awareness, the adrenalin buzz of impending action. More than that — fear of what might happen to the weak, to those she is supposed to be helping to protect.

Now she reaches for her CVCID unit, nicknamed 'Sid', one of the most popular and indispensable pieces of kit in a field agent's grab bag, powered by the global TACSAT6 network. Modelled on a popular civilian smartphone, it handles dozens of tasks, from digital scanning to internet access, at the same time rendering both radio comms and the old SP-GPS 'Spugger' location equipment obsolete. Most field agents manage to lose one or two a year, but the units are accessible only by fingerprint recognition and thus pose no security risk. The field agent is then issued with a new machine, and since data is not stored on the device itself, but in the cloud at the DRFS servers, they are up and running immediately.

The unit in hand, she makes a call to the garrison at Kismaayo. Afterwards, she leans into the cockpit, addressing the pilot, 'There's a patrol in the area. We've got ground troops on the way.'

Please God let one of us be fast enough to stop the bastards.

Khadija, still in her folding chair, picnic food spread on her lap, sees the translucent burst of gunsmoke from one rifle after another, accompanied by the firecracker pop of their discharge. Killers advancing in ragged ranks from the forest, spitting fire and death as they come.

Hibo completes his kick for goal just as automatic gunfire rakes across the glade. Khadija screams out a warning. More gunmen emerge. Hibo's ball arcs through the air and into the net. He raises his arms and shouts in triumph, turning to look at Khadija, seeking her praise just as the first 7.62mm rounds tear into his neck and chest and throw him like a rag doll to the earth.

Other children turn to run, and Khadija staggers to her feet, heedless of the danger, calling to them, bullets stitching death like sewing-machine needles. She spreads her arms like a shield as if somehow she might stop that deadly fusillade.

Matthew takes a shot in the head that fells him like an axe to a tree. Khadija is knocked off her feet as he falls, pinning her so she sees only the dying body of the man who just proposed marriage to her, and the legs of the gunmen as they walk this way, still firing, still killing on that stretch of ground where a few moments ago children had been laughing, playing football.

A pair of booted feet pause in front of her. Now, for the first time, Khadija is afraid for herself.

The chopper settles towards the earth, the colours of the river glade enhanced through the lenses of Marika's sunglasses. Dust and rubbish blows like airborne flotsam against acacia trees and thorn bushes in the downwash of the rotors.

The craft throws up a gritty shroud as the skids touch the earth. Marika unclicks her safety belt and half-stands, feeling the blast of heat as she hits the ground, knees flexing against the impact. The others follow, crouched over, running through the dust in their camo fatigues.

Marika sees the first bodies. Dead children spread like litter. Draped like dirty laundry, their bodies lying alone or overlapping. Most have been shot multiple times in the body, some ravaged by physical damage, others seemingly unmarked. Spent cartridge cases strewn on the ground, mingled with blood and orange peels.

Over the years Marika has given much thought to mortality. Seen its most violent forms too many times not to. Sometimes, she knows, you pass too close. Feel death tugging at your sleeves, its shadow deepening. Times like this she feels herself looking into the void, where all the veneers that keep the darkness at bay are stripped away.

There are weapons to fight the pull of death, Marika knows. She stands for a moment in that killing field, eyes closed. Sees the pink blood-glow of light through her eyelids, until that also fades, and images pass before her in a parade of light and feeling.

Years ago Marika learned to collect beauty. Special moments and places. She saves them up, knowing they are the only true defence. Uses them when the time comes to stave off the dark.

A Kenyan voice, strained with panic and anguish, breaks the spell. The men are lost also. They need someone to take charge.

Her eyes snap open. 'Jonni and Kato, take up position on the perimeter. Abasi and I will look for wounded. Hurry.'

They find one, then another. A toddler miraculously spared. A twelve-year-old shot in the abdomen; dazed, unable to understand why blood spills through his fingers like wine. Each is a small victory, a single blessed moment in the overall horror.

Soon a company-strength unit of AMISOM troops arrives, then Kifimbo with three Humvees loaded down with soldiers from the camp garrison, escorting a contingent of medics. Behind come civilians, on motorbikes and in trucks, and then on donkeys.

Marika takes Kifimbo by the sleeve. 'Why did you bring the camp people here? This is a battle zone. How do we know there won't be another attack?'

'I'm sorry, Tajiri, but these are mothers who have lost children. Can you deny them?'

Marika turns back to look at the faces of men and women trying to take in the enormity of this tragedy. Mothers weeping, brothers cradling brothers. Then she looks at Kifimbo, the depth of sadness in his eyes.

'OK. Sorry,' she says, and moves her hand to his shoulder, squeezes it.

There is a roar in the sky. A flight of four Kenyan Air Force Northrop F-5s streak over at low level, shaking the earth. Angry yet impotent. Marika waits until the noise subsides, then says softly to Kifimbo, 'We can't let them get away with this. Time to hunt them down.'

The AMISOM column is a comforting sight. The famed Sledgehammer squad that liberated Kismaayo from al-Shabaab back in 2012. They feinted on land, launching Africa's first large-scale amphibious assault, overpowering the city in the early hours of the morning with few civilian casualties, earning themselves respect throughout the armed forces of the world. Colonel Sedegali, their commander, is a man of few words, with bright, intelligent eyes. 'Load up, load up. Hurry,' he shouts, his men scurrying to the vehicles.

Marika hefts and cocks her UMP, the rows of 9mm cartridges in the box magazine glinting gold through the gap.

Men run for the vehicles, piling on, clipping in ammunition belts and geeing each other up in staccato sentences. Marika joins Sedegali atop the second Humvee, taking a firm grip on a grab bar just as the driver drops the clutch and the vehicle leaps forward.

'Go!' Sedegali calls. 'Your mothers will cry in shame if you do not spill blood for this crime today.'

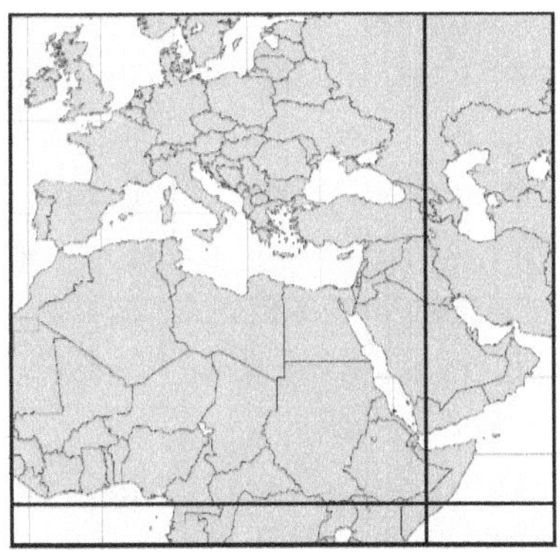

3 SOMALIA

Chakula Refugee Camp

Though the killers are on foot, they have at least forty minutes' start, and the column of Humvees hurtles off in pursuit, hitting potholes, ruts and washouts so the occupants are thrown about like rubber balls.

The road sweeps close to the river, then away again, past a grove of half-grown mango trees, spaced as if part of an orchard. Everything is abandoned. Now and then they see the bloodied body of a villager, proof that they are still on the killers' trail.

This area is empty. The climate has changed here, the coastal belt ruined by salt, the traditional weather patterns changing. Drought follows flood. Extreme becomes normal. There are no 'good' years.

This is the hard face of a hard-hearted bitch of a world, where food and water shortages deepen and new political movements dominate policy and media. In London, Paris and Brussels, right-wing fundamentalists clash with immigrant groups on the streets, and international terrorists find fertile new recruiting grounds. Governments are learning that once an economy is fully developed, and in the absence of war or empire-building, debt is the only way to fund growth. Yet debt can't accumulate forever.

This is the age of remotely piloted aircraft — controlled by a pilot, a sensory operator, and a mission co-ordinator thousands of kilometres away. The MQ-9 Reaper and MQ-1 Predator own the skies, hunting men with guns who have nothing to live for but revenge.

Africa produces warlords and killers with monotonous regularity: Charles Taylor; Joseph Kony; Bosco Ntaganda, the self-styled Terminator. Countless others, spawned of poverty and their own violent environment, preying on a new generation of refugees fleeing rising seas and famine.

Chakula Camp and other camps like it are the rubbish piles of this new world. Each face tells its own story. Some speak of abandonment of dreams, of hopelessness, others of anger, some of hope. Human tragedy is common currency here. Death, broken families, children buried on the dusty trails that constantly change to avoid the roving men with guns who rape and steal.

Yet there is also humour, friendship and love. Singing. Games. Handholding and dreams of other places and worlds. There is hard work. Acceptance. Repentance and faith.

Gangs from al-Muwahhidun, known in the West as the Almohad, recruit from the camp — rounding up twelve- and thirteen-year-old boys, dragging them away to training and indoctrination camps. The Almohad are particularly strong in the Laba Quarter, the vast shanty town surrounding Chakula, controlling the flow of money, guns, the narcotic qat leaf, and even charcoal. Wood from the local acacia trees is used to produce charcoal that sells for anything up to a hundred shillings per bag. The production, packing, transport and sale of this commodity occupies many in the camp.

Tom Roberts, a Canadian public order adviser, asked Marika early in her time here, 'You know what these people want?'

'Food?'

'Yes, but most of all they want their children's lives to be better than theirs. They're not asking for miracles. Just something better for the future.'

Gunfire from the leading Humvee breaks into Marika's thoughts. The dust thickens. The blue tracking bubble on the Sid's map shows that they are approaching Kafee village. The Humvee stops, engine running. Ahead the forward troops have left their vehicles and taken cover, weapons behind a stone wall.

Rifle butts thump against shoulders. Answering bursts. Stone chips and bullets fly. Marika slips down the side of the Humvee and runs, hunched over like the others, ducking down behind the wall next to Kifimbo. She lifts her head in a lull, looking into a wasteland of wrecked vehicles, old concrete culvert pipes, rubbish, with an open sewer winding its way through. A man nearby fires, yet she can't see the target.

'Where are they?' she asks Kifimbo.

His voice trembles, and she can see the fear in his eyes. 'Next time you look, you will see an old van. There are five or six of them pinned down behind it.'

Marika exchanges a glance with Sedegali, now on her other side. 'What about bringing the chopper up?' she asks.

A whipcrack of bullets now, and Marika's eyes are just high enough to pinpoint the muzzle flash.

The colonel shakes his head. 'My men report that they have spotted MANPADS. We can't risk the Blackhawk.'

MANPADS stands for Man Portable Air Defence System, their surface-to-air missiles deadly to choppers. Marika looks at him earnestly. 'Just pop her up into the air, almost on the deck. No point taking any risks, and we'll chew the child-killing bastards to pieces.'

Sedegali gives the order, and the chopper surges forward, comforting and menacing, hovering above the ground. The microgun sits in the open port and beside it a hopper of shining brass 5.56mm ammunition. Marika watches the gunner, keeping her head down as the pilot moves on, seeking a field of fire.

Leaving the relative security of the stone fence, she sprints across the yard then hops lightly up onto the back of the chopper. The gunner is a young Burundian corporal, whose troops have been fighting here as part of the African Union mission for close to a decade.

'In the middle of your field of view you'll see the wreck of a van, OK?'

'Yes.'

'There's some hostiles firing from it.'

'I see them.'

'Take them out.'

A burst of automatic fire clatters off the body of the Blackhawk. Marika ducks again, but then the XM-214 opens up with a numbing, clattering roar, barrels rotating in a blur, spewing out thirty rounds per second, accompanied by a cascade of empty cartridge cases. The van begins to disintegrate. A couple of men run, but are cut down by small-arms fire from the wall or shredded by the microgun.

'OK, cease fire,' Marika calls, leaping straight from the chopper to the cab of the vehicle, then to the ground.

'Follow me,' she shouts, leading the way across abandoned corn fields on the fringes of Kafee village, past the smoking remnants of the abandoned vehicle, bodies lying crumpled and torn around it. She tries not to feel exultation at these deaths.

Finally, tukul shelters made of acacia sticks, then stone buildings, the dirt track giving way to cobbles. Marika goes first, expecting to come under fire at any moment, holding the UMP like a boxer holds his fists, coming around the corner of an ancient adobe building. On the ground is the body of a young, pregnant woman, her kikoi hanging in tatters. There are three bullet wounds: one above her left breast, one in the head, and one in the thigh. Her rounded belly is unmarked, but it is obvious from her battered face and legs that she has been dragged here. Raped and shot.

A shiver of nameless emotion runs though Marika. She falls

to her knees beside the body, feels the woman's chest, then for a pulse in the side of her neck, finding nothing.

Marika lifts her Sid, calling up the medics. Then, buttoning it back into her pocket, she starts CPR, breathing twice through cold lips, then pumping at the bloody chest, swearing softly, her own breath hissing with the effort of each stroke.

Jesus, save her. Fucking save her ...

The medics arrive behind the first clusters of troops. She steps back to give them room to work, wiping blood from her hands onto the sides of her fatigues.

'She's dead, isn't she?'

The nearest of the two medics turns, his moustache half in his mouth, pasted down with sweat. 'Yes, she's gone. But we have a chance of saving her baby.'

Marika grips her UMP and sets off at a determined stride down a dusty alley, that appears to be a main thoroughfare. At first there is no sign of people or livestock. No goats. No chickens. Just a cat moving like lightning through a stone window.

A man on her own side, perhaps Sedegali or Kifimbo, calls her back — a sharp, concerned shout — but she pays no heed. Instead she strides on, into an open marketplace, empty of the fruit stalls, seed sellers, butchers and fishmongers who should be here, plying their wares as they have done for centuries. Instead, two hostiles. She fires a burst at extreme range. Misses. Both turn weapons towards her.

The taller and darker-skinned of the two would be a striking figure in any case, but even at a distance his eyes focus her attention, large and compelling. The face looks familiar, but she can't place him in the shadows and dust.

The face twists into a smile, and he fires a single shot. Marika feels the bullet pass close by, the shockwave leaving her right ear ringing like a bell.

For a moment they stare at each other across an unbridgeable gulf. Whether the assault rifle is empty or not she does not know, but the tall gunman slings it over his back and unclips a grenade from his belt, cocking his arm and throwing it towards her, before turning and running, the other man following.

The arc is too high and the grenade falls short, giving Marika time to shelter behind the raised lip of a stone well, clasping hands over her ears and opening her mouth to help equalise the coming shockwave.

The numbing blast tears at her jacket, but leaves her unmarked. She leaps back to her feet. More AMISOM soldiers arrive in the square now, a storm of dust still billowing up from the blast, larger clods of earth pattering to the ground around her. As the dust clears, one of the two hostiles is just visible disappearing into a narrow laneway. Marika holds the UMP in one hand like a relay baton, and gives chase.

'This way,' she shouts, glancing back to see Kifimbo and two others following.

They pound into an alley, hemmed in by stone houses on either side, the more affluent ones with their traditional tiled or glazed barazza waiting area where guests, in happier times, would wait to be attended. They cross open sewers a hand-span wide at breakneck pace.

Two of the three men with her are good runners, and the fleetest outpaces her easily. They sprint around a corner, stumbling to a halt, reaching for weapons. One of the two fugitives has stopped, chest heaving, his weapon on the ground, standing with his back against the wall of a building, arms extended in the air. His sunglasses have slipped low on his nose and he looks directly at Marika.

She covers him with the UMP, looking for blood or other signs of injury. A soft capture, she decides, but yet, she had initiated the chase swiftly, and not all men can run at that speed for long. The Sledgehammer squad were chosen for their physical capabilities. 'Secure him. I'll try to get the other one. Tie his hands and feet if you have to.'

With just Kifimbo beside her now, she runs on to the next crossroad. From here there are three alleyways to choose from. Of the other runner there is no sign.

Kifimbo holds up a hand to stop her. 'Sorry, Tajiri, but to follow him further would be folly. Not with just two of us.'

Marika stops, placing her free hand behind her head, using the leverage on her spine to open her airway. Kifimbo is right: the man is armed, and the chances of running into an ambush with just two of them giving chase are high. She walks back to where the group of AMISOM troops, now swollen to eight or nine, has the prisoner on the ground, laying into him with boots and fists.

'You cannot blame them,' Kifimbo says. 'These men saw the dead children. Let them have their revenge.'

Ignoring him, Marika lifts the UMP and snaps off two rounds into the air. The men stop and look at her. 'That's enough,' she says, 'get him to his feet. I want him alive.'

As the captive stands, Marika sees that his wrists have been bound with bootlaces, so tight that they have dug into his skin. She can't, however, find it in her heart to want to loosen them.

Marching him through the marketplace and towards the vehicles at the edge of town, she stares at the man's back. Hating him. Knowing in her heart of hearts that she, too, wants to kick his face, make him bleed. Even as they reach the main force and he is cuffed against the roll bars of a Unimog truck in the full sun, stripped of his shirt and with blood from his injured face running down through his light beard and into the matted hair of his chest, she hates him still.

Eight dead and bloodied al-Muwahhidun fighters have been laid out on the street near a makeshift field hospital. It is from there that she hears a cry that cannot be mistaken.

A human newborn.

In this place of death, a life has just begun.

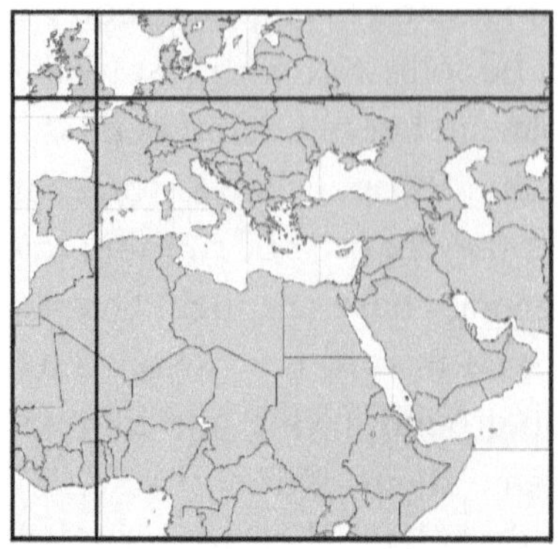

4 UNITED KINGDOM

Test Valley, Hampshire

In England, confused by high temperatures, robins and swallows are nesting weeks earlier than ever before, out of sync with their food sources. Migratory birds such as certain duck species, sandpipers and plovers break the wintering habits of thousands of years. Others — woodpeckers, flycatchers and the song thrush — are rearing fewer chicks as a result of diminishing food supplies.

In London, sweltering through summer, rubbish collection has been privatised, contracted to fee-collecting corporations, and litter grows like mould on the streets and byways; under every stairwell is a dumping ground that overflows and spills out along the footpath. The thirtieth Olympiad is just a slideshow on a forgotten page.

The River Thames breaks her banks on the flood tides and sweeps through Eton, Windsor and Clewer, collecting refuse like a broom, so the tourists standing on the Tower Bridge wear gauze masks to keep the smell at bay. Streets and traffic control systems have fallen into disrepair. Cars and trucks grind bumper-to-bumper down potholed motorways.

PJ Johnson leaves the city, driving just over the speed limit, feeling a sense of relief as the crowded streets give way to open fields. This feeling builds into pleasure over the following forty minutes, until finally he turns off the A303, over a bridge and down a hedge-lined laneway. He catches a glimpse of his face in the rear-view mirror; the new, neatly trimmed beard, so dark it's almost black, still surprising him. He smiles at the new direction his life has taken in recent months.

The crisis at Rabi al-Salah in Dubai, twelve months earlier, and his role in both the storming of the conference centre and the release of two kidnapped girls on Khateer Island had, corny as it sounded when he tried to explain it to his mates in the Special Boat Service, changed his life. He had lifted one of the girls, shot through the chest, with his own arms, and was one of the first into the conference centre. It was he who had wrestled the trigger device from the hands of an idealist seeking death for himself and a generation of world leaders.

Imbued with a powerful new idealism, PJ had turned his back on the Royal Navy with only a vague idea of what he wanted to do next. First he took a holiday on the island of Ibiza that yielded a bit of what passed for love, and a lot of hangovers, then, back home, fielded offers for the security work that many ex-soldiers drift into.

Escorting businessmen and bigwigs around Baghdad, Mogadishu or Tehran, or guarding office blocks and apartment buildings in Kabul is lucrative work, and companies like G4S are always recruiting. Babysitting fat cats, however, did not seem like the kind of new start PJ had in mind.

Before his resignation from the navy took effect, when he was still using up months of accumulated leave, he had a visit from a couple of broad-shouldered young men in suits who took him into the city, over the Thames to the Vauxhall Cross home of Britain's Secret Intelligence Service. Deep underground, on a secret floor that did not officially exist, he was offered a position in his country's newest and most discreet intelligence agency.

It was not the first he had heard of the Directorate of Resource and Future Security — he had worked with a number of DRFS operatives in the aftermath of Rabi al-Salah. It was a hybrid outfit, part intelligence-gathering, part operational. As Tom Mossel, the director, put it: 'This organisation is about the future, not just of our nation, but the world.'

PJ considered Mossel's offer for about three minutes before accepting. Within a month he had recognised this as the best decision of his life. Tom Mossel is that rare blend of thinker and doer, a visionary in his way, gathering a team that blends brilliance with methodical competence.

Six months of intense training, conducted at Fort Monckton in Hampshire, preceded his first operational missions with DRFS. These forays, he suspected, were dummy runs, where he was watched every step of the way.

The generous salary and a joining bonus allowed PJ to realise a long-held dream — some land of his own — somewhere he could be a kid again, and he'd looked long and hard for the right place.

The thought gives him pleasure as he steers down a maze of narrow roads little wider than the car, with lime-green hedges as tall as houses on either side. He skirts the village of Barton Stacey with its castle-like fortified church and charming stone houses. Five minutes later, after navigating yet another twisting route, he stops to open a gate in a stone fence adorned by a hand-painted sign that says 'An Tèarmann'. The phrase is Gaelic for 'The Sanctuary,' a name bestowed on the property by a former owner with big plans but no funds.

PJ looks with pleasure on his two-and-a-half acres. A clear, shallow stream twists through a heritage-listed stand of alder trees. Nearby is a four-hundred-year-old gamekeeper's cottage, once part of King Billy's original estates, built to last of honey-coloured, weathered Cotswold stone. Moss grows in the shadows of the alders, and a pair of grand old oaks.

As he draws closer still, PJ smiles again, the dying sun glinting on the polycrystalline solar panels across the south-facing hip of the roof, pouring power into a battery bank under the eaves. Water is directed from the gutters into two five-thousand-gallon water tanks. He is, for all intents and purposes, self-sufficient. Keeping the gorse and blackberry at bay takes many hours with a brush hook, but he has cleared much of the stream bank, where he goes often, just to think, or to try to catch the brown trout that lurk like shadows near the rocks. They are hard enough to glimpse, let alone fool into taking a fly or lure.

Parking the car, PJ walks down to where the water burbles over mossy rocks. There, in the shadows, he feels his soul recharge. Sometimes, when the breeze blows from the north, especially after rain, he can hear traffic on the A303, seven or eight miles away, but most of the time the sounds are all natural: skylarks and pipits in the trees, the flowing water, his boots making the pebbles clink as he squats near the water's edge, still as fascinated now with water skippers and guppies as he was at ten years old.

Already feeling recharged, he returns to the car, gets his bag and walks to the door. Right at the threshold he stops. Listens. Scans the ground. Tries to identify the source of his unease. Depressions in the gravel that might be footprints. A smell that was not there a few days earlier. A new blossom, or someone's aftershave?

After a minute of listening and watching, he slips the key into the Yale lock and walks into the entry, pressing the alarm PIN into the keypad as he goes. The security system was installed by a couple of DRFS techs at the insistence of Tom Mossel.

Stepping into the house he sniffs the air like a bloodhound. Again he studies the entry. Three pairs of shoes lined up where he left them — brown Scarpa hiking boots, wellingtons, Saucony Cortana trainers. One umbrella in the stand. A couple of caps on their hooks. Windcheaters, one with a faux fur–lined collar. Keys for the outhouses and sheds on their hooks.

Nothing has changed. Still …

He takes another step, opens the door into the sitting room and closes it behind him — again nothing wrong — but he realises that every hair on the back of his neck is standing on end. He feels for the SIG Sauer P226 but it is not there, having been checked in to the DRFS armourer on his return.

There is a registered single-shot Remington shotgun in the bedroom cupboard safe. *Upstairs, damn it*, he thinks, and besides, anyone securing the building would have checked for such things. He picks up a poker from beside the fireplace, an old blacksmith-made utensil that he found in the garden shed and cleaned up. It is a formidable weapon — five or six pounds in weight and viciously pointed.

He climbs one step at a time, watching for trip wires or other devices. He feels that he has stopped breathing, his metabolism on hold. Something of the cat in the economy of his movements.

Reaching the kitchen level, he stops dead, moving only his eyes and neck, running his eyes over every surface. More limestone; thick timbers. Everything built to last.

His eyes settle on a wet ring on the surface of the kitchen bench. The lid of the rubbish bin is ajar. A wry grin cracks across PJ's face, then a shake of the head. 'OK lads, very funny. You can come out now.'

No reply.

'I'm cracking up. Now come out.'

Even though he's sure by now, the laughter comes as an immense relief. He looks up to see two men perched on a window frame some three metres above his head, each holding a can of London Pride in one hand, arms around each other's shoulders. Two of his workmates, and after-hours pals. David and Kutay.

PJ rolls his eyes. 'Whose idea was this?'

David smiles. 'The boss asked us to go around some of the staff residences and check out the security. Thirsty work, as you might imagine.'

PJ turns fast, throwing himself flat against the pantry cupboard as another man comes out of the corridor, not making a sound. In his hand he holds a big silver Colt Commander, the muzzle trained on PJ's chest.

'Bang. You're fucking dead.'

PJ raises his chin. 'Very funny, Ronnie.'

'You would be if I was a hostile, mate. Just be glad I'm not.' Ronnie is tall and rangy, with long arms and an incredible reach that had once helped him win the heavyweight boxing title for 22 Regiment SAS. Like the others, he's wearing civvies: blue Levi's tucked into Cuban-heeled boots, and a black T-shirt with *MEGADETH* in gothic letters across the front. On his wrist is a black studded leather band.

'Someone has to keep you lads on your toes. Too much fun, not enough work.' Ronnie holsters the gun and stands with his hands in his pockets.

PJ knows that, technically on duty, Ronnie has every right to carry the weapon, but few members of the team would pack a firearm for such a minor exercise. 'I'm off for a shower.' He looks up at the two on the window sill. 'If you clowns have managed to get down by then, I'll have a beer with you.'

By the time PJ has showered and unpacked, the sun is below the horizon and the Cree LED ceiling lights are on. He gets a can from the fridge, pops the tab and pours the contents into a glass mug, carries it over to the table where the others are sitting, quieter now. He tilts the glass and takes the first swallow, the bitter flavour easing the dryness of his throat.

David and Kutay smirk at their cleverness. Ronnie sits beside them, reading the paper. The field operatives at DRFS, designated members of 2CG, the Command and Control Group, are few in number, and, in general, socialise together. Close comrades in the field, and at home.

'So tell me, smartarses. How did you get in without setting off the alarm? What's the weakness in the system?'

David raises his eyebrows. PJ likes him a lot — scholarly in appearance, quiet, but dynamite in a scrap. 'The tech boys didn't bother alarming the high windows. It was easy, climbed up the eastern face — water tank, tree, lower slope, then abseiled down the west. Through the window. Not even a challenge.'

'Normal people can't climb like monkeys.'

David grins back, and raises his can. 'To monkeys.'

PJ raises his own glass, drains it, wipes his lips with his wrist, then admits, 'I can't be arsed cooking anything. You blokes feel like a walk down the pub?'

Ronnie clenches a fist, and appears to examine the tattoo of Iron Maiden's 'Eddie' that stretches down the thick muscle of his right forearm. Smiles. 'I've got better things to do than nursemaid you kids.' He slips a silver hip flask from his back pocket and takes a long pull. He is ten years older than PJ, and fifteen older than Kutay. But it's not just the years. He carries tension, like a cable near breaking point.

'I know,' PJ says, 'you'd rather hang out with a bunch of guys listening to twenty-year-old heavy metal has-beens.'

'No one makes music like that any more.'

PJ drops it. Ronnie has been alone for six months, his girlfriend of ten years having left him with a house, a mortgage, and not much else. He hasn't been the same since. 'That's fine. We'll manage, I'm sure.'

Ronnie continues in a matter-of-fact voice, 'Problem is, we all came in my car — left it a couple of hundred yards down the road in some blackberry bushes.'

'Take it, that's no problem.' PJ turns to the others. 'Doss down in the spare room for the night and I'll run you blokes into the city in the morning.' He studies David's face, the only family man in the group. 'Is that OK with you?'

He grins. 'Perfect. Chitrita is over at her mother's for the night with the kids, I don't have to pick them up until lunchtime.'

* * *

In a strange parody of a defensive patrol formation, PJ leads the way, Kutay on one side and David on the other, swaggering in the way of young, fit men on their way for a night out. The destination is the Swan Inn at Barton Stacey village, a not inconvenient distance down a complicated system of lanes.

They eat pasties and keep the publican busy pouring draught ale and whisky chasers, groaning at Kutay's store of clean but unfunny jokes, most of which they've heard before. Kutay was born in Turkey, and immigrated at the age of three. His family are Alevi, a large but often persecuted minority in his country of birth.

The Alevi branch of Islam fascinates PJ. It values inner piety more than external, and espouses humanist principles. Not only are its practitioners permitted to drink alcohol, but they do not make the pilgrimage to Mecca. 'God does not reside in stone temples, but in the hearts of people,' Kutay is fond of saying. He is one of the gentlest men PJ has met, but was also one of the deadliest snipers in the 16th Air Assault Brigade before being poached for the DRFS-run 2CG.

Members of 2CG are drawn from elite regiments such as the Paras, SAS, SBS and the Pathfinders. Capable of rapid response anywhere in the world, they are selected for more than just an ability to fight and to kill. Languages, cultural training, bomb disposal, mine and IED detection. Intelligence and the ability to make snap decisions are part of the selection criteria and a focus of training. Combat is not their primary role, but they all have the skills when necessary.

By eleven pm the publican's daughter has joined them, sipping a watermelon Cruiser, holding hands with Kutay under the table. This development proves too much for the scowling publican, who announces that he has turned the beer kegs off, and that if they wish to continue drinking, they can do it away from his pub and his daughter.

At 0500 the following morning, the phone rings on PJ's bedside table. At first he tries to escape the sound, rolling across to the other side of the bed. Finally, however, he picks it up, listening to the voice dully, propped on one elbow. He climbs out of bed, then throws open the door to the spare room where Kutay and David are spread-eagled on the bed, the latter on his back, mouth wide open, uttering throat-rattling snores.

'Get up, you blokes. I'll make breakfast, and then I'm off.'

Kutay is the quickest to wake. 'What's happening?'

'I'll tell you over breakfast.' He walks to his room, showers, throws a few things into a bag and dresses. Then, in the kitchen, he serves up home-made muesli and toast. By the time the coffee drips through the percolator they are starting to look a little more human.

'OK, let's go.'

PJ shepherds them out the door, switches off the lights, sets the alarm and walks out to the car. A worried frown on his face, he steers down towards the gate, and flicks on the radio to catch the BBC news.

He drops his two friends, both half-asleep, at West Kensington station, and eighty minutes after leaving home he crosses Vauxhall Bridge over the brown and tainted Thames, then parks in the underground complex. Entry is via a swipe card and PIN then, running the gauntlet of discreet body scanners and metal detectors, he arrives at his official workplace.

The Directorate of Resource and Future Security operates out of two secret yet commodious underground floors of the SIS facility. The floor above is occupied by JTAC, the Joint Terrorism Analysis Centre, another new agency under the umbrella of the SIS.

When the building, known in the trade as Legoland, was first constructed in the early nineties, underground space had been left empty for future expansion. Two of these floors were later fitted out and finished for the use of the new DRFS organisation. Being the most recently constructed floors, they lack the contrived modernism of the other sections. They are tasteful, comfortable and pleasant.

The colours were planned by mood consultants, with calm, soft greens and pale pastels dominating, but the furniture, from desks to coffee tables, is stainless steel and glass. The floors are partially open plan, with private offices scattered throughout. A central staircase leads from lower floor to upper, near a staff common room.

The DRFS is a unique organisation, the brainchild of a senior minister in the Cameron government. He pointed out that British intelligence services had no sense of direction — that they identified and responded to current terrorist and military threats, but that it was all too little too late. They did not take into account non-military threats such as popular discontent, ageing populations, water and food shortages, climate change, and the growing number of asylum seekers. His vision was to create a secret and discreet new agency that would have wide-reaching powers to deal with these issues and many more, years before they became a threat. The new organisation would recruit experts from a wide range of fields — economists, strategic planners, climate scientists, as well as a military and security arm known as 2CG, modelled on the CIA's Special Operations Group.

There was no money lying around for such projects, so the planning committee met secretly with what might be termed captains of industry and asked them to help fund it. All businesses want stability, and most agreed to contribute.

The first thing PJ sees when the lift doors slide open is the rather long and uninspiring face of the director's assistant, Will Grace. A face dominated by a bony nose, surrounded by straggly, greasy hair to his shoulders.

'Johnson, I'm glad you're here. Mr Mossel asked me to send you in straight away. He's in the Blair Room.'

Will Grace wears an unbuttoned suit jacket too long for his body, and his tie loose around his collar. He keeps pace with PJ, black jacket swinging like a cloak.

Grace's habit of stalking the main entrance, along with hang-dog eyes and drooping facial skin gave rise to the nickname 'the

Watcher', after the vulture-faced statues that guard The Tower of Cirith Ungol in *The Lord of the Rings*.

PJ stops off at his office, a five-metre-square box of blue carpet and bare walls, dropping his kit, moving to the meeting room with just his Sid, a pad computer and a mug of coffee.

The Blair Room, largest of three meeting rooms, is named after the former prime minister whose legacy required more than a decade of intelligence work to repair. The table is shaped in a half-circle so that no one has their back to the speaker or the 3D screen that dominates the front of the room. The British coat of arms, rendered in tarnished copper, occupies one wall.

PJ sits down, eyes moving to the screen, which at that moment displays a high-definition map of Western Europe.

C4IEW. The latest buzzword stands for Command, Control, Communications, Computers, Intelligence and Electronic Warfare. The SITPOL system takes the lot and rolls it into one package. Set up in three almost identical rooms: Langley, London and Paris, each consists of an OLED screen the size of a small cinema projection, able to project satellite and mapping detail for an area varying in size from a house block to a continent. Target tracking is performed by aerial light detection and ranging (LIDAR) technology as well as radar and satellite imagery.

The screen now shows a live cross into Somalia. The individual on-screen is about thirty years old, bearded, olive-skinned. PJ turns to Tom Mossel, who sits beside the screen on a high stool, his favoured perch. 'Who's this?'

Mossel's voice is even and urbane, his greying hair neatly combed and parted above a square-jawed, mature but handsome face. 'Almohad foot soldier, we assume. Cannon fodder.' He pauses to loosen his tie. 'One of the crew that shot up a bunch of schoolkids yesterday.'

'I heard about it on the news. So our people caught up with them?'

'Yes, Agent Hartmann was involved. Eight Almohad dead and this one captured.'

'Kudos to her. They don't like being taken.'

Mossel shows little overt emotion, but there is a twinkle in his eyes that shows his pleasure. 'No, but it gets better. This one is giving off signals that he might talk — nothing firm, mind you, but Agent Hartmann seems to think he might.'

PJ knows the drill. The prisoner will be playing the usual tough guy routine, but there are always signs. A tendency to keep conversations running, asking questions about what life is like in the West — those kinds of things. Never a dead cert, but encouraging.

Mossel places both hands flat on the table. 'I want you to do the pick-up.'

'No problem. Sounds straightforward.'

Mossel flicks one elegant wrist to bring his watch face into focus. 'I've got a car waiting downstairs, and a 32 Squadron Hawker 800 standing by at Northolt.' He extends a hand. 'Good luck.'

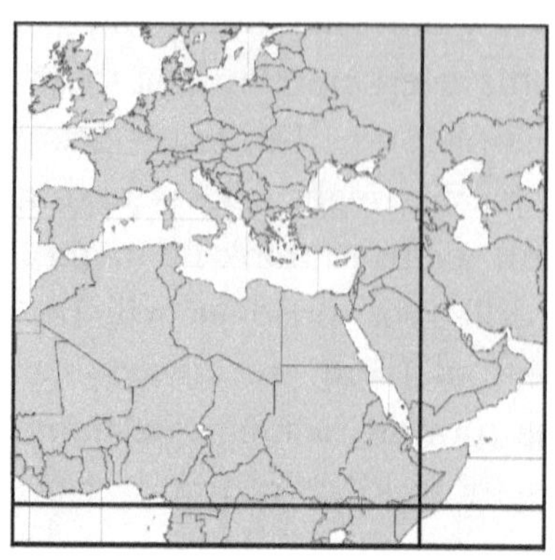

5 SOMALIA

Chakula Refugee Camp

As the plane drones across Africa, PJ sees the patchwork of subsistence farms below, red and dry from the drought, knowing that he is looking down on human suffering only a notch above the people in the camps.

Jatropha and other modern wonder crops have made inroads, provided a source of cash, even here, but at the expense of staple crops. There are no easy solutions to countless problems. Too many people, not enough food, not enough money, governments that want to show the world that they are coping — that they want tourists, want foreign exchange, yet are failing. The spillover of conflict from rogue and failed states does not help.

Chakula Refugee Camp sits just inside the Somali border with Kenya, not far as the crow flies from the older Kenyan camps: Dadaab, Kakuma, Kolobei. Chakula, once they are low enough to see it through the dust-filled air, looks like a grid of countless white squares — UNHCR tents — against the dun-coloured desert. The sheer size of the place takes PJ's breath away.

The airstrip is a wide ribbon of desert that has been cleared of vegetation. The hard packed surface shows tyre marks from regular flights. The pilot takes it with full flaps and engines screaming into reverse thrust almost as soon as they touch down. Even PJ, who has flown in all kinds of aircraft and landed on bush strips all over the globe, finds it unnerving. By the time the plane stops rolling he has a fine sheen of sweat on his forehead.

A desert-pattern-painted Nissan utility and two men are there to meet him, driving out across the apron, stopping beside the plane. The white-toothed Kenyan greets him in Swahili. 'Jambo, Tajiri Johnson. My name is Captain Kifimbo. I command D company, 7th Kenyan Rifle Battalion. We have been on rotation here for three months, and I am assistant to Tajiri Hartmann.'

'Pleased to meet you.'

'This is Tom Roberts.'

PJ's eyes fall on a man in his fifties, lean as a whippet, with pale grey eyes and hands as bony as his face. 'Jambo sana, Mr Johnson. I'm an adviser.'

'Call me PJ, please, everyone else does.' At first he thinks the accent is American, then he changes his mind. 'You're Canadian, right?'

The eyes radiate pleasure. 'I like you already. Well picked.'

'There's a difference ...'

'Of course there is, but a heck of a lot of people can't tell. Anyway, welcome to Chakula Camp. It ain't the end of the world, but you can see it from here.'

PJ smiles, warming to him, and turns back to the African beside him. Kifimbo is around thirty, no taller than PJ, but with a slim build and jerky eyes. His uniform is spotlessly clean and he holds a five-year-old cell phone. His lips are inclined to pout, and he has a preoccupied look as if he is thinking deeply.

'You're Kenyan, you said?' PJ asks.

'That's correct. From Mombasa, when I was young, but I went to university in Nairobi.'

'What did you study?'

'Journalism.'

'Really, and you ended up in the army?'

He shrugs. 'It's a good job for me. The way I felt that I could help the most.'

Driving towards the administration compound, tents appear on either side of the track, hundreds deep. Charcoal-fuelled cooking fires burn outside the structures. Women walk along the roadside with loads balanced on their heads. Here and there the monotony of the tents is broken by a dustbowl football field. A row of kiosks. A makeshift prayer hall.

'These people are mostly Somali?' PJ asks.

'Many Sudanese now, too, and even Kenyans, but seventy per cent Somali.'

'Which clans?'

Tom Roberts answers, 'The Darod, Rahanweyn and Digil. All Southern people. The fighting has been bad since the Almohad came. In the last ten years Somalia has been invaded or occupied in parts by Harakat al-Shabaab al-Mujahedin, the KDF, the Ethiopians, AMISOM and now the Almohad. They are even less tolerant than al-Shabaab, and of course the coastal regions are in crisis from the rising seas. Some of the flattest areas have been ruined by salt.'

PJ sees the children running and playing, some stopping to wave as they pass by.

They cross a security barrier into the admin compound, stopping at the third of ten near-identical demountable barracks huts. A woman in fatigues emerges from the main door and crosses the dry gravel of the car park.

PJ feels himself smiling as he steps from the vehicle and recognises Marika Hartmann striding towards him on long legs. They share a quick embrace and a peck on the cheek. She smells of soap, healthy skin and shampoo.

'Hey there, Aussie.'

PJ's smile is genuine. They first met in the aftermath of Dubai, shared dinner and a few beers with the rest of the crew that stormed the conference centre, and some of the other security staff. It was only later that he found out that it was she who had recommended him for recruitment to Tom Mossel.

Since his arrival at DRFS they've become firm friends, both regulars at Friday evening drinks at the latest popular watering hole, the Mansion House Pub in Kennington.

'You still haven't taken me hiking in the Himalayas,' he chides, 'like you keep promising.'

'And you, my dear Paisley Johnson,' she says, resting one hand on his shoulder, 'haven't yet taken me scuba diving in the Seychelles. Like you keep promising.'

There are just two people in the world who call PJ by his given name. One is his mum, now living in Cornwall with her second husband. The other is Marika Hartmann. She had discovered it by chance, leaning over his shoulder as he photocopied personal documents for his file.

'Paisley?' she'd cried. 'Your real name is Paisley Johnson?'

'Yes. Please don't call me that.'

'Why not?'

'I hate it.'

'I,' she had said, 'like it. It's a beautiful name — and not boring. So many people have boring names.'

Marika has addressed him as 'Paisley', or 'Pais', ever since, and he counters with 'Aussie'.

PJ smiles wryly. He is used to her now — her habit of keeping him off balance. 'Well done on the capture, by the way. Got anything out of him yet?'

'Haven't tried, but I do think he's a chance.' Her eyes turn as hard as little black pebbles. 'This bastard was part of a gang of Almohad that shot and killed twenty schoolchildren and four adults, and wounded another ten. Kids that I'd seen playing in the alleys the day before. If it was up to me I'd have him tried in a court of law, then stood up against a wall and shot.'

* * *

The prisoner is lighter-skinned than many Somalis, wears sunglasses with iridescent yellow lenses and his scalp shaved very close. His face betrays the beating he got upon capture. Bruises; puffy left eye; a cut on his forehead.

PJ makes no effort to shake hands or introduce himself. He has come to understand that in the West psychopaths open fire in cinemas and schools, or bury one victim after another in forests. In the Middle East and North Africa psychopaths shroud their faces with cloth, twist a religion, blow up buses and shoot children.

He stands behind one of three available chairs, gripping the steel frame in both hands. The room is concrete-floored, swept clean, with walls of compressed cement sheet, painted a dull green. The hard surfaces make it somewhat reflective, so that a footstep sounds like a drumbeat.

Marika takes a seat, readying her Sid to livestream the interview to London. PJ senses her rising anger as he moves to sit down beside her. Kifimbo stands at the door, making a show of checking the load on his sidearm.

PJ looks at Marika. *Get this over with*, her eyes say clearly.

'Hayye,' PJ begins — 'hello'. He was, during his initial training, required to choose one language in which to specialise, and he chose Somali. The training was conducted regularly over six months, followed by a fourteen-day immersion in a house full of Somali-born instructors, where using even a single word of English was forbidden. These language skills had proven useful on several undercover missions. One was a hostage rescue in coastal Puntland, another an attempt to make contact with disaffected elements of Hizb al-Islam, who had broken away after that organisation's merger with al-Shabaab. The latter mission had proved both dangerous and fruitless, and PJ's language skills had made the difference between life and death.

The prisoner glares back belligerently. 'Your Somali is shit. Talk English. I speak it, OK?'

'Note that the prisoner has indicated that he speaks and understands English at a high level and requested that the interview be conducted in that language,' PJ says, turning to face the Sid. English is better. Saves interpreters back at DRFS, and also having to translate for Marika. 'I have to inform you that this interview is being recorded — both audio and video. You are being treated as a prisoner of war, and as such you are not eligible to have legal representation at this interview. Both civil and/or war crime charges may be levelled against you.'

The prisoner shrugs off the statement like an unwanted shirt, resuming his uninterrupted stare. PJ is starting to wonder about Marika's assessment that the man is likely to talk.

'What's your name?' Marika asks.

'Go to fucking hell where you belong.'

'What organisation do you belong to?'

Silence.

'Al-Shabaab?'

A short laugh. 'They are finished here. Al-Muwahhidun rule in East Africa.'

PJ watches Marika as she shakes her head and tightens her lips. 'OK. Now you give me one good reason why we don't simply hand you over to the International War Crimes Tribunal.'

The man in the seat cocks his head at an angle and smiles.

'Why did you kill the children?'

There is something sickeningly pretty about his face, almost feminine. When he speaks his eyes become animated. 'The children were killed by American missiles. An explosion. I swear, my cousin saw it happen.'

Marika takes a step forward, pausing at a signal from PJ. 'Don't talk crap.'

'Such things happen every day.'

'Sometimes, yes, but it's not what happened here.'

PJ backs her up. 'Work with us, or we'll dump you back in Kafee, and get the word out that you sang like a bird. How long do you think you'd last?'

The smug arrogance goes. The body language changes. Shifting eyes. A nervous shake of surprisingly smooth-skinned hands. 'You want information? You want secrets?'

PJ looks at Marika before nodding. 'Yes, go on.'

'Do you remember when the mujahedin flew their jets into the World Trade Center in New York and the Pentagon?'

'Of course.'

'Do you remember the London bombings, the Kabul attacks, the Madrid bombings?'

PJ bristles at the rhetoric, but forces himself to ignore it. 'Yes. I remember.'

The prisoner's voice is steady. There is not another sound in the room. 'Then let me tell you that they were just the play of children compared to the devastation that is coming. He is rising again.'

'Who?'

'Istikaan, the man they call the Hourglass.'

PJ glances at Marika, then at the prisoner. 'Keep talking.'

Crossed arms. 'I have nothing else to say. I do not co-operate with unbelievers and apostates.'

PJ looks deep into those dead eyes. It could be an exaggeration, a half-truth, or even just jihadist folklore. In either case, the statement bears further examination. 'Do you know what an extraordinary rendition is?'

The eyes grow even more distrustful. A little shake of the head.

'It's when people like us make someone like you disappear — across borders, across oceans. The subjects end up in a dirty little prison somewhere, where men with no rules or scruples make them talk. Usually they die there. It's a terrible thing, but sometimes necessary.'

The prisoner half-smiles, showing teeth that are unusually clean and white for a Somali man. Qat chewing and lack of dental hygiene ruin most at a relatively early age. Religious prohibitions might have helped in this regard. 'Why are you telling me this?'

PJ leans forward. 'Because that is exactly what is about to happen to you.' The prisoner's eyes widen, but PJ is already turning to Kifimbo. 'I would appreciate if you would get him ready for travel. The plane is waiting.'

Kifimbo grins. 'Of course I don't mind. Well done. Well done.'

PJ leads the way from the room, outside to the shade of a flapping tarpaulin set up on four poles. There, he and Marika stand together for a moment, listening to the sounds of the prisoner's protests as Kifimbo and his men drag him away from the interview room.

'That was enlightening,' Marika says. 'What a slimy bastard.'

PJ raises his eyebrows. 'I thought you said he was ready to talk.'

'Well he did, sort of.'

'The devastation that is coming,' PJ muses. 'What do you think he might mean?'

'Probably planting an IED in Mogadishu. You know how much they hate the Somali government. Istikaan is probably some area commander with a big reputation.'

'Yeah, true. Anyway, we'll get it out of him.'

Kifimbo and his men dump the cuffed prisoner into the caged rear of a Nissan utility, rattling off Surahs in a monotone as he goes. PJ knows that he has to go with them, but it seems to him that talking to Marika is too normal and precious to waste — that stealing a few more seconds is the most important thing in the world.

In the weeks before she left for the camps they had seemed to be drifting closer, and for a moment he stares at her unashamedly. Not as a comrade, but as a woman. Strands of hair spill out of her cap. Her eyes are living proof that brown can be the deepest shade of all.

The strange thing about her, PJ knows, is that she can look as demure as a nun one minute, mischievous the next. Somewhere in between, she leans up to kiss his cheek.

'See you later, then, Pais. I'm late for the patrol.'

'See you, Aussie. Soon, London maybe. You can buy me a pint.'

She smiles back. 'You can buy me one.'

PJ feels strange as he walks to the Nissan, to the hissing creature in the rear throwing curses and hatred like stones at the world around him.

Within an hour of the livestream of the interview hitting London, Director Tom Mossel has a research team sifting through every known item of intelligence about a man called Istikaan, liaising with GCHQ — the Government Comms Headquarters, which monitors terror suspects through SIGINT listening posts across the world — along with all media and other electronic forms of communication.

Mossel stalks the main part of the office, what they call the cattle pens, pacing back and forth. 'I want to know who he is, what he is, and what the hell he might be doing.'

A biographical specialist, using a CIA-developed database known as CREST and hundreds of other sources, attempts to discover Istikaan's identity.

Working with Arabic names and nicknames in English is not easy. Mohammed, for example, محمد in Arabic, has fourteen accepted English spellings. Known or suspected terrorists have for many years been able to use spelling variations on their names to obtain new, 'clean' travel documents. Middle Eastern men may also change their name from 'bin' — son of — to 'abu' — father of — when they produce a son.

Working from a nickname such as Istikaan is even harder. Yet, after many hours of cross-matching possibilities, the researcher is able to determine that a man known as Istikaan was born Zimraan al-Ghazali, in Baghdad, Iraq, attended Kadhimiya District High School, became an office holder within the ruling Ba'ath Party, and was wanted by the International Criminal Court after the fall of Saddam Hussein.

The official records of his working life within the Iraqi administration were marked as: 'Missing, Presumed Destroyed.'

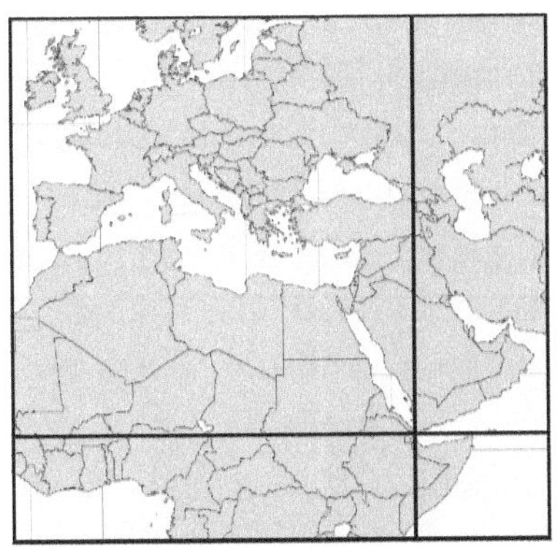

6 DJIBOUTI

Cape Lemonnier

The CIA operates up to fifty black sites across the world, from Afghanistan's infamous Salt Pit to Diego Garcia, a footprint-shaped speck in the Indian Ocean, and the Ukraine. Some, since the turn of the new century, have been located on US warships such as the USS *Bataan*. Acknowledged by George W. Bush in 2006, but rarely before or since, black sites are unfashionable, and few of PJ's 2CG comrades would speak of them with pride.

Cape Lemonnier, home to the Combined Joint Task Force — Horn of Africa, is located at a former French Foreign Legion base in Djibouti, sandwiched between Ethiopia, Eritrea and Somaliland, against the opening of the Red Sea. The base itself is laid out in precise grids and squares, as if it were planned on a sheet of graph paper.

Four-engine C-17 Globemaster jets occupy the tarmac, along with CH-53 choppers, and a discreet Predator drone apron. Comms antennae with multifaceted masts are more common than trees here. Camouflage netting drapes over every structure. A haze of dust from vehicle movement hangs over the landscape.

PJ sees hundreds of huts, pale yellow and steeply pitched, each home to sixteen personnel. From the air, if it wasn't for the drab green colours, the base looks more industrial than martial.

Down on the tarmac a black Ford van waits, manned by agents in dark overalls and darker sunglasses. PJ is more relieved than he might have expected to let them take charge of the prisoner, then ride up front as they speed through a city of tents and Quonset huts.

Finally the van pulls up outside a fenced compound. PJ is asked to produce ID for the first time, followed up with an iris scan and a short delay for verification. Now the van enters the first truly permanent structure he has seen since his arrival on the base. An ugly building, constructed entirely of grey concrete blocks.

A hangar-style sliding door opens on runners and the van idles inside, on smooth concrete now, around a curve and down a level. Here it pulls into a bay where other, similar vehicles are parked. On foot now, they stop at a security checkpoint where PJ is given a temporary pass, then through a series of glass doors, and inside.

Here, the captive is subjected to a thorough series of identity checks. Finger and thumb prints, iris scans and hi-res photographs taken from every possible angle. A physical search includes body cavities and electronic scanning for implants in the body.

The facility makes PJ nervous. He can accept that such a place is a necessary evil, but even now he can hear distressed shouts from the cells below, muffled by the solid construction of the concrete walls and floor. Other things happen, or have happened, here: waterboarding, the modern torture of choice that leaves no marks on the victim.

The CIA case manager, elongated face squeezed between outdated, overly large sideburns, introduces himself as John. He shakes hands like a weightlifter, rolls up the sleeves of his light blue business shirt and sits PJ down in a private office. 'Facial recognition software is the key here. Our database contains more than a billion images — we'll have a shot of him somewhere.'

PJ raises his eyebrows. 'You've got cameras along the River Jubba?'

'Of course not, but those guys move in and out of hotspots. They spend time in places like Qatar and Abu Dhabi, where CCTV is much more common. We also have hidden cameras at mosques and markets in Mogadishu and Kismaayo.'

The American capacity for information warfare never fails to astound PJ. 'How long does it take?'

'We've got some serious computer power. By about midnight we should have him. Then we can pretty much work out everything — family members, likes, dislikes, friends, enemies, education, what he had for breakfast. By dawn tomorrow, you and I will interrogate the motherfucker with the advantage of knowing what brand of toilet paper he uses.'

'So what now?'

'I'll organise some temporary accommodation for you downtown ...'

PJ smiles. 'Downtown?'

'That's just what we call the base rec area. It ain't much — a chow hall and a few stores — but it'll keep you outta trouble till the morning.'

Downtown consists of a double-storey stack of pale yellow shipping containers converted to air-conditioned sleeping accommodation for visitors, six men to a container. PJ carries his kit slung over one shoulder, waiting while he is designated a bunk by number, issued a chit that will later allow him to eat.

By nightfall, having already explored the few shops and worked out at the gym, he is bored of sitting on his bunk and reading pamphlets on base hygiene and etiquette, happy to accept an invitation issued by a squad of reserve engineers from Wisconsin to visit the city of Djibouti on the other side of the international airport. The destination is the French quarter of the town, an earthy blend of Africa, Arabia and Europe.

Sitting in a filthy bar on Avenue 26, a place that reeks of sewers and sweat, men shouting and women laughing in the distance, at a table with men he doesn't know, PJ feels disconnected, drinking whisky already so watered down that there seems little point in diluting it further.

The alcohol does, however, rescue him from the dumps, and he laughs a little with the engineers. The women arrive from whatever dark corner they wait, dusky beauties with the shame of their extremes written on their faces. One comes to sit beside PJ, perched on the edge of her chair so her knees touch his thighs.

She wears a gown and tiara straight from 1950s Hollywood, and make-up that looks like it was applied with a paint brush. When her lips smile her eyes remain calculating, with an element of desperation. Those flecked, citrine-coloured irises tell him that she needs him more than he needs her.

'What's your name?' he asks.

'Kilu. What's yours?'

At that moment PJ just seems too plain. 'Paisley.'

'Ooh, nice name.' She claps her tiny hands in some oft-repeated pantomime.

PJ buys her a bourbon that he knows is just coloured water. He also knows that she is getting kickbacks for every drink someone buys for her. He has spent time in places like this from Iraq to South-East Asia, and knows how the system works.

Other men from the table disappear with their women. They come back alone — flushed of face, clothing loosened; eyes furtive.

Kilu moves her lips close to PJ's ear and says, 'Hey Paisley, you want to screw me?'

The words are calculated to shock and arouse.

Ah, yes, I do. It has been a while, since I, ahem, screwed a woman. He tries to think through the alcohol and the jet lag piled on jet lag. Twelve months, maybe. A couple of times with the nanny, Kelly, after Rabi al-Salah, but then the family she was working for shunted across to New York. Then there was a sister of an old mate from the SBS. A sweet, practical woman a couple of years older than him. They had a few nights in the sack that never really went any further.

Most of the time he can resist temptation. Today it's hard.

Damn you, Marika Hartmann.

That golden skin. Athletic legs. She is just so appealing and he feels guilty that she makes him feel like this, gets his hormones bubbling away.

Yet five minutes on a dirty mattress? With this girl with hunger in her eyes? Who is probably trying to raise half an extended family on what she makes, and can't tell the menfolk where she gets the cash or they will stab her to death for the shame of it.

She leans across, so her head rests against his shoulder. Her soft black hair tickles his neck. Physical desire he can raise in plenty, but no. Not here. Not now.

When she lifts her head and looks at him, asking the question again with her eyes, he shakes his head, then digs out a few notes in US dollars. A ten and a five. Presses them into her hand. 'No,' he says, 'not for me. Not tonight.'

She looks at him, then down at the money. She seems to take a few moments to understand what he has done. Then she stands and walks away. Does not look back, just finds another table. Twenty minutes later, PJ sees her leave on the arm of a US Marine who looks like he is no more than eighteen or nineteen.

At 0800, after a hot breakfast in the chow hall, he is on his way back to the CIA facility. John greets him like an old friend, yet there is something subdued, almost worried, about him this morning.

'So, what did you find out?' PJ asks.

'You had a coffee yet? Yes? Want another one?'

PJ hovers in the generously sized staff room while the CIA man presses buttons on the machine and fills two oversized corrugated cardboard cups with hot coffee, then uses the foamer to add frothed milk. The final touch is a dusting of chocolate powder over the top.

'There you go. Good as any coffee shop in Boston.' He hesitates. 'Or London, for that matter.'

PJ takes the coffee. 'So what did the computers come up with?'

The American leads the way to a table, straddles a moulded plastic chair and waves a hand at PJ to take the other. Once they are settled he crosses his arms, obviously annoyed at himself. 'That's just it,' he says. 'We got nothing.' He raises both eyebrows, then points down towards the cells. 'That son of a bitch in there doesn't exist.'

'OK, so that means he's never been photographed or fingerprinted. That's not impossible.'

'No, but it means he's been careful, or shielded. Or even that he's a brand new recruit from the boondocks, but he doesn't fit that profile. We've ruled out plastic surgery too. We can tell.' The CIA agent smiles for the first time. 'There's one interesting thing. Have you heard him speak more than a word or two of Somali?'

PJ finds himself frowning, thinking ahead of the possibilities this question raises. 'No, only English.'

'Well, last night he did a bit of sleep-talking. Guess what language?'

PJ thinks about it. 'Somali?'

'Wrong. Levantine Arabic.'

The coffee is good, PJ has to admit, but the taste sours in his mouth. 'So he's Lebanese, Jordanian or Syrian?'

'Yes, or Palestinian.'

'In that case, this is not as simple as it first appeared.' PJ considers for a moment. Foreign jihadis have been trickling into Somalia, as they do with all Islamist–West hotspots, for many years. But why would he have hidden that fact?

The American drains his cup, screws it up into a tight ball in his hand, then cocks his wrist and shoots the cup across the room into the brass case of an enormous artillery round that serves as a wastepaper basket. 'In this business, not many things are as simple as they first appear.'

PJ stares. 'Is that shell genuine?'

'Yup. The likes of which will never be seen again. From the USS *Missouri*. Iowa-class battleship. Decommissioned now, of course, so everyone tries to get hold of one. They make great trash cans, as you can see.'

PJ crushes his own cup, smiles at the other man, then sends it the same way, on a looping, high parabola. It doesn't even touch the sides before hitting the floor of the bin with a metallic thump. 'OK, so let's go talk to him.'

The baleful hatred the prisoner transmits like a radar signal has intensified, if anything, since their last meeting. His eyes pass over the American and onto PJ, settling there.

'Where is the woman?'

'Not here,' PJ says.

The prisoner's arms are crossed over his chest. 'From now on I talk only to her.'

The CIA man's voice is soft and soothing. 'That's not convenient right now. It's more important that the three of us here develop a relationship.'

The eyes glow with anger, and the lips take on an ugly pout. 'Shut your fucking lies, OK? I will talk to the woman. Only her.'

PJ turns to the other man, and can see they are both in accord. Sometimes it is best to let these people have their small victories.

At Chakula Camp, Marika sits on a rocky knoll no higher than a single-storey house, facing to the north, knees drawn up. Below her are lines of troughs with women washing, men and children filling containers. Lines of black polyethylene pipe feed the troughs with water pumped from a pool in the river.

Near the Humvee with the machine gun mounted on its tray, Kifimbo wanders between the women scrubbing clothes, chattering, laughing with them, asking questions. The journalist inside him, Marika has realised, has not quite been subsumed by the soldier.

The tablet computer screen is a little unclear beneath the protective plastic case, and Marika tilts it to reduce the glare. The feed comes directly from the DRFS servers back in London via satellite. Image after image. Every terrorist leader on the database, sorted according to country of origin and background. Few of whom she would have expected to find leading an attack in Somalia. Yet, she has become convinced that the African gunman in the market square in Kafee is familiar to her — not from a personal meeting, but from briefings, photographs, video footage of killings and massacres.

She continues to swipe through the images. The top echelon. One after the other: Mukhtar Robow of Harukat ul Ansar, Issa Ossman of Jamiat Ulema-e-Islam, Hassan Turki of Laskar e-Toiba.

Then, a face dominated by sunken eyes that burn with a deep fire. The bony death's-head face she last saw across the Kafee village square is mirrored on the screen.

Saif al-Din. The Nigerian.

Goosebumps rise on her arms. One of the top five most wanted in the world. One of the architects of Rabi al-Salah in Dubai.

You bastard. It was you who killed those children.

Again she looks out at the washing areas, then the outer camp beyond — a sea of makeshift shelters called tukuls, rounded huts made of sticks embedded in the earth, covered with cardboard and plastic bags and other rubbish. There can be no greater contrast with the land of her birth, the Sydney suburb of Bondi with its red-brick affluence and leafy gardens, Mercedes cars and strutting surfers.

Starting out in the Australian Defence Force, in infantry and Special Forces, then the Canberra-based Australian Secret Intelligence Service, she had been recommended for an exchange with London's DRFS by a far-sighted commanding officer.

Marika loved the assignments in North Africa and the Middle East, feeling that at last she could make a difference. Offered long-term tenure, she did not hesitate, and even now she remembers her excitement as she signed a ten-year contract with the DRFS and a lease on a Pimlico apartment on the same day.

To Marika, London is the hub of the world. She loves the Thames and its rushing tides, the aorta of the city, the pulsing rush of energy that had once carried her fleets to all corners of the earth. Contrasts it with what she sees below right now. People caught in the jaws of a medieval society in a modern world.

That's why I'm here, she reminds herself. *Because the world is not fair.*

The Sid shrills beside her. PJ's voice. She is surprised how pleased she is to hear it. Listens to his update on the prisoner's probable nationality and continuing belligerence.

'We have a problem,' PJ goes on. 'He won't talk to anyone but you.'

'Why would he want to talk to me?'

'Who knows? Sometimes these people get the mistaken belief that they can trust a particular individual and not another, even within the same organisation. London's organised transport from Arba Minch. Shouldn't be more than a couple of hours away.'

'No problem. I'll be ready.'

Marika is packed and ready to go in an hour, finishing off with a shower, washing her face and rubbing with a flannel. Towelling off, she enjoys five minutes in front of the mirror, brushing her long brown hair, braiding it so it will sit flat under a hat or helmet if the need arises.

Finally, she hefts her kit from her cot: a Bergen pack and the UMP firearm stripped for travelling. She has trained herself to live with very little. Her life is a backpack of things. Toothbrush. Hairbrush. A smartphone that she uses mostly as an iPod, her Sid taking care of most other duties in the field. The tablet computer and keyboard case for reports and longer communications. Fatigues and mufti for a week. Battle garb. A book. Hardware: sidearm, ammo, cleaning kit.

Preoccupied with her thoughts while Kifimbo drives her to the airstrip, she holds her question until he stops the Humvee, and they perch together atop the seats while they wait for the C-130. Airborne dust masks the sun. The afternoon light red-orange, surreal.

'Kifimbo,' she says. 'You know the baby that was born in Kafee — to the mother who was shot by the Almohad. Do you know where he is? Is he in one of the hospitals here?' The child had been on her mind, off and on. If anyone could find out it would be Kifimbo, with his journalist's instincts and extensive social network.

'Why would I have concerned myself with such a thing?'

'Find out for me, let me know, will you?'

'OK. I will find out for you, out of respect for that baby's dead mother, and those other children, lying dead on the river flat ...' He is silent, again, forehead scored with deep lines as he holds one hand over his eyes, wipes it across as if to remove something from them that cannot be removed.

Marika knows that look, having seen it many times before. 'I'm here to talk about it, if you want to.'

He makes a sound that might be relief, and Marika understands. The Kenyan soldiers are a hard bunch. Machismo is a prized quality. Few would talk about what they have seen and done in the dirty business of war, or admit to being affected by it. Counsellors are seen as a ridiculous luxury.

'The dead children,' he says finally, 'I will never get them out of my mind. Every night I revisit that place. I see their little bodies.'

Marika places a hand on his shoulder. 'I'm the same. You wouldn't be human if it didn't affect you.'

Kifimbo makes no sound. He lowers his head, covers his face with both hands to hide the evidence of his grief.

'Can I tell you something?' Marika asks.

'Yes.'

'You have to collect the good things in your life. You have to use them. What's the most beautiful sight you have ever seen?'

Kifimbo lifts his hands away. 'I am from a place called Lake Nakuru, in Kenya. Have you been there?'

'No, but I've heard of it.' One of the Rift Valley's famous volcanic lakes.

'Well,' he says, 'it truly is beautiful. Blue and still like a mirror. Around it are three hills. We call them Enasoit, Honeymoon and Lion Hill.'

Marika smiles, letting him fill her head with images. 'Go on, please.'

'In winter, millions upon millions of flamingos come there, in a show of colour that must be seen to be believed.' He cracks a smile, white teeth dull in the opaque light. 'Their pink wings and bodies, rising and falling from the waters. I can think of that, perhaps?'

Marika returns the smile. 'Sounds perfect to me.'

'I'll try that for a start, and if it doesn't work I'll think of my mother, or maybe dawn in the hills, when I was a boy and my father made porridge for us.'

Marika lays her palm flat on his forearm. 'That's the idea. You use the good memories. The special things. That's what you use, against ... the bad.'

'Thank you. I will remember.'

'Otherwise it will get you down. It will drag you in.'

The plane is coming now, a speck in the sky growing larger. Marika squeezes the hard muscles above Kifimbo's wrist. Further talk is unnecessary.

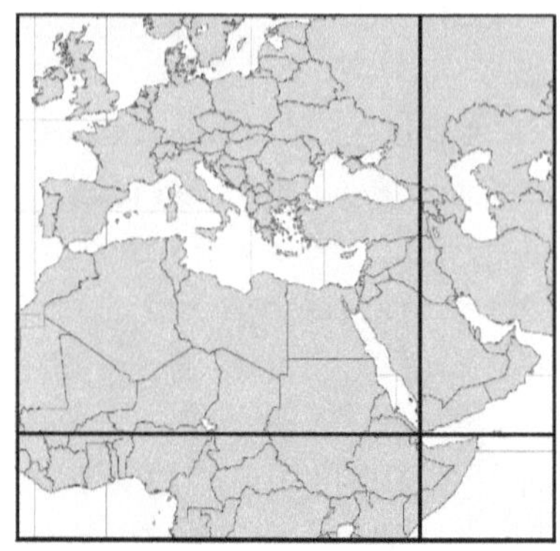

7 DJIBOUTI

Cape Lemonnier

The interview room is built from the same concrete blocks as the rest of the installation, painted off-white, with thick paint drips like tears frozen in time. The room contains just three chairs. No desk. The door has a mirror-like glass panel that Marika realises allows for one-way observation of the room.

The prisoner's face reacts as they enter before returning to what might be deadpan disinterest, though Marika suspects that it is not. His left cheek remains swollen from the beating handed out in Kafee. His posture is nonchalant, but his eyes don't leave Marika's as she settles down into a chair. PJ takes a seat, glancing at her in clear invitation to speak first.

'Good morning,' she says. 'I won't say that it's nice to see you again, but you asked for me, so I'm here.'

His head tilts back, lips parted, showing his teeth, rolling his eyes, accentuating the bloodshot whites. 'I hope that you have come here ready to get me out.' The prisoner fixes his eyes on PJ, then jabs a finger at Marika. 'I want to be alone with her.'

'No.'

'I want to be alone with her or you get nothing. Do you understand? I will speak to this woman. No one else.'

Marika turns to PJ. 'I don't mind.'

PJ stands, his expression antagonistic, but leaves the room, turning once as the door opens for him. Pointing to the observation window. 'I'll be very close.'

When they are alone the informer waves a hand at the Sid unit on the desktop, still recording.

'Switch that thing off, for the moment at least, or I'll say nothing.'

'I can't ...'

'Turn it off or I'll never say another word to you.'

Marika considers the request. The room will be wired up anyway. The need for information, in this case, is more important than protocol. She pauses the recording. 'Listen, I'm a busy person. I don't have time to play these games. Do you know anything else, or are we wasting time?'

The prisoner laughs, but there is an artificial ring to it. 'What do I know?' He leans forward. 'How about this? I know your name. Marika Hartmann.'

Marika's breath stops. How did he know? Had someone let it slip during the interrogation at Chakula, or in transit? She doubts it. They are always careful. She keeps her tone relaxed. 'Big deal. But just out of interest, how do you know that?'

The smile widens. 'We are not stupid. We gather intelligence, just as you do. I know that your home address is 3/56 Eccleston Square, Pimlico, London. Your cell phone number is 0739 3784593 ...'

Marika feels as though a drawer full of her most intimate belongings has been emptied on the floor of the room, but she keeps up the bravado. 'Anyone can look up a phone book. If you know so much, tell me about Istikaan, the Hourglass.'

'The Hourglass brings death wherever he goes. That is his business. He leaves a trail of corpses ...'

'Give me something specific.'

'If I tell you more, will you get me out of here?'

'If it proves to be as important as you say, yes.'

The prisoner folds his arms across his chest and glares. 'OK. This is what I will give you. Go to a place called al-Guin in Syria, you'll see what Istikaan does — what he has done. The latitude is 34.272778. The longitude is 39.624648.'

'How did you know that off the top of your head?'

The prisoner taps his temple. 'I have what Westerners call a photographic memory. I remember everything. When I leave this room I will recall every detail. The clothes you are wearing. Every word you uttered. That is my skill. That is why Saif al-Din values me ...'

'Repeat those numbers, please, while I record them.' Marika switches the unit on, opens the audio app, recording while he repeats the numbers. 'Al-Guin, you said?'

'Yes, a village in the Eastern Desert of Syria.'

The informer leans forward over the desk so his face is close to hers. His skin is paper-thin, almost translucent, and she can see veins up near his hairline. She expects him to ask her to stop recording but he says nothing. It occurs to her then that it is not the audio he is wary of, but the video.

'No wonder you look sad, Marika. You were very hurt when your Somali boy was killed. What was his name again? Madoowbe?'

Marika doesn't bat an eyelid, but inside she is in turmoil. This man knowing her one-time Somali lover's name angers her far more than it unsettles her. Arms folded, she glares back at him. 'Is that the best you and your so-called intelligence-gathering can do? Do you know anything useful?'

'I know many more things. I remember it all.'

Marika keeps her voice cold. 'You'll hear from me after we look into the information you have given us. Maybe then we can start to talk about a deal.' That said, she signals to the observation window. The door opens a moment later. She brushes past PJ and keeps going into the room beyond. Stops in front of one of those grey block walls, fighting her deep rage that the man in that room has dirtied a memory.

Madoowbe was one of the most physically beautiful men she has ever known. Marika had not loved him in the conventional sense — knew him for only a few days. Together they had parachuted into Puntland in a desperate race to find the one woman who might save the lives of hundreds, locked down in that conference room in Dubai.

They had shared one night in a desert cave, made tender love at a time when she had not known if she would live another day. Then, just hours later, he had given his life so she had time to escape the swarming shifta — the ubiquitous bandits of the interior. She would never forget Madoowbe.

PJ arrives beside her. 'Are you OK?'

Marika glances at him, sees the concern in his frown and worried lips. She lifts the Sid she still carries in one hand, placing a call to DRFS, pressing the hotkey with her thumb while keeping her eyes fixed on PJ. It takes a few moments to be routed through to Tom Mossel. There is no attempt at banter or a greeting. Just silence while he waits for her to talk.

'We have been compromised,' she says, 'at the highest level.'

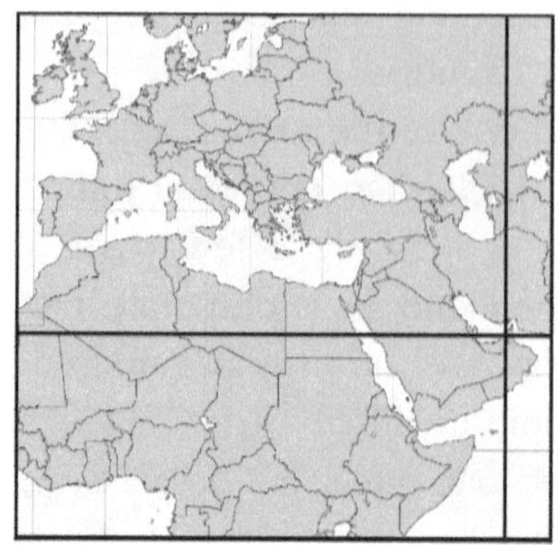

8 UNITED ARAB EMIRATES

Dubai

The car is a stretch Mercedes, with four doors on either side. The finish is a perfect glossy white — a feat that Saif al-Din suspects must require several washes a day in the ceaseless dust of Dubai. Sheikh Zayed Road is, as usual, mayhem, but in the smooth, air-conditioned limousine, the outside world is immaterial.

Soon they will reach the airport, and from there fly to Syria for the next stage. Across from Saif sits Istikaan himself. No longer a young man, but impervious to pain or privation. A man in Saif's own mould. In a car behind are six trusted mujahedin, posing as bodyguards.

Saif's cover as a rich Nigerian playboy is solid — the Emiratis are used to this new class of African millionaire. Dubai, moreover, is a travel hub without peer. Commercial airliner is the fastest and cheapest form of international travel. A solid alias makes using it possible.

Saif's face has been subtly changed by silicone inserts behind his cheeks and above and below his gums. His facial hair remains, but trimmed into sharp angles of the kind worn by flashy Americans and their imitators.

He has reason to be satisfied so far. Things have gone well. The killing of the children was a goad that the AMISOM troops and their advisers could not resist. They are predictable. Indefatigable, but predictable.

At that moment Saif feels a sudden and terrible pain in his head, precise and agonising. Screaming silently, he holds a hand to his temple.

Beyond the y-shaped mark, deep inside, is a tiny sliver of shrapnel, lodged there from the Phoenix weapons system as cannon rounds tore his launch apart during an attack on a kufr warship one year ago. The hiding place on Khateer Island had been discovered by the Special Forces devils. Yet Saif had realised that a ship must have brought them there, and he sought it out on a boat filled with explosives.

He had pointed the bows of his bomb-laden launch into the sides of that iron monster. Then he had jumped aside. He remembers floating in the water, a needle-like pain in his skull, watching a fireball consume the kufr warship.

A Saudi doctor declared the wound, deep inside his parietal lobe, inoperable. The sliver of steel brings on terrible headaches, troubling him most when he is anxious, or tired, and right now he is both. Ultimately, according to two of Riyadh's finest physicians, the wound will take his life. A matter of months, perhaps, a year or two if he is fortunate. There is no time to waste.

With urgent fingers he reaches into his pocket and unrolls a square of cloth, revealing dozens of dark, pea-sized pellets of raw opium, prepared for him by an Afghan unani herbalist. He turns so Istikaan can't see him, takes one and slips it into his mouth.

Relief comes like a wave on a beach. The water rushes and retreats, until finally, the tide floods in. The warm water carries him away, his body tingling in every extremity.

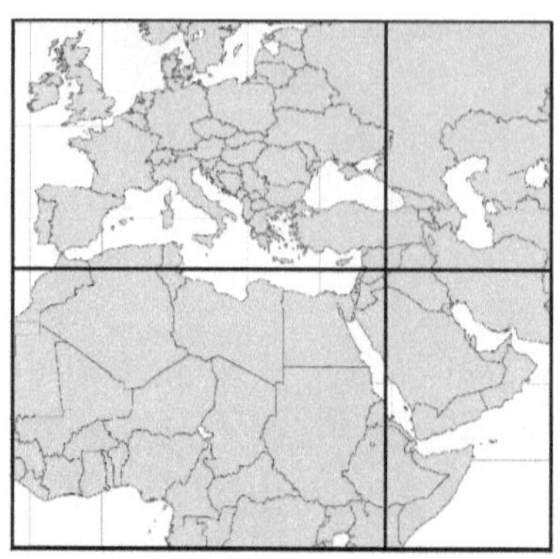

9 SYRIA

Morani

From the tarmac, PJ and Marika are carried by military vehicle to a helipad and a waiting Eurocopter Super Cougar, one of five donated by France to post–civil-war Syria's Air Force.

Hands over head to keep her hat in place, Marika runs under the rotors and grips the door handle. The dust is blowing hard today, the entire horizon obscured to some degree. The door closes and chilled air replaces heat. Marika settles back in the seat, PJ beside her. The chopper lifts off, bearing them away into the south. Neither has spoken more than a few words since their arrival here. Marika passes the time fiddling with her Sid, catching up on the news feeds and operational updates that bleed in from all around the world, in between watching the city slip away, replaced by desert.

Marika and PJ share an occasional observation, but even in silence, she finds his presence comforting. When he isn't looking she studies him surreptitiously. He is square-jawed and handsome, stocky and sure on his feet. It had been she, meeting up with him after Rabi al-Salah, who'd suggested that he be recruited into

DRFS, knowing from experience how rare the mix of qualities he possesses can be.

After a little less than an hour in the air, the co-pilot checks that they are buckled in for descent. Out the window is a dull desert landscape. A small village.

'Doesn't look like much.'

The chopper slows, the rotors churning dust as it settles towards the earth. As soon as the skids make contact one of the crew throws open the door. Hot, dry air blasts Marika's face as she adjusts the straps of her Bergen pack and slides out, hurrying away from the influence of the rotors, where she waits for PJ beside a tussock of sharp-bladed brown grass.

'Looks like one hell of a place,' she says, when he appears.

PJ raises his eyebrows. 'If this is a wild goose chase I'm going to give that prisoner of yours a kick in the arse he'll never forget.'

They ride into the village of al-Guin atop a Syrian Provisional Government Unimog truck, past scattered herds of goats and eight-year-old boys with sticks, hissing at their charges, over-large shorts flapping around bony legs as they run to catch an errant kid. Gaunt old men around camel-dung fires look up belligerently as they pass.

Here, Marika knows, they are outsiders, lumped together under the term *kufr*, sometimes anglicised to *kaffir*. The word means someone who doesn't believe in the Islamic God or his messenger, often conveying undertones of contempt. Long applied by Arab slave traders against Africans, it has become a racist term in parts of that continent.

The village itself is silent and torpid. Donkeys, camels, hens. Sullen men sit in groups in the shade, seemingly devoid of energy. A prayer hall takes central place in this village of whitewashed straight columns and smooth arches.

The driver of the Unimog is an English-speaking Syrian. He spits off the side of the vehicle, dark glasses reflecting the scene like a mirror. 'These are Najdi Bedouin people. They keep to themselves, pretty much.'

The people are unexpectedly friendly, however, and it takes only a few minutes to find an English-speaking Bedouin who professes to know a place nearby where Bashar al-Assad's elite 4th Armoured Division had once guarded a mysterious installation.

The site is less than ten minutes' drive away. Marika and PJ, led by their guide, walk in silence through ruins. The steel frames and concrete slab floors remain in place, but are twisted and tortured as if it was not just fire that destroyed them, but powerful explosive blasts. Overall, Marika estimates that there might have been as much as three thousand square metres under cover, including living areas. Someone wanted them destroyed utterly.

Marika addresses the villager who guided them to the ruins, holding up her Sid to capture the response. 'Tell me about Istikaan. What was he like?'

The speaker's lips curl, and his eyes narrow. 'Yes, very bad. Killer.'

'Why did he kill?'

The man tugs at one end of his moustache and shrugs. 'Don't know why. This man kill everything. That what he does.' He points first at his eyes, then his ears. 'A labourer they do not notice after a while. I hear and see many things.'

'Did you hear or see anything that might help us to locate Istikaan now?'

The heavy brows fold over his eyes in thought, then a slow shake of the head. 'One day I remember Istikaan was angry because a man — a Kurd — back in Iraq make trouble for him. Bashar al-Assad send death squad after the Kurd.'

'How was he making trouble?'

'The Kurd go to the Americans and tell them of atrocities. He say that Istikaan had killed his wife and sons — back in Iraq.'

'How?'

'Don't know. Men went to kill the Kurd but they came back, ah … no good. Istikaan was very angry.'

'Do you remember the Kurd's name?'

'No, but he come from big lake, in Kurdistan.'

'Lake Dokan?'

'Yes,' the man grins, 'Lake Dokan, for sure. And he was only man who ever swim that lake from one side to other.' He shakes his head in wonder. 'They say five miles across. I should live to see such a lake, and man who can swim so far.'

The forensic team is flown in from Manchester, UK, and earthmoving machinery organised from the nearest city, Morani. Marika quickly becomes used to dealing with the polite intransigence of the Syrian Provisional Government, representatives of the original Free Syrian Army and National Coalition fighters who defeated the al-Assad regime in one of modern history's most bloody civil wars.

In just one of many distractions, a member of a small government inspection team, flown in to collect bribes as much as inspect anything, managed to step on a horned viper that bit him on the ankle. The swift action by his comrades to machine gun the offending reptile to death failed to help the potentially fatal bite. Damascus being out of anti-venene he was medivacked to Ankara, Turkey, where his life was, apparently, saved.

They camp each night under a cluster of date palms, and around the firelight the driver of their truck proves a dab hand with the guitar, singing wistful songs of revolution and glory, most of his own composition.

'That one,' he would say, grinning, 'got one thousand two hundred and twenty-three views on YouTube. Soon I will be famous, and rich.'

With the initial difficulties overcome by the judicious use of bribes and diplomacy, the operation is in full swing by the third day. Marika stands with PJ, watching an energetic yellow Cat excavator lift loads of sand with each scoop and deposit them, with a dexterous flip, onto a pile. The forensic team, broiling in orange overalls, work with brushes and cameras in the ruins behind them, but Marika's attention remains fixed on the pit as the excavator bucket catches on something, lifts, then scrapes a two-metre swathe across the floor of the pit, exposing brown and white — a skull, a rack of rib bones. The operator, skilled at this kind of delicate work, does the same thing alongside that first scrape, removing just a thumbnail's thickness of soil. Dozens more skeletons; hundreds perhaps.

The machine operator lifts the bucket, swivels it away to one side and cuts the engine. The silence is overwhelming. No one speaks. The soft moan of the desert wind is the only sound.

Marika fights the desire to turn away from this grisly sight. They knew what to expect, of course. The forensic specialists had combed the site with hand-held detectors that use alumina-coated capillary tubes to sniff out amines in the soil — nitrogenous compounds generated when bacteria break down human remains.

'Bingo,' PJ says.

Yet there is no pleasure in his voice, nor in his eyes as they climb to the floor of the pit. The smell down here is beyond earthiness. Marika stares down at grinning bare teeth, domed skulls, spines of the skeletons piled on others below. Parts of them are blackened, or even charred, and it is obvious that the bodies were burned either before or after being placed in the pit.

'I've never seen a mass grave before,' she says, 'not in person. It's not pretty.'

'My first, too,' PJ murmurs. 'I can't believe the smell, even after years underground.'

Marika walks forward and looks down. Her eyes fall on an almost complete cadaver, less charred than the others. It is a woman with long hair, part burned away, coiled around her head and impregnated with ash.

The lips are twisted into an endless scream. Nostrils fused into one dark cave. Marika recoils and drags her eyes away.

Men and women in overalls enter the pit, carrying pressure-sealed bags. They get busy choosing specimens: skulls, particularly those with shreds of organic matter attached. The desiccated sand has delayed the decomposition process. The samples will be subjected to exhaustive testing back in the laboratory.

Marika shakes her head and swears under her breath, bile washing at the back of her throat as the specimen bags are sealed, then packed into plastic tubs.

It is a mistake, she knows, to spend too long in places like this. A person can get used to it. Even the smell. 'Let's go.'

'With pleasure.'

The sides of the pit are steep and soft, so that their feet sink deep with each step. They scramble over the top, however, and walk towards the ruined buildings, stopping in the shade of a few scraps of tin that cling to an iron girder.

'So what do you think they did here?' Marika asks.

'I don't know. Forensics will work it out. Until then we're just guessing.'

PJ's Sid hums with that muted ringtone most of them use. He gets it out of his pocket and holds it to his ear. Walks away while he talks.

'Some good news,' he says, returning a minute later. 'Our friends in the CIA have been running images of Istikaan through the system. They got a match with a photograph taken three weeks ago, apparently. I'd better go and check it out.'

'That is good news. Meanwhile I think it's worth me trying to track down this Kurd. Can we compare notes in a couple of days?'

PJ folds his arms over his chest. 'Definitely. You still owe me a pint, by the way.'

Marika knows that he's trying to lighten the horror they both feel, but it is not easy to raise a smile. The beautiful things in her life are becoming harder to remember.

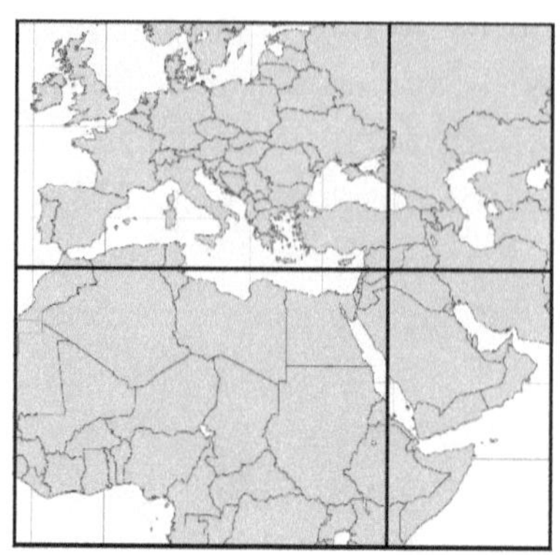

10 SYRIA

Damascus

Saif al-Din watches the Syrian manoeuvre his compact Audi into the depot car park, lock-up with a press of a button, then walk towards the entrance door, sorting through a ring of keys as he does so. Saif is anxious to make the move, but it is best for the man to be inside before they do so.

Hidden in the hedge are six of his own al-Muwahhidun, mostly Somalian, along with the Ba'athists who are partners in this mission. Saif does not fully trust this mixture of Iraqis and Syrians. The Ba'athists smoke, and hum music, in defiance of his warnings. They watch humorous videos on their phones, some of which show lewd women.

The overall leader of the Ba'athist contingent, Karim Yussef, is an Iraqi who boasts often of the fight against the American occupation and their puppet government. He is a Sunni Muslim but even so, Saif distrusts him, for instinctive reasons that he cannot yet fully articulate.

By way of passing the time Saif checks the load of his Norinco QSZ-92 pistol. Works the slide to pump a round into the chamber, then slips on the safety before returning it to his pocket. Checks his watch. Three minutes have elapsed since the owner of the depot went inside.

He turns to look at Istikaan, kneeling beside him. 'You do not have to take part in this.'

Istikaan shakes his head. 'I will not shy away. I will follow.'

Saif stands, looking out for the others, counting them in the distant glow of dawn as they emerge from their hiding places.

All have faces masked with shemagh cloths, leaving just slits for eyes. They wear jeans, gloves, and jackets. Saif walks ahead of the others, holding his pistol in one hand.

The door is unlocked, and Saif opens it, walking through into a carpeted office space, the Norinco sweeping before him. The rooms, however, are empty, even the toilet cubicle.

Through another door and into the concrete floored warehouse behind the office. A vast area filled with trucks, workbenches and tools. As they enter, the owner lifts his head from under the cab of a truck. Saif raises the Norinco. 'You! Get away from the truck. Hands up.'

A spanner falls with a metallic clang. The owner steps away, eyes rounded, chest rising and falling. 'Please, don't kill me …'

'To your office. Now.'

Back through onto the carpet, and a small, tidy office dominated by a large desk, filing cabinets and papers clipped to the wall. More men wait here. Five, six more.

Saif says, 'Contact the drivers and tell them not to come in to work today.'

'I cannot do that.'

'Yes, you can. Text them all, we know you communicate with them in that way. Tell them that you have a family tragedy.'

The owner lifts the smartphone from the desk, and Saif pushes his head close so he can read the message as he types it.

The owner sends the message, then looks back into the eyes of death.

* * *

They are ready within an hour, and Saif inspects the trucks in the hangar-style factory shed, with Istikaan on one side and Karim Yussef on the other.

Between three and five men stand at ease beside each of the vehicles. Saif studies them, wishing he had brought more of his own men to counterbalance the others. Many are former loyalists of the Ba'athist Regime that ruled Syria up until the revolution. Some were members of Bashar al-Assad's personal guard, others fought in the infamous 4th Armoured Division that massacred the civilians of Homs and Aleppo.

This new alliance unnerved Saif at first, but the advantages are too obvious to ignore. The unlocking of a great treasure in Iraq, the work of a Ba'athist regime of many years ago. And despite their political philosophy being secular in nature, it espouses many similar ideals to the Almohad. Pan-Arabic unity, for a start, and a deep hatred of Western interference.

These men are all hardened fighters with a grudge. The Ba'athists want to punish the West. Al-Muwahhidun wants to expel them from the lands of Islam and exact retribution. The same aim, expressed two ways.

Saif inspects everything in silence, walking from one vehicle to the other. Empty payloads. With his eye for detail he studies everything from fuel supplies in jerry cans and drums to the cleanliness of windscreens and floor mats.

When it is done he moves to front and centre, so all the men can see him. His voice echoes from the corrugated-iron walls as he begins to address them. He tells them of the future. Of how important the next few days will be in the history of the world and the ummah. He speaks for ten minutes, then helps Istikaan into the passenger seat of one of the trucks.

By dawn they will cross the border into Iraq. Istikaan will lead them to a treasure beyond measure.

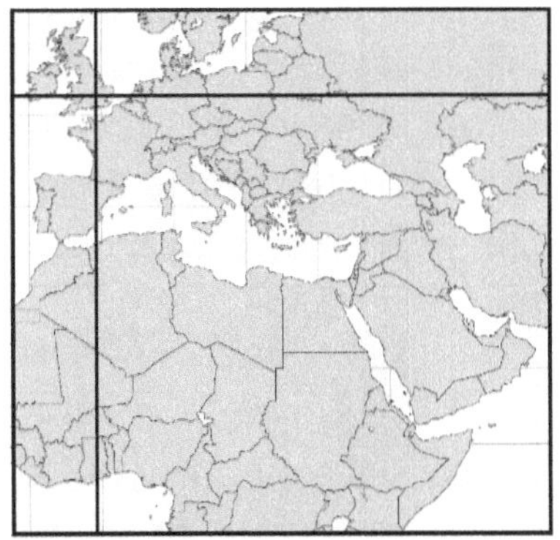

11 UNITED KINGDOM

London

In the borough of Waltham Forest, London, forty-two-year-old shopkeeper Ahmed al-Fahd sweeps glass into piles from the burnt mess that yesterday was a grocery store. His English-born wife weeps from fear.

In a curtained room in nearby Woodford four youths aged sixteen to nineteen, all new recruits to al-Muwahhidun, are shown how to tape a Coke bottle with part of the bottom cut out onto the barrel of a .22 calibre rifle to create a crude silencer, a trick perfected on the streets of Georgian capital Tbilisi against the Russians, and now to be deployed against racist gangs.

The instructor, formerly from Algeria, has been in Britain for just two weeks. He is an expert in the weapons of this kind of war. When it is done he picks up the CZ bolt-action rifle with its beautiful Turkish walnut stock, legal in Britain to licensed shooters, and demonstrates, firing a subsonic bullet into boxes of newspapers set up in one corner of the room. The boys are amazed at how effectively the device deadens the sound of discharge.

In the suburb of Hackney, a pub fills with men, drinking together, beer spilling down chest fronts, singlet tops showing once work-hardened biceps now flabby and unused in long years of unemployment. They sing songs that their grandfathers knew and swear that Britain will again be great once they rid her of the cancer of immigration.

In the Vauxhall Cross office of the Directorate of Resource and Future Security, IT Functional Team Leader Julian Weiss sits behind a wafer-thin SED monitor, fingers crawling over a tempered-glass keyboard. The room contains four benches of monitors in an open square and an orderly tangle of spaghetti-like blue and yellow cables. Five ProLiant 96 Core Opteron servers behind glass, each with 2048 gigabytes of RAM, power the fastest government or corporate intranet in the country.

The design led some wag, years earlier, to nickname the room 'Bear Pit,' a name that stuck. Julian is proud of the Bear Pit. The bears are his, and this is his world — to be shared with others, of course, but they are like-minded compatriots, content to tap away in silence all day if necessary. Any of them can whip out a faulty hard drive and have a new one in place in five minutes, or upgrade RAM in the blink of an eye.

Tonight he pauses to wipe the sweat away in the half-darkness, then to re-tie his long hair into a ponytail to keep stray strands from his face. The servers create intense heat, and due to power restrictions the air conditioner runs only between the hours of nine and five.

The flow of information, however, does not stop. Human and automated sources around the world update constantly, everything routed through and filed away in the databases housed within those servers.

There are hundreds of manual requests for Julian to deal with. Most are security-related, granting access to segments of the compartmentalised DRFS databases to different people. Many of these are straightforward; the more difficult ones where senior personnel might not have access to a particular section of the database require him to route requests through the director.

Julian looks up from the screen across the banks of machines. Bruno, one of his workmates, waves cheerily.

'I'm off home, you going to stay here all night, Juli? Your shift finished at four, didn't it?'

'I'm OK, Raewyn and Paul will be here in a minute.' The Bear Pit graveyard shift starts at eight pm. 'I've just got to finish something. You get going.'

'You're a bleeding workaholic, you are.'

As soon as the other man has gone, Julian's eyes drop to the screen. Fingers blurring, he enters a series of passkeys, the passage through the intranet performed at blazing speed.

Almost everything related to the DRFS's activities can be located somewhere on the databases that he helped develop and implement. Each stage of the network is accessed by a one-time generated code that is constantly reassessed. For example, an employee assigned to a specific operation will be given a passkey for that day that reflects their current task.

Only Julian fully understands the complex, underlying systems that allow DRFS to run smoothly — the thousands of lines of C++ code behind each request for data, each image that appears on the screen. Few outside the IT department understand the data engines that can process millions of requests per second.

The operation he is trying to perform is not difficult, but his daily code does not provide access to it. Generating a new code that allows him to do so is predesigned to create a 'red flag' that will be brought to the director's attention.

There is no way around this without making changes that will be even more noticeable. Not hesitating now, blocking out all other possible choices, all other paths, he begins the process, hesitating when the blinking text asks him for a reason.

SYSTEM GLITCH, he types, the exact wording he has used before — not many times, but regularly enough to encourage

Tom Mossel's alert eyes to glide over it without wondering. After all, it is Julian's job to maintain the system.

The code generator spits up a fourteen-digit figure and Julian copies it with a sweep of the mouse, switching windows with lightning speed and pasting the code into the guard screen of the technical section.

From here it is a simple matter of navigating a series of screens, opening a new tab once to get a serial number … then, finally, he has it.

Exhaling deeply, he changes the last digit from one to three. Logging back out, he stands, reaches for his bag, then leaves the room.

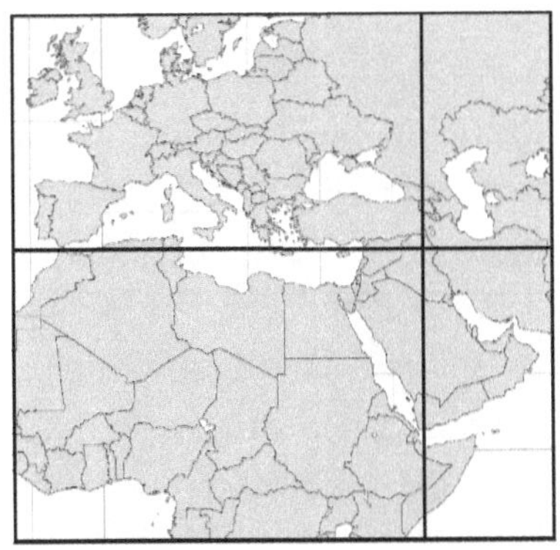

12 KURDISTAN

Sulaimaniyah Airport

They part at Damascus airport, PJ bound for Cape Lemonnier, Marika catching a chartered Cessna Caravan to Kurdistan in North-Eastern Iraq, flying over sites of ancient citadels and battles, the land of Nebuchadnezzar and Beelzebub. Sleeping, head lolling against the window, she dreams of Madoowbe's lean body over hers. The darkness of his eyes, and the lean muscles of his chest and abdomen.

When she wakes the images remain with her, so vivid that she leans back on the seat and savours them, minutes passing before she opens her eyes and looks out the window, left with the feeling that something wonderful has been sullied by that enigmatic prisoner in a cell at Cape Lemonnier.

Through the double perspex she sees Lake Dokan looming ahead, rippled with wind, shining like a sheet of silver. The Little Zab River is an azure vein against a landscape that, from the air, looks no more lush than Mars.

Marika leans forward and shouts to get the co-pilot's attention. 'Can we fly over the lake?' she asks.

'OK. It's out of the way, but we can do so if you'd like.'

'Thank you.'

Marika tells herself that the diversion is important to get an understanding of the geography of the place, yet it is, of course, the traveller in her who can't resist new horizons. She settles back into the seat, head fixed towards the window so she can see the land below laid out in panorama. A land drab beside the dazzling waters of Lake Dokan, a wide expanse despite years of low flows in the catchment. At capacity, the lake covers two hundred and seventy square kilometres. Now, Marika estimates, it has shrunk to just two-thirds of that area, increasingly dwarfed by jagged brown hills.

This is Marika's first visit to Kurdistan, a tribal state within a state, terrorised by Saddam Hussein for many years. He had believed that the Kurds were interlopers and criminals and waged an internal war against them, dropping sarin and tabun nerve gas on the village of Halabja, killing thousands. The pogrom that Saddam Hussein brought on the Kurds is still a recent memory in these parts of the country, a sick taste that raises the spectre of holocaust.

Before they land at the stripe of blue bitumen that is Sulaimaniyah Airport Marika wraps a scarf around her head. Dokan township is something of a resort, but women will still be expected to dress modestly. She does not want attention from the authorities.

The airport has mainly domestic traffic, with businesslike and interested staff. A cool breeze is blowing, and a deputation of locals is there to meet her, one short, older driver and two tough looking men with bulges under their jackets — the security detail, she surmises. All are part of a package arranged by a local firm. The three men wear Western garb — jeans, T-shirts, ill-fitting leather jackets in the case of the younger men; an immaculate suit on their elder. All, however, also wear a patterned shemagh cloth wrapped around the crown of the head, arranged with a tail that hangs over one shoulder in the Kurdish manner.

Marika's guide pumps her hand and grins. 'My name is Elend. You are Miss Hartmann?'

'Marika will be fine, thank you.'

He wears a short beard, and has a cigar stub planted between his lips like a prop. This he lights periodically, taking a few puffs before it goes out again.

'They tell me you are looking for a man — a swimmer.'

'I know it sounds silly, and perhaps rather difficult. I am looking for a man who is said to be the first to ever swim across Lake Dokan, from one side to the other.'

Elend starts laughing first, then the two bodyguards. Marika isn't sure that she understands the joke. She endures their mirth for a few minutes, then plants her hands on her hips. 'Why is that so funny?'

Elend smiles. 'That is such an easy thing. You said it would be hard. Of course everyone here knows Pahedar Jiwan. He is the best Kurdish swimmer in history. He went to the Pan Arab Games in Amman many years ago.'

'Do you know where to find him?'

'Yes, of course. I must warn you that he is not the man he used to be, but I will take you to him now.'

Dokan proves to be a beautiful city on the lake and river, with rugged hills as a backdrop. To Marika's eyes it is a mix of old and new, with broad, modern roads and bridges and five-star resorts with swimming pools overlooking the lake. Arab architecture mingles with a uniquely Kurdish style. Surprisingly bushy trees, including pale green willows, crowd the waterfront. Aerials and satellite dishes bristle from buildings both old and new.

Elend drives on, into the old town with its pale grey housing. They pass a coffee shop, men with their demitasse cups out on street-side tables, many of them moustached, black and white the predominant colours of their clothing. Elend shouts and waves through the window as they pass, and some of the drinkers raise their cups.

As Elend brakes, he swings into a car park outside a walled compound with a sign in Arabic out the front. It is a hospital of some kind, or a convalescent home, and Marika feels the first trepidation at what she is about to learn.

Her guide exits first and opens her door. 'Come with me, I will fix it.'

As they walk across the bare dirt of the parking area she can hear frenetic music from nearby, strong with brassy melody. People clapping. The rhythm is compulsive and for a moment she feels a long repressed desire to dance, wishing that she was here on a less-businesslike mission.

Inside the building, every surface is clean, the floors and walls freshly whitewashed. It has the smells and sounds of the insane asylums of yesteryear.

Up close, Pahedar Jiwan, Marika decides, must have once been a good-looking man, square-jawed and chiselled. Now, however, he has jaundiced skin and disturbed eyes.

'So, you are Australian?' Pahedar asks.

'Yes, born and bred.'

'You look like a swimmer.'

'I am, actually.' Marika smiles. She had swum at state level, for years rising before dawn, her father and mother taking turns to drive her to the Sydney University Aquatic Centre in Darlington for squad training, and later, personal coaching. Butterfly had been her most successful stroke, but it was freestyle she loved.

'It would be great for the children here to see you swim, especially the girls, who lack role models like you.'

'I'm not sure if I'll have time — but I'd love to help if I can. I looked you up on Wikipedia, by the way. You swam at the Amman Pan Arab Games and they say you could have made it at Olympic level, but you withdrew from selection. Why?'

A bitter smile and long slow shake of the head. 'Because I valued my life. The head of the Olympic Committee was Uday Hussein, have you heard of him?'

'Of course.' Saddam's eldest son. Famous for owning more than a thousand luxury cars as much for his litany of human rights abuses.

'Uday was even more of a sadist than his father. The Olympic Committee had its own prison where Uday and his cronies raped and tortured athletes who failed to perform. Why would I, a Kurd, want to volunteer for such a thing?'

Marika's eyes flick from his face down his body. He is skin and bone, and there are scars all over his face and neck. He notices her appraisal.

'Two years,' he says, 'in Abu Ghraib Prison does things to a man. Many didn't last a month.' He looks at her. 'Guess how old I am?'

'Sixty?' This is an awkward question at the best of times. She guesses low so as not to risk offending him.

'I am not yet fifty.'

Marika feels a strong wave of sympathy. Forcing herself to sound professional takes effort. 'I work for the DRFS, a directorate of Britain's MI6. We are trying to track down a man known as the Hourglass: Istikaan.'

The relative silence, with only the dance music as background, is torn by a scream of terror, in a nearby room, one that begins with low, resonant notes. Then, like a hand running left to right along the keys of a piano, it rises to a terrifying pitch, finally breaking into a long series of sobs.

The energy and strength sags out of Pahedar. He closes his eyes, long black lashes meeting the weathered skin of his cheeks. Rests the back of his hand along the timbers of the chair as if seeking support. 'All of us here are veterans of the Mukhabarat, the secret police, and their prisons. For some of us the nightmares last all day.'

Marika can hear muffled voices now, someone trying to comfort the still-sobbing man.

'His name is Salih,' Pahedar says. 'The Mukhabarat took him and his son and tortured them together for eight days straight. At the end of it his son had no skin from his neck to his waist. They had removed his eyes. Do you know why?'

Marika shakes her head, horrified.

'Because Salih had written a letter of complaint to a local official in charge of roads and transport in the area, criticising the level of service.' Again the scream, more soothing voices. 'After his son was gone they chained him in a room for six months. Every day at midday they would take him out and beat him.'

All she can do is shake her head. 'Why?'

'Because they were psychopaths, and Istikaan was the worst of all.' Pahedar lowers his head as if gathering strength. 'I had hoped to never hear his name again.' His eyes, it seems to Marika, have changed colour, from dark brown to deep black. His voice is that of a man with nothing left. 'I will tell you what I know.'

She pulls out her Sid. 'Do you mind if I record? I might need to find a specific detail later.'

'Please, go ahead.'

Marika sets the audio app to record and places the unit on the bench next to her.

'I had just returned from the Pan Arab Games,' he begins. 'Three years married. My wife and I were living in a tiny village near Awazha. I gave swimming lessons, and my wife had just given birth to my second son.

'Kurdistan was not an easy place to live then. For two decades Saddam Hussein enforced sanctions against my people that left us starving. His hatred bordered on the nonsensical. We had no hospitals, no infrastructure. He tried to starve us to death. But even that was not enough. You have surely heard of the attacks, the killings. The al-Anfal campaign where he and his deputy, 'Chemical' Ali, and their troops used conventional weapons, chemical weapons, and air strikes to kill or displace more than one million Kurds. Of course you have heard how they dropped sarin gas on Halabja, leaving it a town of ghosts, but you have not, I suspect, heard of the evil that came later.'

'No, tell me.'

'The Mukhabarat came to our village in the night. The most secret division — those most loyal to Saddam and the family — bought with privilege and selected only for their willingness to deprave the human race to its lowest depths. They were called Amn al-Khas, the Special Affairs Unit, commanded by the favourite son, Qusay Hussein.

'They cordoned off the village. Piled us into covered trucks. Men, women and children, all handcuffed together so no one could escape. Every soul in the village. They left no one. Our last sight was of flames from our burning homes licking up into the sky.

'The trucks drove all night. No drink, no food. They would not stop to allow people to relieve themselves. The smell of excrement was foul and the boards of the truck wet with urine. We held the little ones and prayed. Finally the trucks stopped in a desert valley.'

'Do you know where?'

'In the west of Iraq somewhere. There was a good moon that night and we drove west, I'm sure of it.'

'Any distinguishing marks? Anything that might identify the site.'

'The place we were taken to was underground, but there was a building set in the hillside. It had strange things on the roof.'

'Aerials?'

'Yes, but other equipment also. Something that spins in the wind. I don't know what it was.'

Nothing, not even another outbreak of wild rambling from elsewhere in the centre, can break Marika's spell of concentration. 'So what happened next?'

'Istikaan addressed us. Told us we were special. We wondered what would happen. They took us to a series of cells. Families, everyone in together like cattle, so that there was barely room to sleep. Every day they took small groups away — never to return.

'One day the guards called out my name, that of an old man, a girl and her mother. They took us to a room where we were given injections. They were not Kurds, either, but Ma'dan — marsh people from central Iraq. We started to feel disorientated — I had smoked hashish once or twice when I was a teenager and it was a little like that, but stronger. I think it was intended to make us docile so that we would not fight or struggle.

'I can remember nothing after that. The next thing I knew I was in a hospital bed in Baghdad, under heavy sedation. Later I found out that I was there for three months. I was told that my wife and children had died in a village fire, and that everything else was my imagination.

'I refused to believe it. They took me to Baghdad Central Prison — Abu Ghraib. I was imprisoned there until the Americans liberated it. I cannot describe the cruelties I endured.'

Marika shifts on the seat, eyes fixed on his, feeling a shiver of anger and compassion all at once. Pahedar's hand has started shaking so terribly it is hard for her to resist reaching out and holding it still. 'I'm sorry,' she says.

'I never saw my wife and children again. I tried to find them as soon as I was released. I was threatened with death if I did not stop asking questions and I had to go into hiding, even once Iraq was free again. I know that Istikaan killed them, but I do not know how or why. I also know that he would have killed me too, but that whatever he did to the others did not hurt me. I believe that God spared me for a reason that I cannot yet fathom.'

'What else can you tell me about Istikaan?'

'I know that he moved in the highest circles of the Ba'athist Party that ruled this country. He was a confidante of Saddam Hussein himself. If you have the opportunity, please, kill him without mercy. Kill him twice, three times over and send him to hell where he belongs.'

Marika feels Pahedar's pain, so strong that it's like a third person in the room. 'There is a process that people like me have to follow,' she says. 'It's slow, but as a good friend of mine once said, it is the only thing that separates us from them. You can be assured that I will do everything I can.' She extends a hand. 'What you have told me might be crucial. Thank you.'

'Be thankful that you live somewhere that good people prevail. Do not let history paint Saddam Hussein white. He was the Adolf Hitler of the modern age. The American invasion was wrong, also, but do not let that hide how Saddam Hussein covered this country in blood.'

'I'll remember.'

As Marika leaves that place, she wonders how she will ever forget.

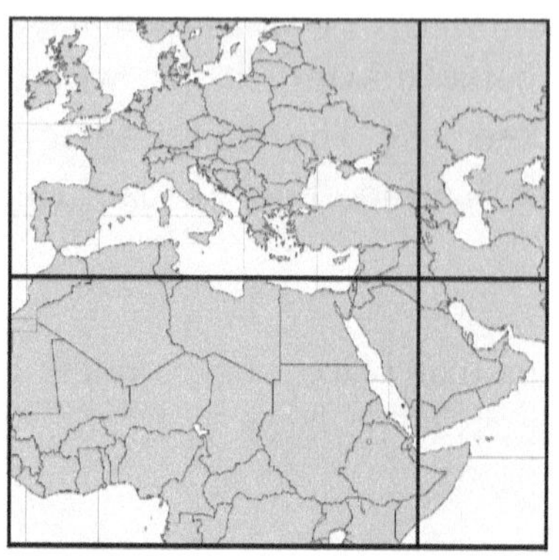

13 IRAQ

Baghdad

Iraq. The cradle of civilisation. The ancient land of Mesopotamia. Ruled by the Ottomans for four hundred years, then drawn into the British Empire who installed an unpopular puppet-king, and drew borders based on political expedience and convenience.

Rocked by coup after coup, and a series of ineffectual governments, Iraq was raped by a brutal megalomaniac and his secret police. A generation of youth died on the battlefields in a terrible and useless war against Iran.

Initially seen by Western strategic planners as a useful counterweight against Iran, opinion turned against Saddam Hussein when he invaded Kuwait, precipitating the first Gulf War. Afterwards, he played a masterful game of 'chicken' with the UN, disclosing just enough of his illicit weapons programs to keep the UNSCOM team from pulling out, telling his secrets bit by bit and letting the inspectors 'shut down' obsolete and superfluous installations.

The game changed after 9/11 when two hundred thousand American boys with guns poured into the country. They had little collective sympathy for the people they called hajjis — the Iraq version of 'gook', and gave Abu Ghraib another chapter in a history that was so deeply marked with blood it stains two great countries forever.

Western powers realised, after the first flush of victory, that the war was far from over. President Bush's 'Mission Accomplished,' declaration from the USS *Abraham Lincoln* in 2003 was not just premature, but an untruth. A new chapter of brutality emerged. Collateral damage. Civilian casualties. Sectarian war.

Pentagon-sponsored Special Police Commando units, recruited from Shia revenge groups like the Badr brigades, tortured dozens, if not hundreds, of Sunni insurgents in the darkest days. Atrocities continued from both sides, and suicide bombings rocked Baghdad on a weekly basis, even after the main American troop withdrawals of 2011.

Even now, Marika reflects, as she walks through the lobby of Baghdad's newest five-star hotel, this is still one of the top ten most dangerous cities in the world. Just days earlier a suicide bomber had detonated a car packed with explosives outside a Shia market in the suburb of Shula, killing twenty-six people, and wounding three times that number.

This dangerous edge to the city, however, is hard to imagine in the luxury of the Rotana Iraq, on Az Zaytun Street in the heart of the Green Zone. Rendered walls in ochre and white pay homage to traditional building styles, and the furnishings call to mind an opulence not normally associated with Iraq. Only the view out the window — across the US Embassy compound to the river — reminds Marika that razor wire and guardhouses are only a short walk away.

Within an hour, fresh from the spa-sized tub in her room, she walks into the lobby, through the glass-fronted wall into the bar, past a water feature that includes a curtain of water so perfectly chiselled it might be glass. PJ is up on one of the high stools, inspecting a freshly poured beer in the same way a carpenter might check his tools before tackling an important task.

Marika props herself with one hand on the shining glass bar rail. 'You look like you're going to enjoy that.'

'Oh, I am. They only have American beer at Cape Lemonnier. Here they've got Stella on tap.'

Marika grins and signals to the barman. 'I'll have one too, please.'

PJ's first sip leaves a smear of froth across his lips, which he wipes with the back of his hand. 'How did you go?' he asks.

'You first. What have our American friends come up with?'

'A good lead. The facial profiler picked up a shot of Istikaan in the port city of Chabahar, Iran.'

Marika frowns. 'Iran? That seems a little strange.'

'Indeed it does. The shot was taken at a hotel. But there's more. He was with another man — guess who?'

'Saif al-Din.'

PJ raises his eyebrows. 'Well done, Aussie. You *are* on top of things today. Saif al-Din had made an effort to alter his profile — cheek pads or something. We only identified him at the second level, as a possible associate.'

Marika smiles. 'So are we going to check it out?'

'Not you, just me. Tom Mossel wants you back in London, along with our prisoner. Despite still saying that he'll only talk to you, he's indicated that he wants to do a deal, provided we get him out of the clutches of our CIA friends and onto British soil. Anyway, what did you come up with?'

'To cut a long story short, Saddam Hussein was rounding up Kurds and shipping them off to a secret establishment run by Istikaan — something, I imagine, along the lines of what we saw in Syria.'

There is no pleasure in PJ's eyes, 'Tell me all of it.'

Marika tells the Kurd's story in low tones, then says, 'The whole thing sounds horrible — like something the Nazis did, or Pol Pot.'

'It has the same ring to it.'

'The link between Iraq and Syria is interesting, don't you think?'

PJ sucks in his lips, whether as a reflective gesture or in order to extract every molecule of flavour out of the beer she isn't sure. 'Remember that they were both ruled by the Ba'athist political party. Iraq and Syria almost merged back in the late seventies, but Saddam took over in Iraq and wanted power all to himself. He canned the idea.'

'Syria and Iraq almost merged?'

'Yep. Well Egypt and Syria did merge, for a while, but not many people remember that. It was part of the Ba'athist philosophy — unifying Arab countries into a single powerful entity. Saddam Hussein preferred to do it by force.'

They eat at the restaurant on the ninth floor, on an outdoor balcony that seems to float over the city itself, high enough for a light breeze that keeps the air cool and sweet. For all that time they talk of other things, but work is always there under the surface.

Marika laughs at his stories of his time in the forces, which he tells with the verve of a natural raconteur, making night-exercise mix-ups and inexplicable orders sound like comedy routines.

After the meal they walk around a city block. Things are much safer here than they were five or ten years earlier, and being with PJ she knows she has nothing to fear. Between the two of them, both packing concealed sidearms, they could cope with anything bar a patrol-force attack.

However, the easy conversation of earlier in the evening has disappeared and there is a tension between them. When they get back to the hotel PJ walks her to her room. They stop outside the door.

'Well I guess I'll see you for breakfast,' she says, 'before our flights.'

PJ smiles, 'Yeah, see you then.'

'I'm tired.'

'Me too.'

For just one tantalising moment she thinks he is going to try to kiss her, but then he stands back and shakes her hand.

'Be safe,' he says.

'You too, please, be safe.'

Still holding his hand she leans forward and kisses him once on the cheek. Turns, opens the door, waves once then closes it behind her. On the other side she stands, back against the door, a surprised expression on her face.

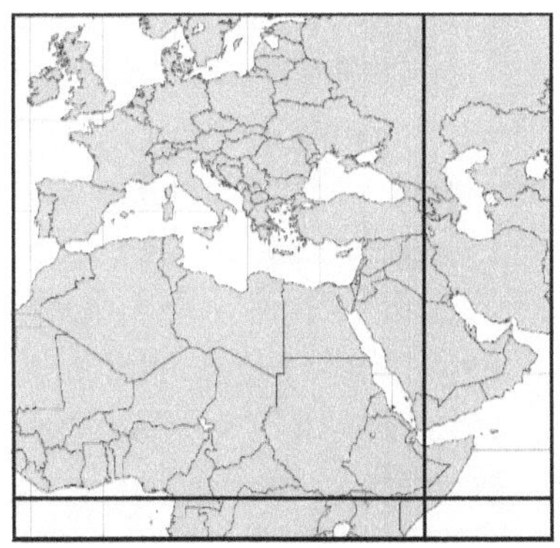

14 SOMALIA

Chakula Refugee Camp

Kifimbo finds himself missing the energetic Marika. For a while he felt like he might be part of a solution, but there are so many problems. The world, it seems to him, is a dam wall under pressure at a thousand points, so that as soon as one hole is plugged the next begins to leak. He remembers his promise to find the dead woman's baby, but days pass before he has time to do anything about it.

Finding the baby takes eight or nine phone calls. Like many young Kenyans, he uses his phone constantly, smoothing his passage everywhere he goes in the camp — organising meetings and appointments with the tap of a few buttons and a sentence or two in Swahili. In both Kenya and Somalia, cell phone towers are everywhere. SIM cards, calls and text messages are affordable even for many of the refugees. Kifimbo's network is wide, and the child, born of a woman already deceased, has attracted gossip in the camp.

On patrol, later that morning, Kifimbo rides atop an M50-armed Humvee, past waving kids with runny noses, hair cut short, with skinny legs and round bellies, wearing T-shirts that advertise everything from Coke to American universities.

The Humvee passes through the barbed-wire border, entering the shanty town that was once a fringe area but is now larger than the camp itself, kilometres of alleys and cardboard huts, rusty corrugated iron, mkokoteni hand carts, women carrying twenty-litre water cans on their heads, children peeping shyly out from behind the bony legs of their mothers.

Kifimbo feels a growing sense of anger and disgust at this ghetto of refuse and human waste, this corner of the world that is almost beyond help. Despite food supplies trickling into the new port facility at Lamu, the giant LAPSSET project in Northern Kenya, the humanitarian effort is failing.

Journalism has given Kifimbo an eye for detail, along with the ability to look at the world with other eyes. So many perspectives; so much pain. He had studied for his diploma at the University of Nairobi, working mornings and evenings as a delivery boy, rising at dawn and writing assignments deep into the night.

He can't help but search for words to describe children with the bloated bellies, blade-thin chests and twig arms of the hungry, and the haunted looks of those who have just arrived, wrinkling their noses at the stench of human faeces, seeking out a patch of ground that they can call their own.

For ten minutes, Kifimbo rides in silence down these narrow passages that cannot be called streets, zigzagging haphazardly past the Qatari tenements. These prefabricated units were paid for with a donation from the government of Qatar and built using imported tradesmen. Most have been stripped of interior and exterior linings, windows and plumbing that never had a water supply to connect to. Now, eighteen months later, they resemble a bombed-out Mogadishu apartment block.

The patrol enters the Laba Quarter, the most derelict precinct of the camp. Deeper and deeper they penetrate, through narrower and narrower alleys. Soon there is no way to proceed by vehicle — the passages are too narrow and cluttered. Kifimbo is forced to leave two men to guard the vehicle and continue on foot. Three of them walk in single file down a track between piles of garbage and tukul structures made of acacia sticks, clad with cardboard boxes or cheap plastic sheeting. The air is dulled by a haze of hearth-fire smoke and a constant hum of sound — hammering, singing, chatter, livestock, and occasionally a spluttering motorbike engine.

The voices are not all Somali, some are Sudanese. Families fleeing the ongoing conflict between north and south, and between tribes in Darfur. Kifimbo hears three or four discrete languages as he walks on, winding around rubbish and avoiding faeces and sullage pits. He passes a woman squatting beside her tukul, a dung fire burning, cooking something in a pot made from an old, blackened peach tin with a clever wire handle. He passes two women nursing a youth on a bed of rags outside their tukul. The older woman's arms are bird thin, her cheeks sucked in. She eyes Kifimbo with a guardedness that belongs to those with so little to keep them from death that they fear any variation in routine. She touches Kifimbo's leg as he passes.

'My son, he has the cholera.'

'I will pass word to the medic station. Help will come.'

Kifimbo walks past young men with the faces of old men. Side passages lead in all directions, the trail winding around and along until it seems that this place never ends, that all of humanity is here, where the NGOs and agencies cannot feed and protect them. They will stay here until tents are found and allocated to them. Only then can the programs start. In the meantime these people are dying.

One or two children start to follow them, holding pretend AK47s, aping the soldiers' walk. That number grows to three dozen or more, not making a sound, stopping when they stop, walking when they walk.

The passage through that hell of dispossession ends with a pile of refuse and boxes. Kifimbo stops and stares. Rubbish piled higher than his head. Twice that high. The buzzing of flies. This is the camp waste dump that provides resources for these desperate people.

Kifimbo starts asking questions of everyone he sees. Trying to find the woman by name. Yet they have not wandered far off the main path when he hears a baby's cry, turning to see a young woman with a beautiful face. Angular and perfectly sculpted, with hair no longer than a boy's. She holds the baby in her arms, rocking it gently, crooning softly, glaring at Kifimbo as he approaches.

'Hello,' he says, slinging his rifle over his shoulder, 'my name is Kifimbo. Is this the baby taken from the dead woman at Kafee?'

'My name is Haro, and yes, this is my cousin Khadija's baby.'

'Please, can I hold him?'

With a flash of dark eyes she hands the baby across. Kifimbo takes the warm infant in his arms, knowing how to support his head, take his weight. He has handled babies all his life. Brothers. Sisters. Cousins. Nieces. Eyes closed into wrinkled slits, the baby starts to bawl. Swinging from the hips and crooning gently, Kifimbo persuades him to stop, and for two or three minutes he holds him, smiling, inhaling the milk and baby-sweet smell of him.

Another minute passes before Kifimbo returns the baby to his surrogate mother. 'Thanks for letting me hold him,' he says, 'he is a beautiful child.' He stares for a few final seconds. 'What's his name?'

The young woman's face mists like a mountaintop at dawn. 'I call him Rajee. In Somali that is our word for hope.'

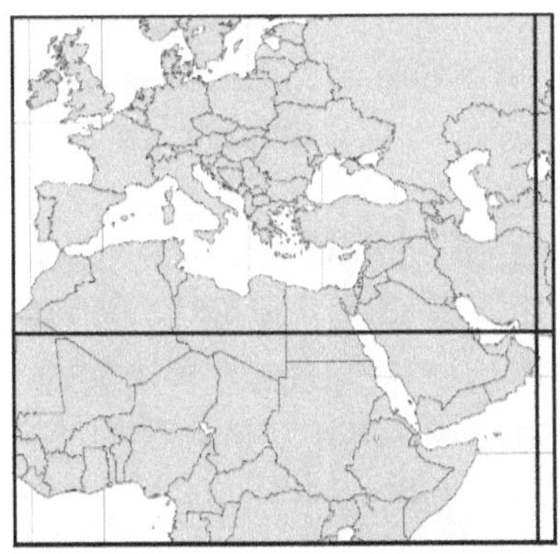

15 IRAN

Chabahar

War between the West and Iran lasted eight months. It began with Nato-led 'surgical' air strikes on nuclear installations and critical infrastructure. The lessons of Iraq had been learned. There was no large-scale invasion, but a number of battalion-force insertions that targeted key cities and bases.

Iran was no pushover, however; with a technological capacity that had seen it produce home-grown missiles and even launch a satellite, it was ready to fight back. Shahab-3 missiles struck Tel Aviv, a Turkish Nato base, and an American installation in Saudi Arabia. Iran's blockade of the Strait of Hormuz held. Soldiers on the ground resisted fiercely.

Three months into the war, a new political force led by the member of parliament for the city of Arak, Abbas Rajeel, was able to depose Mahmoud Ahmadinejad and effect a peace treaty with the West, but the damage was done: millions of refugees on the march. Iranian industry in ruins.

Even now, sanctions persist, and there are skirmishes with Nato troops on the border with Turkey almost every day.

On station just off the port of Chabahar, PJ, mindful of this recent history, is well aware that the peace is uneasy, and that the coastline and borders are more heavily guarded than at any other time in Iran's history.

Light cloud cover has moved in with the breeze, making the night warmer than the previous one and much darker. PJ is onboard HMS *Cressie*, an Archer-class patrol boat seconded to the DRFS, one of the latest versions built by the Ailsa shipbuilding yard. At just twenty metres in length, with a beam of around one-third of that, it boasts state-of-the-art comms equipment, a 20mm cannon mounted on the fo'c'sle and armour plating around the bridge.

PJ lifts his eyes to the sky, unable to pick out any stars, realising that it is not cloud obscuring them, but dust, blowing in off the Arabian land mass to the west. He can smell it, redolent of exotic lands.

The dust clouds only heighten his sense of unease, waiting for something he does not yet know the nature of. Chabahar is just over the horizon, with its long concrete dockside where hundreds of dhows take to the hard at low tide, swinging on their moorings at high.

This is the city where Istikaan and Saif al-Din were photographed by a clandestine hotel security camera, eighteen days earlier. In just minutes from now, PJ will go ashore to find out why they were here. There is, he knows, nothing random about what these people do.

PJ looks up to see the gangly frame of the executive officer walking down the side deck, one hand on the rail more from habit than necessity. 'Mister Johnson, the captain says to tell you that we're approaching your departure point.'

'Thanks, XO. I'm coming.'

PJ follows the other man back around the superstructure, up the steps and into the bridge. *Cressie* has its bridge set high, over the aft cabin area, scarcely big enough for half a dozen men.

Susan Quayle, the captain, is an imposing presence. In her mid-thirties, she is originally from the tough Tyne Dock district of

Newcastle, England, a strapping woman with wrestler's shoulders and screwed-up eyes from years of staring into bright, sunlit horizons.

She glances up at him. 'That's as close in as I'm going. Better get yourself ready.'

'Thanks, I appreciate you coming in this far.'

'Yeah, well, some of us have got better things to do than drive civilians around the place.' She spits the word *civilians* as if reserving it for special vehemence.

PJ heaves a sigh under his breath; he had been warned that *Cressie*'s skipper was unhappy about the Special Forces secondment, and the ribbing hasn't stopped since the moment he stepped aboard. 'I'm no civilian, actually. I was in the RN until six months ago. Special Boat Service.'

Quayle rolls her eyes skyward and makes a *pff* sound with her lips. 'So what do you want me to do? Throw my bra at you?'

The XO and bosun's mate chuckle, faces lit by the glow of the instruments. 'If that's what you want to do,' PJ says, smiling, 'go right ahead.'

A few more chuckles, then silence.

She turns to the XO. 'Give orders to launch the inflatable, and get this bloke out of here before he says something that might actually be funny.'

PJ puckers up. 'How about a goodbye kiss?'

Quayle bends over so that her fatigue trousers stretch tight over a generous rear end. 'Kiss this if you like.'

'Thanks for the offer, but no thanks. See you later, anyway.'

'Don't kill too many of the poor bastards. Sanctions've just about finished them off, from what I hear.'

PJ follows the XO back down onto the main deck while a two-man crew operate the davits, swinging a black inflatable out over the water. In total it is just 3.6 metres long, tiller-steered with a fifty-horsepower Yamaha outboard. Perfect for a night-time run in to the coast.

PJ wears clothes that will pass anywhere — jeans, open shirt, and over the top a traditional, coarse-knitted woollen sweater. In a belt strapped around his abdomen he carries the Sid, a large quantity of cash in US dollars, a Gerber knife, and in a holster, a SIG Sauer 9mm handgun. More money has been sewn into the hem of his shirt. In the Middle East money for a bribe can make the difference between capture and no capture, or even life and death.

The crewman starts the outboard as soon as they hit the water, warming it with a twist of the throttle. The motor's underwater exhaust and four-stroke technology make it almost silent, as well as powerful — carrying them in at a steady speed.

Ten minutes later they lose the ocean swells, passing into the calmer waters beyond a breakwall. The row of dhows on the dockside gets closer until the masts appear to touch the stars. The smell of shellfish and seaweed deepens. The helmsman uses the cover of one of the larger vessels to get PJ in almost all the way.

'Good luck, mate,' the helmsman whispers, and PJ rolls up his jeans and swings over the side, his feet touching the muddy bottom, sneakers immediately filling. He turns the inflatable, points it back out to sea and gives it a shove to send it on its way.

Standing stock-still, he studies the shore. There are few people around. After a minute of looking he decides that he can see no immediate danger and sets off through knee-deep water that becomes progressively shallower until he reaches a set of concrete steps, climbing to the edge of what appears to be a ghost town. He sits on a concrete barrier, pulls off his shoes and squeezes them out as best he can before continuing on, orientating himself according to the map he studied back on *Cressie*.

One old man shuffles past, and PJ mutters, 'Sa-laam.' He is conscious of his pale skin here, but the beard helps, along with a deep suntan. Besides, few Iranians are darkly pigmented.

The man returns the greeting and stops, as if they might chat, but PJ walks on past the boats. Like so many other places, the lower city floods on high tides, so no one lives here any more.

During the day, PJ knows from satellite photographs, it will fill with people doing business, fishermen departing and returning, but there is a layer of fine sand all over, deposited by the high tides that inundate it daily. It's not until he has moved more than a hundred metres up that he reaches a dry street, with lights on in buildings on either side.

Now he can hear voices. Television sets. Soft Eastern music.

Here also, down half a block, comes the first warning that this city has so recently been a war zone. An Iranian army guard post. Men standing around old oil drums with fires burning inside, assault rifles held casually in hands.

PJ slips through the shadows, every sense alive, every muscle taut. This kind of stress is familiar to him. The secret, he knows, is to be part of the background, part of the clutter. To stand out is to die. He tries to play a role — not someone potentially lucrative like a businessman hurrying home, but just another desperate case.

The ground rises into a small hill so that the port area is laid out below. From here he can see the dhows in their moorings, and more fires. It is a good place to get his bearings.

The ground drops again and he comes to an intersection. Three youths stand on the centre line of the road, laughing and skylarking. PJ stops, staring, feeling the crunch of broken glass under his shoe. Working his way up a block or more until he can cross will take time, but there is no way to do so here. Distracted as they are, the youths will soon spot movement.

The adjacent building is the ruins of something from the colonial era, when Portuguese ships stopped at the port — offices perhaps, some of the columns that supported the entrance still standing, others crumbling and damaged. PJ uses them for cover as he moves on down the road.

He has just passed that building, quickening his pace, when there is a shout.

The language is either Farsi or Balochi, the local dialects, neither of which PJ understands. Those youths are trouble. If they suspect he is a Westerner they will cause a scene.

PJ's heart freezes, but he doesn't miss a beat, continuing to walk. But then comes a single shouted word, and the commanding tone is obvious. He stops.

One of the youths has produced a handgun, waving it menacingly at him. Not youths out having fun, but off-duty soldiers or police, wandering the town. The penalty for being discovered as a Westerner has just gone from aggravation to death or imprisonment.

Despite the armistice, there is no love lost. Sanctions and war brought famine to the populace. PJ thinks quickly. Phrasebook Farsi would not help him now even if he knew enough to get by.

Facing the three, one with the handgun still levelled at him, PJ lifts a single finger in the universal symbol: up yours. He smirks, then pumps his hips rhythmically. This is the act of an equal. Of a comrade. It means *I am on my way to see a woman. I don't have time for you.*

This makes the three laugh, and before they can start a conversation he walks on, crosses the road without further attention and hurries down an alleyway crisscrossed with clotheslines high above. Ahead he sees the lit doorway, guarded by a shortish man with massively oversized forearms and a pugnacious face, stepping towards him as he approaches.

PJ breathes a sigh of relief. He is still in danger, but this danger has a different smell and feel, more predictable, less chaotic. He follows the man through the stone passageway and up an unlit set of stairs, past rooms that smell of shisha smoke and male sweat.

Finally his guide beckons him through a doorway with a toss of his chin. The room is lit only by an array of candles. There is a pair of narrow single beds, both neatly made, and a woman on a cushion beside a low eating table. Standing, she takes PJ's hand. Probably forty or more years old, she has high cheekbones and crisp, intelligent brown eyes. Her long black hair falls straight, past her shoulders.

'Hello,' she says in perfect but accented English, 'my name is Mariam.'

PJ does not offer a name, just stands, waiting while the woman walks back to the door and talks to the man who brought him upstairs. The door closes and he is gone.

'His name is Naser,' she explains. 'He is trustworthy, by the way; he has saved my life several times.'

PJ smiles crookedly, still a little dazed by the proximity to her perfume. This woman is older than him in years, yet she is undeniably attractive.

'You are not what I was expecting,' he says.

Those almond-shaped eyes dance. 'No? You expected a man, and instead found a mature woman. I hope you're not disappointed.'

'Not at all.'

She reaches out and takes his hand. 'Now come. You must be hungry, and thirsty.'

The balcony overlooks the sea from a distance of several city blocks. The Western-style table is of sturdy walnut, and Mariam brings plates of salads, spiced meats, and a glass of fruit juice that he downs in three long draughts.

From this vantage point, PJ can see other candles burning all over the city. 'No lights here?'

'No. The power outages come and go. Ten hours so far this time, but they can last for days.'

Power outages are common these days. Even in England. Infrastructure maintenance needs have outstripped financial and resource capabilities. The Iranian government is struggling on a number of fronts, and the lack of power here doesn't surprise PJ.

'This is delicious, thank you. You're not eating?'

'I have already, thank you.'

While he eats she sits on the chair next to him, asking no questions. He finds his curiosity piqued. 'How long have you been working with us?'

'Ten years.'

'Even through the war?'

'Yes.'

'Do you mind if I ask why?'

'The Komiteh took my first husband. He was a professor of political science at the University of Tehran. He became one of the organisers in the election protests in 2009. They came one morning while we were having breakfast at a restaurant in Tehran. I haven't heard one word from him since.'

'I'm sorry.'

'It was a long time ago. I have learned to live with pain, but I disagree with a government that rules through fear.'

The pile of food defeats even PJ's enormous appetite, then they spend an hour discussing options for the following day. Finally, he stretches and yawns.

'Where do I sleep?'

Mariam points back into the one-room apartment. 'There are two beds. One is yours.'

PJ raises his eyebrows. The two single beds are separated by less than a metre of space.

The bathroom is down the hallway. Tiled in blue, it has an Iranian-style squat toilet, but a standard shower as well as a large bathtub. Mariam has laid out a brand new toothbrush and soap in a packet. The water is not piping hot, but warm enough considering the balmy temperature.

When he returns to the room Mariam is already in bed, to all appearances fast asleep, facing the other way. He strips to undershorts and climbs into his allotted bed. For a few minutes he lies awake, listening to the sounds of this strange port city, before being carried away to sleep.

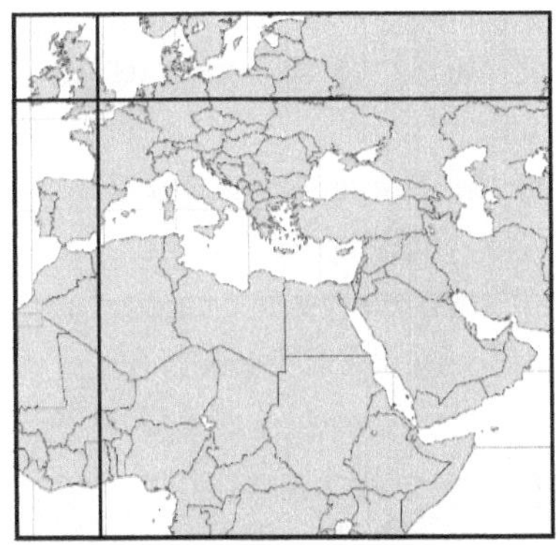

16 UNITED KINGDOM

London

Marika wakes soon after dawn. The sun has risen, but the light remains low and eerie. Out the window the plane trees of Eccleston Square gardens begin the slow burn of autumn; they will change colour a hundred times over the next eight hours.

Now, while dew still drifts down, she pulls her hair back into a ponytail, changes into track pants and a fluoro-yellow T-shirt with dark green stripes. Sitting on the front step she ties the laces on an almost new pair of Gel Nimbus runners. It might be cool at first, but before long the run will warm her body up, and a sweater will only hamper her.

She is tired and jet lagged, having landed at Heathrow a little after eight the previous evening. The plane was a Gulfstream V with a history — once known in Intel circles as the Guantanamo Bay Express. This aircraft was originally registered to a fictitious American company called Premier Executive Transport Services, and now used openly as a CIA workhorse.

The agency had made no bones about their preferred option — packing the Almohad prisoner off to one of several countries that would interrogate him in return for favour or payment. Countries such as Jordan specialise in proxy torture. Tom Mossel, however, will not countenance this.

'We do things by the book. Whatever the stakes. We'll find out what he knows in our own way.'

There are several secure sites in England for political prisoners, potential defectors, traitors, informers. This one is a house in O'Donnell Road in Lambeth, run by an elderly same-sex couple who appear to be kind old men. Both are, however, ex-Paras and know more about tradecraft than a dozen of their younger counterparts.

Going by the trade names Trevor and Ben, they have a fearsome reputation in the business. Protective of each other to the point of paranoia, they have never lost a 'visitor', and were the first choice to host the prisoner. The pair had even, after learning of the suspected origin of their new charge, spent a few days boning up on Levantine cookery.

Marika had supervised the fitting of the tracking collar — actually a bracelet these days, yet almost immoveable without an angle-grinder, which few people would care to risk so close to the radial artery.

Still thinking about him, she leaves the flat, closing the door behind her, taking the steps to the ground floor and out onto the footpath, turning right in the same direction as she would walk to work. The mist shows as a tunnel of light in front of each passing vehicle, headlights of the traffic already running down Belgrave Road. Marika crosses to the far side, down past rows of boutique hotels, at which point she slows to attach her iPod earphones and switch on one of several running playlists.

At first she takes it steady, trying to find a rhythm that is somewhat strange to her after weeks of running on unsealed tracks. The paved surface is easier on the leg muscles, but she can feel the impact in her shins. The surface is damp from light rain that has fallen through the night. Each pace feels like an epiphany, and the more it hurts the better she feels, moving on past white facades, brass plaques and coloured awnings.

Her mind is free to roam, and she thinks of PJ. There have been a couple of dry operational updates as of the previous night, but Chabahar is all but a war zone. If the Iranian military catches him, he will not leave alive. The thought that something might happen to him feels like a grenade in her heart, fused and primed.

Once or twice she passes other runners, a cyclist or two, then a young mother pushing a baby in a three-wheeled high-speed stroller. The first busy road crossing; she jogs on the spot while waiting for the green signal, then over the road and into a café strip. Baristas in aprons bearing Harris or Vittoria logos sweep around the tables of footpath cafés, smiling or scowling as she goes past. Marika is too focused to respond, driving her legs onward, hating the rubbery slackness and unresponsiveness of her muscles. A nagging pain manifests itself in the upper arch of her foot.

Marika turns along the river, the Thames embankment walk that fringes the bank of both sides. The river moves higher each year, closer to the concrete barriers that were designed to last forever but that will soon be inadequate.

The Thames is in ebb, streaming down to the sea, moving almost as fast as she is, but in the opposite direction. This, to Marika, strengthens the sensation of speed. Passengers pouring down the walkway towards the Clipper station turn to look at her as she passes, and for a fraction of a second they transform from innocent commuters to a crowd of al-Muwahhidun gunmen on a raiding party. The sudden feeling of being unarmed is so akin to being naked and defenceless that she fights the urge to turn and run headlong.

Continuing down the path, her eyes fall on a stretch of green grass. For one terrifying instant the area is not empty in that morning light, but bloodied with the broken bodies of children, with the brown river beyond.

Marika stumbles. Stops running, closes her eyes, leans over, hands on her knees. Fighting it. Bringing up the memories she needs. The Budawang ranges at first light. Bodysurfing North Bondi, just as the wave's power takes control, blue crashing into white. The cinema on a Saturday afternoon, popcorn spilling over from cardboard cups.

Marika looks out at the grass. No children. Just a dozen pigeons huddled into a patch of sunlight poking through the skyline.

By ten they have whisked the prisoner from the safe house and to the deepest floor of the Vauxhall Cross facility, where three interview rooms are kept for this purpose. In some ways Marika would have preferred not to have to face him again, but he refuses to talk to anyone else.

These interview rooms are well known in the intelligence community. The brick walls are whitewashed, illuminated by a rectangular array of harsh fluorescent tubes. A polymer table and two chairs are situated at the back end of the room.

There is no question of the interview being conducted in private. The field agents who brought the prisoner from the safe house take up station at the back end of the room, along with a pair of analysts. The prisoner appears to accept their presence, sitting in the designated chair at the table and looking across at Marika as she does the same. She points back up at her entourage. 'They're staying, OK?'

He shrugs. Says nothing.

Marika studies his face. They have still not identified him by name. There is little she can use to surprise him, only some variations in his approach to prayer that one of his sharp-eyed minders noticed, which may or may not be significant.

'Look,' Marika begins, 'we've done our part. You're in London. You're staying in luxury with people prepared to cater for every reasonable request. You've got a mosque nearby, a coffee shop. People to take you there. You've got everything you could possibly need. Now I want everything. I want to know more about Istikaan. I want to know why he and Saif al-Din were in Somalia together, and why they were seen in Iran a few weeks ago. And, I want to know your source in the DRFS.'

The eyes fix on her, glossy dark brown under the lights. His lips tilt into a sardonic sneer. 'How are your parents?' he asks.

A needle of concern pricks her spine. 'Don't fuck with me,' she growls.

'Your sister too. I've seen her photograph ... over in Sid-e-nee — a very attractive woman.'

Marika feels her heart stop. *Bloody Facebook!* Her younger sister is a budding model, just yesterday she had posted a portfolio of her latest shoot for a local jeweller.

'Leave my family out of this,' she says at last.

The prisoner raises his eyebrows. 'They live in a nice safe little corner of the world ... or so it seems.'

'Shut your face. You are in my power, not the other way around.'

A questioning look. *You think so?*

She bristles, 'We've played your little game. You gave us a little titbit of information. We checked it out. You got something in return: we got you out of that cell you hated so much. This stops here, today. You tell us everything in that photographic memory of yours and you get a new life, within reason.'

The prisoner smiles. 'You are making a lot of assumptions there.'

Looking into that face, Marika is almost too angry to speak. Controlling herself with an effort, keeping her words measured, she says 'You're not Somali, are you?'

'The place of my birth does not matter.'

'You have been observed at prayer. You are Alawite, aren't you?'

'My faith is a private matter ...'

'We know you speak the Levantine dialect. You could be Palestinian, Lebanese ...'

Arms crossed. 'None of your business.'

'But you're not. You're Syrian.'

An instant of transparency in those eyes tells her that she's right. 'You're one of those bastards who turned Homs into an abattoir, aren't you? Who slaughtered families because they dared to say that the al-Assad regime was cruel and wrong.'

The prisoner does not answer the question, instead directing a barb back at her. 'You want me to tell you about your lover, Madoowbe, don't you? You want to hear his last words, the location of his grave?'

Don't begin to trust him, not for a moment. Whatever else he has done, he killed those children in Somalia, without conscience, and he would kill you too ...

'The shifta took your Somali boyfriend alive,' he goes on, 'they mutilated and tortured him until dawn, they began cutting off his extremities ...'

'Enough,' she shouts, 'or I swear to God you'll rot in a cell until you die.'

The prisoner's manner changes, becoming thoughtful rather than provocative. 'Let me tell you a story, Marika Hartmann. One that will answer many of your questions. There is something coming. We have called it the Tide of Saleh, after a story in the Qur'an. Do you know it?'

'No.'

'Of course not. The story is about a man called Saleh, a pious man, one of God's favourites. He is sent to remonstrate with the Samood people, who have become rich and powerful and Godless. They demand a sign to prove that he has truly been sent by God.' His voice rises and falls melodically, like a Sunday-school teacher telling a story. 'God does as Saleh asks, and a camel appears from out of the bowels of the mountain. Do you know what the bad Samood people did then?'

Marika folds her arms across her chest.

'They killed the camel.'

'Get to the point.'

His voice drops, eyes swimming with passion, 'God punished the Samood. They fell dead in their strong and beautiful houses. Only the people who believed in God and listened to Saleh were saved. Istikaan believes that he has been sent, like Saleh, to destroy the Samood. He told me that himself. He is an unusual man. Even I am still unsure of his true nature. People say that he is a walking corpse. They say that his family was killed by the Americans. They speak of him with hope, as if he is a prophet who will deliver them from their ills.'

Marika places her elbows on the table. 'Let me get this straight. Istikaan sees himself as Saleh in the story?'

'That is correct.'

'And we Westerners are the Samood?'

'Also correct.'

'Where and how is this going to happen?'

A slow shake of the head. 'I am in London, but I am being babysat in a room with two old men who watch me even while I use the lavatory. That is not good enough for me, I am sorry. I want to feel secure before I tell you more.'

Marika's voice comes out as a hiss. 'What do you want?'

'I want a house, near the sea, with internet and telephone, someone to prepare my meals and clean. I want around-the-clock security. I want one hundred thousand English pounds in a bank account in an appropriate name. I want a genuine British passport in that same name. When I have evidence that you have these things ready, then I'll tell you how the Ba'athists have allied with the Islamists. Of what is hidden in Iraq, what is now ours to claim.'

'That will take days ... a week, at least. The answer is no.'

'You don't have a choice. This is not negotiable. I do not yet feel secure or happy. I need proof that I will get what I ask for. As soon as I go out into the world I am vulnerable.'

'The things you know about me ... you must have a source of information in the DRFS. Tell me who your source is, as a sign of good faith.'

'Not yet. When I have my passport and cash, and I've seen photographs of the place you have chosen for me. I am partial to blue, by the way ...'

Marika stands up and pushes her chair in. 'I'll talk to my boss. He may prefer that we send you back with the Americans so they can find someone to beat it out of you. You'll be notified.'

The prisoner's eyes rise to meet hers. 'Saif al-Din says that you are immoral.'

She is inclined to leave, but he knows how to play her. Knows that she will listen. 'You're lying. Why would he waste time even thinking about me?'

'Because you are a threat to him.'

Marika shakes her head with a forced laugh.

'Saif al-Din says that you are so steeped in sin you can never escape. He says that you must renounce sinful music, dancing, immoral books. He says that if you do so, perhaps he and you can be friends.'

Marika turns to the guards. 'Get this bastard out of here.'

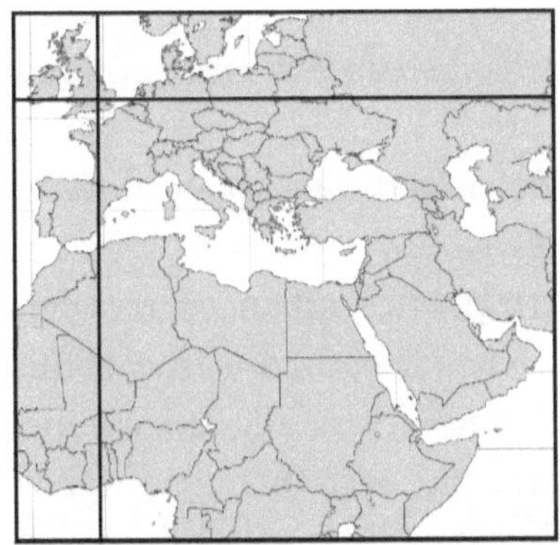

17 UNITED KINGDOM

London

Marika rides the escalator up from the basement, running the interview over in her mind. With an effort she dismisses the prisoner's final statements as a deliberate attempt to distract her. She forces herself to focus on the facts he imparted.

When I have evidence that you have these things ready, then I'll tell you how the Ba'athists have allied with the Islamists. Of what is hidden in Iraq, what is now ours to claim.

Marika has a small private office on the second level with her name on both door and desk, and a black HP workstation linked to the network. First she deals with operational messages and any emails that can't wait.

Then, delving into the database, she starts to read some general background on the Ba'athist movement of Syria and Iraq. The first surprise is that their founder was a Christian, Michel Aflaq. Scan reading where possible, moving from article to article, she learns that Saddam Hussein was inducted into the party by Aflaq himself.

She learns how armed Ba'athist militias fought hardest against the American occupation of Iraq, and how their numbers were bolstered after the Syrian civil war by remnants of al-Assad's forces, bringing heavy weapons and hundreds of new fighters into the fold.

Yet why have they allied themselves to the Almohad and their vast reach across the globe?

In Middle Eastern politics, alliances are often more about who a particular group hates less than a true confluence of ideology. Saddam Hussein, a Sunni, was aligned via the Ba'ath Party with members of the Alawite sect in Syria. Iran aligned itself with al-Assad's regime because they hated the Sunni majority of Syria more, and he was repressing them.

The Tide of Saleh. Something hidden.

The name itself suggests that this hidden weapon is unlikely to be conventional, but would more likely fall into the category currently known by the acronym CBRN: Chemical, Biological, Radiological and Nuclear.

There have been many attempts at CBRN mass murder by non-state groups over the years. Most, fortunately, have been foiled by security services. Dhiren Barot, for example, tried to make a radiological weapon out of hundreds of smoke detectors containing Americium-241. Abu Musab al-Zarqawi, an Iraqi, purchased twenty tonnes of chemicals, planning to make a tanker bomb that would create a toxic cloud capable of killing the inhabitants of a medium-sized city. Abdur Rauf, a Pakistani microbiologist, obtained anthrax spores and associated equipment on the orders of Ayman al-Zawahiri, then Osama bin Laden's number two man. Almost six hundred instances of the trafficking of nuclear material were documented by monitoring agencies between 1993 and 2011.

OK, but why Iraq?

After a quick search on the database, Marika opens an e-book on her desktop screen. White cover, red title with three gold stars at the top. A version of a title first published in 2004, written by Hans Blix, leader of the UNMOVIC inspection team charged with finding and rooting out Saddam Hussein's famed weapons of mass destruction. Marika recalls scanning through it years ago, after the American invasion.

Hans Blix was a respected opponent of America's invasion of Iraq, but his point was not that Iraq had never had the WMDs that were used as a pretext for war. It was common knowledge that they did. Only that some, many or all of them had been destroyed, and that his team was not given sufficient time to finish their work.

'The problem,' he wrote, 'was that the Iraqi side had no solid documentary evidence about the quantities that had been destroyed. It claimed that all documents had been destroyed along with all the chemical and biological weapons. This could all have been true, but it was also possible — and this was our concern — that documents had been hidden and quantities of chemical and biological weapons had been squirreled away.'

Blix made the case that chemical and biological weapons programs were well documented, but by 2001 the UN inspection programs had been largely successful in forcing Iraq to dismantle them. In his opinion Saddam Hussein probably never had a nuclear capability advanced enough to pose a danger to the West.

Marika goes back to the database. More writings and statements by other inspectors. Richard Butler, Scott Ritter. The common thread was a frustration at the ability of Saddam Hussein's government to thwart their efforts, and an acknowledgement of the seriousness of the WMD programs. Most of the inspectors went on to become vocal critics of the Iraq war on the basis that the stocks had been largely destroyed and the inspection programs were working.

Yet somehow, over time, the general public had come to believe that there never had been any WMDs in Iraq. History, Marika knows, for most people, is a heavy blanket thrown over fine detail, but having read what she just read, she is surprised to find such massive gaps in her own knowledge of what really happened in Iraq.

Reading more widely now, the post-war image of Saddam Hussein as a beaten old man with long hair and beard in a prison cell is far from an accurate summation of the man and his life. She reads accounts of tortures, beatings, the killing of political opponents. The destruction of entire villages, even in Iraq itself. Attempted genocide of the Kurds. Pogroms against Islamists, communists, homosexuals, and always, always, anyone who dared to criticise him or his Ba'athist regime. Chemical weapons used not once or twice, but on many occasions.

Between 1992 and 1998 UNSCOM inspectors supervised the destruction of almost half a million litres of Iraqi nerve and mustard gas chemical agents. Marika reads an interview in the *New York Times* with a survivor of the sarin and tabun gas attacks on the Kurds: 'Everybody tried to escape. People vomited. Their skin burned. Some people lost their minds.'

A final article is titled: 'Iraq's Forgotten CBRN — Potential for Use of Legacy Weapons by Non-State Actors'. Reading it, Marika notices the fine hairs of her forearm stand out in goosebumps. The article refers to precedents, such as in February 2007, when an al-Qa'ida team hijacked trucks, piled them high with drums of legacy chemical weapons, cylinders of chlorine gas, petrol and explosives, triggering them in Anbar Province and parts of Baghdad. The toxic 'cloud' killed over a hundred people and severely affected almost a thousand.

Marika opens a blank document and starts to type, gathering and organising the information gleaned from her search.

FACT: Iraq was just one of many nations pursuing the development of anthrax as a biological weapon. Britain had been cultivating anthrax for forty years already, America for fifty, Russia and Japan for at least that long.

FACT: A new, highly virulent anthrax strain, Vollum 14578, was produced by Professor R.L. Vollum, of Oxford in the 1940s. It was tested on the Island of Gruinard, just off the west coast of Scotland, by placing spore canisters on poles and exploding them with small bombs. The effect was then measured on herds of sheep tethered at strategic distances. Most of the sheep died rapidly and were then incinerated. The Vollum strain was so potent, and the spores so long lived, that the island was rendered contaminated and uninhabitable for almost half a century.

FACT: Vollum strain anthrax remains the most usable, the most easily manufactured, the most suitable for weaponisation, and one of the most lethal pathogens in existence. It is the easiest to control, and is thus much more suitable for bio-warfare than exotic viruses such as Ebola. It also has a storage life spanning many decades.

FACT: Iraq possessed at least two inhalation chambers that were used for testing anthrax on mammals.

FACT: During UN inspections, Iraqi scientists admitted to having produced 8500 litres of concentrated anthrax, but claimed that all stocks had been destroyed back in 1991. A weapons inspector noted that there was 'no convincing evidence for its destruction'. The country had, however, purchased enough growth media from German suppliers to grow three times this amount. These further stocks were never found, nor was the missing growth media.

Marika stops reading, and closes her eyes, using her right hand to rub over them gently, then picks up the handset. The author of the article is a former member of Hans Blix's UNMOVIC inspection team, and the email address is with a London provider. Getting a telephone number for him shouldn't be too difficult.

18 IRAN

Chabahar

The Mahee Hotel is a dull and nondescript building in one of Chabahar's main streets. It has a scarcely noticeable street-front, and a small sign painted over the window, so it might easily be missed.

'Remember,' Mariam instructs, 'don't say a word of English, or you will make us stand out. Let me do the talking. I will not translate, either, or it will look suspicious. Just leave it to me and I'll explain what has happened when we leave, OK?'

'Fine, you're the boss.'

Today Mariam wears the modest and demure garb of an Iranian wife, with a roosari scarf around her head and a loose dress that flows all the way to her ankles. His own, more Westernised outfit attracts no comment.

The presence of armed forces in the city is even more glaring than it was the previous night. Soldiers stand in groups with automatic weapons. The war may be over, but Iran is still on high alert.

Passing through the hotel doors, they enter a tidy lobby with an alcove waiting room through the doors on the right. Reception is attended by one lone man. They walk together to the polished timber desk. PJ watches as Mariam passes the man a US ten dollar note. He leaves through an adjoining door.

PJ looks around, trying unsuccessfully to spot the hidden surveillance camera that captured the images of Istikaan and Saif al-Din.

An older man who PJ assumes must be the manager appears, a grey goatee beard sculpted around his lips and chin. He wears an impeccable three-piece suit that would be forty years out of date in London.

Another long conversation, before the manager waves them through to a small conference room. Inside, they sit at a polished table large enough to seat twenty or more. The manager then makes a show of crossing the floor in his black patent leather shoes, looking out the door both ways, then closing it firmly.

Mariam slides across two hundred US dollars, a lot of money here, followed by two thousand rials. The latter is one of the world's most worthless currencies, but easy to use without raising suspicion.

The manager's eyes rest on it, at first with alarm, as if he has seen a snake, but then a smile creeps across his face, exposing the yellowed molars behind his white-painted front teeth. He sorts the cash into four different piles and distributes it around different internal pockets in his suit and shirt.

After a gesture from Mariam, PJ holds out his Sid, displaying the picture unearthed by the CIA. It's a grainy shot, but shows the two faces well enough.

More talking, then the manager stands up, and leaves the room. PJ feels his hand creep to the butt of the pistol inside his clothes.

'It's OK,' Mariam assures him while the man is gone. 'He recognises them both.'

The manager returns a moment later with a hardback book — the guest register — sits down and starts flicking through it. He opens it to a page so both Mariam and PJ can see, pointing to an entry in Arabic.

PJ uses the Sid to photograph the page, then the cover. This done, he passes it back to the manager. More talk in Farsi.

Again the manager leaves, taking the book with him. PJ's eyes widen. 'Where's he going now?'

Mariam places a hand on PJ's arm, looks deep into his eyes. 'Relax. He just remembered that the hotel driver took those men in the photo somewhere. He's going to ask where.'

The manager returns with an address written on a piece of paper, shakes hands with PJ, then walks them to the front door, making it plain that he would like them gone from his hotel, presumably so he can start spending the money. Out on the street Mariam insists on dawdling — browsing and chatting as if they are in no hurry. Finally they climb back into her car, a nondescript white Subaru, where Naser sits dutifully in the driver's seat. PJ slides in beside her in the back.

'It's OK, you can speak English now,' Mariam says. 'Naser doesn't understand it, and I told him you had lived in the West.'

'So what's that address the manager wrote down? Mean anything to you?'

'Not much. I know it's in the industrial precinct.'

She leans over to the front seat and talks to Naser, who starts the car and eases it into drive. Once into the traffic flow he switches on the radio, flooding the cab with Persian music.

'Naser loves his music,' Mariam explains.

PJ's eyes are focused on the roadway, the ribbon-like streets, tall narrow buildings crowding them like a Western city pushed together, made exotic by the domes of mosques and tall minaret towers.

Naser drives robotically, never showing emotion, never interacting with Mariam unless she asks him a question. They pass through residential areas and scattered shopping districts into the rural outskirts of the city.

Finally they reach an industrial estate, with the container cranes of the modern port of Shahid Beheshti in the near distance. Some of the factories they pass have been ruined by Coalition bombs, the debris piled by earthmoving equipment so rebuilding can begin.

Naser stops the car, and points, as if to say, 'Here it is!'

PJ looks. The site is a complex of buildings, all behind a high cyclone fence, topped with razor wire. The car park is full of vehicles, and the closest building has a large concrete loading dock. There is a sign out the front in Arabic.

'Al-Sefeed Medical Manufacturers,' Mariam reads.

'Interesting.'

The main factory building is clad with corrugated iron on both walls and roof. A brick office stands out the front. The company logo — a ferocious black bear — looks out of place on the cheap factory façade. Dozens more sheds are lined up behind the first, some connected by walkways.

'What do you want to do?' Mariam asks.

'I don't think waltzing in there with a fistful of notes will do the trick. We should come back after dark.'

'It's a big place. Where would you start?'

'The office, but I'll need you to help go through the documents. Are you up for a bit of burglary?'

Mariam smiles, and he wonders why he hadn't noticed the mischievous spark in her eyes until that moment. 'I am up for anything.'

PJ has a last look at the chain-link fence. 'Do you know a good hardware store?'

'Yes. There's one on the way home.'

'Can you take me there?'

'Of course.'

Again she leans over to talk to Naser, who hurls the car into a U-turn.

At a small store that sells everything from nails to paint, PJ selects a pair of sturdy bolt cutters, a cordless drill with an assortment of driving and drill bits and a pair of LED flashlights. The salesman assures him, through Mariam, that the drill will have at least fifty per cent charge straight out of the box. At an adjacent discount store he buys a cheap sports bag and a dark sweater.

Mariam does the purchasing in both instances, obviously pleased with her efforts, for she smiles all the way back to the car. They have scarcely settled into their seats before her cell phone rings and she answers, talking in Farsi while Naser drives them back towards her apartment.

Finally she ends the call and sits the phone back on the console. 'This is not good. I have just heard through one of my contacts that the Komiteh are looking for a Western agent here in Chabahar.'

PJ feels a chill. 'How would they know that I'm here?'

'I don't know. The hotel manager, perhaps. I would not put it past him to try and get payments from them as well as us, or at least to make a report on us to curry favour. We will have to be very careful.'

As they drive towards the main part of town it is high tide, and PJ is amazed at how the sea rises above the level of the docks, small waves pushing around flooded buildings. Children play in knee-deep water, fishermen drag their nets, and life appears to have adapted to this new reality.

'It's OK here in Chabahar,' Mariam comments, 'there is enough elevation to keep most of the city alive, but to the north-west of us, in the lowlands, whole regions have been flooded.'

They have just turned into the street PJ recognises as Mariam's when her expression changes, her eyes focusing on something further down. More thoughtful than frightened.

'What's wrong?' he asks.

'Nothing, maybe,' she says. 'It's just a new car that I don't know.'

PJ follows the direction of her gaze. 'There's no one inside.'

'Of course. It's nothing, forget it. Now that I think of it, one of the men on the fifth floor said he was getting a new car — he was boasting about it last week.' She lowers her voice as the driver begins the manoeuvres necessary to force the car into the car park. 'He's always trying — you know what some men are like. They think that women will fall into bed with them because they have a shiny car …'

Back at the apartment PJ sends through an update on the Sid, then kills a few hours sitting on the balcony, dozing, drinking peppermint tea, looking out at the Gulf of Oman and the ships coming and going from the harbour.

Mariam goes out for more than an hour, returns with a string bag full of fruit, meat, and packages.

'We will eat well tonight. What time do you want to go back to the factory?'

'What time will they close?'

'They might work until seven or eight pm.'

'Midnight, I would think, maybe a little later.'

PJ brings up the mapping app on the Sid and studies the factory and its environs. Now, just as in his days with the Special Boat Service, knowledge of topography, streets, hills, dead-ends is vital.

By five in the evening the breeze that has blown in off the sea all afternoon has dropped, leaving the air still and muggy.

Mariam cooks one of the tastiest meals of PJ's life, cubes of goat meat in an exotic mixture of spices.

'Sorry, no wine,' she says, holding a fork loosely in one hand. 'It's almost impossible for a local to buy without attracting attention. Especially here. In Tehran there are places … when I was with Ebi we would drink wine with our friends,' her eyes go dark and dreamy, 'have dinner parties, talk about the world, play at being intellectuals.'

'How long were you married?'

'Ten years.'

'No children?'

'No, we tried, but it didn't happen. I don't think either of us was too upset. We were a little too indulgent — full of ourselves — to be good parents. I think Ebi started to get full of ideas, dangerous ideas, and became obsessed with proving himself. I was too chicken.' She smiles and starts to collect the plates. PJ stands and helps. There is no sink in the flat, and she washes up in a plastic tub. He dries and stacks the few dishes and cooking pots.

She puts the things away, turning often to look at him. There is nothing he can think of to say. Then, when they have finished, she stands in front of him in the dim room for a moment. Strangely, she takes him in her arms, as if to comfort him, rubbing the flat of her hand over the small of his back.

'The job you do is a very difficult one,' she says, 'and no one learns of your achievements. You want to make the world safe, don't you?'

'Yes.'

'So do I. The things we do are very important, and no one will ever know.' She releases him then. 'It's best that we get some rest. OK? I'll set an alarm for three hours from now.'

PJ coughs, attempting to shake the choking, strangely guilty feeling their intimacy has aroused in him. 'I'll have a shower first, I think.'

When he comes back from his shower she is fast asleep, turned away from him on that tiny, narrow bed.

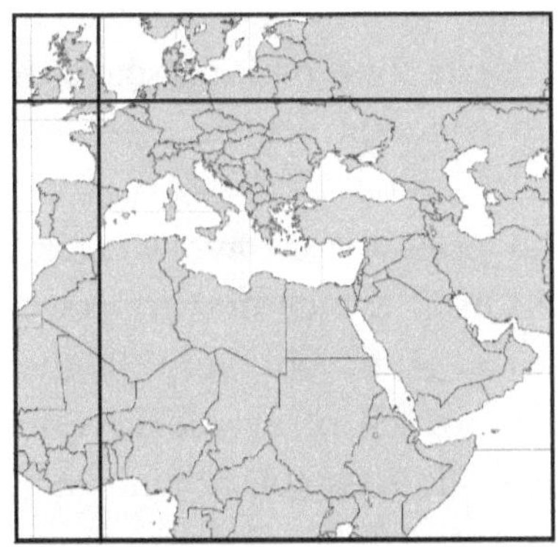

19 UNITED KINGDOM

London

Marika takes one of the little Honda hybrids from the car pool, heading north through the broken suburbs. Smashed shopfronts and burned-out cars are common, after some of the worst violence since the 2011 riots.

Faces with shattered expressions look up as she passes, and Marika knows that there is no answer to this conflict. Nothing that will solve it in a day or a night. Human beings, she believes, have the right to live safely, without fear, in a community of their choosing.

The thought is a pertinent one. The previous evening a van-load of 2CG operatives arrived to carry out twenty-four-hour surveillance of her flat, in the light of DRFS's most serious security leak in its history, and veiled threats against Marika. According to Tom Mossel, ASIS, Australia's Secret Intelligence Service, have also commenced surveillance on members of her family back in Sydney.

Finally she passes into the commuter belt of rural Essex, the car rocking over speed bumps at the entrance to a café strip that includes a theatre and government offices. Easing her foot off the accelerator she looks for a parking space, squeezing between a Range Rover — a common vehicle here — and a tradesman's white van.

Stepping out, she looks at the rows of cafés, takes the Sid from her pocket and calls him. 'Which one are you at?'

Petersen's voice is gruff, but very English. Sounds like a diplomat, she thinks, which of course he once was. He directs her down to a quaint little establishment on the corner, leaving her wondering why they could not have agreed to meet there in the first instance.

A big man, grossly overweight, with a full grey beard and glasses, Petersen waits in the gap between the potted hedges that surround the café. He raises one hand in a subtle recognition signal.

'Tradecraft,' he says when she comes up to him.

'Sorry, I don't follow you ...'

'It is a policy of mine not to broadcast my future whereabouts. That's why I kept the name of the café quiet until the last minute.' He takes her upper arm between thumb and forefinger and steers her through the gap in the hedges towards a table. He holds out a seat for her then sits with his back against the wall of the building. More tradecraft; always protect your rear.

The waiter appears in a black T-shirt and apron, looks first at Marika, pencil poised. She orders a long black in a mug, with a dash of milk on the side. Petersen a double-shot soy latté. His preference doesn't surprise Marika. From what she could glean online, Jeffrey Petersen is a single man-about-town at the age of sixty-three, with a popular blog, and ten thousand followers on Twitter; a darling of the café set.

'For forty-one years,' Petersen says when the waiter has gone, 'I did everything this government told me, no matter how hard, no matter how dangerous. Even married the right woman.' He looks down at Marika's cleavage. 'We're divorced now.'

The coffee arrives and Marika toys with hers, pouring in a little milk.

Petersen empties three paper tubes of sugar into his mug then attacks the complimentary chocolate mint with relish. 'So,' he says at last, 'you're SIS?'

'DRFS, to be exact.'

'Ah yes, the latest manifestation of secret-agent tomfoolery this country pours so much money into.'

'You disapprove of intelligence work?'

'Not totally, but if we spent as much on diplomacy as we do on secret programs the world would be a better place.' Petersen takes a deep sip of his coffee, somehow avoiding immersing his moustache in the process. 'So, to what do I owe the sudden attention?'

'You were a member of UNMOVIC?'

'Ah, there's an acronym I haven't heard for a while. United Nations Monitoring, Verification and Inspection Committee. Had a certain ring to it, didn't it?'

Marika smiles, realising that the banter hides an erudite brain.

'UNSCOM then UNMOVIC. All those bloody acronyms that meant the same thing — keep an eye on Saddam Hussein, the biggest bastard the Middle East has ever produced ... and that's saying something. I was invited to join the UNMOVIC team in 1999, after UN Resolution 1284 decreed that the inspection program needed an overhaul. Me, Hans Blix, Rachel Davies, John Scott, Alice Hecht — a Belgian, one hell of a good operator. Nikita Smidovitch — he'd been with UNSCOM from the start, another great operator — I shared a few vodkas over the years with Nikita. They gave us the funding, the titles, the power, but in the end they — Bush, Cheney, Blair, Howard — didn't want to listen. They wanted war, regardless ...'

'I read your article,' Marika says. 'It seems to suggest there might be legacy biological weapons hidden in Iraq.'

Petersen snorts through his nose, then strokes his chin through his thick beard. 'I wanted the powers that be to recognise it as a possibility. Chemical weapons have been turning up in Iraq for years. In 2009 the government located a couple of bunkers filled with chemical weapons, including armed warheads and some production facilities. It didn't make the news, really. Very little of it was useable, and it didn't really qualify as the WMD Bush and Rumsfeld wanted so desperately to find. It wouldn't surprise me if a few vials of anthrax turned up somewhere, if not in Iraq then in Libya or Syria, and that could be the start of something rather frightening.'

Marika's eyes follow a sparrow, hopping from one end of the café hedge to the other. 'Iraqi scientists did produce anthrax, didn't they?'

'Of course, but you have to remember that they were not alone. All the major powers developed bioweapons. The only reason the British didn't use anthrax on the Germans in World War Two was that after their experiences with testing on Gruinard Island they realised that its use would render German cities uninhabitable for decades. It was too terrible to contemplate. That's why most countries abandoned their programs before they signed the Biological and Toxins Weapons Convention in 1972. Of course Russia, Britain and the US keep seed stocks of just about every known strain, to this day.'

'Iraq didn't sign the convention?'

Petersen's breathing is getting heavier, whether from excitement or talking too much, Marika can't tell. 'No. Nor did Syria, Iran, and North Korea. Rogue states, desperate for deterrents. And Iraqi scientists, led by the famous 'Dr Germ' were really only carrying on the work of the British, who, along with the Russians, had found that the most effective bioweapon was a fine powder of Vollum strain anthrax spores, mixed with bentonite powder, that could be released from an aircraft, spreading for hundreds of kilometres. There are a trillion spores in one gram of this powder. Theoretically enough to kill twenty million people.'

Marika feels weighed down with this knowledge. The numbers are enormous, the potential hard to grasp. 'So Iraq kept going when most other nations stopped, right?'

'Iraq's program was a matter of record, over at least a twenty-year period. My fellow inspectors deemed it to have been largely dismantled by the mid-nineties. Yet at least 8500 litres of viable Vollum strain anthrax spores, with a shelf life of three decades or more, were produced. Massive quantities of growth media were ordered and never accounted for. The Mukhabarat quite possibly ran secret anthrax production sites, some of them underground.'

Marika holds her coffee cup level, 'You're scaring me.'

Petersen cocks his head at an angle. 'I'm sorry, but you are delving into the machinations of a psychopath. You also have to understand the ramifications of this — when and if you do find something. If there is a hidden, viable bioweapons site, certain people will try to use it to justify the invasion of Iraq. They will come out of the woodwork — apologists for Bush and Blair. The media will be all over it. It's best that no word of this leaks out.'

Marika shakes her head. 'One single, possible WMD site doesn't justify a million refugees, hundreds of thousands dead, ten years of occupation.'

'Correct. Israel has biological weapons — one of their best kept secrets, but no one's going to invade them over it. Look, we have always acknowledged the possibility of a hidden program. If there is one out there, given a few more months we would have found it too.'

Marika feels the need to play devil's advocate. 'You don't think war was justified because of the brutality of Saddam Hussein's regime?'

'No, but I also hate seeing his regime whitewashed. Saddam was a control freak with a pathological hatred of almost everyone different from himself — Shi'ites, communists, Kurds. He maimed, tortured and killed anyone he suspected of being a threat. If he'd had the weapons and manpower he would have taken on the rest of the world.

'In 1980 he invaded Iran without warning. That war killed half a million people, all because Saddam wanted to be the dominant Gulf power and thought that the Iranians were too distracted by their revolution to fight back. A little-known fact is that he used chemical weapons — lots of them — in that war, as well as against the Kurds.' He pauses to drink more coffee, take a bite of a spiral chocolate stick. 'Then, in 1992, he invaded Kuwait, again with no warning.'

'Was he a threat to world peace in 2003?'

'That depends.'

'On what?'

'On what you find in Iraq.'

Marika takes out the Sid, brings a photograph up on the screen. Finding this image took hundreds of hours of work from the research team. It shows a man standing outside what look like brand-new buildings in the Syrian desert. There are half a dozen others in white coats or army uniform. The image was found in a personal collection in Bashar al-Assad's fortified palace, near the Alawite stronghold of Latakia.

'This is an Iraqi scientist, taken in Syria. Does that surprise you?'

'Not at all. They had a close connection. One Iraqi general has written a book alleging that all of Saddam's CBRN programs were moved to Syria before the invasion, which was why al-Assad had such huge stocks,' he grunts, as if at an unpleasant memory, '...and what a headache they've been for us.'

'Do you recognise him?'

Petersen peers at the image for thirty or more seconds.

'He looks familiar. What's his name?'

'Zimraan al-Ghazali, otherwise known as Istikaan, the Hourglass.'

'Oh, I met him. I'm sure I did — in Iraq.'

Marika feels a rush of excitement.

Petersen goes on, 'He was a meteorologist.'

A meteorologist?

Marika's theories appear to crumble into dust around her feet. The overwhelming feeling, however, is one of relief. That all her suppositions are wrong. That Istikaan and the prisoner now in a safe house in London are just a couple of crazies who will be easily thwarted. 'I don't think so. We know he studied microbiology ...'

'Not when I met him. He was in charge of a remote weather station. Al-Hajjuf, I think it was called.'

Remote weather station. Marika can hardly breathe, thinking back to Pahedar's words: *The place we were taken to was underground, but there was a building set in the hillside. It had strange things on the roof.*

Aerials?

Yes, but other equipment also. Something that spins in the wind.

Julian Weiss sits in the train carriage, arms hugging his body, eyes searching the crowd, flicking from people inside to others standing on the platforms as they pass the late-Victorian drabness of North Dulwich, then Tulse Hill. Passengers enter and leave, but nothing registers with him, his mind is a closed space.

One at a time they had been called into an interview room. Three men and a woman on the other side of a desk, none of whom Julian had ever met before. Even in the DRFS and the wider intelligence network there are always layers within layers. The Directorate of Internal Affairs. The agents who watch the agents.

Other employees had come back from the interview and told Julian what to expect, giving him time to prepare. He knew they had not already pinpointed him or they would have arrested him. They used questions designed to trip the unwary, artfully worded pitfalls. Places. Times. Hinted at surveillance.

Tom Mossel knows ... the train says as it rattles over the fishplates. Julian tries to keep himself together, to face the prospect that the men who came to see him all those weeks ago may not have been who they said they were.

Julian has a phone in his hand, not his personal phone, but a cheap prepaid he purchased from the Orange shop at Victoria station. His thumb is still on the send tab, resting there until the device bleeps and a return message comes through, a couple of short sentences. A place and a time.

The meeting is more than he could have hoped for at such short notice. He feels like he is drowning, staring down at his loosely laced running shoes, all the while his life flashing before his eyes. One month ago he was a young man with a social conscience coupled with a great job where he could make a difference. Now everything is at risk, his world is falling apart.

Julian was pleased and flattered when they first approached him. He had been a member of the local group EnviroCarers for three years, but his sympathies have long been with the left. They said they were from Earth First. Real activists. Julian had always wanted to be a real activist … used to dream of being like Che Guevara. He wanted to save the world. This seemed like a chance to start.

When he applied for a job at DRFS, he made no secret of his politics. There in the interview room, he found himself involved in a thirty-minute earnest, almost heated, discussion with the director, Thomas Mossel, on clean energy. In the end Mossel had shaken Julian's hand. 'I like a young man with convictions, even when they're a little different from mine. That's the trick. Find the thing that gives your life meaning, stick it on a pole in the sand and defend it to your last breath. You have to start with the Civil Service Fast Stream selection board. Do we have a deal?'

Just a couple of months ago, at a regular meeting of the EnviroCarers at the Bishop pub in Dulwich, a newcomer had sat silent and dangerous in a hoodie. His voice was accented, his skin a shade darker than olive. He said little while they talked of protests and plastic packaging, waste, the bee crisis and a dozen other topics.

After the meeting, the new man joined Julian for a pint. Yet he seemed to know only a little about the causes the group was into, and was not like the others — more physical than talkative.

They had exchanged a few texts before Julian had a call one night just before he finished work. His new friend was in the city, and wondered if Julian would like to catch up for coffee.

There, over an espresso and an impassioned plea for change in the world, this virtual stranger told of his work for Earth First. Of how it is hard and dangerous, but that real men need to risk everything if the world is ever to change.

'If I asked you to do something for me, would you do it?'

'Depends what it is.'

'There is an employee at DRFS who I would like to be given a higher security rating.'

Julian felt the blood drain from his face. 'You don't know what you're asking. I can't do that.'

'Listen, she's one of us. Knowledge is power. Information is power. I represent people who have the ability to provoke far-reaching change. Sometimes men like you have to get down off your comfortable fence and get your hands dirty.'

'You want me to upgrade someone's security classification so they can access information. What is he, a cleaner, an office assistant?'

'Administrative Assistant, Level Three, and it's a she, not a he.' His hands came together on the table in a parody of prayer. 'All we want is for her to access the general daily briefings that get sent to your intelligence officers.'

'So you want them to have OP3 status. That will stand out like a sore thumb, if anyone notices ...'

'How would they? And you can always say it was a mistake. Mistakes happen. Do you have convictions, Julian, or are you just playing at this? Do you want change or are you just a white boy joining a fashionable cause, eh?'

Julian picked up the coffee cup and drained it in one swallow.

'What's this person's name?'

Julian looked her up. Sought her out. She was a nothing, a dark little woman who typed, photocopied and bound reports with clever little plastic bindings. He hovered near her desk, watching. He caught her eye, imagining that she smiled back. There was nothing frightening about her. That was when he decided to do it. They never exchanged words, but Julian felt that he could trust her. That they shared a secret link.

The demands grew stronger. One of the department managers died of a heart attack. They wanted his account resurrected, with clandestine access for their contact. For two weeks now they have been getting high-level operational updates. They can access the database. Staff details. Julian had never in his wildest dreams suspected that he was feeding information to a proscribed organisation — a terrorist group. Until now.

Treason was, up until 1998, a hanging offence in England, and even now it carries a penalty of life imprisonment.

Julian steps off the train at West Norwood station, and looks both ways as he walks out of the station and south onto Knight's Hill Road, all the way to Cotswold Street. There, on the corner, stands the Norwood Hotel, with its solid plaster columns, arches and peeling brown highlights. The front bar is quiet, mainly older men in close-clustered tables watching West Ham play Tottenham on the big-screen TV.

The man he has come to see sits at the bar near the big brass taps. He turns to watch Julian enter. The eyes are cold and frightening as he nods towards the rear courtyard. There are others out there. Four or five men, all in those hoodies.

Julian and his contact settle into the seats at the table, facing each other. Julian studies him. Notes one detail that he hasn't seen before, a tattoo on his forearm, an eye with a map of the world behind it, crosshairs centred on the Middle East.

Noticing Julian's gaze, the man covers the image with one hand. 'Now, what's so important all of a sudden? I was at work, you know.' The others say nothing, just sit like vultures around a kill.

Julian is trying to control the urge to run. 'I've done everything you told me to and more. I want to stop now.'

'This is not a game. You're a man, aren't you?'

'Of course I am.'

'You think we can change the world without risk?'

Julian says nothing, doesn't nod or move. Knowing he is in this up to his neck.

'It's too late for you to walk away. You're an accessory, you know that, don't you? They could put you in prison for that. Every filthy old crim in there would want his turn with you — God — you've got a body like a girl. They'd line up for you.'

'What more do you want from me?'

'Not yet, soon. Don't even think of disobeying us ...'

Julian feels his breath come faster, and a general dizziness.

'Go home. Sleep. Wait. You will be told when we need you.' The other man reaches across and grips Julian's hand in a parody of a handshake, squeezing with the power of a vice until Julian feels the bones of his fingers compress to the point of splintering. A demonstration of strength. Julian feels soul and body deflate. 'Do you understand?'

'Yes.'

'Then go, and do as I tell you.'

'You aren't really in Earth First, are you?'

'Fuck the earth. This is about higher things. Not dirt and trees and fucking animals.'

The man in the hooded jacket stands, lifts his chin as if daring Julian to contradict him, then moves away. The others follow, crossing the courtyard without a backwards glance. Julian's eyes, by then, are shut. Blackness closes in from all directions.

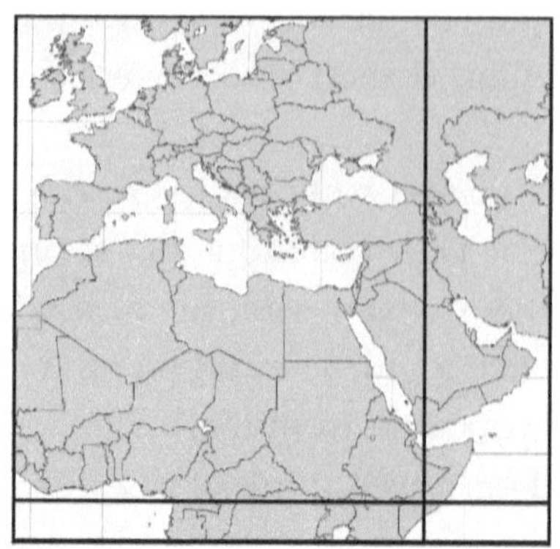

20 SOMALIA

Chakula Refugee Camp

Kifimbo finds that out on patrol, or even lounging in the barracks room playing cards, his mind wanders often to the Somali woman with the baby. That forlorn little survivor of a murdered mother interests him, but not as much as the woman who now cares for him. Many Somali women are beautiful to his eyes, but this one is lovely; very tall, with willowy limbs. While she is probably malnourished she does not have the starved look, not yet anyway.

One Sunday after church he fills a rucksack with soap, a loaf of bread, and bottles of clean water. He borrows a Yamaha motorbike from his company sergeant, then rides the machine through the main compound gate and deep into the Laba Quarter.

There is a lot of dust right now, with the short rains still two months away, the ground churned up by donkey, foot and occasional vehicle traffic. Even with the motorbike engine buzzing away he can hear voices; singing, shouts and calls.

They can see from his uniform and the rifle strapped to his back that he is from the garrison. Many people wave. Most of them inside the wires crave the security that the garrison brings.

Passing through the gate, out into the shanty town, however, the stares are not so friendly. The people are poorer here. There is more activity in the struggle to survive. Charcoal haulers and sellers, vendors of black-market foodstuffs. Husks of corn roasting on smoky fires, on sale for a few shillings.

Into the alleyways of the Laba Quarter he drives, dodging children and filth. Once or twice men duck furtively away when they see the uniform. Finally he stops the motorbike outside the tukul, kicks down the stand, lifts off his rucksack and unslings his rifle. Carrying both, he walks to the opening and calls softly.

The young woman comes out, alone, and stares at him gravely.

'I've brought you some things.' Kifimbo smiles at her.

He leans the rifle against a junction of branches in the wall of the tukul and searches in the bag. 'Look. Soap. Shampoo. A bag of maize flour. Olive oil.' Most prized of all, a tin of tuna fish from South Africa.

Her eyes move from each item to his face. One after the other. A fly circles her left eye and dives for the corner. She brushes it away.

'Thank you,' she says at last. Not effusively. Kifimbo knows that effusiveness is not the way of these people. 'I'm making cha,' she offers, 'would you like some?'

Kifimbo feels his gut clench with fear. Cholera and enteric fever are rife in this part of the camp. Drinking water, even in tea or coffee, is always a danger.

'I will boil it well,' she adds, obviously seeing his discomfort, 'and bring it out to you.'

'Of course I will have cha,' he says, regretting his initial hesitation.

Kifimbo does not try to follow her into the shelter, but he can hear the sound of pots rattling, then a baby's tired cry. While he waits he looks around, greets passers-by in Swahili or the general Somali greeting: sabah wanaqsan.

A few minutes later the young woman comes out with a mug in one hand. He takes it and drinks. 'Thank you. That's very good cha.

'How long have you been here, in the camp?' he asks.

'Since the time of the long rains. What about you?'

'A little longer than that.'

'Do you like being a soldier?'

'Sometimes.'

'Better than being ...' she begins, but does not finish, merely gesturing at the tukul and its contents, clearly meaning ' ... *what I am.*'

He tries to think of something else to say, but can't. Inactivity makes him drink the cha very fast. When it's gone he can no longer think of a reason to stay. He passes her the cup.

'That was very good.'

'Thank you.'

'Perhaps I might visit you again another day.'

She says nothing, but waits, watching as he walks back to the motorbike, kicks the starter.

Kifimbo waves as he shoots forward down the path, past the mounds of refuse that make up the Laba Quarter dumping ground.

Marika is already feeling harried as she strides back towards her flat at a warming pace. It is after ten pm, and the air is too cold for her light blouse and jeans. It has been a long day, but the walk home is necessary to clear her head.

Entering Ecclestone Square, she sees the now familiar unmarked DRFS van parked about five doors down on the other side of the road, in the shadows of the trees. Tinted windows make it hard to see inside the van, and she wonders idly who is working this shift.

Climbing the steps, and opening the door, she switches off the alarm, walks through the corridor, down carpeted steps and into the kitchen. The flat is cold, but the kitchen icy. Finger on the light switch, her senses start to scream danger. The fluoro tube flickers before emitting a steady stream of light, illuminating an entry hatch cut into one of the windows with some kind of diamond-tipped instrument. The alarm relies on movement of the sill. By cutting the glass they circumvented it neatly.

Marika freezes. This is not just the possibility of a burglary, but of someone inside, waiting. Behind a door. Under a bed. In the bathroom. There is just one place in the kitchen big enough to hide a person. The pantry cupboard. Eyes fixed on it, Marika backs away to the bench, then reaches behind her to remove a broad-bladed santoku knife from the block.

Edging forward, she holds the knife underhand, adrenalin shooting into her system. She grips the handle and pulls, feeling the flood of air as she does so. Nothing inside but shelves, and a stale spice smell.

Still holding the knife in her right hand, she whips out the Sid with her left. Presses the contact app. Not wasting time on preamble — there is no need, both her location and identity are logged — she speaks in a low voice. 'Someone either is or has been in my flat,' she says, then breaks contact.

The reply comes less than thirty seconds later. 'Wait.' Then, 'Go to the front door and open it.'

Marika walks back along the corridor, watching the closed doors on either side and the stairwell warily as she does so, then opens the front door. Three men from the van are already halfway up the front path.

Ronnie is first, despite his age, still the fastest runner, and his black eyes settle on her for a moment. As always, he has procedures down pat. Loves them. Knows every regulation. The smell of Altoids mints wafts ahead of him.

'Where's the entry point?'

'Kitchen window. End of the corridor, down the stairs.'

Marika closes the door behind them. One man moves down to guard the entry point in the kitchen. Kutay and Ronnie work their way from the bottom up, both with drawn sidearms. One covers a door with his firearm and twists the handle, then the other kicks it open, accompanied by a loud shout of, 'Hands on heads.'

They search the rooms. One after another. Within three minutes they have cleared the lower floor; dining and lounge rooms. Marika wanders into the latter first, shocked at the mess. Her collection of CDs and DVDs destroyed, each snapped in half. They are hardly used in these days of digital downloads, but they are hers, built up over a lifetime. Gifts, impulse purchases. Most dating back to childhood and youth.

Books torn from the shelves and ripped into pieces. These are even more a part of her. A modest collection, but well loved. Xavier Herbert. Peter Carey. Books of home, of wide open spaces. Books that take away homesickness. Books that affirm to her that there is a goodness to life as well as what sometimes seems like endless evil. A box set of George RR Martin. Anna Funder. Hilary Mantel. Bradbury. It feels to her as if they have torn out a part of her soul. A collection of words that will never exist in the same way again.

In the dining room, every bottle of spirits from the little bar has been emptied all over the carpet. The brandy stench overrides the others. Creamy liqueurs make the worst of the mess.

Kutay and Ronnie tramp back down the stairs. 'The place is clear,' Kutay says. 'But there's shit everywhere.' He waves a hand at the discarded bottles. 'If you think this is bad, wait till you see upstairs.'

Marika walks upstairs, dreading seeing what they have done. The reality is worse than she expected. Her clothes emptied out on the bed. Everything see-through or revealing cut jaggedly with scissors. Blister packs of the contraceptive pill scattered all over the floor.

Ronnie walks in behind her, and she turns at the last moment. He has this uncanny way of walking absolutely silently, even when silence isn't necessary.

'What a complete and utter clusterfuck.'

'Piss off, Ronnie, this is my flat we're talking about.'

'Exactly. This is your shit. You're knee-deep in it — cultivating fucking informers who'll only talk to you, getting personal relationships happening, and this is the crap you get in return. Problem is that the rest of us end up coated in it too.'

'You were in the van, you were supposed to be listening.'

His face switches from sandstone to red granite. 'Are you accusing me of not doing my job properly?'

'Speaks for itself doesn't it?' His eyes are murderous, but she doesn't stop there. 'I'm not the only one saying it, Ronnie; the rest of them are saying it behind your back.'

For a moment she thinks he might respond, but instead he brushes past her, out the door without turning. She stares after him, wondering if she pushed a little too hard.

Kutay comes up beside her. 'Don't let him worry you, he's just got the shits because we didn't hear the break-in — we fucked up.'

'That's his problem, not mine.'

'Lucky you weren't home.'

'They knew I wasn't home. They didn't want to hurt me. Just to send me a message.'

'What message is that? That they're a bunch of sick fucks?'

Marika shakes her head. 'No. They want to tell me that I'm a bad person. Immoral.' Her voice drops to a whisper. 'And that they can kill me whenever they want to.'

BOOK TWO

'One of the bunkers has been tampered with. The integrity of the seal appears intact, but it seems someone is interested in trying to get into the bunkers.'

US Military Cable, Iraq 2004

Released by Wikileaks

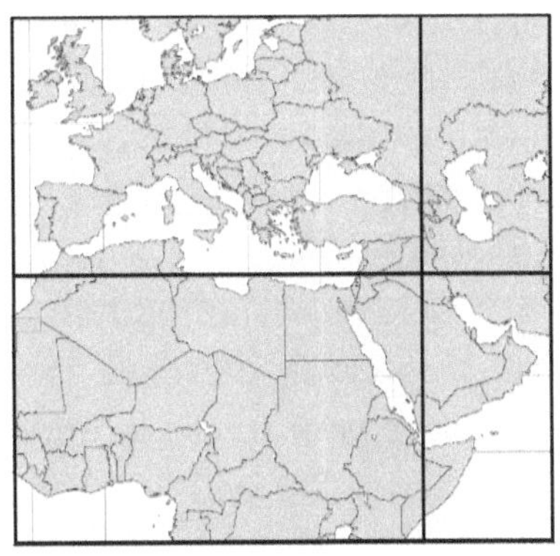

21 **IRAQ**

Jabal Sinjar

The column of trucks stops at an oasis on the Wadi al-Mani, a dry tributary of the Euphrates that flows once in a generation, near an ancient Persian crossroads town where caravans passing east once provisioned and rested. Where Xerxes marched through on his way to Greece, and an outpost of the Abbasid state of the ninth century.

There is no sign now of past glories, just dust, torn vehicles and the lonely frames of burnt-out houses shattered by American missile fire. This is a place abandoned and forgotten by the world, an outpost of no strategic value, home only to date palms and juniper bushes.

As the trucks pull to a halt in a swirl of dust, Saif watches the figures jump out of the rear. Each holds an AK47, their faces hidden behind sunglasses and tightly wrapped black shemagh head cloths.

Other armed men appear from the ruined buildings, and Saif watches them suspiciously. Some of these men are Syrians. Western Iraq is a haven for armed gangs of displaced Syrian loyalists, particularly here, close to the border. Others are Iraqis, remnants of the Ba'athist-aligned militias that have been engaged in a war of attrition against the secular Iraqi government. Labelled al-Qa'ida by the Western invasion forces, many are in fact members of al-Nakshabandia, some of whom protected Saddam Hussein up until the Americans captured him near ad-Dawr.

Karim Yussef barks orders at the men. 'There is no time to stand around talking. Bring your trucks in under the palms. Your men may refresh themselves. We will leave after maghrib, when the sun sinks.'

Saif finds himself bristling at the other man taking the liberty of issuing orders. He, Saif al-Din, is in command. Using all his self-control he says nothing, merely nods and moves off. Inside, however, he is seething: *Do not imagine that you will be giving orders for long*, he thinks. *You are just a guide. I am the leader of a new world.*

The smartphone in his pocket hums. He takes it out and looks at it: more updates from the London Ba'athists, who have opened up an incredible source of information deep inside the SIS.

They are worthy of respect, Saif grudgingly admits. Well organised and funded with oil money salted away for years, stolen from the people of Iraq and Syria by despotic leaders. They are also hard men who do not shrink away from violent action — on his request they invaded the home of that obstreperous woman, Marika Hartmann, highlighting her sin for the world to see. Soon he will command that the lesson be more severe. He will see how arrogant she is when staring death in the face.

Saif puts away the phone then walks back to the trucks, where the men have gathered, with Istikaan at his side. Conscious of the time, close to sunset, Saif turns to face qibla, then, in the prescribed manner, he touches his left ear with his right index finger and the same on the other side.

Speaking aloud, taking the role of the muezzin, he intones the call to prayer, the adhan.

Allahu akbar, Allahu akbar, Allahu akbar, Allahu akbar,

Ash-hadu alla ilaha illallah, Ash-hadu alla ilaha illallah.

The men come together in a line, fall to their knees, heads press to the earth, rise. The Asr is a silent prayer, and Saif's thoughts fill his head.

The second and final rakat of the prayers comes, brevity permitted because they are travelling.

We will not be cowed, Saif thinks. *We will fight. We are unique. Our culture is our pride, and we are not afraid.*

Soon we will have in our hands a weapon of such magnitude that it will change the balance of power across the world. And God will be on our side.

22 IRAN

Chabahar

PJ had identified the cul-de-sac from the map. Eight hundred metres from the back of the factory complex, across open, lightly wooded grassland. Here Naser pulls up the car and PJ takes the light sports bag from the trunk, closes it.

'Tell Naser we'll be ninety minutes,' he tells Mariam. 'If we're not here he's better off just going home than getting caught as well.'

Mariam consults with Naser, leaning in through the driver's window. She, too, is dressed in dark clothing. Black jeans, T-shirt and sweater. Both of them have dark hair, so balaclavas are unnecessary, as well as looking suspicious if they are spotted.

'You ready?' he asks.

Her white teeth shine in the starlight. 'Ready if you are.'

They run together across the grass, Mariam easily keeping pace with him.

PJ times their progress to the rear of the compound with his Sid, masking the display with his body and hands, placing it back on standby to conserve batteries — it has been impossible to charge the unit without power.

Two and a half minutes. He stops short, waving Mariam to the cover of an aarak tree with its fleshy green leaves and drooping branches while he studies the factory complex.

From here it looks even bigger than it appeared from the front. Eight, ten factory buildings, including the office-warehouse closest to the street.

'There are guards,' Mariam says. 'I can see one of them.'

'Where?'

PJ follows the line of her pointed finger. Yes, a single figure on a chair near a rear entrance. 'Well spotted. He's probably supposed to be walking around. Might even be asleep, but we can't count on that.'

'Where should we go through the wire?'

'Not here. We'll work our way around further, get out of his line of sight.'

'OK, you decide, I'll follow.'

PJ leads her back forty or fifty metres from the fence, moving around the perimeter three times that distance before creeping back in, finding that not only is the guard no longer in sight, but that this is the closest point to the main office building. 'From here on just do what I do,' he says.

Slithering to the edge of the wire, he uses the bolt cutters to make a neat hole in the chain mesh. When Mariam has wormed her way through behind him he replaces the cut-out portion so that only a close-up inspection would detect the change.

Now he stops still. Listens and watches until he is satisfied there is no one else in the shadows there. He turns to Mariam. 'We're going to get up and run until we're in the shadows beside that shed, OK?'

'Yes, fine.'

They run, minimising their time in the open. PJ heaves a sigh of relief now that they are sheltered by the bulk of the factory. Open ground is never your friend when you are trying to avoid detection.

He doesn't stop moving, working alongside that building, then across another small open space. They are now adjacent to the main office and warehouse complex, passing by what must be an open lunch area for employees. Tables, stinking ashtrays. Bins that reek of orange peels and rotten fruit.

Back into the shadows, still moving, PJ begins to look for a possible entry point. Most of the corrugated sheets go all the way from ground level to roof, but under the barred windows they are just a metre and a half long.

He leans down, takes the cordless drill from the bag. Chooses a hex-head driving bit, inserts it into the chuck and tightens it by hand. He tests the trigger and is rewarded with an energetic rotation. He starts to remove the roofing screws that hold the sheet in place. By keeping the revolutions low, he suspects that the drill will be inaudible at a distance. There are eighteen screws altogether and he places them in a neat pile on the ground.

The sheet is partially overlapped by another. It takes effort to wrench it out, but finally it comes clear and he leans it against the wall. He feels inside to the back of the internal cladding. Using the bolt cutters as a ram he punches hard, several times, before he breaks through. Then smashes out a hole as far as the battens on either side.

'You go first,' he says to her.

Mariam does not argue, just crawls through. PJ grabs the bag of tools and follows, then reaches back through and pulls the sheet of tin loosely over the hole.

They have come up underneath a workbench. PJ can see Mariam crouched there, waiting for him. They have bypassed the usual entrance alarms, but there may be infrared beams placed at body level. Unlikely, but he crawls forward, takes out the flashlight and uses it to study this portion of the warehouse. Pallet racks of goods reach from floor to peaked ceiling. Forklifts sit at random angles where they finished the day's work. PJ swings the beam looking for alarm activators. Finds none.

'OK, we can walk, but if we get separated, meet me back here.'

They walk down the silent rows between the shelves, many of them stacked with plastic cubes of liquids, shrink wrapped on pallets, or cardboard cartons. Mariam reads and whispers the contents to him, shining her flashlight on the labels. 'Saline solution, petroleum jelly ...'

Finally, the door that must lead to the office. PJ tries it. Locked.

Mariam's face shines up at him. She is brave, he has to admit, and is good, solid company. 'Can we break it in?' she asks.

'Probably.' Next to the door is a glass observation window, installed, PJ imagines, for management to check that warehouse employees aren't sitting around smoking or drinking tea when they should be working.

The office is dark, lit by a single security light. PJ shines the flashlight through at a sharp angle, examining the doorway. Almost misses it, just a bump above the door where wires enter the jamb.

'Damn,' he says, 'it's alarmed.' An old-fashioned magnet contact type, he decides, but still enough to make this harder. He raps the door with his knuckle. Thin ply, no better than cardboard. 'I was hoping we could make it look like no one had been here — but there goes that idea.'

Walking back into the warehouse, his eyes fall on a vast wrapping table. At the back of the table is a low shelf, on which sits an inch-thick ledger. At one end is a huge roll of stretch wrap, at the other a screwed-down serrated blade, obviously used to cut the wrap.

'Here,' he says, 'hold the flashlight for me.'

PJ chooses the Phillips head screwdriver bit from amongst his drill attachments, winds it on. The blade comes off, complete with a wooden support that takes five more screws to remove. He is left with a cutting blade, not unlike that of a hacksaw, half a metre in length.

'Perfect,' he says, moving back to the door, first drilling a ten millimetre hole, then attacking the wood with the makeshift saw. This is not easy work, and within a few minutes he is sweating and swearing under his breath, while Mariam holds the flashlight.

The end result is a narrow tunnel that goes from the floor to a height even he doubts will admit his body. He sends Mariam through first, however, and she has no trouble. He follows, arms first, shimmying his way through the tight space.

On the other side, they emerge into an office the size of a meeting hall. Desks, chairs, shelves. The filing cabinets are in rows against one wall.

'Jesus,' PJ breathes, 'I didn't think anyone used those things any more.' There are computers also, HP machines with clunky black monitors, but it is obvious from bulging in-trays and the sheer number of filing cabinets that this is far from a paperless office.

Mariam walks from one end of the filing cabinets to the other, using her flashlight to read the labels in turn. 'Invoices ... accounts receivable. Look here; orders ... and they're organised by date.' PJ follows the direction of her flashlight beam. The current year takes up three full drawers. 'What date were they here again?'

The photo of Saif al-Din with Istikaan at the hotel was logged by the CIA. 'July 2.'

'OK, that translates to the month of Tir, in the Iranian calendar, the twelfth day. Doshanbeh — Monday. The Islamic year 1401.' She rifles through the middle drawer. Her fingers are remarkably dexterous considering the long, red-painted nails. 'Here, look, that's it. How many orders a day can they have?'

There is a single manila folder of sheets and Mariam lifts them all out, then sinks to the floor. PJ watches as she goes through them, pausing to lick her finger so as to make contact with the sheets. Some she lifts out and puts to one side.

'What are you doing?'

Mariam stops mid-stream, finger poised halfway through a sheaf of papers. 'This company does business with lots of customers. I'm separating the ones that relate to firms that I've heard of, or government bodies — many of them are large hospitals, universities, doctors' clinics — we can rule them out, can't we?'

'Of course. Good thinking.'

While she continues to work, PJ walks to the front windows, parts the curtains and looks out to the same street they had parked on that morning. There are no vehicles. No sign of any guards. Even so, he has the distinct feeling that time is against them.

He walks back to where Mariam is on her hands and knees. She looks up at him. 'I've narrowed it down to five.'

'We may be barking up the wrong tree. They may have just bought something over the counter. Or maybe they didn't come here at all.'

Mariam ignores him. 'Only three of these are business names. Two are just men's surnames.'

PJ falls to his knees beside her, and watches as her face lights up like a stadium at night. 'Can you remember what names they registered under at the hotel?' she asks.

Excitement begins as he fumbles for the Sid. 'I took pictures of the page.'

He starts scrolling through images, up to the most recent, magnifies with thumb and forefinger, then holds it for Mariam to read. 'Ansar al-Hassan.'

The battery indicator on the Sid is showing just a single bar now. Lower than he has ever gone with one of the units.

Mariam jabs her forefinger at an order docket. 'Ansar al-Hassan. It's the same. We found it.'

'What did they purchase?'

Her face falls. 'I'm sorry. I don't know what they are. Chemical names. I can't translate them. But there is a lot, hundreds of litres, thousands of kilograms.'

'It's OK, the boffins back home will work it out.'

PJ lifts the Sid, takes photos of the page, hoping that the battery on the unit has a decent reserve. 'Does it say where it's being shipped?'

'No, nothing. Just that transport will be arranged.'

'What the hell does that mean? There must be packing dockets, or something like that.'

Mariam points out a signature and date written over the printed docket. 'Look, that's today's date. They sent it out today.'

Frustration building almost as fast as excitement, he exhales through his lips. Whatever Saif al-Din and Istikaan ordered left this warehouse just hours ago. 'There has to be some record somewhere — despatch dockets maybe.'

Mariam is already up, walking again along the filing cabinets, checking the labels. 'Nothing like that,' she says at last. 'What about the computers?'

'They'll be password protected, I'll bet on it, but we should give it a try.'

He walks to what must be a supervisor's desk. Switches on the HP machine, waits while it whirs and flickers, the ubiquitous Windows logo coming and going — an outdated version. Windows 8 with its grid of square apps. This switches automatically to a desktop view, with a box and Arabic script underneath that can only be a request for a password. He looks down at the Arabic keyboard.

Mariam has come up behind him. 'Do you want me to try a few things?'

'Why not — we've got nothing to lose.'

PJ hears a noise from out the front, the clink of a chain. He freezes.

'What's wrong?' Mariam asks.

'I don't know.'

'What should I try?'

PJ talks as he moves back towards the front windows. 'Try the manufacturer's name, try 12345, try anything.' At the front window he parts the curtains again and looks out. A vehicle has pulled up out the front, a black Mercedes SUV. Three men have left the car and are talking to a third — a man in a security uniform. Either the same one that was sleeping out the back, or another one.

PJ runs back towards Mariam. 'We've got company. Any luck with that?'

'No, none.'

'Leave it now, anyway. Too late.'

'But we don't know where the shipment is going?'

'That's bad luck, but we've got goons out the front. I've never seen your Komiteh before, but those guys have that secret police look about them. Turn the screen off. Quick.'

Again Mariam has the ability to grasp the situation without fuss or comment. They grope through the relative dark, using just the faint, reflected glow of headlights to crawl along the floor to the door into the warehouse. Mariam squeezes through the hole first, then PJ.

'Walk fast,' he tells her, 'don't run. Walking is quieter, and they might be listening.'

The warehouse seems larger than it did before, and PJ wonders how they are going to cross the open ground outside, this time, without being spotted. Finally he recognises the long bench under which they entered, and he crawls under. 'I'll go first this time, in case they're out there, OK?'

He pushes aside the sheet of tin, pokes his head through, then looks out. Clear. He slithers through, waits for Mariam. She does not come.

For a few seconds he remains patient. Then the first tentacles of worry start tugging at him. She was only just behind him, for Christ's sake!

He looks back through the hole. Whispers as loud as he dares, 'Where are you?'

Just emptiness, his heart in his mouth. From out the front of the building the sound of a gate opening. In a moment the Komiteh are going to drive in here. Start patrolling the place.

PJ feels exposed. Is Mariam not all she appears to be? He rejects the idea almost as soon as it occurs to him.

Mariam has, quite simply, vanished.

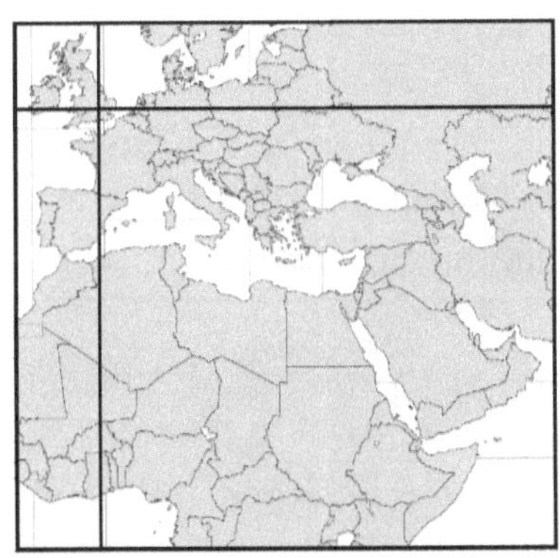

23 UNITED KINGDOM

London

Marika is asleep when Mossel calls. Within seconds her orders bleed in on the Sid, her bedside clock showing 4:57 in red LEDs. She breakfasts while reading the updates, washes the dishes, then jumps up to finish packing.

The serviced flat in Pembridge Gardens, Notting Hill, isn't home, but her flat is now a danger zone, and she suspects that she may never live there again. This fact has affected her more than she would have expected. Through her travels, the thought of returning to her beautiful flat has always been a comfort to her.

As units go, this one is clean and cosy — freshly painted walls in pale yellow, glass tables, modern light fittings — yet she leaves it without regret, locking the door and taking the stairs, emerging into the pre-dawn light just as a silver Vauxhall Astra glides to a halt outside.

Traditionally, mission day means a car with a driver, and Marika enjoys those last few minutes to get her head together, check and send messages, even just sit back and watch the dark streets slip by. The sun has still not risen when the car leaves the A40 down the link road and passes through security at RAF Northolt.

The Hawker 800 jet, with its pale wings sweeping back from a compact frame, sits like a resting bird on the tarmac. *A fast bird*, Marika thinks as she hurries towards it, *a gull, perhaps, or even a falcon.*

Beside her walk the two Royal Air Force Police guards who met her at the car, accompanying her through the abbreviated version of Customs she is required to negotiate, a peremptory check of her weapons and documentation despite her priority passport. No one is prepared to wave anyone through these days, especially not those carrying firearms.

Loaded down with her kit, Marika runs through a list in her head. Her UMP, taken down into three pieces, and a thousand rounds of 9mm ammunition; webbing, combat smock/jacket, Alt-Berg desert boots, everything in the new pixellated CADPAT pattern, developed in Canada by pattern generation software that incorporates neuroscience and the latest clutter metrics technology.

There are other items in her kit: SOPHIE thermal imaging equipment in a foam-lined hard case. Fifth-generation, full-colour night-vision goggles, or NVG, manufactured by Tenebraex. These ultra-compact units are strapped on over the wearer's eyes, far lighter and more usable than the old helmet mount equipment. For protection against bullets and shrapnel she has one of the new lightweight BAE Systems projectile vests, made of layers of shear thickening fluids sandwiched between Kevlar.

Nearing the plane, she recognises the tall figure of Tom Mossel consulting with a man in grey uniform, who must surely be the pilot. A group of men and women in combat fatigues stand nearby.

Now, as Marika approaches she appraises the group. David, the thirty-one-year-old with his scholar's glasses and narrow wrists. Kisira, a native-born South African, with the longest legs Marika has ever seen, and rangy shoulders that betray amazing physical power. Sara is of slighter build, but agile. Kutay, second-generation British from Turkish stock.

Kutay and David are PJ's best mates, regulars at Friday afternoon drinks in the pub at Kennington. It is rare for all of them to be in London at one time, but any number of others float in and out of the group and there is always a crowd, people to laugh with, to forget the burden of responsibility for a while.

David is the first to greet her, gripping her free hand with his own long fingers. His lean body is deceptive, biceps swelling below his rolled-up sleeve.

She moves along the line: Jay, 2CG's expert in EOD, Explosive Ordnance Disposal. Of medium height, he sports a handlebar moustache, and despite his superb fitness, Jay always manages to carry weight around his middle. A pair of Bollés perch on his close-shaved head.

'Hey there, boss.'

'Good to see you, Jay. How's that old Jag you've been doing up?' Apart from a well-known love of cars, Jay is fiercely protective of his private life.

'Almost done. By Christmas, for sure.' He beams, and Marika smiles back. The sixties vintage E-Type Jaguar has already been christened 'the Jayguar' by the tight-knit little group, and photos of the restoration are commented on eagerly as they are posted online.

'Kisira. How's things?'

'Sore shoulder from all those shots, but OK.'

Health Branch, Marika is painfully aware, had assisted with arranging a suite of injections. Comforting, but without knowing exactly what strain of pathogen they might come up against it was impossible to know if they were truly protected.

Next, her eyes fall on Ronnie. His presence is a surprise. Normally he would be a team leader, and since Marika has that role he can only be 2IC. Being placed under her command will irk him considerably.

'You're on this one, Ronnie?'

'Seems that way.'

Then you're going to have to do things my way, she wants to say.

Ronnie is old-style Special Forces. Hard-drinking, hard-fighting, impeccably fit and, up until a few months ago, undeniably competent. Since then, there have been a few incidents — nothing major — small things that others have covered for him. But enough for that slight loss of confidence. Confidence in your comrades, Marika knows, is paramount in this business.

Marika feels a surge of anger that Mossel has placed her in this position, commanding a more experienced man — especially one she has never really got along with. She finds it hard to keep her voice level as she walks over to Mossel. 'Ronnie's my 2IC, sir?'

'Yes.'

'He's not happy about it.'

'I know, but this is an important one. I wanted someone like him to back you up.'

'He's a dinosaur.'

Mossel's eyes darken. 'He's a good man, Marika. Along with PJ he's the best fighting man we've got.'

'He doesn't like me.'

'Leadership isn't a popularity contest.' He pauses, then moves on as if the previous conversation never happened. 'I have some news I need to share with you before you fly out. The pathology lab have just finished full analysis of tissue samples taken from the dead at al-Guin, the Syrian site. It was slow, but had to be undertaken in a BSL-4 laboratory.'

Biosafety Level Four, Marika recalls, is the strictest and highest standard of containment for organic material. Only a handful of labs in the United Kingdom are certified to that standard.

The director places a plain folder in her hands. 'Hard copies are more secure at the moment.'

When the Hawker has levelled out at thirty-two thousand feet Marika opens the folder. The title is the kind of science-speak she would have expected: *Pathological and Immunohistochemical Investigation into Tissue Samples Taken from Cadavers in al-Guin, Syria.* Then two lines of names.

The abstract tells the story.

'Nine out of the eleven cadavers sampled showed haemorrhagic mediastinitis and serosanguinous pleural effusions consistent with infection and death caused by anthrax spp.'

Even though much of the report is hard to understand she reads through to the conclusion, where one paragraph makes her shudder.

'Early indications are that up to one hundred and twenty cadavers may be present in the pits. Speculation on why it was deemed necessary to infect such a large number of living specimens with this pathogen is outside the scope of this report, but may be offered on request.'

Marika closes the report and turns to the window, watching the puffs of grey and white cloud. She paraphrases the final words of the report in her head. *Pay us more money and we'll tell you what we think.*

Finally, hand curled around the stainless steel and vinyl arm rest, she tries to think about the good things. After a while, however, she closes her eyes. On the verge of sleep the images move beyond golden beaches and mountain peaks.

Marika doesn't want to think about PJ. In this job looking out for your own safety is hard enough without taking on the wellbeing of another.

Despite herself, in that innocent state between wakefulness and sleep, when all the defences have been kicked down, she finds her soul calling out across the world to God knows where.

For Christ's sake, Pais, be careful.

24 IRAN

Chabahar

When PJ has almost given up hope, Mariam comes slithering through the gap in the wall. The strength of his relief is like a flood of warmth into his veins. In her hands she carries the huge ledger he last saw on the packing table.

'Where did you go?'

'I just thought of this — it's the … I don't know the word … sending register. It was on the packing table.'

'Well done.'

PJ slips the ledger into the sports bag. 'Now let's go.'

They run together across the clear space and are almost at the wire when PJ hears a shout. He turns. Three men run towards them across the grass. A vehicle is trundling over the gutter of the carpark, headlights stabbing through the night.

'You first,' he says, falling to his knees, skidding. He's watching her go through the gap in the wire, pushing the bag through just as the first gunshot rings out from behind. Then he is down, wriggling through, shouting at Mariam to run.

On the other side he picks up the sports bag and sprints across that patch of grassland, past aarak trees and scrub. He can hear the sound of Mariam's breathing, but he has to moderate his pace a little for her to keep up.

At first he can hear voices, pursuit, but this tails off. The Komiteh operatives will know the layout, are probably heading back to their vehicles. PJ stops and looks back, he can see the shape of one man not far behind them. Smart move on their part, leaving him, probably their fastest runner, on their tail.

'Anyone there?' Mariam grunts out.

'Yep, one. The others will have gone for their vehicles.'

Ahead he can see the car, and Naser must have noticed that they are being pursued. The starter motor whines and the engine fires. Headlights click on. PJ finds himself silently thanking Mariam's efficient right-hand man.

The runner is within pistol range now. PJ considers pulling out the SIG Sauer and taking a shot, but he has found in the past that starting a gunfight is much easier than finishing one. Mariam is here, and the best option will be to get out as fast as possible.

He reaches the car first, opens the back door just in time for Mariam to pile in. He is barely in the door before the car takes off, and the man who was chasing them on foot is reaching out for the door handle when PJ slams down the manual lock. The tyres screech as Naser steps on the gas.

PJ knows exactly what will happen next. 'Get down!' he shouts, taking a grip on Mariam's sleeve, dragging her down just as a bullet hits the rear window, spraying glass fragments like water droplets, exiting through the side window, passing close to where Mariam's head had been just a second earlier.

Another gunshot, but no impact as Naser struggles to control the wiggling back end, careering into a gutter, lurching back onto the road, then screaming away at speed. Half a block down he throws the car into a turn, down a narrow side street, then back onto the main road, joining the traffic flow.

Almost as soon as they reach the beltway Mariam reaches in PJ's bag for the book and a flashlight. PJ is amazed how cool she appears to be for someone who has just been shot at. Flicking on the light, she starts turning the pages.

'I was right,' she says, 'it's a register. They record everything they send out in here.'

PJ shakes his head to dislodge small chunks of glass that have settled in his hair, then turns to look through the rear window, now marked with a single hole surrounded by glazed cracks. There is no sign of pursuit. Not yet. He turns his attention to Mariam. 'You clever thing. You just might have saved the day.'

'Hey, look, here it is. They delivered the consignment to the old port. A dhow called the *Ghudwa*. It was only today, so it might still be there.'

'Can Naser take us straight there?'

Mariam leans forward on the seat and speaks to him. Then back to PJ.

'That's fine. I also have a contact there — I might be able to find out exactly where the *Ghudwa* is docked.' While she produces her phone and makes the call, he looks back through the window again. Rounding an obtuse bend far behind is a black Merc.

'We've got company,' he says to Mariam who, phone to her ear, turns to look. He can see the fear in her face, then she shouts something to Naser. Someone obviously answers the call, for Mariam starts talking, her face increasingly distressed. She ends the call abruptly, puts the phone away. 'I know where we need to go.' She talks to Naser again. Then to PJ she says, 'It's OK, I have a plan.'

PJ is looking at the blue-hued headlights of the Komiteh vehicle behind them. Then another one, perhaps half a kilometre behind. 'I hope it's a bloody good one.'

Naser is driving much faster now, and PJ starts to wonder, judging by the acceleration and handling, if, like Mariam herself, the car has more under the bonnet than meets the eye.

She seems to read his thoughts, 'My car has a WRX engine and gearbox, in a standard Impreza body. Do you like it?'

PJ reaches up to pull another shard of glass out of his hair. 'I'm impressed.' Yet, as the car careers back towards the city, PJ remembers the army checkpoint up ahead and wonders if they will have been warned.

Naser, however, takes a minor road at speed, swinging the car into a turn that is much too sharp, tyres screaming as they enter what looks like a quiet, residential neighbourhood.

Mariam's voice is urgent, 'Soon Naser will take us down a side street and stop. You and I will have to be ready to get out. From there we will walk the last couple of hundred metres. OK?'

'What about Naser?'

'He will lead them away from us.'

'What about him?'

'Don't worry, just be ready.'

The car takes a circuitous route through narrow streets. The two black SUVs come close, directly behind, then drop back, unable to compete with the superb driving skills of Naser, and the incredible power and acceleration of this seemingly innocent little Subaru.

Naser shouts a word, accelerates. Takes another corner at speed.

'Ready, now,' Mariam screams, and the car brakes hard. PJ throws the door open and slides through, propelling himself out and behind a large iron skip bin. Mariam is behind him, and the Subaru sprints away, rear door closing from the momentum of its acceleration.

Crouching behind the skip bin, they see first one SUV, then another, scream past in pursuit. They wait another minute, then Mariam squeezes his hand. 'Let's go.'

'How far to the dock?'

'Not far. Just a few minutes.'

Mariam is right. PJ can smell the sea as they walk. From a rise overlooking the docks she points out an old jetty descending far out into the sea near a promontory of land. 'One of those dhows just there will be the *Ghudwa*. I'm sorry, but from here you are better off alone. Besides, Naser will need my help.'

PJ knows that she is right. The dhow is potentially hostile. This is his department. Mariam has done enough. He reaches out and hugs her briefly.

'Thank you for everything.'

'No problem, it's my duty.'

'What about the Komiteh? They'll know who you are, they'll go to your place.'

'I'm not crazy enough to go back there. Naser and I will move on. We have places to hide. Alternative identities.'

'You and Naser have an interesting relationship, don't you?'

'He is my husband.'

PJ is so stunned he can scarcely stutter out a reply. 'Husband? Didn't you say he was taken by the Komiteh?'

'That was my first husband. Naser is my second.'

'Where did he sleep while I was there?'

'In the car. It would have been inhospitable not to have a bed for you.'

He grasps both her hands in his. 'I hope I can repay you one day.'

Mariam smiles, leans forward to kiss his cheek, then stops, frozen, as they both hear the sound of a powerful engine on a nearby street. The Komiteh will not take long to discover the ruse. 'Now go,' she says, 'hurry. Both of us have dangerous times ahead …'

PJ starts to walk down a narrow lane towards the port, feeling that he has just made one of the best friends of his life.

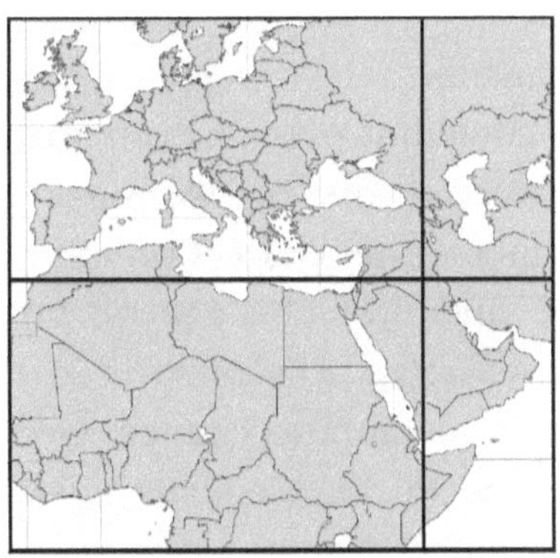

25 IRAQ

Hawija Arban

Saif al-Din's face is drawn, eyes aching deep in their sockets. They have travelled through the long hours of darkness, holed up during the day, forced into close confinement with a large number of men, not all of them emotionally stable.

There have been good moments, yes. Prayers on the roadside. Thirty men on their knees, foreheads pressed to the ground, the murmur of voices low and sweet in the night. There was also a brief firefight with members of the Iraqi Army, mechanised infantry in two Mobile Strike Force Vehicles. The dead were buried away from the road. Six torn bodies hefted and dumped into shallow graves. The two bullet-scarred MSFVs, one torn apart by an RPG, they left just off the side of the road — wrecked military vehicles are part of the scenery here.

Saif al-Din has been watching Karim Yussef, the leader of the Ba'athist contingent, over the past few days. During that time a shocking truth has become clear. When delegating tasks to the men, the worst and most repugnant duties go always to the darker Africans. He speaks to the Algerian, Egyptian and Pakistani members of the group with respect, almost as equals, but to the black men with contempt.

Saif feels that contempt extend even to himself, though it has not been as overt. At first he was surprised, but now rage has begun to simmer in his chest. Confined in close quarters, they are all tense and tired. Even now, however, he cannot sleep, nor let himself relax. The prize is so huge that he can't bear to leave even a moment to chance. God has given him a finite amount of time to complete his mission on earth. The splinter of steel in his head moves ever closer to the vital parts of his brain. To squander even an hour with unnecessary sleep would be sinful.

To keep himself awake he squats and unrolls the square of cloth all al-Muwahhidun fighters carry. Inside is a fifty millilitre bottle of oil. He lays his AK47 assault rifle out on the cloth and begins to strip it. This is a skill he first learned from the soldiers of Boko Haram long ago in Nigeria.

This particular weapon was supplied by the Syrians, an Egyptian copy of the venerable Kalashnikov design. The original Russian models are the best, but they are getting hard to come by. The parts are identical, and the stripping and cleaning method is the same. This is automatic. A task completed a thousand times, on desert sands, the decks of boats, in tents and hotel rooms.

First he removes the magazine, then the top cover of the receiver and the spring assembly. Bolt carrier. Gas tube. Oiled and placed on the clean cloth. The cleaning rod from its well beneath the barrel, then the oil kit from the hinged, spring-loaded hiding place in the rear of the stock.

Saif works the cleaning rod, with its fine, lightly oiled wire brush, up and back twice then gives the stock a light coating of machine oil from the cloth. Satisfied, he packs the kit back into the butt and begins reassembly.

He has just finished repacking the magazine with fresh rounds, when a gunshot rings out. The sound comes from one of the adjoining rooms, muffled by thick stone walls. Saif pushes the remaining rounds into the magazine before standing and hurrying towards the source of the gunshot.

Karim Yussef is already on the scene, beating a man around the head with his fists, shouting and berating him. 'Idiot! Fool!'

'Stop.' Saif demands. 'What has he done?'

Karim Yussef stands back, points to the offender, now bleeding from the nose and lip. 'This fool just discharged his pistol into the wall of the room. He says it was an accident.'

The culprit is a Somali, from the south of that country, with coal-black skin. His eyes plead with Saif. 'I apologise, Sayyid. It was a mistake.'

Karim Yussef turns on the hapless offender again. 'Idiot, you want to bring police to investigate the noise. You want the cause to fail …' The Iraqi lifts a hand to strike the man's face once more.

The blow never lands. Saif catches the aggressor's wrist in his free hand. 'Leave him, there is no harm done, and he's my responsibility.'

Hatred blazes in Karim Yussef's eyes.

Saif glares back. *This man is a bigot. One who looks down on men of black skin.*

'Let go of my wrist. Now,' Karim Yussef growls.

Here, in the dusty basement of a house in the town of Hawija Arban, rank with the smell of men's sweat, fire smoke that cannot escape and the stench of boiling curried meat, they face each other.

'You do not command me, or my men.' Saif lets go of the wrist but is conscious of the AK47 balanced in his right hand and the dagger in its hidden sheath. Yes, the knife would be better. There is more satisfaction with the blade. 'Leave him alone or feel my displeasure.'

'You flatter yourself. Raise a hand against me and you will never leave this country alive.' The threat is bad enough, but the Ba'athist commander adds *'takruri'*, an Arabic word meaning 'black slave', a deeply offensive term that has its roots centuries earlier.

'I will kill you for that,' Saif hisses, 'when this is all over.'

'We will see who will kill who, takruri. But for now I will feed my men, and yours, saving my anger for afterwards, when my knife will learn again of the resilience of black flesh. It is many years since I killed a slave.'

Saif makes a noise that sounds like something between a cough and an exclamation of rage as the other man moves away, trying to control the impulse to kill Yussef now. He even chooses the place on his back, just to one side, below the rib cage, angled up to rake the kidneys and push on into a lung. A mortal wound, yet one that might allow him to live for an hour or more, choking on his own blood and fluids.

Looking down, he sees that his hand is shaking, and through sheer effort of will he makes it stop. His headache is just beginning, an exploratory needle before the iron wedge that will follow. Now, he too will feed his men. Then he will find a private moment to take one of his precious store of pellets before, at his command, they move out to the trucks and away into the night.

26 IRAN

Chabahar

The vessel is similar to many others around it — a shu'ai rigged dhow, twelve or thirteen metres long, carvel-hulled with a raked single mast and ventilation slits below the gunwale.

The name *Ghudwa* is painted near the bow on both sides. There is a guard, standing at the gangway, and PJ stops well short, watching, heart beating fast. Even from where he stands he can hear the sound of a diesel engine deep in the bowels of the vessel, and cooling seawater spitting overboard. The *Ghudwa* is about to make way. He has no choice but to try to get aboard. The guard starts throwing off ropes, and there is a clunk as the helmsman engages reverse gear.

Hurrying now, PJ climbs off the jetty, over the gunwale and into the nearest dhow, crouch-running down her length, mindful not to trip on hatches and stays. At the stern he climbs down, sits on the wide duckboard.

First he drops the sports bag into the water. It sinks quickly with the weight of the bolt cutters. He removes his shoes and socks, then eases into the water, swimming around past the intervening vessels.

A boat, however, is never still. Each vessel rises and falls with the gentle surge of that protected portion of sea, squeezing fenders between hull and dock. Every movement has an individual sound, yet always in harmony with the rhythm of that sea.

The *Ghudwa* has motored clear of its berth, backing up to gain space. She is high-wooded, and pointed at both ends. PJ can hear the mechanical beat, revving up as they warm the engine. The stern of the dhow is close. He can see the broad platform just above water level a few strokes away. Hears the engine clunk back from reverse into forward gear, then the churning of the prop resumes. The approach has gone from safe to risky and he changes direction, making for the corner as the hull begins to move forward.

There is no longer any need for stealth, covered by the noise of propeller and engine. PJ touches the hull, loses it, strokes out, desperate for a handhold on the vessel, misses again, then powers after it in a desperate freestyle. There is nothing here to hang onto apart from the rudder, which he lunges for with one hand stretched so far it feels as if his shoulder joint might crack with the strain, finding a handhold just as he realises that this is his last chance before the task becomes impossible.

One hand, then the other, closes around the hardwood rudder. He feels himself dragged forward faster as the wash pushes at his body and the hull reaches waterline speed of around ten knots.

He can hear nothing, do nothing against the racket of the engine, just holds on, biding his time, knowing that once clear of the port they'll stop the engine. They will not motor all night when there is a wind to sail by. Fuel is too expensive.

PJ searches with his eyes, hands and feet for a way of pulling himself up by a less noticeable route than straight up the rudder itself, a method that will see him enter the boat over the transom.

There is another concern — that the helmsman will notice the extra drag on the rudder, and someone will come to inspect. With this in mind, as soon as he senses movement he drops further back into the water, maintaining contact with as light a touch as possible.

A difficult and uncomfortable hour passes before the engine stops, and the silence is a huge relief. There are no voices. At this time of the night, there will be just one man on watch, calling for help if a major adjustment in sail is required, but otherwise handling shipboard duties on his own.

PJ uses feet and hands for purchase as he climbs upwards. Near the top he stands, peeping over the transom into the dhow's interior. He feels like a voyeur.

There is a man in the main cabin, back turned. He appears to be eating something, perhaps dates, from a bowl on a wooden chart table beside the wheel. A charcoal brazier smoulders away on the deck behind him, and also burning incense sticks, a combination of scents so strong it is hard to discern anything else. Light from the cabin spills all the way back and PJ knows that entering the boat from here is too much of a risk.

Working his way to the starboard side, hanging onto the gunwale itself, he finds a foothold on the thick rub rail that runs fore to aft along the vessel midway between waterline and deck. Moving forward is precarious and slippery.

Amidships, adjacent to the cabin yet hidden from view, PJ swings his leg over the rub rail and eases his left foot down onto the deck, willing the helmsman not to turn around, nor anyone else in the main cabin to be wakeful or alert. Even as he steps aboard he sees an automatic weapon leaning near the wheel, close to hand. If these men are indeed Almohad, they will carry sidearms also.

The hatch that, PJ assumes, leads to the cargo hold is just aft, deep in shadow. He falls to his knees, scrabbling for the huge iron ring that serves as a handle. Not wasting any time, he heaves, fearing the squeak of rusted hinges. The noise, however, is not enough to alert the man on watch, and he continues, slipping inside, easing his feet down the steps then closing the hatch so that it shuts with a faint thud.

PJ finds himself in absolute darkness. Damp and humid, the hold reeks of diesel fumes and bilgewater. He slips a hand into a pouch in his webbing, retrieving the waterproof flashlight. He doesn't yet switch it on, instead trying to determine if there is anyone in the hold. Dhow designs vary, and in some vessels the hold continues into a claustrophobic and low-ceilinged sleeping area, with knee timbers every metre or so.

On the companionway, half-sitting, half-standing, completely immobile, he registers each sound as if on a checklist, ticking it off as non-threatening. Slap of water on the hull. Groan of timbers. Traffic sounds from the shore. A cough from up topsides.

No human sound from down here, but as he descends, his senses are hit with a new smell — dried dates, cloyingly rich. The oppressive atmosphere deepens, and PJ finds it hard to believe, after a few minutes here, that anyone would choose to sleep in the hold rather than the breezy main cabin above.

He slides the SIG Sauer handgun out of the holster, half-opens the slide and inverts it to get any residual water out of the magazine, barrel and action, then holds it ready, right arm extended, while his left switches on the flashlight and sweeps the area.

No hostile faces. Just general freight in heavy, palletised cardboard boxes. Dates in huge bales, hundreds of them. Yet the hold is by no means full. PJ spends a few minutes moving the flashlight beam.

Searching all the bales will be a huge task, and there is also a chance the more sensitive shipment might be elsewhere — in the captain's cabin, perhaps.

Yet why would they hide it there? Where better to carry illicit cargo than in a mountain of other goods? Besides, getting access to the other sections of the dhow will be much more difficult.

His close study of the contents of the hold gives him two places to start, and both are in the most cluttered and crowded areas: logically, the best place to hide contraband. He begins to make his way over to the far corner. Each bale will have to be examined, and even before he starts, his hands are sticky from the dates. He struggles to hold back a sneeze, knowing that any sound might give him away to the men sleeping and watching just metres away.

Finally, before beginning the search he removes the Sid from his pocket, rubbing the machine between his hands, warming it, trying to get the battery primed for one last effort. For more than a minute he continues to work at warming the unit, then tries the power button. The British coat of arms glows dully. He waits, then opens the main message app.

On board dhow Ghudwa, *leaving Chabahar Harbour with consignment.*

The message sends, and the screen blanks out, battery exhausted. The feeling of being alone is almost overwhelming.

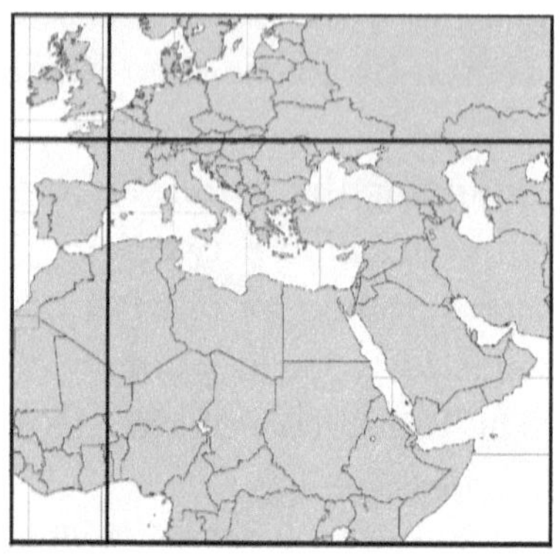

27 FRANCE

Paris

In Clichy-sous-Bois, in the eastern suburbs of Paris, a crowd estimated at five thousand boils through the streets, smashing shopfronts, invading homes, tearing burqas from women and beating up Muslims and Sikhs. Organised groups retaliate and the violence escalates into a full-blown street battle, including small arms.

The first detachment of the Compagnies Républicaines de Sécurité on the scene is inadequate, and they have little choice but to take cover while the situation explodes. Within a few hours the violence has spread to eight other suburbs as well as the cities of Lyon, Strasbourg, Toulouse, Marseille, and Lille.

The president issues a statement calling for calm, suggesting that the riots are the work of a small number of members of right-wing organisations joined by disaffected youth. The media headlines shout: 'Émeute Raciste; Racist Riots'. Police are criticised for not doing enough, then criticised for doing too much.

In London, a right-wing group calling themselves the Crusaders plan a night attack on the suburb of Waltham

Forest. Fifty men will drive to three pre-arranged locations, burn houses and tear burqas from women down three main thoroughfares, before converging to fight whatever forces turn up to challenge them.

In the United States of America, black neighbourhoods of Chicago, Los Angeles and New York have malnutrition, childhood mortality and life expectancy rates comparable to the West Bank and parts of North Africa.

The latest fad, begun by rapper celebrities, is DNA testing to discern what African tribe their ancestors came from. Having the result tattooed on their skin is a new form of tribalism. Violence tears cities apart, and police shooting rates rival those of Iraq.

Some states attempt to change the way the nation votes, banning those with criminal records or those who don't possess a particular type of identification card. A new elitism. Widening inequality.

An attempt to raise the debt ceiling is defeated once again, and spending cuts deepen an unavoidable recession. The long, slow decline in health and education standards has begun, yet government priorities lie elsewhere. The National Security Agency spends eight billion dollars a year, intercepting almost two billion personal and business communications every day, looking for the proverbial needle in a haystack. Presidential election budgets exceed one billion dollars per candidate, enough to feed one million Africans for a year.

Back in 1981, President Reagan signed Executive Order 12,333 banning assassinations as a mode of warfare, intelligence or otherwise, but by 2013, assassination via drone or Special Forces unit had become the favoured method of waging this new asymmetrical war.

The death of civilians, collateral damage from drone strikes, is a growing cause of anger and radicalisation across the world.

* * *

In Chakula Refugee Camp, Kifimbo has been unable to get the Somali woman, Haro, out of his mind. He finds his sergeant, Antoni, in the canteen and offers him a cigarette.

'Can I borrow your motorbike again?'

Antoni slips the cigarette between his lips, bends down so Kifimbo can light it, then blows smoke straight up with pursed lips. 'My good friend Kifimbo, can't you see that nothing good will come from chasing Somali tail in the camp?'

'I just want to help her.'

'You want to help her into your bed.'

'That's not true. She is a friend. I want to help her. Can I borrow your motorbike, or must I walk all the way there? If I walk, when I get back I'll be too tired to play poker. You won't win your money back if I'm too tired to play.'

Antoni digs the key from his pocket and hands it across. 'Take it, visit the woman — I hope it is worth it.'

This time he finds her at one of the stone berkaad, the traditional water collectors that dot the camp, near the front of a long line of women and children with buckets. Hers has just been filled and she is walking back towards her tukul, the bucket on her head and baby Rajee on her hip.

At first she stops when she sees him coming, then keeps walking. He falls into step beside her.

'Sabah wanaqsan,' he says.

'Sabah wanaqsan.'

'I've come to visit you again.'

'I can see that.' There's a sardonic twist to her lips, but, it seems to Kifimbo, also pleasure.

'I brought you some things.'

'That is very kind of you.'

'Some things for the baby, too.'

'Thank you.'

Back at the tukul he again takes items from his rucksack. Again she accepts them with a simple thank you. Olive oil. Real bread from the officers' mess. A packet of salted peanuts that he's saved for a week.

Haro invites him to come inside. At first tentative, he ducks through the opening. The interior is quite dark, but he settles onto his haunches. The smells of breast milk, of cha, of charcoal smoke and human odours are like home to him.

He contents himself with watching her make cha on the brazier, careful to show that she brings it to the boil before pouring the steaming and fragrant liquid into coloured plastic mugs.

They drink in silence for a few minutes before she lifts Rajee to her lap and frees one breast. Kifimbo watches the baby take one dark nipple into his mouth, then his jaw move rhythmically as he suckles. To him it is the most natural and wonderful sight in the world.

Kifimbo wonders if one day that baby boy will carry a gun. Like so many others. Wonders if the cycle of violence will ever end.

He tries to think of something to say, settling on, 'It was lucky for Rajee that you had milk.'

'Yes, lucky for him, but sad for me that I lost my little girl.'

'How did she die?'

The young woman shakes her head. 'We were travelling. It was hard. She died in the night.'

'I'm so sorry to hear that.'

'We all are. But how long must the bad times continue?'

'I don't know. I'm sorry.'

'Again you say that you're sorry, but you're not to blame. Why must people like you — good people — keep apologising for the bad.'

There is a sound at the door, a double slap with an open palm on the tukul wall near the entrance. Haro calls out in Somali, answered by a man in the same language. A moment later two men duck through the entrance.

The young woman looks up at the first of the two newcomers and they talk for a moment in Somali, too fast for Kifimbo to understand, before she turns back to him.

'This is my brother, Dambe, and his friend, Itaal.'

Kifimbo has seen faces like that before. Barely disguised suspicion. The memory of past betrayal. Kifimbo can see it all. He knows that such people lash out because they have themselves suffered the lash too many times. Itaal is a little older, one cheek puffed out with qat.

'Hello, Dambe,' Kifimbo says.

'Hello.' Arms crossed, jutting lower lip. 'What are you doing here?'

'I am drinking cha, as you can see.'

'A smart mouth. Typical of a Kenyan. What tribe are you?'

'That is not your business, but if you must know I am Kikuyu.'

Dambe shrugs, 'You are all the same to me.'

Then why did you ask? Kifimbo thinks, but Dambe has not finished.

'Finish your cha and then you stay away from her, do you understand?'

Kifimbo is not afraid of the man — after all, he has a handgun in the holster at his side, while the Somali is unarmed. Besides, Dambe is thin, with a frame that could be pushed over, it seems, with a finger.

'When I have finished my cup I will go, but not because you told me to.'

The brother scowls, but he and his friend duck back through the opening, their voices receding into the general clamour of the camp.

'They saw your motorbike,' Haro says, 'and wanted to know who was here. Forgive my brother. He is protective of me, and has many problems.'

For Kifimbo, however, the mood is broken. He drinks in silence, until just leaves remain, and he stands to go. 'I might be able to get you out of here and into the camp. Would you like me to try?' His mind races ahead. Maybe he could get her a job in the administrative compound — the kitchen, perhaps. Then he could see her whenever he likes.

'No. Dambe is the only family I have. I won't leave him. Now, you had better go before he comes back. He has a bad temper.'

'I am not afraid of him.'

'I know you are not, but I have seen enough fighting.' There is a pause, then, 'It is best that you do not come here.'

Kifimbo feels a shock. Why would she say such a thing? Hadn't he brought her good things? He feels an unwelcome prick of anger. *If she does not want me, I will not come back.* Yet even as he swears in his heart that he won't ever think about her again, he asks the question. 'Why?'

'Because you are Kenyan, and I am Somali,' she says, as proud as a queen, rather than a young woman at the extreme of poverty and circumstance. 'What you want can never be.'

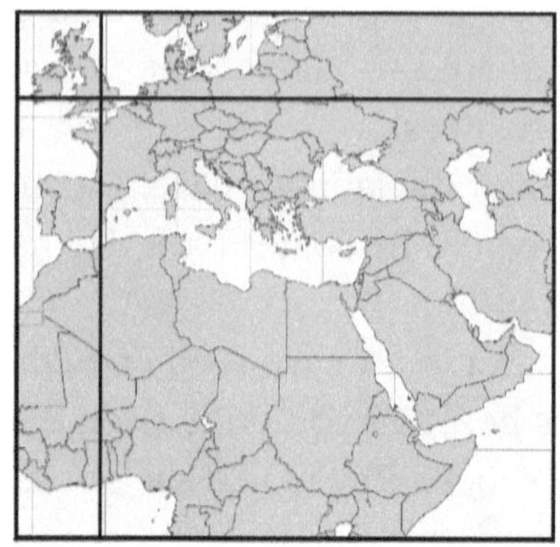

28 UNITED KINGDOM

London

Tom Mossel has a strong sense of history. And history is easy to believe in as his driver takes him past Westminster. Architecture that would be impossible to duplicate now.

The wealth to build this city was looted from America, Africa and Asia. The gold, silver and diamonds of the world flooded into this country for two hundred years. Stolen from dozens of colonies all over the world, who could not stand against the British military machine with its veneer of justice, underneath which simmered a controlled savagery. The grandeur of London was purchased with the sweat, blood and toil of the working class, by one of the most unfair and unequal societies in history.

The National Security Council, responsible for oversight of the UK's revamped CONTEST anti-terrorism strategy meets in a small room in the complex adjoining Number 10 Downing Street. Once referred to unofficially as COBRA — Cabinet Office Briefing Room A — the room is rectangular in shape, wood-panelled, a SITPOL screen situated at one end. The expansive maple table seats twenty-four, and a few more at a pinch.

Chaired on this occasion by the Home Secretary, the meeting is attended by representatives of relevant departments and security organisations, each in touch via local-area-network with their own back room of advisers. CONTEST is an overarching strategy, combining the four work streams of Prevent, Pursue, Protect and Prepare.

Mossel delivers the briefing as always, succinctly and without humour or emotion. 'One of our assets has identified a shipment of chemicals outward-bound from a factory in Iran. Most are used for the production of bacterial growth medium and others, our analysts believe, can be mixed with bacterial spores to be broadcast as an aerosol.

'At the same time, we have identified a site that may provide evidence of an old Iraqi special weapons program. We believe that the site may also be known to a Religio-Political terrorist group with a history of violence and mass murder. I am asking you, gentlemen, to authorise a covert fly-in as we have not yet been able to secure permission from the Iraqi government. In the meantime I, in concert with the Foreign and Commonwealth Office, will continue to work on the Iraqi government. In fact, I will probably fly to Baghdad as soon as I leave this room.'

Stunned silence. Blank faces.

'My other request is that we should now initiate Code Amber stage one.' This is a heightened state of preparedness for a CBRN attack — airport scans for substances, increased surveillance on the movements of suspected insurgents.

One of several senior public servants from the Home Office raises his hand. 'Isn't that jumping the gun? We don't have firm evidence that—'

There are times when Tom Mossel loses his patience. People sometimes forget that under the unflappable English exterior there is a hard man also, one who was on active service through much of the Cold War, lost a wife on the job, and has killed men, once or twice with his bare hands. When Tom Mossel gets angry it begins on the inside, is manifested in his eyes, then his face in general. He glares at the young politician and the force of his anger burns across the room like a laser.

'If you want to play politics, don't do it near me, and don't do it now. There's too much at stake. If potentially catastrophic loss of life doesn't worry you, let me assure you that Britain cannot afford a CBRN attack, at any level. The kind of attack this group might be considering would be an economic disaster. Prevention is our only chance.'

Tom Mossel had done the sums. The 2001 US Mail anthrax attacks, for example, affected just twenty-two people, killed five, yet cost half a billion dollars to investigate and clean up. Teams of laboratories tested millions of items of office waste. There were seven thousand hoax calls from the public. That entire campaign was planned and orchestrated by just one man with access to a lab. A legacy weapon wielded by a powerful network with well-established tentacles in Britain could cost billions, quite apart from human lives lost.

No one speaks against Code Amber. Both motions are carried unanimously. Both are significant.

Code Amber means that known affiliates of al-Muwahhidun will now come under intense scrutiny. Facial-profiling computers at airports, meeting places and hotels around the world will report every sighting. Software will compare and track travel patterns for the last year or more. Tiny sensors at travel hubs and events measure a phenomenon known as microexpressions. Experienced, trained terror operatives can learn to hide emotions, but microexpressions are facial giveaways of intense stress, often lasting for mere fractions of a second.

Some machines use sophisticated sensors, from a distance of several metres, to take blood pressure, skin temperature, and pulse readings, while also making an assessment of surreptitious eye movement and breathing rates.

Others 'sniff' out CBRN agents being smuggled through airports and borders. Portal shield bioweapons detectors in the

London Tube and cross-channel tunnel can detect eight of the most likely biological agents.

As he steps outside past the iron fence and onto the paved footpath of Downing Street, his official Jaguar cruising down from outside the Cabinet Office to meet him, Mossel feels a measure of satisfaction that he has woken the machine up to the threat. Now it is up to him and his organisation to neutralise it.

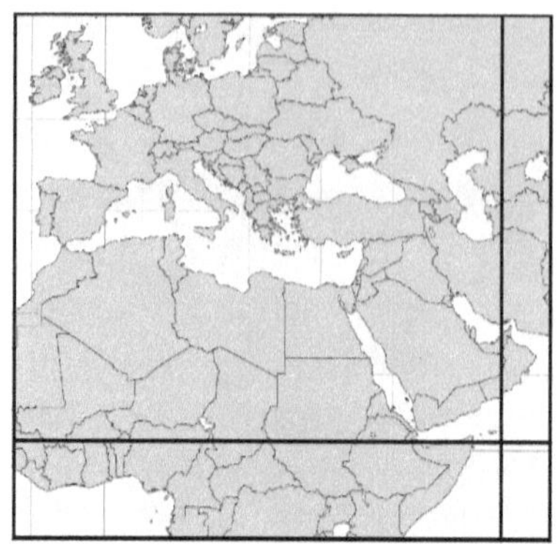

29 ARABIAN SEA

Offshore

After countless hours of searching, PJ's hands and clothes smell like dates, and he has an overwhelming desire to be free of them. There is no way to be certain of the time, as the Sid is out of batteries, the screen lifeless and dark.

The search, arduous as it was, has not been fruitless. The first item of interest he found was a weapons cache, in eighteen separate crates; at least two hundred North Korean-made assault rifles chambered for the standard 7.62mm short round, a dozen RPG tubes manufactured in the same country, and a copious supply of ammunition for both.

He was then forced to go through a dozen bales of dates before finding the next items: five larger wooden crates with Arabic and English lettering on each face, proclaiming the country of origin as the Islamic Caliphate of Iran. Again he levered up some boards with his knife, careful not to snap the blade.

The first two crates contained eighteen blocks of Iranian-made countermeasure flare launchers. Made to defend aircraft against missile attacks, they can be mounted on any aircraft, and discharge dozens of individual flares that emit massive heat signatures, confusing ground-to-air and air-to-air missile guidance systems. From what PJ can remember, these decoys throw out foil chaff to confuse radar guidance systems as well. They are a worrying inclusion in the dhow's manifest.

On his knees beside the next crate, he shines the beam of his flashlight on banks of blue twenty-litre chemical containers. He lifts out one by the handle, again using the flashlight to study the label. Arabic letters, then the English below: beta-propiolactone. This translation had not appeared on the invoice statement in the office, but might be useful now. He goes through the crates. Tryptone. He opens one more crate to be certain. Yeast extract — glycerol.

Any one of these chemicals in isolation would mean little, but PJ knows what to look for. These are the active ingredients of laboratory growth media. Enough to have raised a flag from any of the world's intelligence services.

PJ closes the crates then rocks back on his haunches, certain that what he has just seen is the material required for the laboratory production of a large quantity of pathogen.

Moving on, beside it are four one-tonne bales that are as hard as stone to touch, yet when he slips his knife into the top, sawing away to get twenty or thirty millimetres of access, he finds that the contents are a fine, soft dust, feeling like cosmetic powder between his thumb and forefinger. In the torch light it is a pale brown-pink colour, and smells of earth when he raises a smear of it to his nostrils.

Bentonite. A specialised form of powdered clay. First used by the Russians as a delivery mechanism for anthrax spores, the incredible fineness allowing it to drift large distances, enveloping cities.

He fumbles again for the Sid. This has proved to be a vital cargo. London needs his position. Again he starts to rub it between his hands.

Please, just once more …

The unit is capable of an emergency burst transmission that will take less than a second, instantaneously uploading all data in the machine to London, in particular his current location.

He tries the power button. Nothing.

Voices.

Footsteps.

There is scarcely time to put away the useless Sid, close the crate, and duck into his hiding place. Preparing this space was one of the first things he did, hollowing out a body-sized gap between two one-tonne bales of dates. He has a glimpse of bare feet on the companionway steps before he burrows deep into the stinking cave.

The voices are muffled by the cargo, some in Arabic, others Somali. There are six or eight of them, at least. Too many to fight.

'If he is aboard already, he will be in here ...'

'How would a kufr agent have got in here without us seeing?'

There is some further grumbling, footsteps on the timbers of the hold, then, 'Saif al-Din says that he is here, and therefore he must ...' A stumble and a curse as someone loses their footing.

PJ feels his heart sink at the words. *Saif al-Din says that he is here ...* The feeling of fear, not for himself, but for the entire organisation, is sudden and numbing. That unauthorised access to the DRFS database was no temporary hack, but ongoing and complete.

They know everything.

For a moment the knowledge is so consuming he cannot think or act.

Their lines of communication must be extraordinary, if information can take such a rapid route from London. One of the world's most secure organisations has been blown wide open.

He hears the action of an assault rifle slide. They are armed with automatic weapons and ready. The voice again. 'Get to work. It will not take long if we hurry.'

PJ tenses at the sound of men grunting, and of bales being dragged. There is a very high likelihood that his hiding place is about to be disturbed. The only possibility of escape is to get *inside* one of the bales of dates.

Almost choking from the smell, PJ slides the slender Gerber knife from its hidden sheath and slowly works it into the burlap skin of the bale, using the razor edge of the knife in a sawing motion from left to right, opening it up to the width of his shoulders before resheathing the weapon and trying to wriggle forward, into the bag, using his hands like those of a swimmer to part the dates.

The sounds of shifting cargo loom closer as he disappears head and shoulders into the bale, almost choking as he squirms his way inside, dates pressing on his face, into his eyes and lips. Getting his shoulders into the bale represents a tremendous effort, and he is forced to stop for a moment and subdue the sense of panic rising through his system, attempting at the same time to get the SIG Sauer from the holster on his belt.

'Stop, Hassan, I heard movement. Is it a rat?'

PJ stops, motionless, feeling his chest heaving beneath him. Dates still pressing against his lips and nostrils. Each breath is a torment. Getting further into the bale is impossible. His free hand has only managed to delve halfway towards the butt of his pistol. The other still clutches the knife.

He feels the bale gripped and dragged by half a dozen hands.

'Sayyid, this one has a tear in it. Look! The dates are spilling.'

The bale stops moving. A shout. 'What is that?'

'The kufr agent — look.'

PJ tries to move now, desperate to slide back out of the bale so he can fight. The pressure of the dates is strong, however, and getting out is little easier than getting in had been. Legs kicking frantically, he starts to slide out.

The sound of a rifle being cocked. 'Stab him. Get your knife. Kill him.'

PJ feels a sharp steel blade glance upon his rib cage, tries to roll, but knows also that he has just microseconds before they either stab more successfully or they start shooting, or both.

'No. Get him alive.'

Strong hands grip his ankles, dragging him physically out from the bale, his head thumping against the deck as he falls. Then they are all over him. Hands, sweating faces, pushing him face down on the deck, while all the time the others shout in Arabic or Somali. Someone stomps on the hand that still holds the Gerber knife, pinning it to the deck.

'Frisk him, hurry.'

'Get cord to tie him with.'

'What if there are others in there?'

'Have a look, but the message said that there was just one.'

They gather his hands, wrist to wrist, on his back and tie them together. Other hands run over his body, taking the handgun and dead-flat Sid.

A man on each of his legs, they drag him towards the companionway ladder then up, with one man standing below and pushing. Out onto the deck, rolling him over. Another man, beard long and thick, black whiskers curling darkly, holds up a cell phone to record the capture on video.

Someone slaps his face, then, with pincered fingers, grabs his chin, making PJ look into a pair of bloodshot eyes, sneering lips, and a row of brown teeth.

'Sathaan,' he says. 'You are the devil, and now you will find out how it feels to die.'

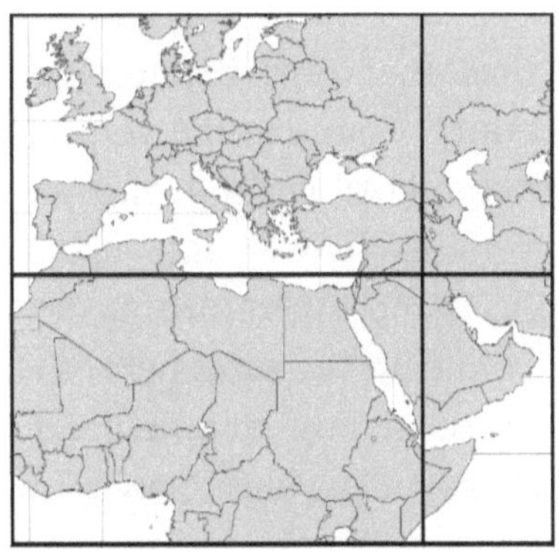

30 IRAQ

Al-Hajjuf

Up until now the contingent of Ba'athists has guided the convoy, using their up-to-date knowledge of military installations and infrastructure to avoid trouble. The near-empty trucks glide through the deserted streets of the desert city of Kubaysah, lined with squat clay-walled houses, and on towards the remote region of Qasr Khabbaz, date palm fronds against the night sky. Not long after midnight Istikaan wakes, and Saif, still at the wheel, becomes aware of his tension as they near their destination.

Istikaan is quiet, subdued, and Saif senses the nostalgic pang of this return for the Iraqi to the land of his birth. Saif understands. Every man has a place, a home, and there are threads that bind the two together — no matter how long he has been away. The place where he attended his first Madrasah, where he learned to fear God. Where he kissed his sister's best friend and giggled about it to his friends. Yes, the land of a man's birth is an enclave in his heart, for all the years of his life.

'Stop now,' Istikaan says, 'just ahead of here we must turn.'

187

Saif takes his foot off the throttle and lets the speed bleed away, pulling off onto the verge before stepping on the brake and changing to neutral. Counting the vehicles as the headlights arrive and line up behind. All waiting, engines running.

When all four vehicles have caught up, Saif shifts into first gear, revving into the change, then turning onto a small track that leads off into the darkness. The sand here is soft and the wheels of the truck lose grip constantly, spinning and churning.

Mostly the road tracks straight ahead, occasionally with diversions around what must be deep troughs and steep hillocks of sand.

'How far from here?' Saif asks.

'Less than an hour. We are very close.'

Saif warns the others. The headlights pick their way through the night. Once, a desert rat scuttles across the roadway, and another time they are forced to slow for a goat herd, a boy of no more than ten or eleven, whose multicoloured livestock fill the roadway, panicked and bleating. The boy tries desperately to control them, shouting and using his crook to turn the recalcitrant animals away from the road.

Without a word, Saif stops the truck, walks out with his rifle and approaches the boy. Then, at a distance of ten paces, he shoots him twice in the chest and leaves his body there on the sand before walking back to the truck.

'It is best that no one carries word of our passing,' he says, closing the door.

Istikaan nods in agreement. 'I agree. It is best.'

More than once they almost get stuck, but Saif is an African, with skill in the sand, knowing when to rev the diesel hard and when to gentle through. At one point, when the wheels begin to dig their way in, he uses forward and reverse to rock the vehicle like a child's cradle, gaining momentum with each movement until the truck moves off down the track.

Finally they grind over a hump into a bowl-shaped valley several kilometres across. Istikaan raises himself on the seat. 'Stop here,' he says, 'this is the place.'

Again Saif brings the truck to a halt, engaging the handbrake, letting the diesel engine idle. 'Are you sure?'

'I could not forget it. Not even at night.'

Men pile out from the backs of the trucks. Some of the Syrians and Iraqis light cigarettes. Istikaan and Saif alight from their own vehicle and stand together.

Istikaan points to the south. A ruined building is visible in the vehicle headlights. 'The bunker is in the hillside just behind it.'

'Will it take long to penetrate?'

He taps the side of his head with one finger. 'No, once the earth around the entrance has been dug away it will not take long. I know the way, and how to unlock the hidden doors. The secret of al-Hajjuf will soon be ours.'

Karim Yussef approaches, sauntering with that arrogant stride. By his side walk two other men — no better than bodyguards. They are like clones of the same man, with full beards but clean-shaven on the upper lip, their shemaghs cloths worn loosely to expose the hawk-nosed ferocity of their faces.

'Killing the boy was the act of a fool,' Karim Yussef hisses at Saif.

'It was necessary. He might have told of our passing.'

'We have passed a thousand children since the trucks rolled into Iraq. Should we kill them all?'

'No, but he was close to our destination. I deemed it necessary for him to die.' Saif says nothing further, but follows Istikaan away before he loses his temper.

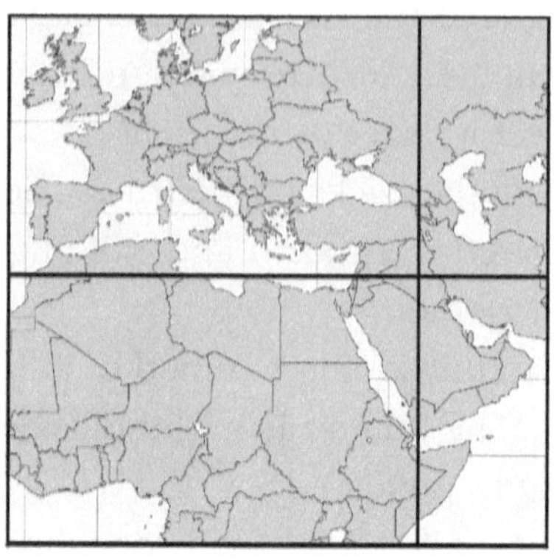

31 IRAQ

Qasr Khabbaz

The Lynx AW159 Wildcat heli troop carrier sweeps low across the desert. Two more fly at either side; Marika can see them at the extremes of her vision, shadows in the night sky, flying so low that their passage raises clouds on the ground like fast-moving dust devils. Adrenalin surges through her veins.

Tom Mossel's words echo in her mind. *I'm on my way to Baghdad, but until I get clearance for this mission you should regard this as a black operation. You may be fired upon. You may not fire back.*

Marika glances at her team on the bench seats, with their longarms and greasepainted faces. Each agent also has a full Bergen field pack with sleeping and cooking equipment plus rations for twenty-four hours, leaving no clear deck space.

The heat of their clothing is only bearable for someone trained so often in CBRN response that the physical discomfort can be subverted. The first layer is a CPU, Chemical Protective Undersuit, with zippered front and a skin-tight hood. Above that is the Kevlar/Shear fluid vest, then a tightly zippered battle jacket, designed to offer at least the same level of CBRN protection as a standard First Responder Kit.

Before hitting the ground they will each fit black latex over-gloves and the Dräger PAPR, Powered Air-Purifying Respirator, incorporating an HC-COM comms unit, connected via Bluetooth to their Sid, carried in a padded pocket designed for that purpose. Standard NVG — night-vision goggles — are worn above the respirator.

There is more to Marika's mood than just the dread-excitement-fear of impending action. Tom Mossel also confirmed that London has lost contact with PJ Johnson. Not only that, but one of the Islamist websites on the DRFS monitors is boasting of a capture in the Arabian Sea. 'We believe he boarded a dhow called the *Ghudwa*, on the trail of a cargo of laboratory equipment including the chemicals necessary to turn bacterial spores into a weapon of mass murder ... we are being told that he is now in the hands of the enemy ...'

... boasting of a capture.

That's what they do. Boast. Hurt. Kill.

Marika does not want to think about specifics. North African and Middle Eastern torture methods are known to her. They are direct and bloody.

Guilt and sadness overwhelms her. Yet what can she do but try to put him out of her mind? No matter how difficult that might be. She looks at David, sitting beside her. She has worked with him before, many times, and appreciates that he doesn't feel the need to chat. He sits forward, knees apart, eyes fixed on the screen of his Sid.

'Last-minute orders?' she asks.

He holds the Sid up, displaying a hi-res shot of a woman and two children of around five and seven. All three are dark-complexioned, particularly the woman. South Asian ancestry. Marika has never met David's family. Like many people in this game, he keeps his personal life insulated from this world.

'I've told you about Chitrita,' he says, 'and the twins. Jordan and Mukulita.'

'They're all beautiful.'

'Yes, I think so too.' He makes a sad little laugh in the back of his throat. 'She didn't want me to come, this time. Dreamed that she saw me bleeding to death, and nothing she could do would stop it.'

Marika is silent. They never know which will be their last trip. They don't lose many, but enough.

He goes on, 'My wife doesn't understand me, but I can't just ride the tube and sit at a desk every day while the world heads for oblivion like it's on greased fucking rails ...'

There is a sudden swoop in Marika's stomach as the Lynx rises over a low ridge of hills, the ground clear in the moonlight, stony and barren. On the other side from her sits Ronnie, stonily silent, the only one of them who always looks as tidy as if he is about to step onto a parade ground. Marika has never seen him dirty — not for long, anyway.

Kutay is beside him, a canvas case on the deck in front of him holding the Barrett .50 calibre sniper rifle that he is as good as married to. This weapon is accurate for up to a kilometre or more, and he is a freakishly talented trigger-man.

Right now, in his own reaction to nervousness, he is telling one of his jokes. They rarely get much of a laugh, but always have a calming influence.

These two breakfast cereals walk into a bar, right? Then one says ...

David taps away at his Sid for a few seconds before zipping it away. 'What do you think the chances are of hostiles at the site?'

'At the briefing, they—'

'I know what they said at the briefing. What do you think?'

'Fifty–fifty.'

... an' she says, you don't think we fuckin' had a corn flake here before ...

The talking stops at a shout from the cockpit. 'We have aircraft on radar, converging fast. Five of them.'

Marika unclips her lap belt, stands, squeezes in between the two pilots, staring at the radar screen. From the speed of the blips she realises that they are jets, probably Iraqi Air Force F-16s.

The F-16s are an antiquated US-made machine, refurbished and delivered to upgrade the Iraqi Air Force some five years earlier. Antiquated or not, they will be equipped with Sidewinder air-to-air missiles, and can call on five times the speed of the choppers.

'We're being challenged,' the pilot says calmly. 'They're telling us to identify ourselves or they'll fire upon us. What do you want to do?'

Marika swears under her breath, trying to think. 'Tell 'em we're US Army. Joint manoeuvres with the INCTF.' The Iraqi National Counter-Terrorism Force, Marika knows, is one of several US-trained Special Forces battalions in the country. The most likely to be conducting a covert training op.

'They won't buy that.'

'Try it, anyway, then get down lower. It's a dark night. They won't see us.'

'Lower? Jesus Christ, we're already flying beyond the edge of sanity.'

'Just do your best.'

Marika brings out her Sid and issues two terse instructions. One is a pre-rehearsed order that will see the flight disperse on three different vectors and then rejoin at the target site. The other is to get down low, right on the deck, flying under power lines if they have to.

This is a hard order to give — at such low altitudes there's a strong chance that they will lose at least one aircraft and all personnel on board, but they must get through. This is too important.

The other aircraft break away like predatory insects. Individual evasive action is up to each pilot, and Marika feels the airframe tense and vibrate, groaning with strain as they decelerate and turn sharply. This is a manoeuvre intended to make the jets overshoot, at which point they will be unable to find the scattered choppers either visually or on the radar.

Now the ground is so close that a slow response by the pilot will be disastrous. The pilot flies by eye, relying heavily on the FLIR — Forward Looking Infrared screen — on the dash. Up ahead is a lit-up house with palm trees reaching higher into the sky than the chopper seems to be flying, and the skids appear to brush a wire fence that encloses the place.

The co-pilot turns to Marika and grins, jabs a thumb at the pilot. 'No one else in the world can fly like this bloke.'

Both, of them, Marika knows, are from the elite 657 Squadron, Army Air Corps, detached on special duties. Seasoned at flying SAS and other elite troops on black ops, they are the best in the business.

This knowledge helps temper Marika's fear as the headlong flight continues. Ahead is a row of towering iron power poles, lit by streetlights, and still the chopper does not rise. Marika finds her fingers digging deep into the hard back of the seat as they fly under the wire. Flying this close to the deck in the darkness is the most thrilling and exhilarating ride she can remember.

'They've lost us,' the co-pilot says. 'They're scattering, trying to get a search pattern together.'

'Any sign of the other friendlies on the radar?'

'One popped up a minute ago, but nothing now. They're invisible.'

Marika purses her lips, nodding to herself. The dispersal might work yet. 'How long until we reach the target?'

'Thirty-five minutes on this route. Wadi al-Atr is coming up. We'll get down into the dry river bed and even Jesus wouldn't pick us out on a screen.'

* * *

The government of Iraq, post-Saddam, has a chequered history. Organised into eighteen governorates, the country is ruled by a Council of Representatives and a largely symbolic Presidency Council. From the time of the American occupation this government has struggled for legitimacy and credibility.

Thomas Mossel walks into the cream-coloured convention centre that houses the Iraqi parliament. Security is tight, including metal detectors and body scans, followed by a grilling about the purpose of the visit and a slow photocopying of identification.

It is after midnight, and many of the staff appear to resent this unscheduled visit. Rolling eyes, staring belligerently. Keeping Mossel waiting at every turn.

Waiting beyond the third security check is an Iraqi plain-clothed security operative and a red-cheeked Englishman. Seemingly all legs and no trunk, bent in the middle like a hinge: Rawson Zimler, the High Commissioner.

Mossel shakes the proffered hand. 'Good evening.'

'Likewise, old chap. Warm night, eh?'

'Rather warmer than London, no doubt about that.'

They are escorted onwards by a moustached man who talks almost constantly into a short-range communication device, peering from the corners of his eyes at the two Englishmen as if expecting them to turn violent.

The High Commissioner fills Mossel in, voice grim, as they walk. 'There's a whole bunch of diplomatic backwards-ing and forwards-ing going on. I've got the Prime Minister to agree to twenty minutes with us.'

'That will have to be enough. He works late, I'll give him that.'

Zimler makes a face. 'Well he doesn't generally get here until the mid-afternoon. If he didn't work till midnight he wouldn't get anything done at all.'

They climb a set of steps, and the security man directs them to an antique lounge chair. Mossel is under no illusions about just how important this is. He has waited in many offices like this — knows the games that men like to play, particularly when facing one of the major powers. Making the West look small is viewed as strength in this part of the world.

Ten more minutes pass before the door opens and a man in his sixties in a tailored suit and pointed, tooled brown leather shoes walks out. 'I am sorry to have kept you waiting. I'm sure you understand how busy things can be for me.'

'Of course.'

Zimler introduces him: 'Mr Prime Minister, this is Thomas Mossel. He met with your ambassador in the UK yesterday. His name may be familiar to you?'

'No, sorry, it does not, as they say, ring any bells.' A wave of the hand. 'No matter, come in.'

The office reeks of wood and incense, the colours brown and red, an Iraqi flag unfurled on one wall. The cedar-framed window looks down on floodlit lawns, wire, and men with guns marching in perfect ranks as if purely for the benefit of their PM.

'I'm sorry I can't offer you coffee. My assistant has gone home for the night.'

The note of smugness in this statement is not lost on Tom Mossel. 'There's no need. I'll get straight to the point, if you don't mind. We are here on behalf of His Majesty's Government. We need permission to send a covert mission into your airspace.'

The Prime Minister's eyes remain steady. 'I suppose I should be pleased that you have decided to ask permission.'

The High Commissioner breaks in, 'I might remind you that it is some years since we have conducted an operation into Iraqi airspace.'

'So you tell me, Mr Thomas Mossel, what is going on here. You are asking permission rather too late. I have already had word of unauthorised aircraft over our Qasr Khabbaz region.'

Mossel is well aware that the Iraqi government remains corrupt, with leaks at every level. There can be no possibility of telling him everything. 'Sir, we have identified a threat that goes beyond your borders, requiring urgent attention. The site we have identified is in a remote region, clear of villages and other civilians. We request permission to send in a team of analysts, with military escort, via aircraft. We estimate that they will be on-site for just a few days.'

'Analysts?' the Prime Minister asks. 'May I ask what they will be analysing?' Mossel can almost see his mind working, sensing advantage. No one rises to the top in post-Saddam Iraq without political acumen and an aptitude for ruthless bargaining. The Prime Minister's hands open wide, the gesture of a priest, or a peacemaker. 'Why do you not just tell me what you want to do? Give me the co-ordinates and I'll have my military investigate.' He points at the phone. 'All I have to do is make a call and it will be done.'

'Our intelligence is sensitive,' Mossel replies, 'and we need to be able to act independently. With all respect, you do not have the personnel with the expertise necessary in this case.'

The Prime Minister raises his chin. 'This is my country. Not an ant moves in this place without,' he thumps his chest with one fist, 'my permission. Iraq is no longer your vassal, your battleground.' He cranes his face forward. 'Not a blade of grass blows in the wind without me knowing about it.'

This seems to Mossel a rather ambitious boast in one of the most lawless and corrupt countries on earth.

The High Commissioner, a career diplomat, bows. 'We understand that, sir, but we have many reasons to wish to undertake the mission ourselves. There are international ramifications of importance to us, and ultimately you as well.'

The Prime Minister smiles for the first time. 'I understand. Your request is *important*. In that case I too have some *important* things I have been meaning to ask from your country. We shall see what your answer is ...'

When Tom Mossel leaves the building twenty minutes later, he has committed a company of engineers to help rebuild a bridge in the town of Gammas, a massive discount on a potential order of custom aluminium-hulled patrol boats from Abels Shipbuilders in Bristol, and promised a favourable review of the British Foreign Aid budget for Iraq.

Zimler turns to Mossel as they step into the chauffeur-driven BMW. 'The PM is going to have some harsh words with you and me over this.'

'You just leave him to me. He's a lamb, really. Besides, you heard the man. Free access. Full co-operation.' He claps the High Commissioner on the back. 'That's compromise, old son. You should know about that.'

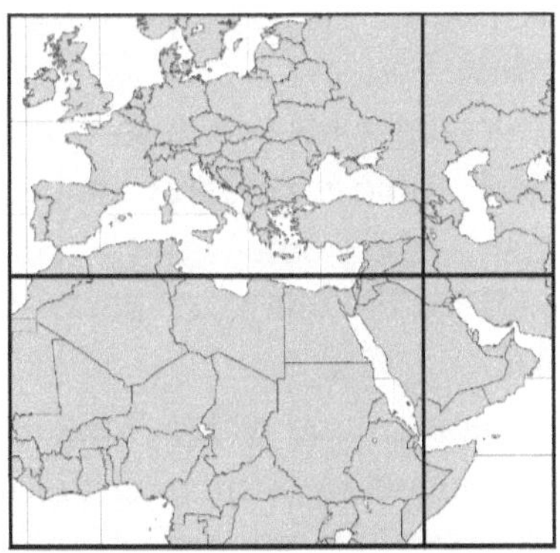

32 IRAQ

Al-Hajjuf

Istikaan has a strange feeling as he stands near the bunker entrance. It is many years since he was last here. Men with shovels are already digging, Saif al-Din haranguing them, urging them to work harder.

'Our sources have informed me that the kufr are on their way,' Saif al-Din calls out. 'We must work faster, and be gone before they arrive.'

Istikaan is surprised to find his hands shaking with excitement mingled with fear of death and failure. He hugs his chest with his arms like a boy.

The weapons of retribution are at hand.

Almost every night he dreams of how the enemy will die, of how their last moments will be, aching for breath, haemorrhaging. Not hundreds of them, not thousands, but millions perhaps, hundreds of millions, the agent of their last moments falling in minute particles from the sky — out of sight and smell.

For decades he has felt that he holds the power. The desire to use it is something that has grown along with his knowledge of the world. His hatred of the West is a writhing, multiple organism like the hair of Medusa.

As a child, he was tall for his age, heavy in the hips and belly, giving him an unusual, almost womanly shape.

'Istikaan, Istikaan,' the other boys chanted. *Hourglass. Hourglass.* So named for the shape of his body, the heavy hips and fatty boy-breasts.

He spent his childhood alone with a book, or with his second-hand Tasco hobby microscope, watching the tiny creatures that lived in water and on food. At the age of nine he could identify spirillum bacteria from cocci, and would spend hours watching paramecium feed and whirl in a droplet of swamp water. In his leaving examinations he topped the Kadhimiya District in chemistry and biology, and won a scholarship to Baghdad University to study biotechnology.

His PhD thesis was completed in 1990, on the genetic structure of certain disease-causing pathogens, and soon after he was recruited into the Ba'ath party by his uncle, a local party organiser who moved in the highest circles. Istikaan was shrewd enough to know that joining the Ba'athists would be a powerful career move.

He was working on agricultural crop diseases at the Muthanna State Establishment and seemed set for a distinguished future when the president sent troops into Kuwait, and UN Resolution 678 authorised 'all necessary means' to expel Iraqi forces from the neighbouring country.

At this stage, Istikaan was married, his family living in a government-provided house in the Baghdad neighbourhood of Kadhimiya. He lived in men's accommodation in Muthanna from Monday to Thursday and spent weekends at home.

At first the far-away war impacted little on his life. Then, one Friday evening he returned home to find his house in ruins. His mother, wife and two children dead, laid out under blankets. A misdirected Coalition smart bomb had done the damage.

After the war he was sent by the regime to an indoctrination camp near Damascus, Syria, a country then under the control of the al-Assad family, who were also members of the Ba'ath Party.

Al-Ilkhan training base was a thrilling terror.

The instructor's eyes glowed like burning coals. 'You are a man now, but let me take your mind back to childhood. Picture yourself as you were then. I want you to imagine the moment at which you were most afraid.'

The moment I was most afraid …

Istikaan thinks back, parting the years like curtains, picturing the boys who met him on the way to school, took his lunch and stole the one hundred fils coin his mother had given him, then smashed him to the ground, forced his mouth open and smeared goat shit through his lips and he was crying and trying to breathe and the smell of faeces was foul in his head …

'Istikaan, Istikaan. Hourglass. Hourglass.' They took his lunch. They told him he was an abomination. They punched his nose in the schoolyard, and kicked his ankles in school corridors.

He heard again their laughter echoing from the green linoleum floors and peeling white ceilings. He gasped aloud with the force of this memory. 'Oh. God, I was afraid, yes.' So afraid he'd peed, and the urine had run down his legs and they had laughed and thrown stones until he fell. Dust and sand clung to the wetness …

'Do you hate the boys who did this to you?'

Eyes closed tight, fists like hammers. 'Yes. I hate them!'

The voice softened. 'Good. But let me tell you, that your hatred for them must be nothing compared to what you feel for the enemies of God. I want you to remember how your bride looked as she lay dead, and your daughters covered with bloody sheets beside the ruins of your home … innocents slaughtered by the coalition of Jews and unbelievers. Tell me how you hate them.'

His voice broke into a squeak. 'I will not rest until they lie dead, in their locust-like millions — this plague that Sathaan has sent to infest the earth.'

Back in Iraq, Istikaan was transferred to al-Hakam Technical Research Centre, north of the city, to work under the direction of the infamous Dr Rihab Taha, better known as 'Dr Germ,' widely rated as one of the most dangerous women in world history.

The facility was conducting broad-spectrum research on a number of pathogens, some designed to cause mass mortality among urban populations such as botulinum and anthrax. Others — wheat rust, for example — would cause crop failure and famine in the target countries.

Anthrax had long been identified as the most suitable candidate for biowarfare. Its spores have a very long life span, at least thirty years, and the mortality rate in humans, when inhaled as an aerosol, is over ninety per cent. Death, moreover, can occur within seventy-two hours. Spores of the deadly Vollum strain, developed by an English Professor of the same name, were kindly provided by the British government.

Istikaan headed up a new division specialising in the genetic engineering of bacterial pathogens, berated and forced to work at a frenzied pace by the violent mood swings of Dr Taha, who frequently punctuated staff meetings with chair throwing and other histrionics. Meanwhile, the new factory oversaw the production of 8500 litres of Vollum strain spores and a similar amount of botulinum.

Fatal tests on live animals, including donkeys and primates, were performed in a German-designed three-cubic-metre inhalation chamber. Istikaan felt no pity. He saw this as a necessary part of ensuring these weapons would one day be used on the real enemy. On one occasion, when a colleague confided his private disgust at what they were doing, Istikaan reported him to factory security. The man was carried off to Abu Ghraib and never heard of again.

There were two focuses to the research: the weaponisation of new and exotic strains, and the genetic manipulation of bacterial DNA. In 1997 Istikaan spent six months in Russia's Stepnagorsk

Scientific and Technical Institute for Microbiology, controlled by the infamous Biopreparat.

UNSCOM weapons inspectors were active at this time, and the site, officially producing chicken feed, could not escape their notice for long. The new research, however, was seen as so promising by senior Ba'ath party officials, including Saddam Hussein himself, that research was moved first to the Daura Foot and Mouth Disease Vaccine facility, then the secret bunker complex beside a little-known meteorological station in the desert.

Here Istikaan enforced a draconian regime of strict silence and worship. Twelve scientists lived in a shipping container buried into the hillside, sleeping on bunks welded to the walls. Conditions were tough, yet, away from the prying eyes of UNSCOM, and later UNMOVIC, progress continued. There were whispers that no one left al-Hajjuf except in a coffin, and a melancholy pervaded the place. The suicides angered Istikaan. Morale suffered as a result. Yet al-Hajjuf was a doorway from which there was no return, a black hell that most men could not live with.

As if his feet have a mind of their own, Istikaan finds that he has wandered towards the ruins of the meteorological station. He can see the beam where he found the hanging corpse. The author of the letter from beyond the grave.

The letter that sits waiting in a safe place at Ka Tirsan for the day he has the courage to read it.

To the Living from the Dead …

The note that has become a scar in his psyche. The thing he cannot overcome.

To the Living from the Dead …

Ten years passed with him saying, 'I will read it tomorrow,' before he recognised that he was afraid.

To the Living from the Dead …

Ten years to realise that he is terrified of what the dead will say.

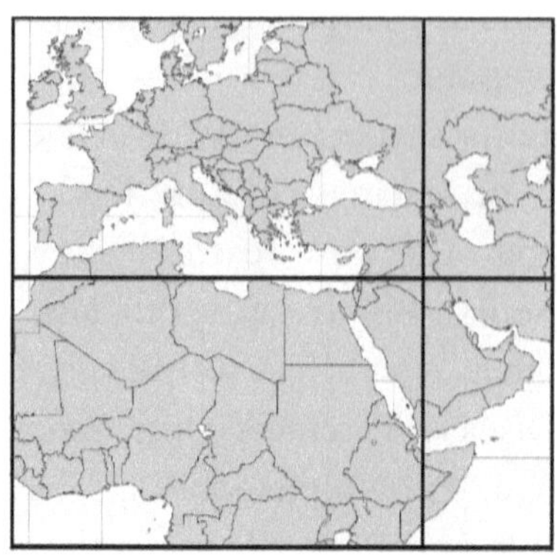

33 IRAQ

Al-Hajjuf

The darkened landscape becomes a blur, and after a few minutes of blinding speed, on a direct vector across a deserted countryside, the Lynx rockets down into the steep-banked walls of a dry river with occasional trees that loom up at lightning speed.

They almost collide with a camp of nomads, camels and children scattering in all directions. The burning sticks of a campfire glow burning hot with the fanned flames, then coals scatter in all directions from the wind of their passing.

Now the movement becomes even more erratic as the pilot follows the wadi floor, twisting unexpectedly with the valley cut through the desert. Then, abruptly, they leave it, rocketing cross-country again.

Marika gives the order to gear-up, and all around her members of the squad don masks and gloves, and check their weapons, seemingly oblivious to the rocking craft. Then, however, the news of a deal comes through from Tom Mossel on the Sid, and she feels a weight off her shoulders: they no longer have to fear the Iraqi armed forces along with the Almohad.

'You can cut out the subterfuge now,' she informs the pilot through the Dräger, 'they've called off the dogs.'

After a final, smooth five minutes at one thousand feet the Lynx clatters over the lip of a valley. The pilot's voice comes through the Dräger: 'Advising heli-team commander that we are landing, orientation due north. I repeat, due north.'

Marika reaches down for the buckle release in her lap. 'Seatbelts off,' she shouts. More clicking metal releases as the Lynx drops, plummeting like a bird with folded wings, then stopping, hanging a metre off the ground. Again the pilot's voice, more urgent now. 'Disembark.' Like all chopper pilots he is nervous on the ground, anxious to get back in the air where he and his crew will provide, if necessary, close fire support.

Marika is first out, then David beside her, into a swirling cloud of dust that she feels in her nose and lungs, stinging her eyes. The others follow: Kutay, Sara, then the rest of the team. Ronnie at the back.

Following standard operating procedure, they take up prone firing positions on the earth, forward of the chopper, scanning out into the darkness. Marika knows that the others are as tense as she is, waiting for muzzle flashes and incoming fire.

Remaining in this position until the choppers are back in the air, Marika is the first to rise to one knee and study the valley through the NVG. No hostiles are visible, and she gives the orders they are all waiting for, dispersing her team into different roles: securing the perimeter of the valley, guarding the LZ, and her own squad who will proceed to the bunker itself.

Marika is pleased to find that already she has merged the actuality of the hollow with what she studied on the map. The choppers remain in the air and, at a radioed order, they flick on powerful floodlights that illuminate the landscape.

An irregularity on the earth catches Marika's eye and she walks twenty metres, squatting to examine tyre tracks embedded in the dust, overlaying footprints. A cigarette butt. She picks it up and holds it under her nose. Still fresh.

Ronnie moves up beside her and looks down at the tracks. 'Road tyres, commercial vehicle — ten tonne at least.'

'Yeah, someone has been here, in the last few hours by the looks of it.'

Holding his SA80 by the butt under his armpit, he claps sarcastically. 'Smart cookie.'

Ignoring Ronnie, she looks up the hillside to what must be the ruins of the meteorological station. The cladding has long ago been cannibalised, leaving just beams and girders standing like a matchstick grid. Nearby is the yawning entrance of a tunnel, freshly disturbed earth spread around it.

They've been and gone, she says to herself. *We're too late.*

'I want pickets on the high ground at all four points. I'm on my way up.' Then, turning away from Ronnie, she lifts her Sid to her lips. 'Kutay, move up here.'

A moment later he runs up, the Barrett held in both arms — no lightweight, but he makes it look easy. 'I want you here on fire support,' she says, 'keep a close eye, and if you see so much as a twig out of place let me know.'

'Will do.'

'OK. Red Squad, come with me.' She waits for them to form up, spreading out in patrol formation; David, Kisira and Jay. She is happy knowing that Kutay will be covering them with the Barrett. Not to mention the choppers if things go to hell.

The ruin, she sees as they get closer, is just that. Bare beams and floors. The fresh wound in the earth nearby is of much more interest. As they approach there remains little doubt that this is a bunker entrance. Her suspicion that they have been beaten to whatever lies hidden here deepens.

Marika stops the squad, and sends Jay on alone, rifle slung, equipped with a hand-held device called a HHA scanner. This unit is able to give a presumptive warning of biological material in suspension. Marika watches, almost unable to bear the tension of waiting.

Minutes pass before he comes back.

'Is it clear?' she asks.

A shake of his head. It is impossible to read his expression through the mask, but there is a tenseness to his movements that wasn't there before.

'Nothing's coming up in the air samples. But they've left a bloody great IED in the entrance, with IR beams rigged to trip it.'

His voice sounds distant and ethereal, part auditory, part through the comms unit in the helmet. 'Is it dirty?'

'I don't think so. Looks like a couple of kilos of C4.'

Marika slithers forward until she too can see it, plainly visible in the freshly dug entrance to the bunker. They have made no effort to hide the device. She studies it carefully. The trigger beams are arranged to cover the entrance.

'So if that bunker contains anthrax spores and the C4 goes off?'

'We'll be evacuating a couple of hundred square miles, but not before a few thousand villagers get infected. This place would take decades to clean up.'

'What do you need, Jay?'

'I'll have to bring in Dirty Harry.'

Dirty Harry is Jay's nickname for the tracked disrupter unit, waiting in the hold of one of the choppers for just such a deployment. 'What then?'

'We burn the fucking thing with avgas down in the valley.'

'OK, let's go for it. Get the chopper pilot over here with the disrupter.'

'We also need to get all personnel back at least as far as the LZ.'

'We're suited up.'

'Yeah, but I've seen these things blow. Shrapnel will punch through respirators like they're not there — tear them right off, even. If that bunker is packed full of anthrax we're fucked, right?'

Marika swallows. 'OK. I'm onto it.'

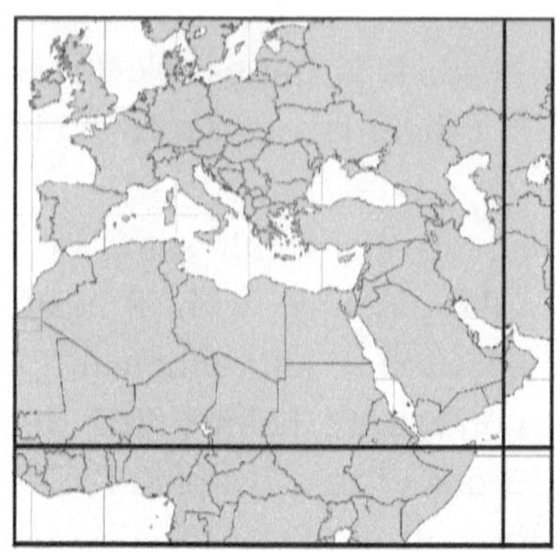

34 ARABIAN SEA

Offshore

The motion of the dhow has become like a second heartbeat to PJ. His arms and face are coated in sweat. The tiny storage compartment is hot, the air thick and gloomy.

When they threw him in here, he remembers seeing, before unconsciousness took him, a crack of light around the door and a single knothole through which a feeble eye-dot of light penetrated. Now even those tiny promises are gone. Therefore, he reasons, it must be night.

As for their position he has no idea, nor how much time has elapsed. Only that there are deep pains all over his head and body where they beat him, coupled with a thirst that threatens to steal his senses.

The questioning lasted for a long time, but like all DRFS field agents he was prepared. He disclosed a false, but watertight, checkable identity, then embarked on a series of stories that had, months earlier, taken two DRFS analysts weeks to devise, and another week for PJ to commit to memory. Meaningless facts.

Difficult to check statistics. He repeated himself. Made them think he was indispensable.

Yet they wore him down until he could no longer remember, and they no longer believed him. That's the danger now. They don't believe what he says.

PJ sits up, shakes his head to try to clear it. Apart from the groan of ropes and timbers, and the slap of water on the hull, the dhow is silent. The crew will be asleep, with one, maybe two men on watch. His wrists and ankles are free of ropes or cuffs. If ever he will have a chance, it is now.

The temptation to return to sleep is strong, but instead he crouches. The room is barely large enough to kneel. He starts to feel around on the floor. Nothing. Bare. He still has all his clothes, even the money hidden in his shirt.

The knife, the handgun and the Sid have all been taken, of course. There is no way of knowing east from west, nor even the bow of the boat from the stern. This fact, for a man accustomed to leading patrols in unknown terrain, is disconcerting.

Half-sliding, half-crawling on his knees, he explores each wall in turn, trying to identify which one has the door, running his fingers along the timbers, looking for the telltale crack. He finds it on the third wall, feeling both vertical and horizontal jambs. Once he has done so he feels for an internal lock. Nothing. He swears under his breath and moves his hands along to the other side.

No lock, just heavy metal cylinders, cold to the touch. Hinges, each with an inner bolt. For the first time he feels a measure of optimism. Yet he has no tool to force the bolt through.

Again he goes back to the other walls, feeling all over with his hands, concentrating all his senses on the flat pads of his fingers. Perhaps ten minutes of close observation passes before he finds what he is looking for: a splintered end in the timbers. Using his nails he begins to work at it, tearing, ignoring the pain.

Finally he manages to lever up a splinter of wood twice as long as his finger and snap it off at the base. The effort has made the sweat flow even more, and he wonders how much longer his body will be able to produce moisture without any water.

Turning back to the hinges, again feeling his way in the pitch darkness, he starts with the lower hinge, forcing the splinter of wood against the stubborn bolt.

He compresses his teeth hard together with the effort, bringing the strength of wrists, forearms, shoulders and biceps into forcing the bolt through. He feels it start to move. Once the flattened upper end of the bolt is shy of the cylinder he is able to use thumb and forefinger to lift while the other hand pushes.

Slowly it rises, until with a sigh of release from the surrounding timbers the hinge pops. He rests for a moment, waits for a full minute in case someone on the other side has heard, then starts to work on the other hinge. This one is harder, as it holds the weight of the door. Five minutes have passed and he has skinned his knuckles twice before the bolt comes out.

He starts to push the door through, moving it just far enough out to admit his body. Heedless of the splintery ends of the timbers, PJ worms through until his head is outside. The air is fresher here. He drinks it in greedily as he folds his body through the small gap, exits, then pushes the door back so it again sits flush.

PJ goes cold, the sweat on his skin chilled as if by an ice bath. Attached to the door is a string that extends down the corridor. A crude alarm, almost certainly attached to a tin of stones or similar.

For a second or two he cannot react, just waits. There are two choices. One is to get back inside and pull the door closed and try to reinsert the hinges before whoever is listening arrives. Yet seconds pass and he does nothing, just crouches, waiting.

There is a possibility that the string has not moved the alarm object far enough to wake the listener, and this seems more and more likely. He counts to thirty in his mind, and still nobody has come.

The extreme muscle tension softens, and he looks around the narrow passageway, looking into a small cabin, lit by a pale

12-volt fluoro tube. A cheap plastic work light. There is a man sprawled on a bunk, breathing noisily.

A handgun sits on a wooden shelf on the other side, beside a couple of books and loose-leaf pages. Cartridges lie scattered beside it, as if the owner has emptied a pocketful of ammo there. For just a moment PJ considers getting the gun, but he can see no way of reaching the shelf without walking on, or at least kneeling on the bed. That is not possible without waking the sleeping man, and then he would have to be shot, alerting the rest of the ship.

Deciding that stealth is the better plan, PJ waits and watches, then moves on down the passageway. Even out here he can't stand to full height, but has to walk bent over.

At the bottom of the companionway that leads to the main cabin is an open blister pack of plastic water bottles. A few empties have been thrown beside it.

PJ sinks down, takes one bottle out, opens it and pours it down his throat. The water, coupled with the breeze drifting in down the companionway, refreshes him to a level he wouldn't have believed possible a few minutes earlier. He starts to climb the steps, then pauses halfway up to listen.

Just a suggestion of a sound down below. Feet touching deck, perhaps. He cannot be sure, but speed is important now. Gingerly, crouching, he moves up the rest of the way. Five steps, one at a time. Peers over the top and into the gloom of the main cabin, lit by LED strip lights.

There is a man standing beside the wheel, fixed in place by a loop of hempen rope. He leans one hand against the dash, looking through the windows at the sea. His back is to PJ.

PJ stalks forward, halfway there, already deciding on his approach. Taking him by the throat will be the most silent. Before he can act he hears a commanding shout from the top of the ladder. Turns to look into the muzzle of an AK47 trained on his chest. It is not the man he left sleeping just a moment before, but another.

The helmsman turns also, fumbling for his own weapon. Finding it and driving a round into the chamber, cocking it with a loud metallic click.

PJ freezes, waiting for them to shoot, but instead the man he was about to kill runs forward and drives the butt of his rifle hard into the side of PJ's head, pushing him to the floor. He feels as if his skull has cracked through.

Another man looks down on him, squats, takes out a handgun and screws the barrel hard into PJ's temple, face twisted angrily. PJ expects him to fire, flinches, fades away in that moment of recognising that death is at hand.

Then another voice, in Arabic.

PJ's knowledge of that language is perfunctory, but he recognises the words for 'tomorrow', *gha-dan*, and 'kill', *quatl*. The man holsters the gun, and PJ understands that they will kill him tomorrow.

35 IRAQ

Al-Hajjuf

Lowered from the Lynx on a pair of cables, 'Dirty Harry' is an explosive disrupter unit made by Ideal Systems in North Carolina. About the size of a hospital trolley and equipped with a pair of caterpillar tracks, it is electrically powered via deep cycle batteries and remote controlled.

More modern units use a laser to take out IED and ICD initiators. Dirty Harry fires a .357 Magnum cartridge. Jay swears by it.

Once the unit is freestanding and has undergone a series of tests, Jay sets up behind a polycarbonate screen near the ruined bunker, opening and booting a laptop computer. 'You shouldn't be here, you know,' he says. 'Violation of Render Safe Procedures and all that. Better off going back down with the others.'

'I want to watch, if that's OK.'

'You're the boss. If you want to.'

The process of manoeuvring Dirty Harry into position takes a good ten minutes. The disrupter unit is not built for speed, but makes light work of the broken and steep terrain. Suddenly, Jay goes from lighthearted and distracted to tense and exacting.

The screen view changes to a camera shot of the IED, with a set of crosshairs. 'That's the aiming point,' he says. 'I sight this in every month. No more than a millimetre out at ten paces.'

There is a sudden smell, and Marika realises that Jay has begun to sweat. Not just a little, but copiously. The undersuit is made of one-way breathable fabric, and Jay must be perspiring right through it. He no longer talks, just moves the image of the crosshairs on the screen with the laptop's arrow buttons.

'C4's the best ordnance to work with,' he says. 'You can drop it, shoot it, burn it — just about anything and it won't explode. It needs a combination of heat and shockwave to fire. Once I take out the initiator, it's safe as plasticine.'

Marika nods, she has trained with PE4, the British version, and has even heard of infantrymen burning small amounts to heat food.

More silence. Infinitesimal adjustments. 'OK. I'm ready to fire.'

'Go ahead.'

The sound of the .357 Magnum discharge is muffled, almost lost in the background noise of choppers and personnel movements down in the valley. Marika, braced for a secondary explosion, does not move, just watches the screen with Jay, as smoke disperses. 'How did it go?'

'Yep. Got it. I'm going to shoot those IR beams right off, if you can wait another minute. You never know.'

'Whatever you think.'

This process, however, is rapid, taking out first one, then the other unit, leaving them splintered and broken. Jay grins up at her. 'I hereby declare one IED now fully fucking neutralised.'

Dirty Harry safely back in the Lynx, one of the other choppers, floodlights blazing, carries the IED in a sling, two or three kilometres away, on the extreme edge of the valley. There it is doused with half a tonne of avgas before being ignited with a tracer round.

Flames leaping high in the distance, Marika follows Jay into the bunker, sweeping ahead of them with the HHA unit, through the entrance and into the space beyond, the flashlight beam finding not bare earth walls but polished stainless steel and glass. This is a sophisticated bunker, purpose-built at substantial cost, buried underground for security and to keep the prying eyes of the world away. A feeling of nausea comes on as she does a complete circuit of the entrance area, making sure Jay is satisfied there are no more mines before calling David and Kisira through.

Marika says nothing, just walks the space between the racks. Empty shelves, storage cupboards. Glass-fronted, sealed partitions with arm holes so a technician can manipulate items inside without coming into contact with them. Banks of refrigerators with perished rubber seals. UV sterilisation units. More storage.

An office. Desk arranged with in-trays, even a telephone. The place was sealed so tight that there is scarcely a layer of dust. A framed print on the wall depicts Saddam Hussein looking imperious in full army uniform, and his full title down below, in Arabic and English script: Field Marshal Saddam Hussein Abd al-Majid al-Tikriti.

On a side wall, a series of photographs have been clipped up like X-rays in a doctor's surgery. They show a dying man. The time stamps on the shots show a period of several days.

Marika walks back out into the main bunker. A connecting door leads deeper inside, and from here there are no wall or floor linings, just concrete over cavities hacked out of the earth.

A compact room, with tubes and electrical conduit running to both walls and ceilings, a pressure sealed door at the front and a perspex viewing screen. Marika feels a chill. She has seen photographs of smaller versions of this same unit uncovered by UNMOVIC at other sites. An inhalation chamber. She shines the flashlight beam through the perspex. The interior is bare, stainless steel.

Moving on, she heads down another adjoining corridor, opening into a cavern-like space. The bars are what she notices first. Half-inch textured reo bar running vertically, with cross members of the same material welded at top, bottom and middle. Marika stops cold. Needs to get out into the air and away from this claustrophobic hell hole.

Something catches her eye as she sweeps the flashlight around. She stops, focuses and looks. In the beam of her light is a skull, backbone still attached, curved as if curling into a ball and screaming a final scream.

Those, Marika soon realises, are not the only human remains there. Her eyes pick out the rounded dome of another skull, and then another. The spines and rib cages are intact.

These people were still alive when they sealed up this bunker. Whoever ran this place knew they were here and left them to starve to death.

A vein begins to pound in her forehead and a shiver starts in her abdomen, working its way up to the base of her skull. This is how it feels to be part of the food web, just another creature dying and decomposing without meaning. No more important than a mayfly, living for just a single day, its only purpose to reproduce, to pass on the genes.

Standing still, one hand curled around a rusted bar, she closes her eyes. The summit of Mount Kenya. Terracotta roofs and green grass. Cicadas. Watermelon in the park. The cliffs at North Bondi ... migrating whales in a dappled afternoon sea. Love.

Our ... lives ... are ... important.

Another minute passes before Marika's eyes open and her feet start to move. The flashlight beam dances ahead like a spectre. This is, it seems to Marika, the single most evil place on the face of the earth. Dachau, Auschwitz, the killing fields of Cambodia, and now al-Hajjuf. The earth itself is contaminated by it.

Only with ruthless self-control can she prevent herself from running, down through the corridor, past the stainless steel racks and shelves. Finally the bunker entrance looms ahead and she blunders outside, flames from the burning IED still leaping high across the valley. Two of the three choppers are on the ground now. The third remains in the air, sweeping its lights around the valley perimeter.

David is on guard duty at the entrance. 'What do you think?' he asks.

Marika is unable to answer, breathing hard, filling her lungs with air that reeks of burning explosive and death.

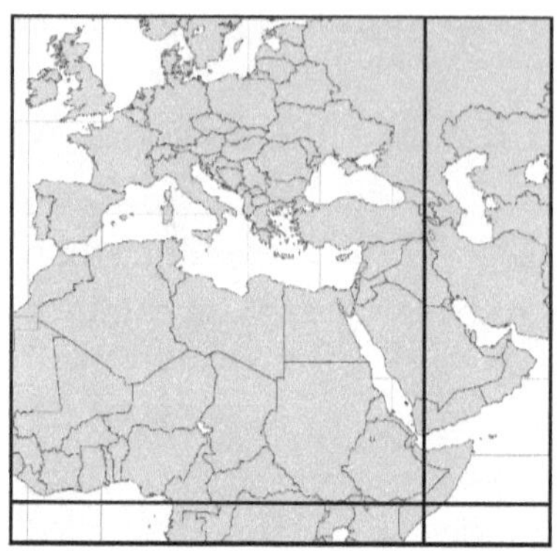

36 SOMALIA

Chakula Refugee Camp

As fast as engineers can locate new water-supply bores and pipe trough and tap systems for the inhabitants, the Laba Quarter grows and spreads outwards into the base of the Muraayad Hills.

Newcomers build traditional water-catching surfaces called berkaad, of smooth local stone. But during the rains water runs off across the ground, over human faeces and litter, carrying a cocktail of parasites and pathogens, one of which is an inoffensive-looking bacterium called *Vibrio cholerae*.

When the people of the camp drink contaminated water, spores settle deep in the small intestine, feeding there, the colony growing, releasing a powerful toxin that triggers an abnormal release of water. The result is a chronic form of diarrhoea.

The first symptoms, apart from the watery discharges themselves, are abdominal cramps, fatigue and insatiable thirst. More and more water is consumed, worsening the infection. Eyes turn glassy or sink deep into the skull, sufferers can no longer cry as tear ducts dry up. They release only a small amount of urine, or none at all.

Body organs cease to function. The kidney and bladder shut down first. The sufferer lies down for the last time, and death comes to many.

This is cholera. The blue death. Scourge of the camps.

An untreated person may produce ten or more litres of diarrhoea a day. Without oral rehydration therapy many die in torment, in a bed of foul-smelling secretions.

To combat the disease, drinking-water supplies are chlorinated heavily, but there are many water supplies and they cannot always be reached regularly enough by a force of volunteer and paid workers overwhelmed with food distribution, latrine-digging and rubbish disposal.

The dead are carried by truck to the camp cemetery where the gravediggers never stop, and the rhythm of the shovel blade is a grim reminder of what awaits so many of the world's poorest people.

The screen of the cell phone brightens in Saif al-Din's hand as he switches it on. A risk, but a necessary one. It is crucial to know how close the kufr are to them.

The machine vibrates. A message comes through. Terse and direct. Saif reads it and frowns, annoyed — their source, it seems, has been closed down. This information makes him more nervous than before. He switches off the phone then turns to the driver. 'Pull over, Isaq.'

Now that they have the cargo it is prudent to split up the more senior members of the team. Istikaan is travelling in a separate truck and Saif misses his company, saddled instead with this much slower-witted specimen.

Isaq does, however, have the ability to follow orders. He brakes the truck and pulls over to the verge. Saif watches in the rear-view mirror as the others follow suit, throwing up a screen of dust as they stop in a line. Soon it will be light, and the kufr might be looking for them by air and land.

Yet, if the kufr know the nature of the cargo, will they risk a drone or missile attack? Fear, Saif knows, is the most useful attribute of the weapons they are so close to being in a position to deploy.

Saif exits the truck's cab, boots thumping onto the bare road verge. All along the line, doors are opening. Drivers and passengers drop to the ground. The Iraqis and Syrians smoke and consume soft drink from cans. Some even listen to music on earphones. Controlling the urge to rip the wires from their ears, Saif lets them come to him, forming a rough circle. Some of the Ba'athists have remained in the trucks because so many armed men in one place would stand out, even in Iraq.

'The kufr are looking for us,' Saif tells them. 'They know the nature of our mission. It is time to split up and prepare the subterfuges. We have practised this. Go to work. Now.'

Men hurry off to each truck and begin the process of transformation. One has its sides replaced with red Coca-Cola livery. One has adhesive signs placed on either side of the cab, telling the world that it belongs to TA'AZ Construction Company, one of the biggest such firms in the country.

Instead of looking like a cohesive unit, they will soon seem different — like any roadside resting place for truck drivers. Preparations take almost an hour, and Saif becomes impatient. One or two vehicles pass by, staring at this unusual agglomeration of trucks and activity.

When they are all ready, diesel engines rumbling, Saif calls the drivers together one final time to issue directions. They are just twenty kilometres east of a major crossroad. Some of the trucks will travel east, all the way to Baghdad, before heading south. Others will go back, to the south, then east to Karbala. Others will use minor desert tracks to reach al-Qurnah, at which point they will follow the mighty Shatt al-Arab River, that behemoth birthed by the spread thighs of the Tigris and Euphrates. All will take pains to stay apart from the others.

From a cardboard carton Saif hands each driver a small GPS navigation device. 'These units have been programmed,' he tells them, 'delivering a different route to At Tannamuh, a city near the mouth of the Shatt al-Arab. Be there by maghrib — sunset. No earlier. No later. Do not attract attention. Obey all road rules.

'Turn off all cell phones or the kufr might track you. Do not turn them back on until five minutes before the appointed time. This is very important. And finally, each truck is, as you know, wired for destruction with sufficient explosives to destroy the vehicle and broadcast your cargo over a large area. Your martyrdom will not be in vain.'

He looks to the sky. 'Go with God, my brothers, and let us triumph for His glory.'

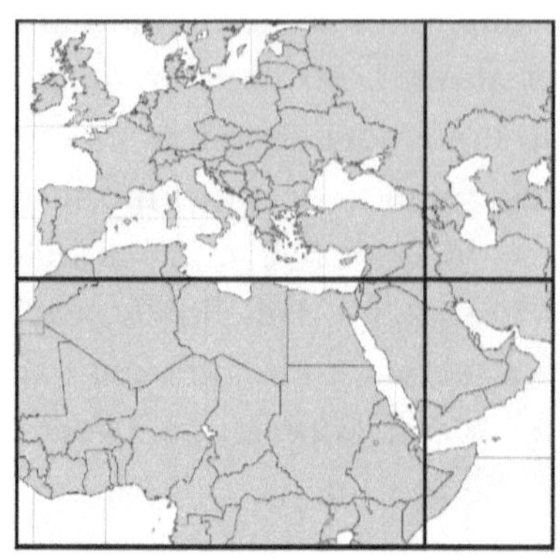

37 IRAQ

Al-Hajjuf

Accommodation on-site is a British military twelve-by-twelve-foot tent, with canvas lace-together doorways and net-covered soft vinyl windows. Each tent is occupied by four personnel, three in Marika's case, sharing with the two female members of the team, Sara and Kisira.

Female company is good for Marika. A refuge from the machismo of the males; their arm wrestles and endless stories of conquests, both martial and sexual. Time to talk about things the men would roll their eyes at, and Marika would rarely give a thought to — the hot male celebrities of the moment; relationships. Sara is ebullient and happy, Kisira quiet, but the previous evening they had lain in their respective stretchers, talking and laughing. Marika felt the dark places, so recently explored, veer far away, until it didn't seem to matter at all that they were so close to this place of death.

Marika's first stop after changing into fresh clothes and breakfasting is an open pit, where twenty labourers scrape and move the earth with shovels. Heavy equipment will take days to organise. These are locals, happy to earn good wages for the intensive labour.

Up close, the pit is similar to the one they found in Syria. Marika takes a series of photographs with the Sid and sends them through to London. Again, the remains are charred, more thoroughly here than at al-Guin.

The labourers were told to stop when they hit bone, so the work now focuses on expanding the pit outwards. At this stage there is no end to the carnage in sight. Marika has her arms crossed over her chest, a look of sadness on her face. There are hundreds, maybe thousands of bodies here. Why?

They located the mass graves with the same amine detector units as were used in al-Guin. Four more potential sites are yet to be excavated. Each could be as extensive as this one. This is a crime on a terrible scale.

Unable to watch any longer, Marika leaves the site, moving towards the bunker. Al-Hajjuf is alive with activity: equipment and personnel arriving constantly. A Chinook disgorges its payload onto the valley floor. The Fuchs CBRN reconnaissance vehicle rolling out from the giant chopper's ramp has a strange appearance, with a wedge-shaped nose and six heavy wheels.

The bunker entrance is heavily guarded, with sandbagged emplacements on either side. Marika signs in with a Royal Marine sergeant, one of a company flown in to guard the site. A strong chemical smell wafts out from inside. Overnight it was pumped full of paraformaldehyde, and all surfaces sprayed with chlorine bleach to kill any residual biological material in the centre. There is no further need for the CBRN protective equipment.

Inside, Marika moves past the laboratory areas to the office, now the domain of a SIBCRA team, flown out overnight from their base at the UK Defence CBRN Centre in Wiltshire. The SIBCRA team are equipped to sample and identify biological, chemical and radiological agents. Three men are at work in here. One is cataloguing personal effects, dropping them in ziplock bags with Dymoed labels: photographs, a rock-hard pack of chewing gum; even paper clips, a stapler, erasers.

The others are on their knees beside the filing cabinet. Marika walks up beside them. One man passes her a sheet of paper. 'Have a look at this … it's scary shit.'

Letters and numbers denote what must be strains of pathogen, hundreds of them, recorded in order … C35, C36, C37, FH201, GJ56. Each has anything from a few lines to pages of notes in Arabic. Passing the sheet of paper back, Marika feels the gorge rise in the back of her throat.

Even outside, heading back towards the tents, she cannot shake the feeling of physical illness. The nausea makes her feel more vulnerable than usual, so that when the Sid vibrates in her pocket she braces herself for more bad news.

Lifting it up to read, the text in deep red indicates that the status of her team has changed to the highest state of readiness.

Efforts underway to locate shipment. Trucks stolen from Syria, details to follow. DEPLOYMENT IMMINENT.

Marika scrolls through to Ronnie's contact icon, presses it, waits until he answers. 'Have everyone on five-minute readiness.' Then she hangs up before he has a chance to say anything. The sooner this is over and they are out of each other's hair the better.

Again the message tone sounds. The text that comes up is from SYSOPS, a generic account used by duty controllers. She reads the words, all caps, and at that moment she realises the extent to which the DRFS comms and information system has been compromised.

She is too angry and confused to call Mossel. Just forwards the message back to him with the highest priority flag. She looks at it one final time as the message box shrinks and leaps out into cyberspace. The message is amateurish, really, the equivalent of a spiteful fifth-grade classroom note, but in some ways that worries her more — the unpredictable nature of these people. The willingness to act from pure bravado.

IMMORAL BITCH, PROSTITUTE OF AMERICA. SOON YOU WILL DIE ALONG WITH EVERYTHING AND EVERYONE YOU LOVE.

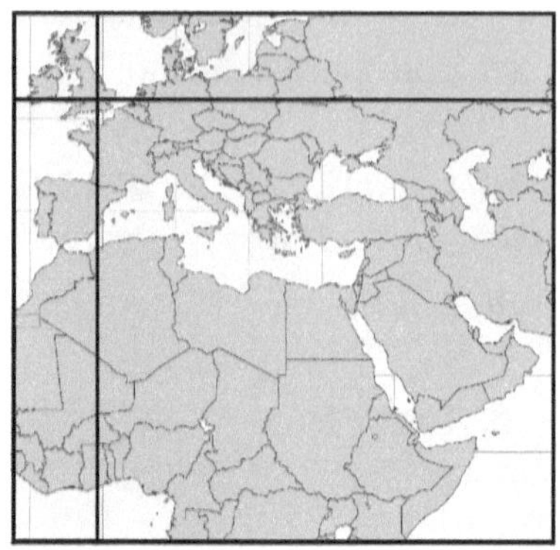

38 UNITED KINGDOM

London

The Omaçã café on Black Prince Road, occupying a converted three-century-old stone cotton store, serves the best felafel and the second-best vegan pasta Julian has ever tasted. Sometimes, for a special treat, he eats the noon meal there instead of in the crowded lunch room at Vauxhall Cross. Limited to an hour, he phones his order ahead, walking the ten minutes past the Spring Gardens and the Railway Arch, just as they heap his spinach tagliatelle or basil and pine nut risotto onto the distinctive, kiln-fired plates. Sometimes Leisel meets him, her favourite red jacket on the back of her chair, drinking her smoothie through a straw and eating carob drops while she waits for him to arrive.

Today, however, he needs to get out of the office to think, to clear his head. The meal is tasteless, the waitresses mere wraiths, moving in and out of the heavy fog that appears to surround him.

One hour later, hurrying back to work, running a few minutes late, his state of mind isn't any better than when he left. No sooner has he slipped back into his chair behind the twin twenty-eight-inch screens than the Watcher appears at the door. Will Grace, with his long nose and perpetual scowl. His hair appears to have left greasy marks on the shoulders of his shirt.

Julian looks up. Even from here he can smell the disgusting reek of sausage roll and tomato sauce on the man's breath. He keeps the vile objects in the freezer in the lunch room, piles of them. Zaps them in the microwave and devours them wrapped in paper towels to stop them falling apart. Julian shudders at the thought.

'Weiss.' The Watcher takes on many roles, depending on the mood of his boss. When Tom Mossel is trying to wheedle the best out of an operative, his assistant acts in the same way. If an agent has come back from a successful mission, the Watcher might go as far as bringing him or her small gifts, leaving them on a desk wrapped in ribbons and gold paper.

Now, however, his voice is commanding and harsh. This is not a good sign. 'What is it?'

'Mr Mossel wants to see you.'

'Can you tell me what for?'

'He'll tell you.' A pause. 'Come on, he means now.' The words are accompanied with an emphatic wave of one hand.

Julian's palms moisten. He has never been summoned like this before. Generally if Tom Mossel wants to talk to him he comes down himself, or just calls through on an internal line. He considers running — making an excuse to get away from the Watcher and his greasy breath. The toilet — anything. Then leave this place forever, down the elevators and out of the building.

They would track him, of course. There is no point. Instead he stands and follows, hurrying down the corridor and up the stairs.

The Watcher knocks on the director's office door, opens it. 'Mr Mossel. Julian Weiss is here.'

Julian walks in, standing in front of the desk. 'You wanted to see me, sir?'

'Yes.'

Mossel swings in his chair, gripping a pen in the fingers of both hands, holding it up in front of his chest. 'This is worse than we thought. Someone is inside our database. Whoever it is appears to have full access. How is this possible?'

Julian doesn't trust himself to speak, just shakes his head.

'The someone we are talking about just happens to be one of the most active and brutal terrorist groups on the planet. The lives of our people are at risk right now because of it.'

Julian feels like he is going to faint, waiting for the accusation. He coughs into his sleeve. 'Yes, sir.'

'This is your responsibility.'

'Yes sir, I will ...'

Mossel's eyes bore into Julian's. 'What will it take to withdraw every security protocol we have and reissue them all?'

Too early to feel anything approaching relief, but the ground is firming beneath Julian's feet. 'A lot of work, sir, but I could do it in eight or ten hours.'

'Make it five, if you can.'

'Yes, sir.' Julian feels like a man who has slid through the hangman's noose at the last moment. *Mossel doesn't know.* Even better, the horrible men with their hoodies and dark frowns will no longer have access to the database. He has no choice but to follow orders. They will understand that, surely.

'Well, come on then, get to it.'

'Yes, sir. I'll brief the others and we'll get cracking straight away.'

Later, in the Blair Room, Tom Mossel runs his eyes over the SITPOL screens, the bank of consoles operated by experts.

He has some reason for optimism. He is still smarting at the extent of the security breach, but it has happened before, albeit to a lesser extent. A few years earlier a hacker group called Anonymous went close to accessing the system. On that occasion Julian Weiss and his technicians had contained the problem. Surely they can do so again.

Things on the ground are also a little better. They now, at least, have full Iraqi co-operation. Nato partners have issued their own CBRN alerts and activated sophisticated detection systems.

Ultra High Temperature Missile systems are being deployed across the Middle East. These UHTMs are designed to destroy biological stocks, producing temperatures sufficient to melt plate steel, over a large area, killing any living thing within that radius.

SITPOL shows, at the moment, a high-definition map of Western Iraq. The map is constantly updated from reconnaissance and satellite photography as well as civilian and military cartography. Radar, infrared and spy satellites that snoop for General Packet Radio Service (GPRS) phone signals all contribute to the system.

The screen image zooms in on North-Western Iraq, settles for a moment on the pencil-lead grey of Lake Tharthar, then crosses over the ribbon-like Euphrates, all the land cinnamon-coloured — desert sucked of moisture.

Red blotches indicate vehicle movements that might be regarded as suspicious, including those of trucks over a couple of tonnes. Meanwhile, Iraqi police are setting up roadblocks and will search all heavy vehicles. When the all-clear is given the marker will change to a dull green. On the other hand, further intelligence on a particular vehicle or group of vehicles will change the marker to orange, singling them out for further investigation, aerial surveillance or ground-force apprehension.

Ever since the first trials, Mossel has been in awe of how well it all works. The high-range resolution images are crisp and clear; and using ISAR, Inverse Synthetic Aperture Radar, they can tell a motorbike from a scooter driving down al-Rashid Street, Baghdad. Information comes from other sources, too, everything from pattern recognition software to physical observation.

Mossel takes a seat and waits, arms crossed. Identifying the Almohad trucks should only be a matter of time. He accepts a mug of coffee and a Portuguese tart from Will Grace, and tries not to let the information filtering back from al-Hajjuf cloud his thinking.

* * *

Saif al-Din switches off the verbal instruction option, then attaches the GPS to the windscreen via suction cup, adjusting the angle so that he can direct the driver. For the moment, however, traffic is thick in the approaches to the city of Ramadi. More trucks. Military. Motorbikes. Overcrowded buses with men and children sitting on the window sills and roof racks.

When traffic comes to a standstill the hawkers move from window to window, selling newspapers, tiny cups of coffee and shwarma — rolled flatbread filled with cardamom-spiced meat, labneh and tabouli. At first Saif had thought urban areas more worrying than the open road, but now he can see the anonymity of it — the truck is just one more among many.

Finally, the traffic begins to move again, and the driver changes into third gear on the approach to the bridge, recently rebuilt after a courageous attack by mujahedin in a truck filled with ammonium nitrate explosives destroyed it utterly.

Baghdad lies over one hundred kilometres ahead, and only then will they turn south. Their chances are perhaps better than some of the others. Not only will the traffic be heavier, but this truck now wears the livery of the Iraqi defence forces, and they have papers authorising the delivery of three thousand infantry training manuals to the garrison in al-Basrah. The load is covered with a layer of these manuals, and Saif has a copy on the console to show a curious checkpoint guard.

The subterfuge is solid, sufficient for all but a thorough search.

Over the bridge, they move on through Ramadi. Hotels, businesses and blocks of houses. Everything dusty and brown, but Saif is at home with that. Even the heat that builds on the roof of the cab and shines in through the windscreen as they head east does not bother him, merely prompting him to open the window and slip on a pair of Tag Heuer sunglasses.

Then, as they pass through an area of countless relocatable buildings and car parks, the traffic again slows to a crawl. Such delays are not unusual in Iraq, and might occur for any number of reasons, from a major road accident to a security operation.

Deep anxiety tells Saif that it is the latter. This sixth sense of his — the wild-animal alertness for danger — has not always been right, but he has never failed to obey the premonitions when they come. They have saved his life, many times. 'If this is a roadblock,' he says to the driver, 'just shut your mouth and let me talk, or your stupidity will give us away.'

Over the next thirty minutes, it becomes apparent that this is indeed a roadblock. Saif can see the white police vans with their flashing lights, and the uniformed officers, yet still he does not let nervous worry turn to panic. Ever since climbing from the Indian Ocean and onto the beach off the Khateer Island all that time ago, he has felt the hand of destiny on his shoulder. God has ordained great things for him, and a few policemen at a roadblock will not stop him.

As they near he sees that the security forces are waving heavy vehicles over to one side. The driver babbles, 'We are discovered. This is the end for us.' His hand moves to the door handle.

'Get hold of yourself,' Saif commands. 'Trust in God.'

The driver lets go of the door handle. 'Yes, Sayyid.'

'If we are discovered we will detonate the charges, destroying the vehicle, and send every one of these dogs of America to hell. Do you understand?'

'Yes, Sayyid.'

The queue moves on, and a uniformed police sergeant uses a baton to wave them over into a dusty layby along with perhaps twenty other trucks. Saif moves his hand to the glovebox and removes a wad of US dollars, still sought-after currency in this country.

He is pleased when just a lone police officer appears at the window, a man with a weak, thin face and round eyeglasses.

'Peace be upon you,' the man says. 'We are investigating suspected terrorist activity. Please step from the vehicle and open all doors.'

Saif knows that he can make this offer only once, and better now while he is still in the vehicle, and not in open view where his dark skin may attract attention. 'My friend,' he says softly, 'we are in a hurry today.' He opens his palm to show the wad of notes. 'There's enough money here for a co-operative man to buy a second-hand car.'

The policeman scarcely bats an eyelid. 'I am a co-operative man.'

'That's good to hear.'

The money changes hands with practised ease, from Saif to driver to policeman, who deposits the cash down the front of his trousers.

'You,' the policeman says to the driver, 'step out while I make a show of inspecting the vehicle.' Then to Saif, 'You stay in the cab or they will see that you are black. Your colour might make them suspicious.'

The process takes just a few minutes before the driver climbs back into his seat, then shifts the truck into gear. The policeman waves them on.

Saif hisses air through his teeth with excitement and relief. 'There, did I not tell you it would be easy?'

'Thanks be to God.'

'Yes, thanks be to God ... and the greed of men.'

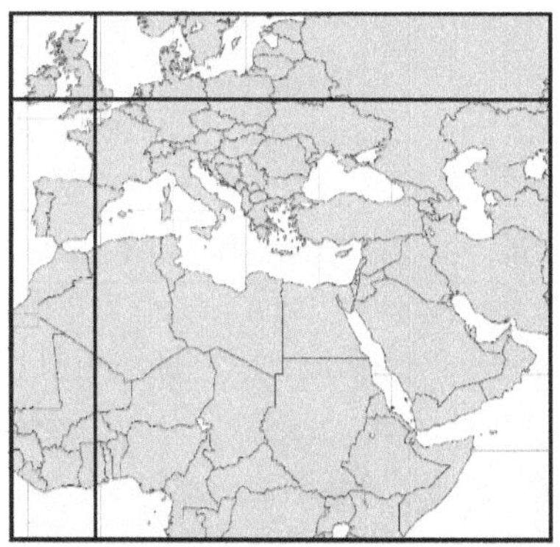

39 UNITED KINGDOM

London

'With the help of the CIA we have identified a convoy of trucks heading south on the Karbala Road near Ar Razzazah.' Tom Mossel addresses the room, as well as the National Security Council via a live feed. 'The Yanks have a Predator RPA en route from Incirlik Air Base, Turkey, and will be on-site in three minutes. The convoy is twenty minutes from the nearest town and if we can identify them in time we will take them out in a fireball so hot that it'll destroy anything in the target area, and I mean *anything*. The drone is carrying Hellfire missiles, and alternatively we have T2KU surface-to-surface missiles standing by from M270 SPLL launchers on the Arabian Peninsula. The warhead, in either case, will be a combination of high explosive and extreme high temperature incendiary material.'

The RPA, or Remotely Piloted Aircraft, is the technological advance that has, in recent years, tipped the balance back towards Coalition intelligence services and was a major factor in the unravelling of al-Qa'ida. Mossel still finds its use breathtaking; a visible and audible terror, a weapon that looks very much like the forerunner of the intelligent machines of science fiction. Drones provide a force projection capability not dreamed of twenty years earlier, when the aircraft carrier was still the spearhead of military power.

RPAs, shaped like low, streamlined fighters, designed without regard for aesthetics or passenger loading but on purely aeronautic principles, are used primarily by the United States, but also France and Israel. The terror of Gaza, they have earned the name *Zenana*, an onomatopoeic Arabic word that means simply, 'buzz'.

In this new world they fly from dozens of bases around the world, from the Seychelles to Saudi Arabia. From one perspective, drones represent an unspeakable evil. Passionless death at arm's length. Tom Mossel understands this. To him, the old-fashioned way — an agent on the ground eyeballing the target before he strikes — is the best way. Yet, RPAs have become an indispensable part of modern asymmetrical conflict. Their advantages in part-surveillance, part-offensive operations such as this one are hard to ignore.

The image on the screen divides into two sections, the left-hand side now a 3D feed from a camera in the drone, speeding towards the brown mass of the desert below. The ribbon of road appears, and then the convoy of trucks. There is a headlong rush, a sudden deceleration, then a swoop as the drone drops in height, falling flat towards the desert floor.

The room hushes as the image relayed from the drone shows more and more detail. Then a collective sigh as the logos on the truck sides become visible: Red Crescent, the Arab world's division of the Red Cross.

'Cancel the strike.' Mossel orders. 'This may be a subterfuge, but we can't take the chance. We've activated Team One. They'll be on-site in a few minutes.'

Viewed through the open side doors of the Lynx, the desert below is mesmerisingly uniform, with occasional dirt roads and settlements, odd groups of camels or vehicles. Then the Bahr al-Milh, the aptly named Sea of Salt, deep and blue. On the other side they are over the desert again, and there are weather reports of severe dust storms that will hamper any search.

Dust storms have increased tenfold in frequency and intensity since climate change tightened its grip on the world. Known locally as the Haboob, they blanket Baghdad eight days out of ten, the worst of them so thick that visibility drops to just a few hundred metres.

This prospect increases Marika's sense of unease. Historically, more ops have been ruined by inclement weather than enemy action.

Ahead looms a ribbon of bitumen. Marika consults the navigator on the Sid, and shouts, 'Too far north. Head south.'

The chopper swings like a pendulum. The centrifugal force pushes her back against the seat. Then, standing, gripping the back of the co-pilot's seat, Marika cranes to look through the Plexiglas. The road is a straight blue ribbon, the line of trucks ahead. The aircraft drops lower until it flies just a few metres above the power lines.

Marika starts thinking ahead. If these vehicles do indeed carry something as deadly as suspected, will they defend themselves? It seems naïve to expect them to allow a few soldiers with guns to search the trucks.

This train of thought is cut short by the helicopter swooping past the line of speeding trucks, where it begins a manoeuvre pilots call 'herding', hovering in advance of the trucks and rearing on the spot in a signal to stop.

Marika grabs the PA mike and moves to the edge of the open doorway, waiting until the lead truck moves closer. The moustached driver, arm out the window, stares up at them, casting anxious glances at his passenger.

'Pull over,' Marika orders in English, hoping at least some of them will understand. 'I repeat, pull over to the side of the road and exit the vehicles. All stand with both hands on the sides of the truck.' She can see the chrome lugnuts on the wheels spinning in a blur.

To her relief there is a burst of dust as the driver slows and brings the offside wheels out onto the verge. The other trucks follow, and the pilot takes the Lynx a stone's throw out from the trucks before settling it down to earth, raising more dust than the entire convoy put together.

Marika is first out the door, UMP in her hands, ready to aim and fire from the hip. The troops who fan out beside her hold their weapons to their shoulders, sighting as they go. The last of the trucks are rolling to a stop, doors opening. Men and some women in burqa move to the truck cabs where they lean over, both hands flat on what must be hot metal surfaces.

It is obvious to Marika that these people have faced this kind of situation before. There is a world-weary belligerence to the way they move — as if to say, 'Hurry up and get this over with.' They don't act like terrorists. In fact, she is willing to bet money that they are not. The presence of women is one obvious sign, but then, subterfuges can be easy to arrange. With Ronnie on one side and David on the other, she approaches the first vehicle in line, addressing the driver in English.

'Who are you, what are you carrying and what is your destination?'

'We are from the Damascus office of the Red Crescent, and we carry important medical supplies.' The driver's chin lifts. 'I must protest at being stopped in this manner. It's my understanding that the English and Americans no longer rule Iraq ...'

'Save the cheek, mate, I haven't got time for it. My team is going to search your trucks. The more fuss you make the longer it'll take.'

'I protest, and warn you that I will be complaining to both the government of Iraq and my superiors.'

'I understand your concerns, but this is an important security operation. If you have nothing to hide you will soon be on your way. In the meantime make sure that no one moves while the search is underway.'

With the crews covered by half a dozen men, Marika unlaces the canvas cover at the rear of the truck and climbs inside. The interior space is loaded with cartons, each stamped with various messages in Arabic, and, often, images too — syringe cases, gloves.

Ronnie looks at Marika, 'Fuck. It'll take hours to check through this lot.'

'Yeah.' Marika stands back, thinks for a moment, then shouts along the line. 'Are all these trucks loaded like this?'

'Looks like it.'

'OK then, we'll unpack some of these damn boxes. Open one of every different type, or any that look suspicious.'

'Again,' pleads the driver, 'I must implore you. We bring urgent supplies for the Khan al-Hammad hospital.'

Marika is not immune to the plea. 'You want us to hurry? Help us, don't hinder us.'

Within half an hour it seems obvious that this convoy are who they say they are. A contingent of Iraqi police show up from a nearby village and examine their papers, confirming from other sources that the fleet of trucks does indeed have a bona fide humanitarian mission.

The doctor in charge makes no attempt to hide his dislike for Marika as the last of the boxes are replaced and secured. 'I hope you are satisfied,' he sneers. 'Lives may be lost by your actions today.'

Marika meets his eyes without flinching, 'I am sorry to have delayed you, but believe me, a large number of lives might be saved if I do my job today.'

Finally the trucks begin to move off down the road, and as the last one passes by, Marika's forehead creases in thought. The earlier vehicles in the line all have a coating of black dust in streaks above the red, where they must have passed through some alluvial plain on the long journey from Damascus. This one does not.

In addition, the others are all International or Volvo eighteen-wheelers. This is a smaller vehicle, manufactured by Hino. Insignificant in itself, but enough to make Marika look twice. She ambles back towards the squad of 2CG, standing together, weapons pointing to the ground.

'Who searched the last vehicle in line?' Marika asks.

Ronnie half-raises a hand. 'I had a quick look at it. They were a bona fide humanitarian convoy — it would have been embarrassing to hold them up any longer. I'd just been through the one before it pretty thoroughly.' He pauses. Guarded. 'Is there a problem?'

'Maybe. Maybe not.'

Marika's pace quickens as she walks back towards the Iraqi cop Humvee. The trucks are gone. She isn't sure why she is bothering to pursue this. The chopper blades are spinning again, ready for lift-off, and the team is starting to assemble beside it.

'Excuse me,' Marika says, 'how many trucks were on those Red Crescent travel papers?'

The Iraqi holds up his thumb and all four fingers from one hand. His index finger from the other. 'Six.'

David and Ronnie have followed her, and they stand beside her as she lifts the Sid and calls through to London. The duty officer comes on the line.

Marika snaps out the question: 'I need to know the make of the trucks stolen from Syria.'

A pause, then, 'Hino, all five of them.'

'Squad, embark,' she shouts, then turns on Ronnie. 'You just let one of the bastards slip right through our fingers.'

His face goes a bright shade of red. 'What?'

'According to the last update those trucks stolen from Syria,' she says, 'were Hinos. All of them.'

'You can't blame me if one of them—'

'We can't afford mistakes like that, mate.'

He starts to reply, but Marika doesn't hear. She is already running for the chopper.

40 WORLD

The Arab Spring is not dead, but many of the seeds remain dormant. Leaders drive around in jet-black LandCruisers while the people wonder when they will be allowed to join the developed world and live without repression.

In Egypt no one is quite sure if they have achieved the *karama* and *hurriya* — dignity and freedom — they fought for in the revolution, as the Muslim Brotherhood, in the form of Mohamed Morsi Isa El-Ayyat, takes control. The effects are immediate. Veiled news readers appear on Egyptian TV for the first time in years. Anti-Western sentiments become more common in news reports, leading to events such as the embassy riots of 2012, protesting a small-time movie made by a Coptic Christian in California. Riots that spread around the world, including in immigrant Muslim communities, tired of being blamed and vilified, yet their reaction stereotypical of the sins they were accused of in the first place.

Groups such as Ansar Bait al-Maqdis, the Partisans of Jerusalem, launch deadly raids into Israel from bases in the remote Sinai.

In Libya there are too many weapons, too many groups. An armed gang murders the US ambassador. RPG strikes target Red Cross compounds.

While al-Qa'ida continued to suffer setback after setback, new organisations filled the void. The Islamic Jihad Union grows in strength. Based in the tribal regions of Pakistan, it was originally made up of Uzbeks, but now draws members from European countries, particularly Germany.

The dynasty of the Almohad is building. The thousand-year-old movement that once conquered all of North Africa and much of Southern Europe has stirred again, and its tentacles are long.

In Europe, in low-income ghettos, a new crusade of right-wing fundamentalist Christians targets Muslims, bringing violence and bloodshed, and the Almohad are there like a shield, retaliating, offering hope.

The art of the IED improves, making them more effective, harder to detect. From early, crude contact or hard-wired switches, clever minds have used everything from garage-door controls to cell phones to trigger their explosives. Counter-terrorism forces found that all they had to do was drive around flashpoint cities like Baghdad or Kabul with a garage-door remote controller, pressing the button, in order to blow up finished and unfinished IEDs, often along with their creators. The cell phone switch has its own problems, mainly that it operates on traceable cellular networks. In recent times the answer has been to use long-range cordless handsets, the best of which can operate at more than a kilometre from the cradle.

Implementation improves — more thoughtful placement, the use of camouflage. Experience and newer theory manuals tell them that damp soils provide a far more powerful blast than dry soils.

So too, do counter-measures attempt to keep pace. A vehicle-mounted camera, linked to a computer, studies changes in roads and terrain. Any new disturbance — a pothole or patch of fresh earth — sounds an alarm, thus alerting the crew to a potential mine or IED. Zeus, a new vehicle-mounted directed energy beam, is designed as an anti-ordnance device to be used instead of small arms or RPGs to explode IEDs still in the ground. FOPEN, foliage-penetrating radar, can spot and track activity deep under cover, including urban areas.

In the meantime, while the creatures of the planet bicker and fight, the world changes, the sea rises. The Almohad know that their time is coming, that the prosperity of the early century was an illusion, and food is short. This is the real issue. The world is running out of the capacity to feed itself.

In Chakula camp there is a grenade attack on a souk in the Laba Quarter. Three, perhaps four grenades, rolled into a busy market square on a day shining blue and beautiful, at eleven am when women and children crowd the ground around the tables and carts.

Kifimbo and his patrol are first on the scene. The wounded kick and scream and bleed. The dead lie, bodies twisted in puddles of blood and dismembered limbs, body parts plastered onto walls and in trees. Tears flow down his face and he cannot think, cannot speak, because the vortex of death is centred on his own heart.

Medics with white latex gloves, splashed bright crimson with blood, work to save the most grievously injured. Camp workers erect barriers to keep screaming family members away. Kifimbo cannot understand why people would do this to their own kind, to anyone. Or how killing can be done with the name of a god on the killer's lips.

Kifimbo has come to love these wonderful, resilient people, and now he is forced to help lay the dead out in rows, and see the tears in the eyes of aid workers who come to help, stunned and unprepared.

Shrapnel and blast wounds. Men and women blinded, staggering about in uncontrolled terror. And everyone asking why,

why, why when all they want is a better life, if not for themselves, then at least for their children.

In that bloody market square Kifimbo's heart weeps. Silently he screams for help, as the blood of people he is here to protect stains his hands and uniform.

41 IRAQ

Al-Anbar

Istikaan, conscious of the pressure-sealed stainless steel flask and associated equipment buried deep in false cargo in the back of the truck, wipes away the sweat that coats his forehead, and wills away the trembling in his knees. The search was a near thing, and the idea of attaching themselves to the rear of a Red Crescent convoy had almost backfired.

At first the idea had been to travel alone, but near Fallujah they had seen the Red Crescent trucks pulled over on the side of the road, checking tyres and resting drivers. It had seemed like an opportunity too good to miss — the secret of camouflage is always to surround like with like.

When the helicopter and armed soldiers had appeared it had been all Istikaan could do not to scream out his hatred at them, but instead he prayed that they would pass on by, and now it seems that those prayers have been answered. Not only that, but their security status has improved — they have been checked, and thus the convoy will pass through from here without being molested again.

Istikaan allows himself to share a nervous smile with the driver. With preparation, planning and foresight, the kufr can be fooled. For all their sophisticated electronics, in the end it comes down to eyes and ears. And those eyes and ears were careless. They had but glanced over the surface. The kufr are surface people. They look not at depth.

As the convoy continues down the highway, Istikaan settles back and makes himself comfortable. He has slept little in the past days. He closes his eyes, but sleep does not come.

There is a sound, increasing. At first he thinks something might be wrong with the truck, something in the engine, but then he hears the driver's anguished cry.

'The helicopter, it's coming back.'

Istikaan's eyes snap open, and he feels that sense of dread returning, along with a strong sense of denial. *It must be that they are travelling this way … a coincidence. They have already let us pass.*

But then the chopper shoots ahead, pulsing down in front of them, forcing the driver to slow, cutting them off from the group.

'Keep driving,' Istikaan shouts, 'they won't do anything. If they know what we have on board they won't risk it.'

'What will they do?'

'Attack us with a missile, but not until they get us alone and clear the area. Stay close to the other trucks, for the moment anyway.'

Istikaan stares ahead, into the south-west, seeing a smudge of brown. Billowing clouds of dust reach high into the sky. 'Ahead,' he says, 'the Haboob. God has sent us cover.' He peers through the windscreen. 'And soon there is a crossroad.'

This time the kufr helicopter swoops down even closer, the black skids almost brushing the front of the cab, so close that Istikaan can see a yellow hazard sticker with bold black type.

The driver jabs at the brakes, but Istikaan shouts, 'No, don't do that. Keep going, they cannot stop us as long as we stay close.'

'We will crash into them,' the driver moans.

'No. Drive.'

Again comes the amplified voice in English. 'Pull off the road.' The order is repeated several times, before becoming more strident. 'Pull over or we will fire upon you.'

Istikaan stares ahead. The billowing dust clouds are no more than a kilometre ahead. Less than a minute at this speed. They will make it as long as the driver holds his nerve. He makes his voice softer, because there is no point bullying the man. He leans out and touches an arm. 'Trust in God, and believe me. Keep close to those other trucks, and when we get into the dust we will lose the helicopter. Yes?'

Hesitation, then a sigh. 'Yes.'

The helicopter rears down towards them again, and looks like it will land in front of them.

'Do not swerve,' Istikaan shouts, 'it is a bluff. Just a few more seconds. Look! Here it comes.'

The helicopter is a beast of a thing, turbines making it bulge on each side, armaments hanging from the stubby side wings — rocket tubes, missiles in clusters of four. Broad-bladed rotors flex as it lifts out of the way, just as the dust comes to greet them, appearing to Istikaan as the encircling arms of God, welcoming them to safety. They enter the Haboob and the trucks in front of them disappear, replaced by the red glow of brake lights as they are forced to slow.

Istikaan starts to laugh, then gives thanks as they move deeper into the cloud. 'Let's see the godless ones track us now.'

Marika sees the towering wall of dust ahead. 'Shit, they're going to get away. We need to drop a marker on the truck.'

'I don't know if we can get close enough.'

'Yes we can! Get down there.'

The chemical marker is fired from a standard 40mm L17A1 underslung grenade launcher attached to a Heckler & Koch G36 rifle. Someone passes the weapon through the cabin to Marika, who lifts it to her shoulder, moving her hand to the extra grip and trigger below the forestock as the pilot brings the craft lower, swaying to the movement. Unable to use a handhold because of her grip on the weapon, only a superb sense of balance prevents her from toppling.

'Closer,' she shouts, 'get me right down there.'

Already the dust is moving in, wispy and confusing shrouds in many shades of red, grey and brown. Wind buffets the chopper.

Now the top of the truck is just a stone's throw away, and Marika knows how dangerous this is — power lines might loom up out of the dust in microseconds, sending them all to oblivion.

She waits, even so, for the motion to settle, then squeezes the trigger, hearing the dull pop of the discharge, watching the projectile burst in a liquid spray across the top of the cab.

'Pull away,' she shouts, and the chopper rises almost vertically with the feeling of being in a high-speed elevator, ears popping. Marika swallows to equalise the pressure. 'OK, follow it now.'

'The Iraqi police are on their tail. We're directing them up.'

'Get them to come up on the truck and force them off the road. We have to get them alone at any cost. I'll tell London to have their missiles on ten-second launch readiness.'

42 IRAQ

Babil

Saif al-Din raises one hand to the scar on his temple and rubs the area. For three hours, since leaving Baghdad, they have driven down the endless bitumen that heads south and east, cutting across the majestic loops of the Euphrates River, following the main channel when possible.

He would love to turn on the cell phone and call the others, yet knows that doing so will be traceable. He might as well raise a balloon high into the air. No. The fate of the others must lie hidden until the time comes.

They have, of course, had the radio tuned to the Voice of Iraq on 1179 AM, and nothing has been said about a security concern. People are used to roadblocks and searches here. They are immune to police, soldiers, choppers and even gunshots. Iraq has been one of the most dangerous places on earth for decades.

A sudden jab of pain spears into Saif's temple, and he feels himself jump in response, taking in air through his nostrils. The driver looks sharply at him.

'Are things well with you, Sayyid?'

'Of course,' he snaps, 'now shut up and watch the road.'

Saif digs into the small bag he keeps at his side, seeking his medicine and a bottle of water purchased with lunch an hour ago from a roadside café. He takes just half of one opium pellet — enough to dull the pain but not enough to remove his mind from the present — then chases it down with a long swig of tepid water. He sees the driver looking at him sideways.

'I told you to concentrate on driving. Do so, or I will thrash you, understand?'

'I understand.'

Istikaan sees the blue light atop the cop Humvee in the rear-view mirror, then the front wheels and the bumper. 'The police traitors are coming up to us, even in the dust.' He picks up the phone and powers it on, waiting for it to acquire a signal.

The driver's frightened eyes roll upwards so the bloodshot whites are visible.

'Didn't Saif al-Din tell us not to use that thing?'

'There is no point holding back now. They are onto us — it may be our only chance.'

Istikaan punches in a number and waits. The number connects to a box that will scramble and reroute the call throughout the Middle East, making the recipient almost impossible to trace, even for the CIA and Britain's GCHQ. Because the routing is different each time, the system works well, with only the caller being vulnerable, and then only if they are already under surveillance.

Istikaan hears a series of clicks, then a one-word answer. He utters a code phrase that Saif al-Din made him memorise. While he waits for the next stage he covers the bottom half of the phone and asks the driver. 'What is the licence plate number on the front of the police vehicle?'

'Ah, I cannot see it well.'

The Humvee, however, now begins an overtaking manoeuvre. 'I can see it,' the driver calls. 'Yes, there is a P, then four, three, eight …'

A voice comes on the end of the line. 'Why are you using the phone? It is dangerous.'

'We are discovered. An Iraqi police vehicle is trying to overtake and block us. Can they be reached? An offer made?'

'Insh'Allah I will be able to get pressure on them. All these dogs carry phones.'

Istikaan dictates the plate number then terminates the call and switches off the machine — there is no point letting their enemies track with it. As he does so the Humvee appears level with the cab and he looks into a wound-down window, the barrel of an M16, and an angry, black-moustached face.

'Pull over,' the man shouts. 'We are the police. Pull over.'

The driver wrenches the truck across but the cop is ready, steering neatly out of the way, then ahead, edging in front of the truck cab, beginning to move back in. The truck lurches across so the right-hand wheels wobble on the dirt verge.

'Do nothing,' Istikaan shouts, 'we are bigger than them. They cannot force us.'

Yet he knows that the Humvee is heavy, with a low centre of gravity, and solid. The manoeuvre has already forced them to slow, and there is now no sign of the Red Crescent convoy. Istikaan feels the first twinge of real alarm.

At that moment the Humvee swerves out, then comes back in at high speed. A desperate manoeuvre, completed with skill, and the force of the impact throws Istikaan's head forward onto the dash, nose first, breaking it as if struck with the flat of an axe.

The truck rears onto its right side, and for a moment it seems that it will roll with the momentum. Istikaan brings his head back up, holding his nose, feeling blood spring from between his fingers, and drip down onto his shirt. The driver fights the wheel, the truck skidding across the dust of the verge. Regaining control, he brings the vehicle onto a true heading, attempting to turn back towards the road, but the Humvee is there like a shepherd to prevent them.

Visibility in the dust storm is limited to twenty or thirty metres, and within a few seconds the sense of where the road is located is lost in the shifting plumes.

The tracking of the marker is not performed on the chopper, but from the Predator C drone already on station, equipped with LIDAR, transmitting a constant update to the plotters in the cockpit and SITPOL screens in the major centres.

'We've got them off the road,' the pilot shouts into the system.

Marika feels herself stiffen with excitement. 'Can we take them out yet?'

'London says no. There's a village up ahead, and they're recommending a thousand-metre clearance area around the IP. We have to allow them to get past it first.'

'That's all they get,' Marika says. 'Then we turn them into a fireball.'

Istikaan wipes the blood away with his sleeve. 'If we are martyred now,' he says, 'it will not be in vain. Our load is a fraction of the total.'

'But you are the key,' the driver says. 'They cannot do the work without you. Let me slow the truck and let you out.'

Istikaan knows it is true. No one can do what is necessary better than he. His death will mean long delays. On foot he will have a chance. 'Those dogs, the Iraqi police, are behind us.'

'They will stop chasing us. They won't want to be close when the kufr destroy us. You must run.'

Istikaan considers this for another few seconds, then acquiesces. 'I'll do as you suggest. May God guide both of us.'

A village appears through the dust, a tiny place of ancient stone buildings. Date palms tower over decaying structures. A boy leading a camel stares as the truck roars through the gap between two such structures. A sickening thud follows as it strikes a goat, heading on into a field, narrowly missing an acacia hut. A toothless old crone shouts abuse, shaking a hand at them as they pass.

Past the village, into corn fields and dry, wilted pasture.

'The police have stopped,' the driver warns. 'I will slow, but not by much. You must leave the truck.'

'Praise God, brother. You are a brave man without equal.'

The driver slams one foot on the brakes. The truck slows. 'Go now, *hurry.*'

Istikaan opens the door, steps down onto the running board and launches himself out into space. The soft sand absorbs most of the impact apart from a slight jar in the knee, and he is up in a moment, scanning for any pursuit, then heading off through the dust towards the village. He, like all of them, has a cache of money sewn into his raiment. With cash in hand, transport can be arranged.

The sound of the truck fades into the distance, but Istikaan does not wait for the sound of its destruction, just walks away as fast as he can manage.

'Target clear,' someone shouts, and while the moment is recognised in several centres, the order is given by Tom Mossel inside the SITPOL room in London. A few seconds later two Hellfire missiles streak out from the wings of the Predator, leaving a stinging trail of smoke behind them.

The chopper ascends like a whirlwind, engines screaming under full throttle and the rotors cavitating as they lose their grip in a turn that finishes with a headlong flight, leaving the impact point as fast as possible.

Marika would have liked to see the missile hit, even from a distance, but knows it will not be possible in this dust. The chopper stops its forward movement and holds station, waiting.

'Ten seconds to strike,' says a metallic voice over the speakers.

The explosion is not as loud as a standard high explosive munition might have been. Yet, seconds later a shockwave rocks the body of the Lynx.

'Did we get it?' Marika asks.

The pilot's voice. 'Yeah baby, we got it.'

There is excited chatter among the team. High fives. Necks craning to see.

Marika waits five full minutes, more than enough for the insane heat of the blast to have dissipated. 'OK,' she says, finally, 'let's get in there for a look.'

The journey takes only a minute or two, and the pilot slowly descends over a blackened area of earth, scorched of all plant life, to hover several hundred metres off the ground. Of the truck there is merely a blackened, twisted, melted iron mess that must have once been bodywork and chassis.

Marika studies the wreckage, happy to do so at a distance. They will not land, not until the area has been checked out. 'OK,' she calls, 'take us away.' She turns to David. 'One down. Four to go.' She punches him on the shoulder. 'Come on, smile. We got one.'

'Yes, that's a start.'

Marika picks up the Sid, opens communications with the SITPOL room. She updates via voice, then asks, 'Any sign of the other trucks?'

'Not yet, only that they're heading south.'

She settles back in her seat, surprised to see that Ronnie has moved back up beside her. Ever since they left the truck convoy he has been sitting away from her, glowering. She wonders if he's going to apologise.

Instead he pushes his face close to hers, lips compressed pugnaciously. His breath reeks of mints, and something stronger underlying them. Hidden but there. 'You ever talk to me like you did back there on the ground, and you and I are going to have a problem. Not just a little problem. A big one.'

Marika looks back at him, knowing that David has heard, and maybe even Kutay and Sara. 'Get out of my face, Ronnie. You're out of line.'

There is no hint of him backing off. She knows that he does not back down. Not ever. She maintains eye contact for a few more seconds then looks away, beginning to suspect that they already have a big problem.

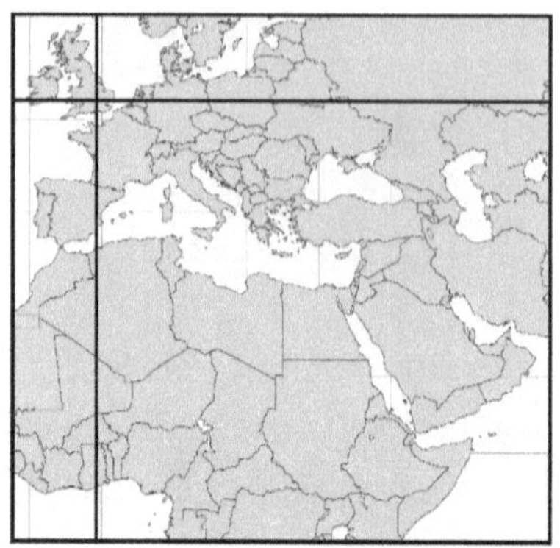

43 UNITED KINGDOM

London

On the train, on his way home, Julian stares at a text message on his phone. The phrase is very simple, all in capitals. Six words that chill him from spine to fingertips.

Ten minutes ago he was on a high. The system is clean again. He was beginning to think of the good things in his life: his girlfriend Leisel; release day for *Diablo V*; the EnviroCarers protest slated for three weeks' time at the Westcon Agriculture building; dinner with Leisel, perhaps …

Now the fear has come back. They know what he has done — that they can no longer access the database. They have reacted swiftly.

He reads the words on the screen over and over again.

Leisel is Julian's first girlfriend, and the thought of her warms his heart. He has never met a human being so alive; all red hair, blue eyes and mischief.

They met at a meeting of the Borough of Southwark EnviroCarers. She worked as a volunteer at the same animal shelter as one of the other members — came twirling in, a hurricane of energy and summer light. Bright and passionate. Loves animals. Likes to drink and dance and have fun, and save the world in between. On her upper lip she has a tiny, white scar, and just the hint of a lisp that she seems not the slightest bit conscious of.

Julian found himself staring. Once or twice she looked his way and he dropped his eyes in case she might think that he was rude. Speaking against the recently expanded South Korean whaling program, she became so passionate that tears spilled from her eyes and a lock of hair plastered itself to the side of her cheek, remaining there for the rest of the meeting.

Their first date was at a French café on Lordship Lane. Soy lattes and vegan wraps out in the sunshine. Julian had learned that she was twenty-four, a year younger than him, and loving her final year of a BA in Liberal Arts at King's College, University of London. 'What happened to your lip?' he asked.

Spread fingers nestled in the hollow of her waist, her arms making angel's wings on either side, she made a coquettish parody of being angry. 'I was born with a cleft palate, silly. Not a bad one, but it needed surgery. That's why I talk funny.'

Julian's face burned with embarrassment. 'You don't talk funny.'

'I do so. I talk like thith!'

'You're exaggerating now.'

'I am not. Now shut up about it, what are you having?'

Text messages, emails and DMs followed. Half an hour on Skype every other day.

A fortnight later, with her characteristic boldness, she asked him back to her place for dinner with a casual, 'So what are you doing tonight?'

'Nothing, really.' Julian decided that under the circumstances, immersing himself in the *Diablo*-world of Sanctuary could not be called something …

'Want to come around? I'll cook you dinner.' Head cocked to one side. 'I can cook, you know.'

'Of course, I mean, yes, do you live alone, or ...'

'With my dad, but he's gone up north for the weekend. But of course, if you don't want to ...'

'I really want to,' he said, and almost added, *more than anything.*

They were deep in conversation when the train rolled into South Bermondsey station. Julian followed her out, the view across red-brick terrace houses dominated by the New Den football stadium and factory smokestacks beyond.

Leisel nodded to friends and acquaintances as they walked, until she stopped outside one of the houses, a renovated semi-detached building. 'Well, this is home.'

Julian ran his eye over the sharp-peaked roof, patterned red and white bricks and porch complete with miniature Doric columns. Leisel opened the front door ushering him in to a full-sized entry, where he left his coat on a carved oak stand. Beyond was a kitchen and lounge. 'Looks nice.'

Her lips were set in a line of prim disapproval, 'Quite bourgeois really, three bedrooms, but we only moved here because of the stadium.'

'Really? You like football?' His face fell. One of the main reasons for a profound sense of relief at finishing high school was the end of PE lessons: tracksuit-clad instructors who promised to make a man of him; morning runs in the cold; footballs that other kids managed to dribble around witches hats but that refused to do so for him.

Leisel aimed a playful punch at his shoulder, grinning. 'Not me, of course, silly. Dad's a bloody football nut,' she said, 'way over the top, he even has United pyjamas — how embarrassing is that?'

His composure flooded back. 'Lots of people like football.'

She rolled her eyes. 'Yeah, but most of them don't feel the need to live on top of a fucking football ground just so they can walk home drunk from a game.'

Julian likes the way Leisel swears. She uses expletives like ribbons and bows, dressing up her sentences like gifts. 'You're nice and close to the city, though,' he said. 'South Bermondsey is only a stop from London Bridge.'

Leisel made a face. 'Yeah, OK, but I'd still rather walk ten fucking miles every day than live here. Now come with me, we're going out to the garden. Then you can talk to me while I cook up a storm.'

'Sounds great.'

Out the back, in an area not much bigger than a volleyball court she had created a mass of greenery, all waist-high in brick beds. There was not a weed to be seen, just seasonal vegetables. Brussel sprouts, lettuces, peas, broad beans. Julian walked from plant to plant, touching the leaves, feeling the healthy vitality of them.

'You do all this?'

'All the gardening. Dad's a builder, so he made the beds — all with old unwanted bricks from tear-down jobs that would have gone into landfill.'

'It's brilliant.'

'If everyone supplied their own vegetables, imagine how much more land would go back to the animals and trees. That's the ultimate, isn't it? Reclaiming the world for nature. We're such terrible destroyers.'

Julian felt a surge of truth at her words. 'Of course we are. Everything we touch, we just ruin.'

'Exactly. Here, hold these.' She filled his arms with rocket, peas, then a twisted turnip. 'I've already got a pumpkin in the kitchen — didn't grow that here, they run everywhere and take up too much room. Me and the other girls have got a patch at the shelter. We grow enough for everyone.'

Back in the kitchen Julian took charge of a chopping board and knife, slicing vegetables to her specifications, watching as she used rice flour and egg substitute to fashion a pie crust.

'You're vegan, too, aren't you?' she asked.

'Of course. Eight years now.'

'Me too. Since the day my Year Ten class did a tour of the abattoirs. It was disgusting ... and the way they treated those animals ...' Her eyes glowed like screens, round and huge, and her lips took on an outraged pout. 'Crowded into stalls and shot with some horribly cruel gun, and they bleed ... Just awful.'

They chatted all the way through the preparations. Julian set the table, lighting a candle and dimming the lights back.

'It's OK,' she said, 'we've got a bank of panels on the roof. The whole lighting circuit runs sustainably.' She stopped. 'But candlelight is kind of nice, isn't it?'

He grinned. 'I think so.'

The vegetable pie, when it came, was steaming hot, solid winter fare, flavoured with mushrooms grown under her house, sliced into precise little rectangles. They washed it down with thick juice so rich with flavours that Julian drank it down to the last gritty mouthful, wiping his lips with the back of his hand. 'Wow, what's in that?'

'Whatever fruit and vegies I can find when I've got the blender out. Anything I can grow or buy. Nice, isn't it?'

When the meal was over she washed the dishes. Julian dried, finishing up while she wiped down the benchtops and left the room. The last few, bigger items he stacked on the side, unsure of where they should go, then hung the tea towel on the oven handle. This done, he followed her into a lounge room, noting that funny, musty smell some lounge rooms have.

The room was dominated by an integrated entertainment system — televised world news on a massive screen.

'I know it's ostentatious,' she explained. 'Bloody Dad again, of course. Has to watch every game of football in the world. Sometimes he's up half the night, and I have to get up and tell him to turn it down five times ...'

'It's a nice telly, though.'

'Yeah, sure. Nice, but unnecessary.'

After half an hour of news, they played two hands of euchre. The house was getting so cold that he shivered.

Leisel smiled sympathetically, and reached out to touch his hand. 'I'm sorry it's cold. Dad usually has the gas heating going non-stop, but it's such a fucking waste of resources.'

'I agree.' Julian wondered where her mum was, having seen no sign of another woman in the house, but he decided not to ask, just concentrated on following suit, trumping when he could, and trying in vain to keep up with the speed of her play.

Finally, she laid her cards down on the carpet. 'Do you want to go to bed? It's nice and warm there.'

The feeling had been growing on him that something might happen, but even so, her words shocked him. No one had ever been so bold with him before. Her tone of voice was such that she might have been asking him for another game of cards.

'OK.'

She cocked her head at him. 'You don't sound too keen. Do you want to?'

'Yes, I do.' *I really, really do.*

Leisel's bedroom was lit by yellow light, with sumptuous bed covers and pillows. She took his hand, smiled, then leaned up to kiss him. His hands went to her waist, but she stepped away and undressed. Her body was white and slim, her nipples tiny and pink.

She helped lift his shirt over his head, then unbuckled his jeans, unzipping his fly and slipping both trousers and underwear down.

'It *is* cold. Quick, into bed.'

The bed was soft and smelled of soap and of her. She snuggled into him and he didn't rush, instead trying to stamp the moment on his memory so he would be able to recall it at will.

When the bed had warmed from their bodies she raised herself and started kissing him again, her lips like sweet, sliced fruit. His hand moved to cover one breast, then the other. She moaned and collapsed half on top, one leg over his, running her hand down to grip him.

Julian was afraid she might laugh at him. He knew he was not large down there, but she said nothing, touched him lovingly, kissed his neck. He wondered what would come next.

Leisel straddled him. Mind-numbing pleasure saturated his senses as she raised and lowered her body, the muscles of her abdomen moving visibly under her skin.

When it was over they collapsed back on the bed and Leisel pulled up the quilt around both of them. One hand moved to his ear, fondling the lobe between thumb and forefinger. She kissed his sweating forehead and held him tight.

The daydream ends. Back on the train, and its filthy window view of the suburb of Norwood, Julian looks down at the text message again. He groans aloud with terror as he reads it.

WE KNOW WHERE YOUR GIRLFRIEND LIVES.

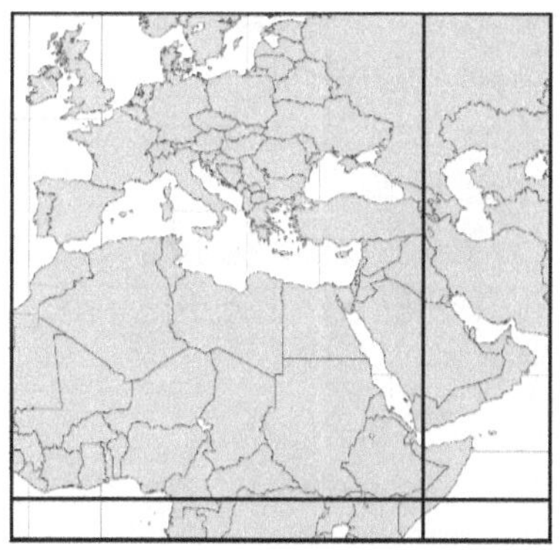

44 SOMALIA

Indian Ocean

The sun is a bucket of dazzling rays poured against PJ's face, as he struggles against the bonds that hold his wrists. Blood fills his mouth. The blinding light is blocked and unblocked by the movement of men on the deck. He can't remember for how long they have been sailing, but it must be several days. Days without food, and with minimal water.

The death he was promised has been delayed, as the crew seemed to derive more pleasure from keeping him bound to the aft rail, day and night. Taunting him, pressing burning incense sticks against his most intimate parts. Emptying chamber pots over his body. Punching and kicking him. His ears rang for hours from gunshots fired just inches from his head, aimed out to sea at the last moment, leaving him wondering if he was dead or alive.

All the time the dhow sailed on, and PJ, in constant view of both sun and stars, was able to ascertain that they were heading south-west towards the coast of Africa. Their speed varied little from a steady six to eight knots.

Now, with a dun-brown landmass on the horizon, the Almohad crew are no longer playing games. PJ senses that this time they will kill him. Near to their destination, there is no longer any reason to keep him alive.

The open deck is hard beneath his body. At least three men stand over him, one binding something tight around his ankles. There is constant chatter.

Tighter, Jamal, tighter …

He is from the pig offal British. Be thankful he did not get the chance to kill us all …

Using the unbalancing force of a large wave, PJ twists and kicks in earnest, but there are too many of them holding him. The manoeuvre fails and the crowd parts. Another man steps up, rifle held barrel skywards, and beats him across the face with the butt. PJ lifts both hands and hunches into the foetal position in an attempt to protect himself.

Another face, leaning down and speaking in broken English. 'You want to find out our secrets, English pig? Take to the grave with you the knowledge that Istikaan, the Hourglass, will save our people. That soon we will own the earth.' The speaker hawks and spits. 'Istikaan is gathering to us a weapon that is more potent than you can imagine.'

There is the clink of iron, and as PJ rolls he sees the pile of heavy chain, and the rope that binds it to his ankle. A scream of terror begins deep in his chest and escapes through his battered lips. He does not have to hear them explain what the chain is for. It's clear that the heavy links are intended to drag him to the bottom of the sea.

Again he tries to fight, an effort rewarded with another flurry of blows, one of which lands like an axe stroke into the side of his temple, stealing his hearing so the sound of the other men comes as just a drone of noise. Blinking, he fights unconsciousness as they drag him across the deck, knowing that to black out now is to die.

They lift him over the gunwale and he hangs above the water. The only thing keeping him there is the weight of the chain.

PJ begins to hyperventilate, breathing like a bellows, completely exhaling to load his body up with oxygen, pumping it through as fast as he can manage.

An arm wrapped with links of chain shows against the sky. The heavy iron splashes into the water. He just has time to take a last massive gulp of air before he is plucked beneath the surface, dragged as if by a kraken below.

First comes a sense of panic so strong it is like an all-consuming wave, a crushing, numbing sensation that he has to use all his mental and physical strength to combat. The speed of his descent is terrifying, passing the first atmosphere of pressure in mere seconds. PJ tries to focus his mind, knowing that coherent thought is a weapon against panic.

What is the world record for survival underwater without breathing apparatus?

Twenty-two minutes, but that was achieved by a long preceding period of breathing pure oxygen.

Who was it?

A German.

What was his name?

Tim ... no Tom. Tom Sietas.

What about a free dive?

The longest free dive with atmospheric air was just over ten minutes. PJ himself, at the peak of his training with the Special Boat Service, has managed six, but that was under ideal conditions, and prepared for with hyperventilation.

Now he will be lucky to last four, with unconsciousness almost certain at five.

Four minutes. Two hundred and forty seconds. As much to settle his nerves as anything he begins to count backwards.

Two hundred and twenty ...

PJ keeps his mind working, remembering seeing what must be the Somali coastline in the distance before he was dragged down by the chain. How far away? Maybe four nautical miles. How deep would it be here? Forty metres? PJ has free-dived to thirty, and some specialists have gone close to one hundred without SCUBA gear. Again he pinches his nose and equalises as he continues to surge downwards, forced to allow precious air to trickle from between his lips as the increasing pressure squeezes his lungs.

Then, as abruptly as it started, the downward plunge stops, his knees ploughing into something soft and gritty — sand and mud. He opens his eyes. The light is strong here, the water blue-green. He guesses that he can't be more than thirty metres down. He tries to half-push, half-flounder away from the seabed, but the ropes on his ankles secure him to the chain, the bonds biting into his skin.

Panic. Waves of it. This time they're harder to counter. The first strong urges to breathe are racking him, and he loses count for a few seconds, estimates what he has missed, then starts again.

One hundred and ninety ...

Hands are the key, but they are tied together at the wrists with sash cord. PJ lets his feet and ankles settle into the soft substrate of the bottom, ignoring the particles that swirl up and obscure the floor. A school of silver trevally flick past, bodies pulsing with each beat of their powerful tails. The bond on his right wrist feels looser than the other and this is the one he concentrates on, flexing his forearm, twisting, pouring all his strength into trying to slide the hand through. The cord stretches, yet not enough to graze past the bones at the base of the thumb.

As one side comes up, the other slips back. He rips and tears upwards, closing his eyes as he feels strong vertigo, the sense that he is about to pass out. Another renewed effort as one hand slips free, then the other.

One hundred and thirty ...

To get back up to the surface PJ decides he will need at least half a minute. He leans over and begins to attack the bonds on his ankles, the ropes here a fine nylon cord, the knots pulled tight by strong hands and the weight of the chain on descent.

Push, don't pull, he tells himself, the old rope man's maxim. His fingers seem to have the dexterity of raw sausages. Blood from his wrist spills in swirls, like smoke, dispersing with each urgent movement, appearing green at this depth. Red is the first colour filtered from the spectrum.

More sediment thrown up by the movement of the chain in the seafloor creates a toxic soup, and his chest heaves with an urgent need for air.

Up until now his natural optimism has pushed him along, assuring him that this can't be the end. That a man with so many thousands of hours of under- and above-water training cannot be snuffed out so easily.

In the past he has faced perils almost as serious as this. He has been in a dreadnought suit when the air ran out. He has been forced to decompress when the oxygen tanks on his back were all but empty. Perhaps, though, this will be too much. For a moment he loses control, his fingers scrabbling at the bonds, trying to force the knot, but the foot is constructed differently to the wrist, the bones of the heel too big to let the rope slip by.

He stops, chest ready to explode, feeling a sob of despair in his chest now.

Ninety seconds ...

PJ takes a moment to compose himself. *You can do this, for fuck's sake. You're a pro.*

His struggles have tightened the knot, but even so, when he works at it he feels it loosen just a little. Just enough. More fiddling, and a half-hitch comes free. Then another. Underneath is a variation on the rolling-hitch, a seaman's knot designed to grow tighter with pressure.

Now confidence replaces despair. This knot was one of ten or more that he had to learn way back in his basic HM Navy Marine training. Fastening and unfastening, both blindfolded and sighted took hours of practice. It appears complicated, but there is a trick to it. His fingers appear to carry a memory of their own. The last loop comes free, and his ankle slips through.

PJ begins to rise, fighting waves of blankness that threaten to steal his consciousness. The brick wall of oxygen starvation is coming earlier than he expected, but of course he has been struggling, using more oxygen than normal.

Within a few metres he is out of the disturbed sediment and into clear water.

Pressing both hands into his skull, he knows that he is at the limit of his strength and oxygen. Trying to keep counting, but the numbers are jumbled and confused in his head.

Fifty, maybe sixty. What the hell does it matter anyway? He is just a speck of organic matter. A few tubes and electrical impulses. Nothing is important. Not even his own life.

He feels the urge to kick towards the surface subside. Stops. Enjoys the sudden cessation of the struggle. What is the journey of an organism anyway but the battle to live? It seems at that moment to be a relief to be released from it.

Random images swim into his head. A butterfly. A cousin's yellow Mini Cooper and a double date with that brunette. The two of them squeezed into the tiny back seats. What was her name again?

It doesn't matter. Nothing matters.

Instinct keeps his legs kicking weakly, but he no longer has the desire to breathe, only to sleep, yet a short distance above he can now see the silver mirror of the surface.

Now he can see the burning orb of the sun far above. It is so hot, so burning hot, that it must be far safer here under the water — cooler, this perfect temperature that wraps him like a blanket.

Head and shoulders slide through the surface of the sea. Mouth opening, lungs convulsing, taking in vast heaving breaths of air, tears streaming down his face before gravity pushes him back down, head going under, eyes open.

A huge effort, and his head is free again. He concentrates on filling his lungs, removing the dangerous carbon dioxide, the odourless, clear gas that builds up in the bloodstream, toxic to an oxygen-starved brain.

For perhaps five minutes he does nothing but tread water and breathe. Strength flows back into his limbs. Reason returns also.

PJ scans the horizon. The sail of the dhow is still visible, perhaps a nautical mile ahead, sailing towards the shore. Soon that deadly cargo will reach land. He coughs, eyes filling with tears, and swears that he will follow, to the best of his ability, while he still has breath in his body.

Day becomes night, and the pole star orientates him, allowing him to swim towards the coast; always south-west, to what must be the coast of Somalia. PJ has swum in Force Eight seas, ten miles from Christchurch to Yarmouth on the Isle of Wight, dressed in fatigues with a water-sealed pack on his back, yet the exhaustion he feels now is beyond any training exercise.

In the distance he can see lights and these become beacons in his mind, driving him forward. He alternates between a survival backstroke and sidestroke to prevent cramps and overusing the same muscle groups. Even so, his shoulders feel as if they are tearing from their sockets, and his skin is soft from constant immersion.

Thirst is a torment, a demon in his cracked lips. His tongue feels like a dry sponge, and the water so warm that he is overheated, as if he has spent hours in a steam bath. There is no way out but to keep swimming, making for the shore.

The moon rises as a pale crescent of silver white light on the eastern horizon, as welcome as a friend, dancing on the wavelets raised by the breeze across the water. Three small fishing dhows, a couple of hundred metres distant, pass by, sails full of wind braced against the raked mainmasts.

They are too far away to consider expending energy in trying to wave them down. Besides, while they would undoubtedly try to pick him up, they would not cut short their fishing trip. On their return to shore they would almost certainly hand him over to a local warlord. Being held hostage for ransom does not appeal to PJ.

Many things prey on his mind in the dark hours that follow. Sharks are more of a danger as he nears the coast. They are well known to frequent jetties and ports, feeding on fish frames and rubbish. He worries also about where the Almohad dhow reached land. Surely they will be docked and unloaded by now.

Somalia, he wonders. *Why here?* The lack of control by the central government, he reasons, makes this an attractive location for a clandestine operation, and the Almohad have a growing presence here.

PJ knows that he needs to get more details of the cargo — especially the missile decoys — to London ASAP. That means finding a way of making contact with DRFS, but there is no question of requesting an evacuation. He needs to find the dhow and where it has docked. He needs resources. A thousand US dollars is sewn into the seam of his shirt, but this was intended for high-level bribery in Iran — all in hundred dollar notes, a denomination that will attract attention here, and not be easy to change.

Another hour of sidestroke, treading water and back-floating passes before PJ is close enough to pick out the sight of a headland thrusting deep into the sea, the white smudge of spray where waves meet rocks.

Within a kilometre of the landmark he is forced to stop and float on his back for ten, twenty minutes, staring up at the stars, drawing strength and fortitude. Then, turning onto his side, he sculls towards the dark stone face, hearing the crash of waves.

The current, however, is sweeping him along at almost three knots. The headland nears and only now does he see how forbidding it is. He stops swimming, treads water, studying the cliff faces, seeing no way to land safely. There is no point trying to get closer, and he relaxes, the salt water and fast current combining to provide such buoyancy that he requires just a gentle pedalling motion with his feet to keep his head above water.

The headland rushes past, and on the other side, in the pale moonlight, lies the fluorescent pale sand of a beach. Further along the coast is more forbidding stone. More headlands. Now he rolls forward, using the last of his reserves to launch into a powerful freestyle that pulls him across the current and towards the beach, estimating the best angle, one that allows him to intercept the beach while fighting the surge the least.

It seems to take forever, but finally he feels sand beneath his feet, stands, chest heaving, arms aching as if they carry hundred-kilogram dumbbells and legs like cooked noodles, half-crawling from the water, yet having the presence of mind to stop before he emerges onto the clear ground of the beach to scan for possible observers.

When he reaches the dry sand, all he wants to do is roll onto his back and sleep, but it is too open here. Nor can he leave the trail of a crawling man leading up the beach. He forces himself to his feet. Walks up behind the beach, into the beginnings of the mangroves. He sinks back down, stretches out his legs and lays his head on the sand.

He is half-asleep when his right leg cramps up. He sobs with effort, reaches down to bend his toes before releasing them and sagging back to the ground. Now, battered and fatigued beyond endurance, he sleeps.

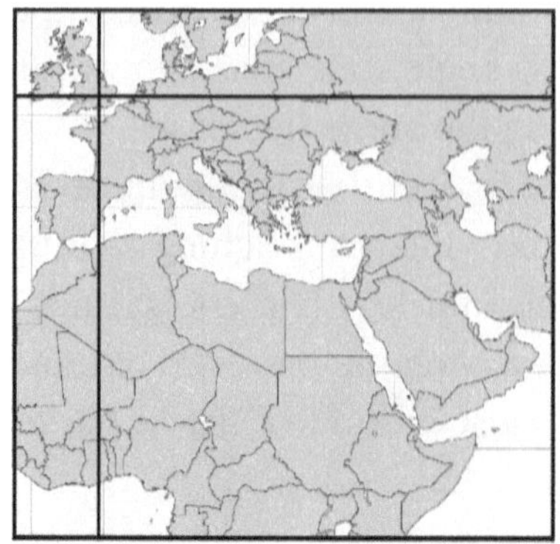

45 UNITED KINGDOM

London

Julian wakes with a sheen of sweat on his skin and a faint feeling of nausea. He reaches for his phone on the bedside table, checking the time, then lies on his back, listening to the traffic that is just beginning to stir, watching the headlights flashing from one wall to the other.

Leisel's head is turned away from him and he wants to reach out and touch her hair, so smooth and soft, but even her presence cannot bring him happiness today. He loves it when she stays at his flat, but right now everything is dark.

They were waiting at the train station as he made his way home. Four of them. Issuing threats, pushing him against a wall. Holding him there. A show of strength that had him quivering with fear.

He can see no alternative but to do as they say. Yet his heart and conscience scream at him that he cannot do that.

Beside him, Leisel half-turns, comes up against his arm. Her eyes open. 'Are you OK?'

'Yes, fine, just awake.'

She snuggles into his embrace, head on his arm, hair spilling across his chest. She reaches up once and kisses him on the side of his lips. 'Something worrying you? You didn't seem to be yourself last night.'

Her lisp is always stronger when she is sleepy. There is something innocent about it. Innocent and frightening. Makes him realise just how responsible he is for her continuing safety.

'I'm fine.'

Leisel places one hand on his stomach, and with her forefinger starts to trace tiny circles in the triangular mat that extends from his pubic hair upwards. Despite his mood, he feels himself becoming aroused. Her finger continues its movement while she talks.

'My uni group yesterday had a talk from a Thai professor. He spoke about a Burmese mountain tribe that has existed for thousands of years in perfect harmony with their environment.'

Her hand moves lower, fingers continuing to dance over his skin.

'They have discovered a way of equitably sharing resources, and subduing aggression. Both genders are equal, and the tribe is governed with an amazing democratic method.'

Her hand stops, then glides lower. Julian gasps out loud. 'Incredible.'

'He believes that if we can apply these principles to our society, we can, over a generation or so, solve our problems and get on track. He lived with them for ten years, and is working on a model that Western communities can emulate.'

Her hand squeezes; teases. Over and over. He groans.

'Imagine that, a whole new way of doing things. Food for everyone. No more war.'

She lets go of him, lifts her nightdress over her head. Car headlights sweep over her body. The image of utopia combined with Leisel's writhing body bring him to a climax so strong it seems to blow his mind.

* * *

Just after dawn a team of six men arrive at the O'Donnell Road premises and collect the prisoner. In his hands they place a genuine UK passport in a fictitious name, a selection of banking documents, and cash.

A pair of silver Vauxhall Astras speed out to the east of London, on the M20 as far as the Sene Valley, then turn down along the coastal strip of the Esplanade and Dymchurch Road.

The house sits back from the sea on one-and-a-half acres. It was once a holiday home for a London banker who saw a reversal in fortunes after the Euro crisis.

The prisoner-turned-informer walks the rooms, nodding in approval. 'This is satisfactory,' he says at last. 'Tell your boss that I am ready to talk, but only to the woman.'

'I'm afraid that she's not in the country.'

'Then get her back.'

In a small office there is a computer with full internet access. Of course, the prisoner knows that every action will be monitored. It doesn't matter.

As soon as he is alone, he starts the computer, visiting a seemingly random array of websites. The final URL is a web-based anonymous proxy software called Iron Gate.

The important thing, from this point onwards, he tells himself, is to avoid using the keyboard. They will have keystroke recognition software running. Instead he uses a shortcut to bring up a virtual QWERTY keyboard, moving swiftly, listening often for any sound of movement. There are cameras and sound recorders everywhere, but he has made the text as small as possible.

There are many methods for the illicit transfer of information. One of the most important is via a process called steganography, where messages are hidden in graphics files posted on websites. Another is the one he uses now, a clever and very simple method known as dead dropping.

Bringing up the gmail website, the Syrian taps out an email address and memorised twenty-nine digit password into the login screen. The account had been set up some months earlier by a third party, physically located, at that time, in a country almost completely off the radar of intelligence services, New Zealand.

The inbox holds a variety of fake emails, all of a totally innocent nature. These are not, however, what he is after. Hundreds of millions of emails are screened daily by America's National Security Agency and Britain's GCHQ. Encrypted emails are especially targeted.

The process of dead dropping involves saving messages in the drafts folder, which can then be opened by a contact anywhere on the planet, in possession of the email address and password. No email has been sent, and thus no suspicious keywords transmitted. The Syrian sees one email in the folder. Opens it. Reads silently then creates a new draft message of his own.

Outside, the security team take up positions around the building. They have been told that the prisoner's life might be in danger from the people he once served.

That's not true. He serves them still.

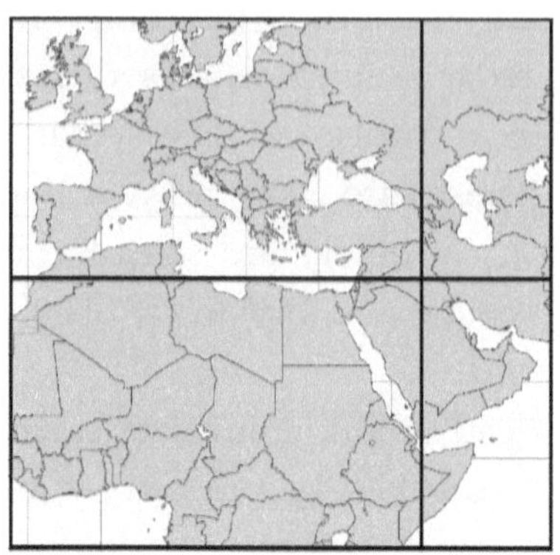

46 IRAQ

At Tannamuh

Afternoon is turning into evening when the truck rolls into At Tannamuh, an outer suburb of Basrah. Saif al-Din notes the palm trees and industrial taint of the place. This is a port town. Trucks carrying shipping containers are common. There are also many people in the streets. Business in the roadside cafés appears to be thriving, many of the customers wearing yellow fluoro vests, workers for the many transport companies here. Glancing at his watch, Saif reaches down for the cell phone and switches it on. A moment later, the device beeps and vibrates as a text message comes through.

There are no words, just a series of numbers in a pre-arranged sequence.

Saif's first act is to forward the message to the others, then he leans forward and jabs the co-ordinates into the dash-mounted GPS, watching a new set of instructions appear on the screen. A location that could not be revealed until now.

'South of the town,' he calls, 'but don't appear to hurry. We can't afford to attract attention.'

The position has been sent through by the dhow captain. Time is now vital. The transfer must be made at high tide, or the vessel will be left stranded and vulnerable.

'We have signals. Two, no three of them at once.'

Mossel hunches forward in his seat, watching SITPOL. CIA spy satellites, focused on the area, are receiving GPRS data and have already profiled the numbers involved.

On the screen three orange signals glow, all of them in or about the river city of At Tannamuh.

'That's it,' Mossel says, 'they're converging. If we don't get them now …' He delivers a series of orders. 'Liaise with the Iraqi police. We want personnel on every dock and jetty in the area.'

Men and women run in all directions, and Mossel feels himself burn with determination. He looks back at the screen and the signals disappear. Have they received information and are switching off their devices again?

Standby or airplane mode is not enough. Once the number is known, any regular cell phone — unlike the CCVID units used by the SIS — can be traced whenever there is a battery connected. If these people are pros they will know that.

Mossel smiles grimly. Now it's just a matter of artfully casting the net.

The Shatt al-Arab River, carrying the combined flows of the Tigris and Euphrates, is more than a kilometre across here, the colour of chocolate milk, with the trappings of industry on either side. It bears thousands of boats, everything from small dhows to hulking container ships.

Marika looks down from her vantage point in the Lynx. The road south from At Tannamuh, leading towards the border with Iran, is busy with port traffic, trucks streaming in both directions.

They are down a little in numbers, it having been necessary to send personnel in a second Lynx to investigate a possible sighting at al-Nesayri. This made it possible for her to offload Ronnie for a while, sending him in to command this foray. This is a relief in some ways — his presence was becoming intolerable — but it also leaves them short-handed. It will not be possible to search all of the trucks, but even so, they have to try. And first they must stop the traffic flow.

'Land on the road itself,' Marika shouts to the pilot.

'Seriously? There's moving traffic.'

'Give them plenty of warning. They'll stop, don't worry.'

As Marika predicted, the sight of the Lynx settling down towards the surface causes a mass braking of oncoming vehicles from both directions. The chopper's skids touch the ground, rotors spinning. Marika is out first, flanked by David and Sara, the others behind.

'Targets are heading south,' she says, 'so, Kutay, start letting the north-bound traffic through on the verge. Nice and slow. The rest of you, we have to check every single vehicle.'

Marika herself walks to a Toyota sedan with a bent radio aerial that contains two businessman types, first in the line of banked-up traffic. The driver's eyes are wild with anger, sunglasses perched on his forehead.

'Who are you and why are you stopping us?'

Marika doesn't feel comfortable here — exposed on all sides, dozens of people in vehicles with her and the team a clear target in the middle. Tactically it is a bad situation to be in, and she shouts at a couple of the others, who are standing together beside the cab of a small truck, to disperse. Clumping makes them more vulnerable.

'Sorry, but this is a joint operation with the Iraqi police. They will be here in a moment. Please wait.'

A police motorcycle eases along the verge, then another, lights flashing. Two Iraqi cops step off and remove their helmets. Both come over and after a quick introduction the more senior man, sensing the driver's intransigence, uses a combination of halting English and hand signals to indicate that he will take over while she keeps moving along the line.

Relieved, Marika notes how much more co-operative the driver is when the Iraqi asks for his papers, has a quick search of the boot, then calls, 'Pass through.'

The car drives off. The man spits out the open window at Marika as he goes, missing by some distance, then revs away down the road.

Jay, jumping down from the tailgate of a truck he has been inspecting, grunts in annoyance, lifting his rifle. 'You want me to give that prick a new arsehole in the middle of his forehead?'

Marika shakes her head, 'No. Settle down. We're going to move down the line, see what's there. Tell Kisira and one of the Iraqis to come with us.'

Up ahead comes the first truck, a gull-grey pantech, a Hino but a different model from the truck they helped destroy up near Karbala. Even so, while the driver displays his papers, Marika opens the rear door and climbs inside while Jay covers her. Inside she finds boxes of goats' cheese. Enormous, pungent cubes that must each weigh four or five kilos.

Marika jumps down, waves at the others, then continues to walk down the line. A lone imam on a bicycle. A couple of daredevil French tourists braving one of the most dangerous countries on earth. A man and his bride heading off to the seaside city of Faw, she still in her white dress.

Another truck, yet another Hino.

They're all the same fucking brand in this country.

This one has red Coca-Cola canvas on the sides, secured by loops and hooks to the side bar. It looks new, and businesslike. If there had been more likely prospects, Marika might have passed on.

She approaches the front driver's door and the window winds down.

Before she can initiate conversation with the driver she hears the sound of footsteps and turns to see David coming up fast. She steps back from the window. 'What's going on?'

'There's a diversion — traffic passing right around this roadblock — a side road.' He pulls out his Sid and shows her the map. 'Down here. Word's passed around.'

Marika swears; already they have insufficient personnel for the job. 'Tell Kutay and Sara to get down there. I'll contact SITPOL and try to get more boots on the ground here.'

Stepping back from the Coke truck, she takes out her own Sid. Talking into the unit, she watches the line of traffic ease forward another twenty metres. She ends the call and shouts out to David. 'We've got two choppers full of US Marines on the way from the USS *Abe Lincoln*. ETA fifteen minutes. Ronnie and the rest of our guys are heading this way now too. They'll be a bit longer.'

Marika looks back at the line of traffic. Ahead there is another truck — dusty sides, as is usual here. Her first impulse is to ignore the shiny new Coke truck and search this one, but a sense of duty has her turning to David. 'I'll have a look at this one coming. Would you just check out the red beast up there?'

He grins. 'Sure thing. I could do with a Coke.'

Marika smiles and walks down to the more nondescript vehicle. Another Hino. The driver winds down the window. He is alone, young, wearing a baseball cap, with dark sunglasses and facial hair shaped to follow his jaw.

'What's your business?' Marika asks.

The man shrugs. 'I am Omar Sayegh and I have a load of mixed merchandise, bound for Khorramshahr. Is there trouble?'

Marika doesn't answer directly. 'I'd like to search the truck.'

'No problem. Just unlace the canvas at the back.'

Marika steps away from the cab, then back along the truck. Even as she begins to unfasten the cord ties she can smell the musty interior, or is it the canvas? Just as she is about to part the entrance and climb inside she hears a shout and a burst of automatic fire from up ahead in the line.

Fuck. The Coke truck.

She comes around the corner of the vehicle at a run, hearing an engine roar as the Coke truck bullies its way out from the line of traffic onto the verge. Then return fire from somewhere in the chaos — she guesses it must be David.

UMP ready at her hip, she is so intent on sprinting after the departing vehicle that the sudden disruption of air around her comes as a surprise. The sound of gunfire is now coming from behind instead of from in front.

Throwing herself onto the road, feeling the thick khaki at her knees and elbows tear and the rough gravel graze her skin, she turns her head back to see the rifle barrel extending from a new tear in the canvas sides of the vehicle she was about to search. Then the truck's engine starts racing, driving off the road, bypassing the traffic, and the chopper.

'Two of them,' Marika screams into the Sid, 'two of the bastards, and they're both getting away.'

Back on her feet, sprinting away towards the fast disappearing trucks and the distant chopper. Half a dozen guns now extend from the back of the second truck, and gunfire rakes across the roadblock.

If I'd opened that canvas, she thinks, *if I'd tried to get inside, I'd be dead now.*

About to return fire, Marika sees a chilling sight. A man kneeling, RPG tube on his shoulder. She knows instinctively why he is there — that they dropped him out of one of the trucks and left him behind to take out the one thing that gives the 2CG team such an advantage.

Even as she aims the UMP and holds down the trigger, she sees the fiery backblast from the rear of the RPG, then the Lynx taking the hit, engulfed in flame, rocking it onto one side.

The man is dying, 9mm rounds from her UMP chewing him apart, but it's too late. She stops firing and turns to look at the Lynx.

That's my chopper, you bastards.

The crew, she sees with relief, manage to emerge from the other side before it falls back onto its skids, burning, while the trucks accelerate back onto the road.

Marika shouts into the Sid. 'We need those Blackhawks here now. Two trucks have opened fire on us. One chopper in flames ...'

Mossel's voice breaks through as she finishes the description. 'We have every jetty and wharf watched. They can't get away.'

The second of the two trucks is now braving a storm of gunfire from Kisira, Jay, and the Iraqi cops, pieces flying off from the bodywork as bullets strike. Muzzle flashes from return fire show from tears in the sides and the rear. It accelerates away, speeding down the road.

Marika feels a terrible sense of failure as she comes up to where David has taken a bullet in the abdomen, blood flowing like red slime from a long and deep tear. She falls to her knees beside him.

His breath is coming in gasps, and his eyes are huge with panic and the onset of shock. 'Chitrita was right ... she dreamed ... I'm gonna bleed ... to death.'

'No one's going to bleed to death. Just a little stomach wound.'

Kisira, the squad medic, takes over, getting Marika to hold a compress pad on the wound until the Blackhawks arrive with a pair of US Navy medics.

'You ever been on an aircraft carrier?' Marika asks David.

He shakes his head, his body shivering with shock.

'Well, these guys are going to take you there. They've got a hospital on board. Operating theatre and everything. Not on these two birds — we need them to chase the bastards in those trucks, but they'll wait with you. Another one is on its way. OK?'

This time a barely perceptible nod.

Marika touches his forehead briefly then strides towards the US Navy choppers. There will be men on board who will judge her for the tears on her cheeks, but she makes no effort to hide them as she steps up into the Blackhawk.

The light is fading.

* * *

A dhow noses towards the northern bank, two men in the wheelhouse illuminated in the glow of the dimmed sonar unit. On the bank, a pair of headlights flash for one-thousandth of a second. The dhow responds with a floodlight mounted atop the main cabin.

The keel impacts the river bed, but always the dhow breaks free and moves on, the captain skilfully avoiding the sandbars and shallows. The vessel is, of course, designed for not only ocean travel, but shallow beaches and lagoons, with a flat bottom that draws very little water.

Finally the nose of the dhow pushes into soft mud a bare few metres from the bank. The two men abandon the helm, throwing a stout hemp cargo net over the portside gunwale and clambering over into knee-deep water and mud that sucks and clings at the legs, followed by others who'd been waiting on deck. With the river slack and unmoving at the top of the tide, and the forefoot touching the bank, there is no need to anchor the boat.

Saif al-Din clasps the dhow captain's hand warmly as he reaches the shore. Two more sets of headlights are coming down the narrow track that leads to the loading place.

'Three of us. Excellent. A good start.' Then, having allowed a moment of self-congratulation, he urges them along. 'Hurry, start the loading. This is the critical moment, where we will succeed or fail.'

'They've disappeared,' Mossel says. 'Where the hell are they?'

He shakes his head in frustration. Every possible loading zone, every wharf and jetty is now filled with troops and police. The trucks have shown up at none of them — not even the highly recognisable Coke truck.

One of the technicians looks up. 'Sir, LIDAR is picking up satellite requests from three vehicle navigation systems in the same location.'

'Where?'

A red pointer appears on the massive screen, now zeroed in on the lower river area. 'Just here. An empty stretch of river bank.'

'Get us a thermographic image of the area.'

Thermographic, infrared imaging shows colours according to the surface temperature along a spectrum from freezing point to above forty degrees Celsius. The coldest temperatures show as black, grading to blue, shades of purple, red, orange, yellow and finally white.

Half the screen changes, becoming a hazy image, the background dark blue, with orange and yellow blobs — humans — moving between larger images that may well be trucks.

'That must be them. Can we take them out?' Mossel asks.

'We've got a series of buildings two hundred metres away. A school — no, a hospital.'

'Damn them, they would have known that when they chose the site. Take too long to evacuate it. Way too long. Get a team on-site, and hurry.'

The Blackhawks hurtle towards the site, twelve-and-a-half kilometres upriver. Two minutes' travel at this speed. It occurs to Marika that there may be long-distance shooting to be done. She loops the UMP over her shoulder, then calls to the troop sergeant in the back of the machine, 'I need some more firepower. Have you got a spare M16?'

'Yeah.' The sergeant opens a rack behind the cockpit bulkhead and passes back a single rifle, then a pouch of magazines. 'We don't call them M16s any more. This is an M4, which is pretty much a cutdown M16A2. Still 5.56mm. Still the best damn infantry weapon in the world.'

In a pub, with a couple of pints under her belt, Marika might have enjoyed arguing that point. Right now, she is happy to accept it as a damn good rifle. The Swedish-made Aimpoint red dot sight above the barrel is state of the art.

'Hey,' the sergeant says, peering at her through the half-darkness, 'you're a woman.'

Marika laughs for the first time that day. 'Thanks for telling me,' she says, 'I hadn't noticed.'

Saif al-Din's nostrils are full of the sulphurous smell of river mud. He knows that somehow, soon, the kufr will find them. They have too many ways and means to remain blind for long.

Two of the trucks are still missing. He risks switching on the phone in case any messages have come through. Nothing. He powers it off. A thought comes to him. Has the Ba'athist leader, Karim Yussef, the racist dog, planned to take the truck's cargo for himself? To sell on the open market or to use in his own name?

Saif moves closer to the river bank, where men slosh through the mud and water with their burdens, grunting with exertion, while more hands reach down to take the load and stow it on board the dhow. Some items are heavy and large, requiring two men at each end, grunting and straining. Others are small, able to be carried in one hand.

After a few words of encouragement Saif calls to the dhow captain, who disappears into the cabin and returns with a Chinese-made FN-6 surface-to-air MANPADS launcher.

Saif walks back onto dry land and assembles the weapon by feel, kneeling, priming a rocket and sliding it into the unit. Finally it powers up, and Saif shifts the weapon to his shoulder, stands, slides the sight forward until it pops up, revealing a monochrome screen with rangefinder sight. He disengages the safety and activates the trigger, moving his right hand to the grip and his left further down the tube to hold it steady. He scans the sky with the screen.

Hurry up, Karim Yussef. If you have double-crossed me there will be nowhere on this earth you can hide.

The non-arrival of the truck bearing Istikaan bothers him to a much greater extent. Everything will be harder without Istikaan —

his absence would delay the operation by many months. Perhaps longer than the needle in Saif's brain will allow him to live.

Arrive soon, my brother, Saif prays silently. This cannot be done without you.

A man appears beside him. 'The loading is done, Sayyid. The men are embarking.'

'How long before the tide drops too far for us to leave?'

'No more than twenty minutes.'

'Then we will wait. If they are not here, we have no choice but to leave without them.'

Day becomes night at pace in these latitudes, and Marika can only just see the second Blackhawk in the grey light of dusk, on station some two hundred metres to starboard. The other Lynx, returning from al-Nesayri with Team Two, will not be far away.

From her kit she takes out the NVG, slips them onto her head, changing the interior of the chopper to TV show surreality. A dollop of David's blood on the knee of her fatigues shows up brightly in the screen.

The Marines are donning full CBRN protective gear, but the kit for her squad was destroyed with the Lynx. There is no question in Marika's mind but to go in without it.

'How far?' she asks the sergeant.

A delay while he asks, then, 'Thirty seconds. You ready?'

A young lieutenant starts barking preparatory orders for landing, and at that moment, Marika is relieved not only to escape the burden of command, but also for the assistance of the Marines.

The headlights of a truck turn down that side road, then flicker briefly. The recognition code. The fourth vehicle out of the five.

Saif hopes that this is Istikaan's truck, but sees in the lights the joyless face of Karim Yussef. Hiding his disappointment, still holding the launcher, he calls out instructions.

'Back right down to the water. It will make the loading quicker. The kufr will be here soon, you can be sure of it. Work like ants, hurry!'

Now he prays for the final truck to appear, but it does not.

This is the kind of situation where the source at DRFS would have been so useful. Unfortunately there have been no new information updates for some time, and the London Ba'athists have so far failed to re-establish the connection. Saif resolves to have stronger words with them when the opportunity arises.

The truck engine roars as the driver backs it down to the water, tyres spinning in the mud, moving until the rear of the truck is chassis-deep in the river.

Then, when the engine switches off, he hears a sound: a helicopter, maybe two, a high-pitched drone at first, then the unmistakeable *swop-swop-swop* beat of the rotors. Saif feels a burning hatred as he stares through the viewfinder, waiting for the launcher's digital infrared seeker to pick up the heat signature from the aircraft, still not quite in view.

The launcher whines in his ear, a sound like an old-fashioned camera flash. Yes, it is seeking. Saif can almost feel the restrained energy.

'They are coming,' he shouts, 'finish the loading. Hurry!'

Two choppers shoot over the hills beyond the river, already close, and now the green light comes on. The FN-6 is tracking. Saif braces himself for the backblast and pulls the trigger.

The flash is blinding, destroying his night vision. He knows that the unit has a seventy per cent single-shot hit rate, and he prays under his breath as he watches the firework trail of the projectile. The chopper takes evasive action, performing a hard break turn and deploying a shower of multicoloured flares. Saif reaches down for the second rocket, looking up in time to see the missile overreaching the target and arcing away into the distance.

Again he fires, again the streak of light. It catches the machine at the end of an awkward turn. The chopper drops in altitude, trying to get into the clutter of the riverside trees, but not fast enough. A fireball lights up the sky as an explosion rocks the Blackhawk's side.

For a moment it seems like it might remain airborne, but it begins to plummet, autorotating on the way down.

Filled with wild exultation, Saif raises the MANPADS tube again, the second chopper is no longer there. It has gone to ground, and there is no longer a tracking signal on the FN-6. Saif drops it and sprints for the dhow. This is no longer a time to fight, but to run.

Marika sees the flash trail of the second surface-to-air missile even before one of the crew shouts. The pilot is taking them down to the ground fast after the first near-miss. The skids just touch earth as the lead Blackhawk explodes, lighting the landscape.

Marika leads her team out at a run, taking shelter behind an earthen flood levee, protecting them from both gunfire and the infrared and heat-seeking electronics of the MANPADS. Her squad of 2CG followed by the same number of Marines: a formidable force.

There is no need for caution, just a double-time run, using the NVG for vision, across a field Marika recognises as some kind of bean crop. Twice she stops for barriers that might have gone unseen by a less watchful person, once a low-slung wire fence in considerable disrepair, and once for a treacherous irrigation ditch filled with a little water and a lot of mud that would have claimed someone to the hip.

The probability that they will arrive too late urges her on. The dice have been thrown, and she prays that they will be in time to see them fall.

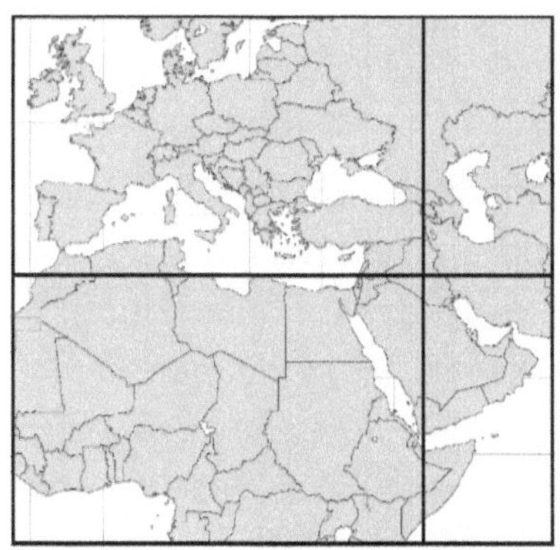

47 IRAQ

Shatt al-Arab River

Saif punches his body through the water towards the dhow, throwing spray as high as his shoulders. Others push the vessel out from the shore.

He feels confident that the kufr cannot search the thousands of boats on the river. Half the population around here live on their dhows. Many are armed and dislike interference. Besides, in just a few minutes they will have moved downriver, over the border into Iran.

As he nears the boat, however, a figure detaches itself from the shore.

Saif recognises Karim Yussef. 'What are you doing? The rest of your men have already gone.' It's true, most of the Ba'athist contingent have melted away along the river bank. Their work here is done.

Karim draws a long knife from a scabbard and holds it extended. 'Ah, yes, but I have business with you before I go.'

Saif stops, teetering to save his balance. 'You fool, you would endanger everything we have done for a personal feud?'

'I promised you a knife in the ribs and I always keep my promises.'

Saif sees that the dhow is now floating free and the last of the men have clambered aboard. The diesel engine starts up, and a surge of mud and water churns out from the big bronze prop. The captain leans over the side. 'Hurry, Sayyid, we must go, while there is water over the mudbanks.'

Saif reaches inside his shirt and draws his dagger — a blade he was given by his friend Zhyogal, who now lies dead in an unmarked Dubai grave. It is a thing of beauty, nine inches of Damascus steel, single-edged, curved and subtly thickening towards the hilt. Saif learned to fight with a knife in Nigeria, where the men of Boko Haram are famed for their skills.

He makes for Karim Yussef, using the uncommon length of his arms in a single wild lunge for the gut. It is a stroke that would have finished most men, anchored as they are in the mud and shallow water.

Somehow, though, his adversary manages to avoid the blow and launch an attack of his own, his knife slicing across the top of Saif's left forearm, cutting deep, forcing him to step back.

'You are a fool,' Saif grunts, knowing that this will not end without the death of one of them. His entire body is now as taut as steel cable, every muscle straining.

'Perhaps, but a fool who will live to fight another day.'

'No.' Saif shifts his grip, feinting underhand, countering the response, then running five or ten steps towards the dhow, unwilling to let it get out of reach.

The deeper water favours his height and will hamper his opponent, who chases him in, pulling up just out of range. Saif lunges to the extent of his reach, feels the point of his knife touch bone and glance away. A grunt of pain from Karim Yussef. *Close*, he thinks, *another few inches.*

Another shout from the dhow. 'Hurry, the kufr are coming! We can see them through the trees.'

Saif ignores the shout. Karim Yussef has cut him, and now Karim will die in return. Saif pretends to break off the engagement and fakes a run for the boat. Out of the corner of his eyes he sees the Iraqi fall for it and go on the attack, slowed by the water. Saif turns, slashing across the other man's neck, hearing the rush of air from the windpipe.

Next he brings the knife down and opens Karim's abdomen in a single stroke from navel to breastbone, lifting the knife against his bodyweight, feeling the slippery rush of intestines leaving the body under the water, enjoying the strange, surprised expression of a man who is still living, yet aware that he is dead.

With a final shake Saif drops the body facedown in the water, extricates his knife, then plunges through the mud and water. He reaches up to grip the gunwale, helped by many hands, then vaults onto the deck as the current catches the dhow and sends it spinning downstream with the tide.

Marika comes out from the trees, sees the abandoned trucks, one having backed almost into the water. She stares out into the dark river. Boats are visible out there in the screen of the NVG. More than one.

'Can you see them?' she asks Kutay.

'There are dhows everywhere. But see that one? Moving away from us?'

'That must be it.'

'Do we shoot?'

'No, wait.'

'Don't ask London, for Christ's sake. You know what they'll say. This might be our only chance ...'

Marika ignores him, but as Kutay predicted, the answer comes back in the negative. 'They say no. Don't shoot. The cargo and the proximity to civilians.'

'Damn the bastards. They have no rules. We have shitloads of them.'

Marika stares out at the dhow as it mingles into the river traffic and the darkness of the night. 'The rules are what separates us from them. Remember that.'

The rising expectation in the SITPOL room collapses into despair.

'Keep the Predator on station, and get every available chopper up and searching. If all else fails we'll try and pick them up out to sea,' Mossel says. 'It won't be easy. Thousands of dhows go out the river mouth with every tide. Yet there is no alternative. We can't vaporise a couple of hundred civilians. Particularly not when we can't explain to the world why we've done it. OK?'

Despite the justification of failing to stop the dhow, there is a feeling that something terrible and significant has taken place. That a cataclysm beyond imagination has just become inevitable.

BOOK THREE

'Iraq undertook a program, run by the office of the president and involving a special MIC [Military Industrial Commission] Unit 2001, either to produce new agent, or test agent that was retained from pre-Gulf War stocks. In 1995, Unit 2001 conducted tests on live human subjects taken from Abu Ghraib prison, using BW [Biological Weapon] and binary CW [Chemical Weapon] agent. Around fifty prisoners were chosen for these experiments, which took place at a remote testing ground in western Iraq … As a result, all the prisoners died.'

— **UN inspector Scott Ritter** in

Endgame: Solving the Iraq Problem — Once and For All

'I personally believe those human experiments happened. One day, the evidence will emerge.'

— **Richard Butler, Chief Executive, UNSCOM**

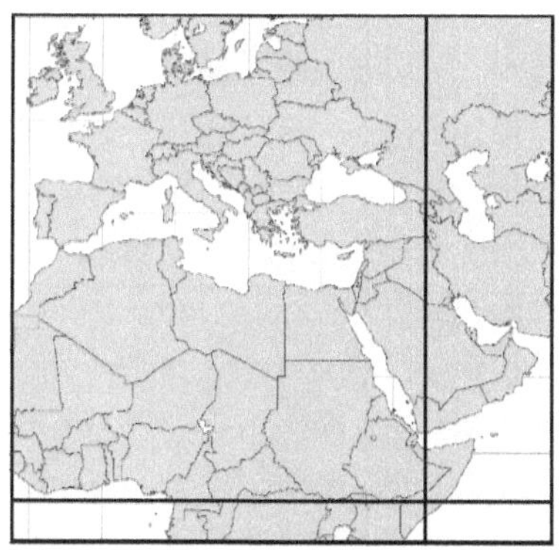

48 SOMALIA

Somali Coast, near Libidh

PJ wakes to the sound of voices. The sun, filtered through a dusky sky, is yet to clear the horizon and the light is murky. He rolls over, his tongue swollen and dry. It takes a moment or two for him to understand exactly where he is, but then his eyes flick open and he rolls to his feet, ignoring the pain, looking up to see a group of armed men moving down the steeply sloping path that leads to the beach, talking loudly in Somali.

They carry automatic weapons and wear desert-lizard camo gear, all with the distinctive shoulder patches of the fledgling Somali government's armed forces. It seems a strange place for a routine patrol, and PJ imagines that a dhow captain spotted him swimming the previous night, or someone saw him arrive on the beach and reported it.

Crawling deeper into the mangroves that line the back of the beach, elbows on the sand, dragging his lower body, he watches the soldiers step down off the last sloping few metres of the track and onto the sand. Two light cigarettes while the third looks first up, then down the beach. He issues instructions to the other two. One man, it seems, is to set off towards the near headland and another in the opposite direction. The corporal will search above the beach towards the fishing village, and the final man, the least competent looking of the group, is to do the same but heading west, towards the mangroves where PJ is hiding.

This last man takes a drag of his smoke, shakes his head, and argues back. 'There is no one here, why should we waste our time with this?' The smell of burning tobacco wafts across.

PJ assesses them. Their uniforms are clean and tidy, yet they handle their weapons casually. The way they talk to their NCO smacks of ill-discipline. They speak standard Somali, with an occasional local word or expression he is unfamiliar with.

The corporal rounds on the dissenter. 'You will do as I tell you, or Captain Ibrahim will hear of it when we return to barracks. Do you understand?'

'Yes, Corporal, I understand.'

'Go then, look.'

PJ has little fear that this group might pose much danger to him — he could probably creep up and tie their shoelaces together if he so desired. Rather, he sees them as an opportunity.

Two carry assault rifles, the other just a sidearm. All have water bottles in a canvas pouch on their webbing belt. Even from his hiding place PJ can imagine the cool water sloshing. The prospect of water drives every other thought from his mind.

The argument resolved, the four men move off in different directions. PJ watches the man with the cigarette saunter towards him a few metres, then turn towards the back of the corporal walking away. He lifts a single finger in an emphatic gesture of defiance. This done, he takes a long drag of the cigarette before slinging his rifle and walking towards the mangroves, scanning from side to side.

PJ allows the man to walk ten, twenty, thirty metres past his hiding place, then makes his move, running hunched over, using speed to cover the unavoidable noise even bare feet make in the sand. His target is unprepared, and the surf is loud enough that he doesn't turn until the last moment, when PJ has already launched a rabbit punch at the base of the neck.

As soon as the man hits the deck PJ takes the AK47 from his hands and lays it gently on the sand, then slides the eyelids back, checking that his victim is fully unconscious. Finally, with building anticipation, he fumbles with the water bottle, unscrewing the cap and lifting it to his mouth, limiting himself to just a small swallow at first, feeling his tongue, lips and the roof of his mouth come painfully alive. The second time he up-ends the bottle and lets the water flood in, knowing from his survival courses that this is a shortcut to stomach cramps, but he doesn't have time to sit in the grass with an unconscious soldier while he waits. Instead he finishes the bottle, drops it, then rifles through the man's pockets.

His wallet is cheap vinyl, with Velcro fasteners; inside is a photograph of a young woman, in a modest swimsuit with her hair free — a photo that would be considered risqué in this part of the world. There is a pair of condoms in plastic packaging in the middle void. Also in his pocket is a half-finished packet of cigarettes. Finally, he takes the man's cap, slipping it onto his head. A man without headgear looks out of place in any Muslim country.

Leaving the man where he lies, PJ decides not to take the AK47. Unarmed, he will attract less attention. Without wasting any more time he takes the path that leads above the beach, the heat of the sun radiating off the crumbling tawny earth, and the glint off quartz and other flecks of mineral. Later, the heat will be far worse.

The track bends back once before the top, and by the time he gets there his thirst has returned in full force, despite the liquid he has taken. There is a sharp pain in his gut that might be hunger, fatigue, or punishment for drinking too fast. He tightens his stomach muscles and concentrates.

At the top he finds a Mazda dual-cab utility painted in pale green, obviously belonging to the squad of soldiers down on the beach. He walks past it. There are no keys in the ignition and hotwiring it will attract attention. Instead he starts walking north along the track that runs parallel to the coast, a hundred metres behind a group of civilians; two women in burqas and children of various sizes.

PJ attempts to match his pace to theirs, not wanting to overtake them. A motorbike appears, moving down the path. PJ raises his right palm as they pass, and mutters the response to their greeting. His growing, dark beard is a wonderful accessory — few men here are fully clean-shaven. He walks on at the same pace, past the rocky headland he came so close to the previous night.

His legs are fatigued, yes, and his body aches from his feet to his chest, yet even so, PJ is surprised by just how easily his muscles move, sensing that there are depths of endurance not quite plumbed to the extremity. He is driven by the need to communicate. He needs a phone, as fast as possible. Not only that, but if he can find where the *Ghudwa* docked he might be able to follow the cargo to its destination.

The track heads inland to bypass what looks like swampland — probably, PJ guesses, farmland just a decade or two ago, before the seas rose. Before long, on the banks of a tidal creek, a small military garrison appears up to the left, with half a dozen buildings and about the same number of vehicles that look similar to the one on the beach. Several hundred metres further on, PJ watches a couple more trucks speed down the connecting road, raising a trail of dust behind them.

At first it seems that they will move past him, but then with shouted voices and a clatter of boots on the steel tray of the leading vehicle they pull up some fifty metres short, skidding on the gravel. He watches dully as one man climbs onto the roll cage of the cab and shouts in Somali, 'Give yourself up or we shoot. Now!'

PJ half-turns. Decision time. He can give up and try to bluster through. But it is not always clear if local troops answer to a central authority. Once they work out that he is English he might well be the subject of a ransom demand, and what might be a long and terrible captivity. He has been involved in three African hostage-rescue situations, and in only one of them were all the hostages freed in the same condition as they were when they were captured.

Up ahead, on the inland side, is more of the mangrove swamp, seemingly endless, fringed with giant candelabra trees. Even from here he can smell the marsh-gas reek of it. He looks back just as a vehicle-mounted DShK gun fires a burst over his head. Known in the trade as a Dushka, this is a Russian-made heavy machine gun, favoured across Africa as a vehicle-mounted weapon because of its devastating power against other technicals and ground troops.

Without turning to look again he breaks into a sprint, heading off the track, reaching the first reeds and long grasses. Then the mangroves swallow him up as he blunders into the mud and shallow water of the swamp.

The Dushka takes longer to resume firing than he expected, and he is well out of sight of the men and the vehicles when it starts. The result, however, is spectacular and frightening.

The heavy rounds explode against the mangrove trunks so that the fleshy timber inside shatters into thousands of fragments. Others strike the water surface, creating waterspouts and constant spray. Worst of all is the concussion of the detonations, and if he remembers his weapons-specifics training correctly these projectiles will be hurtling out at a rate of something like six hundred per minute.

Still, the mangrove forest seems to go on and on, so the best defence is always going to be distance. He blunders forward, falling once, and now he begins to realise what a toll the previous few days have had on his reserves.

Thankfully the water does not get any deeper and he's able to keep up the pace. The detonations cease, and PJ suspects that they have just finished a belt of ammo. Being government troops they will care little about expending shells, and will soon start up again.

Mindful of this, he continues on, deeper and deeper into the mangrove swamp.

Over the next two hours of trudging misery, PJ wonders if submitting to the local authorities might not have been such a bad idea after all. Anything seems better than the suck and cling of mud on his feet and ankles and mosquitoes that swarm around his head so that his skin is angry with bites.

Finally, however he reaches the other side, where the mangroves end abruptly. Here he climbs the side of a grassy hill, with a lone umbrella thorn on the summit, obviously a favoured perch for the local marabou storks, four or five of the morose shapes hunched on the branches.

In the shade of the tree he rests for twenty minutes, easing the pain in his tired muscles. Scrupulously cleaning the mud from his lower limbs. In general, Muslims are more fastidious than Westerners, and don't walk around with dirt on their bodies and clothes. The last thing he wants to do is stand out.

Within an hour, he is on a sandy track heading north, passing occasional subsistence farms, many of them abandoned. Palm trees droop in the stillness of morning.

There is a hill in the distance, and PJ finds himself stopping to stare at it. The peak itself rises two hundred or more metres into the air, and the summit is jagged red. As he walks the foothills of this dramatic but small range he can see all the way to the coast.

He stops to study the terrain. Not far away is a small village. Then on the coast, a port town fringing a bay. A breakwall fingers out into the sea and even from here PJ can see dhows and small boats.

This is the obvious direction in which to travel, and it proves to be almost pleasant after the mangrove swamp. Heading down towards the village, taller trees rise, with thick vines entwining themselves. Monkeys chatter and bark, leaping from branch to branch with astonishing agility. Curiosity gets the better of some of these creatures, coming close to stare at PJ as he walks along a path. He begins to pass huts both alone and in clusters, and farm workers as they pass or emerge from the dwellings.

Finally he enters the village itself. Stone walls, buildings, alleys, wattle huts. A substantial mosque occupies pride of place beside the market square.

PJ is aware that the first priority is to make contact. The loss of a Sid is a 'worst case' in terms of projected agent safety. Checking in has become an operation priority also. Without the unit he has no charts, no idea of his position. Not even the name of the village he has just entered, as there are no signposts.

What strikes him most is how few people there are, in the market and elsewhere. These areas saw a population explosion in the latter part of the twentieth century, but now many have left, unable to eke out a living here.

Stealing or buying a cell phone is the most useful possibility that occurs to him, but remarkably, as he walks through the square, he sees a pay phone in a booth along one wall — that once-common utility that is now confined to selected public places in the Western world.

The phone booth, however, has attracted a line three deep out the front. PJ walks across, takes his place and waits. There is little talk in the queue, but he is able to glean that the local cell phone tower is out, thus the pay phone is the only viable method of communication. A pair of teenage girls, chaperoned by their brother, then a couple of labourers in overalls. No one tries to engage PJ in conversation, though there are a couple of enquiring looks.

The wait drags out — the first caller talks for a long time, then dials again, provoking an outbreak of muttering among those waiting. Once this is done, however, the line moves quite fast, and PJ soon finds himself moving into the booth, closing the Perspex and aluminium door behind him.

There is a special DRFS phone number, committed to memory in the early days of an agent's tenure, for use anywhere in the world, regardless of the network. It costs nothing, all charges reversed.

The voice that comes on the line is unfamiliar to him, and guarded until PJ recites an eight digit code that changes monthly. Muffling his voice with his hand so the others in the line won't hear him speak English, PJ establishes some identifying information including his name, and the theatre in which he is operating.

After several minutes of silence while he is transferred, during which time the growing crowd begins to mutter from behind him, another voice takes over, and PJ issues ten sentences of information summarising what he found on the dhow and his current intention. The voice offers no greetings, no embellishments. In no less succinct a manner it updates him on developments in Iraq and London. Finally it orientates him to his environment. Identifies the port city nearby as the town of Libidh. When it is done the line goes dead. PJ hangs up the phone and walks out of the box.

On the road towards the port, some of the passing traffic are government troops, and PJ knows that they may be looking for him. He resists the urge to hurry, instead attaching himself to a family group on the move.

The farms on either side, down here on the coastal plains, once so fertile, lie abandoned, and the only plants are salt-tolerant thorns and grasses.

The supertides began four or five years earlier, the advance guard of catastrophic climate change. At least once each lunar cycle the sea breaches the old high-tide marks and flows inland. Nothing edible grows here now. Soon these areas will be swampland, like those he traversed earlier in the day.

In the company of strangers, weathering their confused looks, nothing further happens except that the heat of the day intensifies. Within a couple of kilometres he passes the first of several small suburbs of Libidh, little more than transient camps, and he attracts scant attention from roadside hawkers and loafers, avoiding them as so many others would do.

Past a section of higher ground he merges onto a paved bitumen road. Now there are turns to the left and right, farm and industrial compounds, and in the distance a typical East African freight terminal — very little different than it would have been half a century earlier.

Still he walks on, seeing nothing here that can help him. The occasional car comes along, beeping the horn to clear the way, but he is not in a position or enough of a hurry to attempt a car-jacking.

Libidh is an ancient port with coral block and concrete wharves that might have been used for thousands of years, with an archaic stone town behind. A place of narrow alleyways between five-hundred-year-old buildings, frequented by donkeys, cats, and children who greet him with a smile and a vocal 'Sabah wanaqsan.' Silversmiths and artisans greet him outside their shops. The Great Mosque has pride of place in the centre of town, the call to prayer blaring out from loudspeakers high on poles around the town.

The dock itself has hundreds of dhows, able to float even at low tide thanks to shallow drafts. Most are small fishing boats, with some rigged in the Mozambique style, prepared for long sea voyages. Almost all are wood, though he spies an upturned aluminium dinghy that was made in far-away Australia by a company called Quintrex.

Yet beyond all this, PJ knows from experience, are guns, hunger, a dysfunctional economy in spite of the general industry of the population. Hopelessness is common, and the endless chewing of qat is a symptom of this. The town, like the surrounding farmland, would flood regularly, and it is obvious that much of the population now lives behind the town in the low hills there, making the centre a ghost town at night, just like Chabahar had been.

* * *

In the afternoon shade of a harbour marker, PJ looks out along the waterfront, at the dhows rising and falling at their moorings. A gentle breeze off the water gathers the scent of weed and cunjevoi, seabirds and dead sea creatures.

Excitement and desire for retribution burn hard in PJ's soul. *Ghudwa* is moored out in the bay, lit by a masthead LED, yet with no crew in sight. He looks behind him, back along the breakwall.

His next step is not easy to discern. The dhow is floating high — obviously unloaded, the cargo long gone. Here, out along the port breakwall, he is in an exposed position, and government troops will surely still be looking for him.

In modern ports, finding out when and what the *Ghudwa* had unloaded would be a simple matter of breaking into the harbourmaster's office and checking the lading and destination records. Here, no such records are kept, and walking around asking questions is a great way to get shot.

PJ looks further along the bay where a similar vessel is being unloaded by boat, away from the congested dock. The dhow crew passes goods down to a smaller, outboard-powered vessel that plies to and from the shore, where crates, bales and boxes are stacked on the dockside. From here they are carried away on the heads of labourers, possibly down to the roadway where an old truck, donkeys or even camels might be waiting to bear the goods away.

There could be dozens of ferry boats in operation here — small, wide-gunwaled dhows converted for either a putt-putt diesel engine or an outboard. Most transfer passengers between the township and the port. Surely if one unloaded the *Ghudwa* the captain would know something about the cargo, even the next stage of its travel. Asking might well be worth the risk.

PJ settles down to wait. The unloading of the dhow continues for another thirty minutes or more, at which point the ferry boat returns. Now he leaves the rocks of the breakwall, steps down to the narrow passenger jetty and waves.

'You want to hire?' the captain calls out.

'Yes, to the town, please.'

Without another word the captain deftly brings his boat alongside and a deckhand, a shirtless boy of about thirteen, all ebony skin, bone and sinew, grips a bollard. PJ steps on the wide wooden gunwale, then on board, settles down into the thwart seat in the bow and waits while the engine revs and the bow pushes out into the harbour.

As they pass by the *Ghudwa* PJ waves a hand at it. 'A friend of mine had some freight delivered by that dhow. Did you unload it?'

The man with the outboard tiller widens his eyes until they look like those of a frightened cow. Then he spits overboard and exchanges a glance with his deckhand. 'The men who came on that dhow have caused much trouble here. I have had nothing to do with them and, Insh'Allah, will not in the future.'

'They had dates on board. Where did they go, did you hear?'

The dhow captain lifts his free hand and points it inland. 'I saw the *Ghudwa* unload at the dock. Some of the cargo went to local merchants.' He pauses, examines the shore, then points along the roadway. 'Can you see the fine Mitsubishi truck driving along there, coming into the port?'

'Yes.' The vehicle looks decrepit and battered to PJ's eyes.

'That truck belongs to a man called al-Gawain, and I saw much of *Ghudwa*'s cargo loaded onto it yesterday.'

PJ continues to watch the truck near the port. He can see the beach up ahead, the colourful town. 'Where did al-Gawain take the cargo?'

'He travels daily to the Ugedi crossroads, near the village of Kal, that is all I know. I will say no more on the matter.'

PJ looks back at the dock they just left. 'I've changed my mind. Will you take me back again?'

The dhow captain's face screws up unhappily. 'You will have to pay the full two hundred shillings.'

'I can pay US dollars, but I need somone to change denominations for me. Do you know anyone?'

'I can take you to a moneychanger.'

'Good. I just need to talk to the truck driver. Wait for me.'

'OK. What is your name?'

The captain holds out a bunched fist. 'My name is Joe.'

PJ attempts to copy the complicated rap-handshake that seems to be de rigueur here. 'Pleased to meet you, Joe.'

PJ stands at the edge of the gunwale, ready to jump to the dock as soon as he reaches it. Up ahead he can see that the truck has pulled up beside bales of goods and crates piled up on the dock. Men are standing by, waiting to load, and by the time PJ has reached dry ground and walked across the work has already started.

The driver stands in the shade of the truck, arms folded, chewing qat and watching the labourers. The man's eyes focus curiously on PJ as he nears.

'Hello,' PJ says, 'I was just talking to my friend Joe. He said you might be able to give me a ride to the Ugedi crossroads at Kal.'

The driver scratches his beard. 'You're Joe's friend?'

'Yes.'

The driver spits. 'I don't think you are. You look like a white man to me — perhaps the one the government troops are searching for.'

PJ's eyes fall on the holster at the man's side, the butt of an automatic hanging out of it. 'Maybe I could give you fifty US dollars for the journey if that would ensure your silence?'

'One hundred.'

'It's a deal. When do you leave?'

'First light.'

'I meet you here, OK?'

'You give me half now.'

PJ takes out a note, folds and rips it carefully at the halfway point. He hands the driver one half. 'You get the rest when we arrive at the crossroads.'

49 IRAQ

Al-Qushlah, Iraqi Coast

Dawn. Mist lies heavy and thick on the water, whipped away by the chopper blades. The sea is stained brown for miles in all directions from the millions of tonnes of water dumped by the Shatt al-Arab into the sea. Marika feels the downdraught pull at her clothing as she is lowered onto the deck of the Royal Navy Patrol Boat.

Finally, hard steel plate beneath her feet, she disconnects the carabiner that holds the harness to the cable, then waves to the goggled face that stares down from the Sea King. The cable and harness rise and the chopper lifts away, the sound of rotors and engines deadened by the sea and the mist.

Marika rips off the balaclava and sunglasses and looks around, into the scowling face of Captain Susan Quayle, stepping off the bridge ladder and walking towards her. The captain is wearing battle fatigues, and her hair spills out from under her cap in disarray. Her downturned lips push down on her chin, creating an extra fold.

'You're Captain Quayle?' Marika asks.

'Correct,' Quayle says, 'and you're our latest Special Forces action hero. This time a girl version. We've had Ken, and now Barbie.'

Marika shrugs out of the harness. 'Good morning to you, too.'

Quayle crosses her arms over her chest, chin jutting in obvious displeasure. 'You people are like floating turds — just when you think you've flushed it down, up it comes again.'

Marika throws her a look. 'Let me guess, you're having a bad day?'

'You could say that. No one tells me a damn thing. I'm pissed off, sitting in this hell hole of a place. Look at the freaking colour of the water!' She stops. 'So can you kindly tell me what's going on?'

'I'll tell you as much as I can, but first tell me about this contact you sent into London.'

'Come up to the bridge — easier to explain up there.'

Unslinging her UMP, placing it on a weapons rack against the bulkhead, Marika follows Quayle up the ladder and onto the bridge. The bosun and XO are already there. Marika acknowledges each in turn before settling in front of the navigation display.

'OK,' Quayle says. 'We've been watching all night, searched about five hundred of the filthiest, stinking tubs that ever did float, all coming out of the main channel.' She jabs a stubby forefinger at the electronic chart image. 'Now, in the last hour there's been a suspicious-looking dhow sneaking right round in the shallow water, almost as if they knew there was gonna be a mist this morning. Like they tied up somewhere for a few hours until the fuss died down, and used the last of the tide. They're moving slow, not much of a radar signature, like maybe they've taken down masts and aerials. I don't know about you, but that makes me as suspicious as hell.'

'Yeah, me too.' Marika stares at the radar screen beside the plotter. The return is just a tiny blob of red and light blue, overlaid with the chart, moving slowly, hugging the shoreline where the fog is thickest.

'I didn't want to approach it directly — not until you so-called intelligence people'd thought things through.' Quayle pauses, jabs a thumb downwards and towards the stern. 'I've got twenty-nine good boys and a couple of chicks on this tub. I don't like taking them into danger unless I know what the hell is going on.'

Marika moves closer and drops her voice. 'First thing, you need to bring your ship to CBRN state. Suits won't help, but issue PAPR respirators and orders for the crew to check each other for open lesions or sores. Cover them up with sticking plaster. We're chasing an Almohad cell that have got their hands on Saddam-era biological weapons.'

'Jesus. They want to deploy them here?'

'No, we're not expecting any attempt at deployment. Accidental release, though, is possible. They're trying to get clear with them. The deployment will come later.'

'Where?'

'Use your imagination.'

Quayle screws up her face and issues a series of instructions. The bosun's voice echoes over the PA. 'Action Stations. Action Stations. All hands assume CBRN state. Action Stations. Action Stations.'

Within seconds feet clatter on the deck as the off-duty crew rush to their posts. This done, she addresses Marika. 'So, Agent Barbie, what are we going to do about this suspicious vessel?'

'What's your smallest launch?'

'We've got a fourteen-foot inflatable with a fifty-horse Yamaha on the transom.'

'Does it show up on radar?'

'Not usually. Why?'

'I'll take two of your men and have a look.'

Quayle narrows her eyes. 'Don't you dare get any of my blokes killed, OK? I love every single one of them.'

* * *

They launch the Zodiac inflatable over the stern platform, and within a few moments one of the two leading seamen has the engine burbling away, water jetting from the telltale into the sea.

Marika climbs in, followed by a third man toting a G36 rifle. She calls back to Susan Quayle, 'Guide us in with the radar, will you?'

'Sure thing. Nice and slow.'

The engine clicks into gear and after a few revolutions the prop bites, pushing them away into the mist. Marika is in the bow with the safety rope in one hand and her Sid in the other, following the chart, a set of co-ordinates now being broadcast from *Cressie* to SITPOL, then relayed to her.

They have two nautical miles to cover, near enough to four thousand metres, Marika calculates, and the Yamaha outboard drives them along at twenty-five knots, in glassed-out conditions. When they are close she makes the damping-down signal for the helmsman to slow, then points in the direction of the arrow on the Sid's chartplotter.

Saif al-Din has been asleep for forty-five minutes, his most substantial rest in days. When he moves his arm it creaks with fresh stitches in the deep wound inflicted by Karim Yussef, which was dressed on board by the multi-talented Egyptian captain.

Saif smiles when he remembers the fight. It has been a long time since he last engaged in one-on-one mortal combat with a man. There is nothing else like it — the ultimate game, where a mistake means death, and skill, daring and patience mean life. For a moment he savours the feeling before standing and draining his mug of warm mint tea in just a couple of draughts.

The dhow captain comes to him. 'Peace be upon you, Sayyid.'

'And also upon you. Are they here?'

'Almost. We had a text message eleven minutes ago.'

Saif runs his eye over the deck, seeing with approval that the cargo is stacked and ready. 'We must make the transfer very quickly. The kufr will be close. They always are.'

'Here it is. Look, Sayyid. I have never seen a boat like it.'

Saif stands and looks out over the sea, where visible droplets of mist hang in the air as if they are suspended from above. The vessel that appears out of this eerie curtain is one of the strangest Saif has seen; with a narrow beam for its length, buoyancy provided by thick air-filled plastic collars on all sides. At the rear are no less than five three-hundred-horsepower Honda outboard engines, joined with tie rods for steering, fed by under-floor fuel tanks that hold more than three tonnes of gasoline.

This unique boat had been used for running drugs across the Black Sea, the illicit cargo stashed in dry under-deck storage areas. It was seized by Turkish police and put up for auction. Agents for al-Muwahhidun had edged out some stiff competition to win the prize.

Designed to be undetectable by radar, this is one of the fastest load-carrying boats ever made, capable of forty-five knots, even fully laden. Faster speeds are possible in ideal conditions and at full throttle. No large warship ever made could even approach it.

Saif smiles at the cleverness of their plan. This sleek craft would have attracted too much attention upriver. The dhow was perfect for that task, but now the superfast craft will fulfil a role to which it is itself perfectly suited. An express passage across the sea.

With three men standing guard, the loading is carried out at rapid pace. The tension is obvious in the frightened dark eyes, taut muscles, and lack of conversation, so that the laboured breath of each man competes only with the slap of water and groan of rigging on the dhow.

When the last of the load has been stowed, the men board, taking their weapons and some possessions. All are anxious to cast off rather than wallowing here. The mist offers only an illusion of safety, they all know that. Electronic eyes, thermal imaging, and radar all see through it.

Saif al-Din lingers, shouting orders, his voice shattering the silence like a hammer on glass. 'Lie down on the deck; it is best.

'No radar will pick us up then.' When they have obeyed he turns to the last man on the dhow. His name is Rahul, and they are already calling him 'The one who stays behind'. His duty is an important one, and his face is filled with the gravity of what he is about to do.

'Stay with God,' Saif says, then leans forward to kiss him on one cheek and then the other. 'You are the favoured one among us all ...'

He hears the whipcrack of a passing shot before the discharge itself, and then sees the grey inflatable looming out of the mist to seaward.

One of the crew, who in spite of Saif's directions is still standing, takes a round in the throat and falls sideways across the gunwale.

Saif leaps across the intervening space, into the drug runner, with all his strength and natural athleticism. 'Go,' he screams, 'fools, incompetents. Go with all possible speed!'

He lands, both boots thumping onto the deck together, knees folding, throwing himself flat. The five huge stainless-steel propellers churn the water.

The sight of the two boats, rather than one, takes Marika by surprise — there was no warning from *Cressie*. One of the two seamen gets off a burst.

'Aim for the hull,' Marika shouts, 'it's some kind of RIB.'

Men fall and bullets stitch across the hull, but there is no sudden deflation. Marika guesses that it must be foam-filled.

Return fire comes from both the dhow and the other vessel, and Marika feels the air around her burst with high-velocity bullets. 'Back. Quick. We need to bring *Cressie* up.'

The Zodiac turns, accelerating with a powerful roar, and is swallowed by the mist. Marika has the Sid in her hand. 'We have just been fired upon. Suspect boat has transferred cargo. We need aerial surveillance above the fog.'

Quayle's voice: 'How the hell? There's nothing but that one dhow on the radar.'

'The damn thing's scarcely a metre out of the water. You've never seen anything like it. If we can get choppers up here they'll see it on their FLIR.'

Marika feels the Zodiac start to falter. She shares a worried look with the seaman at the helm. The little vessel is taking in water.

'We've taken a hit. I'll have to stop. Can you pick us up? For God's sake, they holed us.'

'On our way.'

The motor chokes. Dies away to nothing.

Again into the Sid, Marika adds, 'Launch another boat, we have to get a marker onto that launch somehow. OK?'

'We'll try.'

'You do that. ETA?'

'We'll be with you in two minutes.'

Marika brings her feet up onto the seat to get her boots out of the warm seawater now flooding into the boat. Sitting like a grasshopper, she crosses her arms over her knees and sinks her head down, then lifts it to lock eyes with the two men, shaking her head, allowing the faintest of smiles to cross her face.

'When things go wrong,' she says, 'they sure do go wrong.'

Still, she is able to lift the waterproof Sid and report developments. Choppers from three different bases or ships are on their way. None of them, however, will be on-site in less than twenty minutes. Too long. That boat with its five huge outboards will be miles away by then.

They hear *Cressie* before they see her, sides tall and iron grey. Now Marika is in water to her waist, and the last thing she needs is to look up into the grinning face of Susan Quayle, leaning over the side.

'Hey, I lend you one of my boats for five minutes and look what you do to it. What the hell do they teach you people at secret agent school?'

A seaman attaches a line from a gantry to the puddled mess of the boat and lifts it onto the deck while Marika and the two men climb a rope ladder.

Quayle turns away, calling out orders. The engines build as full power is applied.

Marika follows the captain up to the bridge, watching the bow parting the mist.

The starboard machine gunner requests permission for a test fire and the hammer of gunfire follows, fired high into the sky. 'They've been getting the odd jam,' Quayle explains.

The radio comes to life, and Marika recognises the call sign, the HMS *Laser*, *Cressie*'s sister ship, patrolling five thousand metres inshore. 'We have probable target visual, closing for positive ID.'

'Hostile vessel at three hundred degrees. Visibility thirty metres.'

'Approach with care, confirm armed hostiles on board.'

'Will do.'

As they close with the target Quayle orders *Cressie* to 'slow ahead', easing through the mist, eerie and strange.

The radio crackles. 'We can see the dhow. No other boat in sight. One crew member visible, standing with hands up. Going in closer with a boarding party.'

Marika feels the panic rise up through her body, snatches the mike away from the captain, and shouts into it. 'Stand off,' she cries, 'I repeat, stand off. Do not approach.'

Quayle looks at her, mystified, for a moment, then Marika sees her face change as she comprehends the situation. But it is too late.

The explosion is so powerful that it burns away the mist for hundreds of metres. In that moment the sea is visible, and there is a fireball in the distance; a shockwave that carries a punch that might have been delivered by a heavyweight fighter, striking Marika at the bridge, half-falling, while Susan Quayle takes the helm, throttles surging as she attempts to turn the *Cressie* towards the explosion-induced wave that will follow.

Marika regains her feet. 'Here it comes.'

The wave is a wall of water three or four metres high, with an even bigger one behind it. At the extreme of her vision Marika can see HMS *Laser*, burning. The shouts of survivors drift across the sea.

For a moment it seems that Quayle will never lift *Cressie*'s bow fast enough, and Marika feels certain that the boat can't weather a wave of this height. The engines roar, and Susan Quayle has the wheel at full lock. 'This is it, hold on,' she yells, just as the razor-sharp bow comes around to meet the onrushing wave head on.

The first one is just a precursor, but huge nonetheless, breaking against the bow in a shower of white water and foam. Someone shouts, but whether in alarm or warning Marika can't tell.

Cressie rears up into the second wave, but it is the third that poses the real danger, tall as the ship's bridge, curling a little at the crest, with a flutter of white foam. The second wave has thrown the boat beam-on, and the engines scream as Susan Quayle tries to turn it back. Too late. The wave hits off centre, and the deck tilts under Marika's feet. She recognises the moment when the point of balance is reached, and the water they have already shipped but that has not yet made its way out the rear scuppers rushes to the critical side, the free-surface effect that has sunk more ships than gun and missile fire put together.

Like a pendulum at the furthest point of its travel, *Cressie* stays at that 'almost' point of no return for what seems like an age. Marika, like every crew member aboard, tilts all her weight to the high side, trying with every ounce of energy to reverse the process.

Finally, when the ship seems lost, the wave passes through, and the hull begins a slow return to equilibrium. Susan Quayle is already guiding *Cressie* over the final, smaller waves, motoring towards the burning wreck of the *Laser*, the bosun's voice again echoing through the ship's PA system. 'Initiate SAR procedures, all crew stand by to pick up survivors.'

Marika feels again the horror of death, that clammy, helpless feeling that they have been outsmarted and out-brutalised.

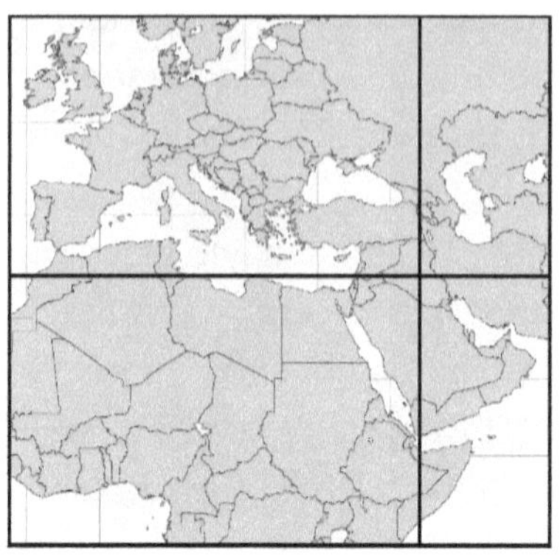

50 IRAQ

Marshes of Qurna

Istikaan is not a young man, but he feels no pain, eats and drinks only as necessary to keep blood in his veins and hatred in his heart. He keeps walking even when blisters cause his feet to slide around in the blood that slicks the insides of his boots. He has washed his broken nose to improve his appearance, but the area is bruised, swollen and tender.

He consults the sun, accepts lifts when offered, crossing desert and road without care — a decrepit middle-aged man, not worth paying attention to.

The landscape changes and he enters the great Marshes of Qurna, fed by the Tigris, dotted with lakes and hidden from the world by the endless qasab reeds. A land within a land, hidden by impassable terrain. The only inhabitants, the marsh people, the Ma'dan, live in this world of water, papyrus and bulrushes, where the modern world scarcely penetrates.

History, Istikaan is aware, has not been kind to these people. After a concerted effort by Saddam Hussein's government to drain the marshes after a Shia rebellion, the marshes have dwindled until there are just a few thousand of these ancient people left. Saddam Hussein was right, Istikaan thinks. The Ma'dan people are a throwback, a people of legend, out of touch with the mainstream of society. The marshes would be better off drained and turned into agricultural land.

As he limps his way along the rough track he hears a motorbike coming from behind. The machine carries two Ma'dan who come alongside at walking pace. The bike is splattered with mud from guards to pillion. The motor idles unsteadily, mudguard rattling as the rider runs wary eyes from Istikaan's feet to his face. He has an old bolt-action Mauser on a sling over his back.

After the customary greetings, the youth asks him who he is and what he is doing.

'My name is Abdul,' Istikaan says, 'and I am a fugitive from the government.' He barely manages to hide his contempt for these people. They make many claims, such as being direct descendants of the ancient Sumerians, but few outside the tribe believe this.

The youth points to Istikaan's battered nose. 'Did they do that to you?'

'Yes. That's why I ran from them ...'

'Bastards. How dare they beat an old man like you? Where are you from?'

'Baghdad.'

'Our village is just up ahead. You can come with us. Have you any weapons?'

'No, nothing.'

'Then you are welcome.'

With the motorbike idling along, Istikaan follows, seeing how bulrushes and grasses give way to slender papyrus reeds. Soon he finds himself walking on a narrow throat of land with water on either side. Once or twice that water comes so high as to flood the path, and in those places the motorbike slips and slides, wheels spinning, throwing mud and slush in an attempt to find purchase.

On some open water on Istikaan's left side he sees a boat called a mashoof, pointed at both ends, a man in the stern poling it along. There is an excited exchange of chatter between the two groups. Another water crossing is necessary, this time ankle-deep for more than a hundred paces. The motorbike gets stuck, and the two youths are forced to dismount and half-push, half-lift to dislodge it.

The next sight is a wonder to Istikaan. Ahead is a veritable lake of water, and on its surface are dozens of man-made floating islands of papyrus. Each is a little bigger than a Baghdad house block. On the surface of each is at least one traditional kibasha hut, dome-shaped like a tunnel. Corrals of sticks, amazingly, fence in small herds of goats. A pile of fodder is at hand for the animals, green among the dry brown reeds.

Women in black burqas and men in white are in evidence on all of the rafts. The cries of children carry across the water, mingling with those of waterbirds.

A deputation arrives in a mashoof to meet him. One man carries an ancient single-barrelled shotgun. The others carry machetes in rawhide sheaths at their sides. They are a warlike-looking bunch, Istikaan decides, primitive and unsophisticated.

'Peace be upon you,' one says.

Istikaan shifts his attention to that individual. He seems young to be the emir, but he obviously has authority. 'Peace be upon you also.'

'These two boys have just told me that you are a fugitive from the government. We are no friends of theirs either, but we don't wish to bring attention our way. What is your crime?'

This has required some thought from Istikaan. If he makes his offence seem too heinous they might be afraid to harbour him. Too trivial, and they might send him on his way.

'I have intellectual differences with the government. I'm a social liberal, and believe in reform.'

There is a general nodding of heads; they have all kept abreast of the waves of reform that continue to sweep through the Arab world.

'You are an activist?' the leader asks.

'Yes.'

'They have beaten you?'

'Yes.'

'I am honoured to meet you. My name is Yasan and I am the emir's son. He is away in another village to meet his new bride. Hah, my father is seventy years old — older even than you — yet still he plucks a virgin from the tree like a fat green date!'

Istikaan smiles. 'Then your father is a man indeed.'

The emir's son takes him by the arm, 'Soon it will be time for noon prayer, then please join us for a meal, humble though it may be. You are welcome to stay with us.'

'If you don't mind, I'll refresh and provision myself, then hurry on. I am on a journey of importance. I must reach the main branch of the Tigris in order to journey downstream as soon as I can.' He makes his voice low and conspiratorial, as if sharing a secret, and the man catches on.

'Me and my cousin will take you by boat to the main river. It will be far quicker than walking.'

Istikaan inclines his head and looks around the village, thankful that he will not be forced to stay here for long. 'I pray to the all-seeing, all-knowing God that one day I will be in a position to repay your kindness.'

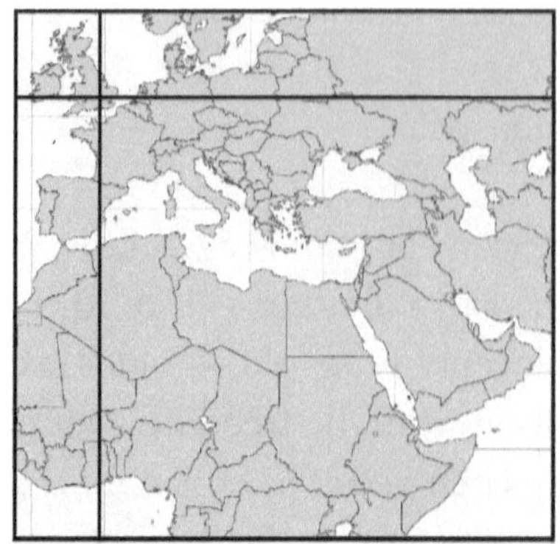

51 UNITED KINGDOM

London

The small family at dinner is different from anything Julian is used to. His own, back in Gloucester, hardly ever ate together. Leisel and her dad, however, talk, bicker and laugh like friends. She doesn't seem in the slightest bit awed or frightened of him.

For dessert there is fresh stewed rhubarb and soy cream heaped into a bowl. The rhubarb is unsweetened but delicious. When they are all finished, Julian helps Leisel dry the dishes. It is strange how this very normal act makes him feel better.

When it's done, Leisel gives him a hug. 'You look strung out. How about a cup of tea?'

Julian is about to reply when he hears the heavy knock on the door. He stops drying a plate, places it on the kitchen bench. Leisel smiles. 'I'll get the door, you put the kettle on.'

He doesn't, just follows her down the hallway, watches as she unlatches the door and it flies open as if propelled by an explosion, smashing her backwards. Before Julian can release the strangled cry that grows in his chest they are in, one grabbing Leisel, then another pounding down towards him, seizing his arm and twisting, using this grip to force him into the lounge room. Leisel's dad is halfway up from the lounge, eyes wild, attempting to fight the two men who run at him, ducking under the first blow, but the second slamming into the side of his head. Julian sees him fall in a staccato burst of punches.

Julian is pushed back down to the lounge, while five men in hoodies prowl the rooms. One goes back to lock the doors. The leader drags Leisel down to the coffee table and pushes her head to the surface.

Again Leisel's dad tries to fight, elbowing and clawing like a cat, but one of the men lashes out with his foot. The blow strikes him on the face with a sickening, squashed sound. The flow of blood is instant, running down and creating a stain on the carpet where he now lies.

The eyes of the man holding Leisel bore into Julian. 'You have not done what we asked you to do.'

Julian's breath is like hot acid. 'I can't, I —'

'You can and you will.'

The face is terrible, bony and hard. The shadows of the hood make it still more forbidding.

'I will break her fingers one at a time.'

'I can't do it,' he sobs, 'I really ...'

The man grips Leisel's little finger, lifting it from the table. Jerks it upwards. The crack of breaking bone is clearly audible, and she screams like a baby.

Julian cannot believe they have done it, but the finger remains impossibly bent. 'Stop,' he shouts. 'I'll do it, just leave her alone.'

The man smiles. 'How soon?'

'Everything is tighter now. There is only one way to get you back into the system, and that's after the weekly GCMS.'

'What is it?'

'It's called the Global Compliance Management System — like an audit. Afterwards I can do things I can't normally do.'

'When?'

'Tomorrow night.'

'We stay here, with her, until it's done, do you understand? Every eight hours we break another bone.'

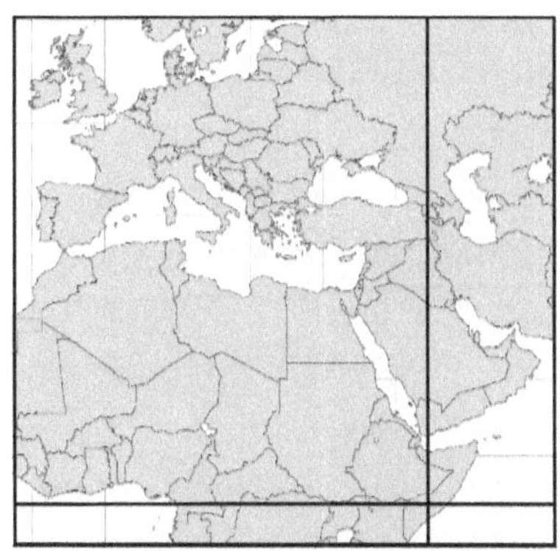

52 SOMALIA

Chakula Refugee Camp

In Africa, major corporations flock to buy land, build mines, and influence politics in their favour. Yet few countries are entirely stable, and plentiful resources come at a price.

Dilemmas and unforeseen consequences confuse experts, and often, there is no clear right and wrong. Collecting and selling archaeological relics, particularly in North Africa and along the Swahili Coast, provides an income to local people living well below the poverty line, but destroys the historical record.

Paid safari elephant hunting provides meat and money to local people, also removing rogue elephants, but is repugnant to Western tourists and aid organisations, both important sources of foreign exchange.

Somali piracy, anathema to foreign shipping, has kept the fishing fleets of the world away, leaving Kenya and the Somali coast with the healthiest demersal and pelagic fisheries in the world.

As the fish run out in Senegal, plundered by the same European and Asian factory ships that now shun Somalia, five thousand fishermen turn to piracy, until that country rivals Somalia in its reputation for unsafe waters.

In Nigeria, Sudan and a dozen other countries, China buys up millions of acres of the best and most fertile land to grow food for its own market. Production is mechanised. Locals find themselves pushed off the land.

The failure of the US corn crop begins with an attempted cover-up, followed by twenty or more unscrupulous companies placing some of the most valuable put options in history with the Chicago Board of Trade.

The disease is diagnosed as a new and devastating form of fusarium, or ear rot, a fungal infection that has until then been confined to a small number of hybrids and minor outbreaks. Now it affects virtually every GM seeded crop in the world.

Corn is the largest staple crop in the world, and prices surge to levels five times higher than a week earlier. Feedlot operators admit that shooting cattle before they starve and stockpiling the meat might be the only possibility.

When Monsanto begins work on producing a fusarium-resistant strain of seed, it is too late, and experts suggest that a new pest will sooner or later arise. 'It's the gene pool,' one explains. 'Too narrow. GM strains cannot adapt to new pests, or environmental change. Summer was too hot and dry. The fungus thrived.'

Across Africa, millions of acres have been planted to the troubled GM strains, subsistence farmers promised higher and faster yields than from their traditional varieties. The World Food Organisation launches an appeal, but the corn failure across North America and much of Europe is already setting off tremors that will be felt around the world.

In Chakula Refugee Camp, one of the doctors, coming back exhausted from a twenty-four-hour shift, tells Kifimbo of a new and widespread outbreak of cholera in the Laba Quarter, of people so dehydrated their eyes bleed and their skin feels like paper. 'That's what kills them,' he says, 'the dehydration.'

Kifimbo takes a Nissan twin-cab in the interests of speed, parking it at a guard post within walking distance of Haro's tukul, hurrying down the alleyways, frowning and worrying more with every pace. The disease is selective, for life continues here — people laughing and arguing and children screaming as they play.

Haro! Please be here for me, Kifimbo says to himself. *How foolish I was to let you tell me not to visit. I should have taken you away with me when I had the chance. Far from here. Slipped away in the night to the home of my family where you could live in dignity. Poverty, yes, but with your head held high.*

He passes one of the berkaad, the stone water reservoirs. Skull-and-crossbones signs warn people in five languages not to drink the water.

Nearby he sees the tukul he has been seeking and walks to the opening. He calls out. No answer. He pushes the hide doorflap aside and steps into the foetid space beyond. The brazier has the smell of cold, smouldered ashes. Haro's brother, Dambe, is inside. In his hand he holds a cloth. His face is racked with grief.

Before him lies a living thing so wretched it is scarcely worthy of the name.

A woman, naked to the waist, lies in soiled bedding. Ribs push through her skin like canvas over tent poles, her belly sunken into a pit. Her breasts are empty pouches of skin and her neck so narrow Kifimbo might have encircled it with one hand. Her hair has been pulled out in clumps, the remainder clinging to the scalp in twisted strands.

How the sight of her wrenches his heart, even before he sees the effect he has on this thing. How she weeps, the frail body racking, yet there are no tears. No liquid to express. The arms wave like the legs of a praying mantis as if to embrace him, yet lacking the strength.

Kifimbo locks eyes with the brother, whose face has lost all hope. The anger of their previous meeting is gone. 'I have nursed her,' he says, 'but I am losing her ...' A gulp like a fish on the beach. 'Haro is the last one, she is all I have left of my blood.'

'Have you taken her to the infirmary?'

'Just yesterday, I walked there, to see the doctors. They said they would come to get her, but have not yet arrived. I would carry her, but I ...' he looks down, 'I am not strong ... I tried.'

Kifimbo knows that the field ambulances are overwhelmed. He moves his attention to the baby. 'Is Rajee OK?'

'So far, yes.'

'Please look after him. I'll take your sister and be back soon.'

Dambe nods, and Kifimbo kneels beside the woman. He plants one knee on the earth and lifts her in his arms. She weighs nothing. Like air.

I am too late, he says to himself. *Too late to save her.*

He walks those narrow alleys with a thrust of determination in his chin. He walks fast, glancing often at her face turned to one side. Once during the journey she voids, and he holds her so the faeces trickle and strain to the ground.

The last part of the journey he carries her on the back seat of the Nissan. He drives quickly, using the horn to clear the streets of pedestrians.

Before entering the cholera ward, Kifimbo is asked to wash and is given a gauze mask and gloves. The hall was built with money donated by school fundraising in the United States. Intended for community events and recreation, it is now a repository for the dying and the dead. The facility is attended by harried medical staff, many of them volunteers with minimal training.

There is just one doctor in sight, on his knees beside a patient, glasses low on his nose, white coat stained beyond redemption. He glances up as Kifimbo enters the room.

'This woman is very sick,' Kifimbo says, 'where should I put her?'

'Anywhere. Find room.'

Kifimbo begins to search down the lines. The lucky lie on so-called cholera beds, elevated platforms with holes at the midsection so discharges can be collected in buckets and disposed of hygienically.

There is no room for her to lie down inside, there is barely room for him to walk. He goes outside to the shade cast by the building, to the rows of people laid out on blue plastic tarps. He lowers Haro, meeting her alarmed eyes, crooning softly, setting her down half on her side, pulling down the kikoi that had hiked up to expose thighs of little more than skin and bone.

He walks back in and finds the doctor again, tugging at his sleeve. 'Please come, she needs help.'

The doctor seems as if he will refuse, but then he nods sagely and follows Kifimbo outside. He kneels beside Haro, listens to her heart with a stethoscope, peers into her eyes, then prods at her abdomen. When he again stands, his face holds no hope. 'We are losing about twenty per cent of all cases, at the moment. If we get them here faster, the success rate is much higher. This one is very far gone.'

'I'll stay, and do what I can.'

'She needs fluids. Watch how the others are feeding liquids to the patients. Ask for help if you need it.' Kifimbo nods. This is someone who understands. Who has given up an easy life in the West to help hold back the tide.

Kifimbo tries his best, but when he attempts to make her drink, her swallowing reflex is gone. She needs an IV, but there are no supplies left. Over and over again he tries, but time is passing by. Night comes and he feels helpless, holding her lips open and pouring the mix of water, sugars and salts down, then turning her on her side so she does not choke.

Haro dies at two o'clock in the morning, just as a pale quarter moon rises like a scythe over the dusty horizon.

Kifimbo stands while an old woman of the Darod clan closes Haro's staring eyes with her forefinger and washes the skeletal frame with clean water, shrouding her in sheets. She recites the Fatihah and kneels beside the bed, crying out God's name.

God, forgive our dead and alive, our present and absent, our young and old, our male and female. God, whomever among us You gave life, let him live with Islam. Whomever among us you took life from, let him die with faith …

When the sun rises he goes back to the tukul. Rajee is crying. Dambe is asleep, and Kifimbo wakes him. His eyes snap open.

'Haro is dead?'

'Yes, she is dead.' Kifimbo tries to swallow away the bitter taste in his mouth.

Dambe looks from Rajee to Kifimbo, then at the ground. 'I cannot care for the boy — Rajee.'

'No. I'll take him to the orphanage. It is the best place for him. He will be cared for.'

'He is yours now. Whatever you decide.'

'What will you do?' Kifimbo asks.

The other man stares back. 'I do not know. Perhaps I will join al-Muwahhidun.'

At the orphanage the children run and play. Some are more silent than others. A kid of nine or ten sits slumped against a wall, one hand over his forehead. His chest swells and recedes with the force of each sob.

One of the volunteers, a young woman in jeans and a T-shirt, has a group of children in a circle, singing that catchy Kenyan folk song, 'Jambo'.

Jambo, Jambo Bwana, Hello, Hello sir, Habari gani, How are you, Mzuri sana.

The director is a kind Sudanese with a very fit body, a tight red T-shirt with Nike in white letters across his muscled chest. He takes Rajee into his arms, holds him up, looks into his eyes, then at Kifimbo.

'You are the child's guardian?'

'Yes, but I can't take him to the barracks.'

Kifimbo hovers, watching while Rajee is fed and immunised. The child's eyes are dark tumbled stones of obsidian, and he has strings of saliva between his lips as he reaches for the breath to scream.

Rajee. Your name is hope. You are just a few weeks old, and you have already lost two mothers.

The nurse takes a folded tissue from her pocket and cleans around Rajee's weeping nose and eyes.

'There, that's better, isn't it?'

Kifimbo thanks the nurse, then walks out into the sunshine. He needs to think of the good things. He forces his eyes shut. So tight he sees stars.

He remembers what Tajiri Hartmann told him. That the only way to hold back the horror of the bad things is with the good.

Seconds pass, then a minute. In his mind's eye he sees a village. Then a lake.

In the shallows, one million flamingos wade. Their plumage is of a hundred shades. Pink, crimson, pale pastels. Splashes of blood-like red, patches of white. When they take to flight, their black-edged wings fill the sky. Curious, curved beaks reflect on the lake. Their cries echo from the hills.

Warmth comes back to his heart. He weeps for a woman he hardly knew, for the family he has not seen for so long, but most of all he weeps for Rajee, the boy called Hope.

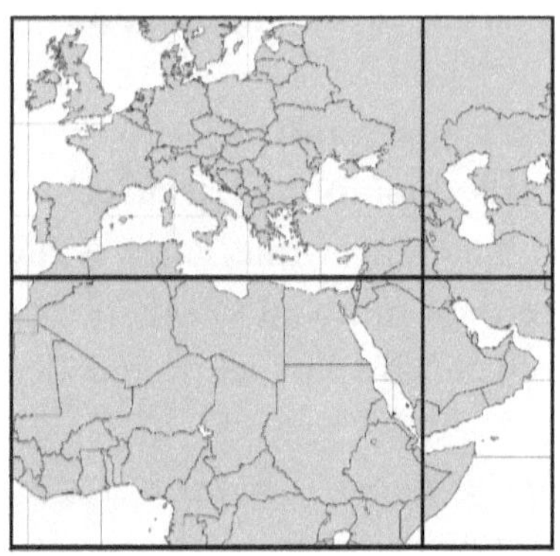

53 IRAQ

Shatt al-Arab

Istikaan is curled up on the deck of a river dhow, half-wrapped in a spare sail, the coarse material rough against the bare places of his skin. Hands, face, neck. The smell of the river and of long-immersed timbers has permeated his clothes and his soul. He is staring up at a sky so clear it is truly possible to see forever and ever, into the future and the past simultaneously.

There is magic in this mighty Shatt al-Arab river — forded by the Assyrians with their chariots, the Parthians, and even Alexander the Great, whose massive army of Macedonians and mercenaries crossed on their way to engage the Persian king, Darius.

Istikaan is aware that he is too late for the rendezvous with Saif al-Din and the others, but there will be other ways. The precious cargo will be in Somalia by now, and that is where he must go. His work is not yet finished.

The Ma'dan, for all their simplicity, proved to be superb guides, taking him to the main river where he was able to purchase passage on a fast river-boat downstream. It is amazing to him that even such primitive people can have such a good command of their environment.

His thoughts are interrupted by the figure of a man peeping around the corner of the cabin. Istikaan closes his eyes, pretending to be asleep. He hears footsteps as the crewman retreats across the deck and disappears below. Soft voices follow. Alert now, Istikaan lifts his head and moves to the ventilation pipe from which the sound emanates.

He is asleep … the money he gave me was folded tight … there will be more … much more … the river is deep here … weighted, his body will never rise to the surface … which of us has the sharpest blade and the strongest arm?

More sounds, and Istikaan realises that the river men are drawing lots as to who will kill him, and that he might have less than a minute before they come up to do so. Of course, even when he first approached them, he had known that this was a possibility — these are hard men who live outside the law, whose cargo is anything men will pay to transport, and for whom money is the sole motivation.

Fighting them off is not an option. He has no weapon, and they are many. He loops a wire-handled plastic bucket over his arm, walks to the edge of the deck then slips over the side, holding onto the gunwale, feeling the tepid water swallow his feet, calves, then, hanging at full stretch, his waist. Finally he releases his grip, immersing himself fully.

Surfacing behind the boat, bobbing in the wake like flotsam, he lifts the bucket with one hand, tilted to break the suction. He empties the water and flips it upside down, feeling the buoyancy of the twenty-litre cavity keeping him afloat. Watching the dhow pass by, he sees the river men spill from the cabin, and then the shouts of dismay as they find him missing.

They line the rail, peering back into the darkness. They look, but see nothing, beginning to remonstrate among themselves for letting him slip through their fingers. Putting them from his mind, Istikaan studies first the western, then the eastern bank.

The former, the Iraqi side, is closer, and he can see city lights up ahead. Holding the bucket under his chin, he begins to kick out for that distant shore.

Physical discomfort is not an issue to Istikaan. In his own mind he died many years ago, surviving only with the purpose of bringing vengeance. His body is a carrier, a vehicle. Hunger, thirst, heat, cold, and exhaustion do not matter. He is a walking corpse in the service of God.

There are no light memories to blend with the dark. Human suffering is an addiction to him. There is a thrill in the methodical taking of human life that cannot be compared to any other activity. Seeing that moment in their eyes when the curtain falls. Crowded together, huddled, not understanding.

The precision of the commands. Subjects dragged from the cells. Placed in the chamber. Doors sealed. Then the introduction of the spores. The precise time noted. Watching them die. Hoping for a faster death. More acute symptoms.

He loved it when they fought. Pushed their faces close to the window and screamed out their rage, smashing at the glass. Eyes fixed on him, and him feeling weak-kneed, more powerful than mortal men should ever feel.

Even in the water, the memory fills his senses. Soon he will kill again, and it will be a slaughter beyond the imaginations of any who have come before him.

The swim inshore takes a little more than an hour, and dawn is coming as Istikaan's feet first touch the bottom alongside a series of fishing boats drawn up on the mud. He huddles up against the hull of the closest, observing the town.

The adhan, the call to fajr prayer by the muezzin, comes over speakers a block or two away. The words are seductive and powerful.

Come to salat ... come to success ... the time of the best deeds is to come ...

The prayers, here in the south, are Shia rather than Istikaan's native Sunni, and he misses the familiar line *Salat is better than sleep.* Even so, it is many days since he has joined prayers led by an imam, and a thrill runs through him.

Cold as he is, Istikaan falls to his knees in ankle-deep water and touches his forehead to the surface. Going through the prayers in concert with an unseen crowd of worshippers feels strange, but when it's over he stands, refreshed of purpose and spiritually renewed. He walks up from the boats, taking the opportunity to enter the town before the worshippers file out from the mosque, when fishermen will go down to the boats and shopkeepers back to their shops.

Istikaan moves up into the town, past a near-empty souk with brick and semi-permanent market stalls cut by walkways. An alleyway becomes a street of retail shops. He knows that his wet clothes will attract attention and his eyes move past a grocer, a hardware supplier, resting finally on the shopfront of a purveyor of men's clothing. There is no window. Just a sign. He walks across and tests the door. Unlocked.

Without hesitation he passes through, entering a smallish space filled with iron racks of clothes on hangers, some Western suits, kandura robes, shemagh cloths, and shoes. Knowing he has only seconds or minutes before the shopkeeper returns he gathers a bundle of clothing and, using a spare shemagh to wipe his water trail from the floor, he retreats into a small, curtain-draped changing room, where he drops his clothing to the floor and dries himself.

Rather than wearing wet underwear he leaves them on the floor, slipping a thoub shirt over his head and pulling on white flowing trousers. He looks in the mirror. This is a good compromise — allowing him to move freely at all levels, even in the West if required to do so.

He rolls the wet clothing into a ball and forces it deep under the wooden bench seat, followed by the shemagh he has used as a towel. Then, just as he is about to step out of the cubicle he hears the jingle of a bell as the door opens, and footsteps as someone enters the shop. There is a singsong note as the man hums a few bars of music and then mutters something to himself.

Istikaan hopes the store owner might go back out to run an errand, buy some food from a street vendor perhaps, but instead, when Istikaan opens the curtain a crack to look, the businessman begins to remove garments one at a time from a cardboard carton, folds or hangs each, then places it on a hook or shelf.

He is older than Istikaan, in his sixties at least, slight of build and somewhat frail, yet he has him imprisoned as if in a cell of stone and iron.

Istikaan feels a sense of frustration build in him. Up until now he has been free to move, however difficult it might have been. Now he has no rear exit, no way of leaving unobserved. Besides, he did not think to get shoes, and on any kind of air transport he will look out of place.

The next step from here is not an easy one — he has thought little further ahead than hiring or stealing a motor vehicle, but how far will it get him? To travel internationally or to get through a checkpoint he needs identification. He again opens the curtain a crack to watch the man bent over the box, rummaging inside.

Moving with stealth, Istikaan parts the curtain and glides into the room, stands over and behind the businessman, joins his hands together into a ball of bone and muscle and brings them down with all his strength on the base of the man's skull.

The businessman hears him and starts to turn at the last moment, but the blow falls hard and square. He collapses to the floor, but he is not yet unconscious, eyes glaring, opening his mouth to scream. Istikaan forces the palm of his hand over the man's mouth, closing his nose between thumb and forefinger, feeling the warm wetness of his breath, moves one knee to his chest, pressing down, yet pulling up against the head with all his strength at the same time, wrenching, using so much force that his arms tremble with strain.

The crack of the neck comes as a great relief, and Istikaan feels the body twitch several times. Face dotted with sweat, he goes first to the door, turning the key in the lock. Feeling safer now he delves into the dead man's back pocket for a wallet, takes it out, then examines the papers before secreting the wallet and its contents in his own clothing.

Then, he takes the man's arms and drags him away, into the dressing cubicle, full of excitement at the killing. It is true that the man was simply in the wrong place at the wrong time.

It feels good, however, to kill with his own hands. To know that he is still capable of it. Cracking a human neck is not easy. It takes strength, technique, and determination. The dead man was a man of faith, Istikaan decides, and he smiles to himself, thinking that perhaps he might have even approved — dying in the pursuit of something that will bring the West to its knees.

With this in mind, Istikaan closes the curtain, chooses a pair of soft leather sandals, slips them on, then unlocks the door and walks out into the day. The city of Faw, he knows, cannot be far away. At that point his contacts within al-Muwahhidun will make arrangements for him. As he walks down the street, he feels strong and confident. Sleep does not matter, it can wait until the task is done.

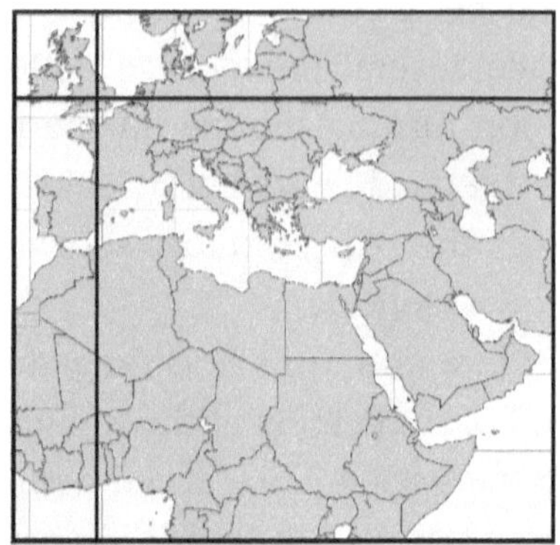

54 UNITED KINGDOM

Sene Valley, England

Flying time from Baghdad to London is generally six hours. This time the Hawker makes it to Northolt in five. Marika rests on the flight, a cold, exhausted sleep that leaves her feeling fragile.

Her transport is a sleek white Mercedes 350 with a divider between front and back seat, a VIP transport that indicates just how important this mission has become. She appreciates the privacy, however, and even more that the driver has been instructed to pull up outside her new flat to allow her a quick shower and new clothes before weaving back out through the city, merging onto the M20, heading east.

Tom Mossel calls, and the sound of his voice is as reassuring as the passing rows of semi-detached housing. To Marika, the director has come to represent what is good about this country. Christ knows, she thinks, there are enough reminders of the bad. For ten minutes they debrief, and Mossel issues some last-minute directives for her meeting with the prisoner.

'Oh and by the way, I've got some news for you — good news.'

Marika's heart beats a little faster. 'What?'

'PJ is not only alive and kicking, but on the job ...'

'Really?'

'I thought you'd be pleased. I don't think there's any question of an extraction for a few days at least, but he's alive and well. That's another one to us, by my reckoning.'

As she ends the call Marika is surprised to find herself smiling. Yet she's still too busy catching up on comms to dwell on the news, or watch the scenery, and the journey passes quickly. The passenger up front chats occasionally with the driver, but neither are particularly talkative.

Her first sight of the sea, however, has her sitting up and craning her neck as the car passes along rows of holiday houses, through a security gate and into a driveway. The prisoner's new abode is luxurious, with its views over green parkland and villages to the sea. A man clipping hedges in the front yard raises two fingers to his temple in discreet salute. She smiles at him, a field agent she has worked with before. A bulge under his armpit shows that he is no gardener.

The prisoner meets her at the door in jeans and an immaculate white shirt. Someone has been shopping for him. She feels a surge of anger. *This bastard does not deserve this.*

He sneers, 'I imagine you've been off killing the babies of the Muslim world. Interfering with governments, starting coups.'

'Listen, mate, I just spent hours on a plane because I was told you're ready to talk. You'd better be, or I'm going to be pretty damn angry.'

He leads her down a faux marble entrance, past a kitchen and into a lounge room. A large OLED screen is tuned to al-Jazeera, the sound turned down very low so the Arabic voice of the newsreader is no more than a rumble. Beside it on the black-glass stand is an elegant vase with a pair of white lilies looking far too stage-managed to be real.

'Sit down,' he invites her.

She settles down onto the soft suede seat and opens her Sid, begins recording without asking. 'Now, no more games. You promised the truth. I've travelled a long way to get it from you.'

'There is one more thing first.'

Marika watches him warily, an edge to her voice. 'What?'

He raises his wrist with the tracking bracelet attached. 'I will no longer wear a collar like a dog. I asked for freedom, but there is no freedom for me while I am tracked like an animal. I won't talk while it stays on my arm.'

Marika doesn't argue, just stands and walks away, pulls out the Sid and calls London. The conversation is brief, and she is back within minutes. 'OK. I have authorisation for the bracelet to be removed. That requires a specialist and it will take him a couple of hours to get here. I don't have time to wait. You'll just have to trust me.'

The Syrian raises one thick eyebrow. 'Two hours?' he asks.

'Give or take a few minutes, yes.'

'That is satisfactory. I will talk now.'

Marika goes back to the lounge and sits down. 'OK then. Talk. Tell me everything, starting with your name.'

'No name.'

'You're Syrian, aren't you?'

A hard, ugly twist to his mouth. 'Perhaps.'

'You fought for al-Assad. That's how you met Istikaan, isn't it?'

He shrugs, says nothing.

'You're one of the bastards who slaughtered children, shelled villages.'

'They are your words, not mine.'

'So why the alliance with al-Muwahhidun?'

'Convenience. They have numbers, infrastructure, they are a state without borders. We need them to deliver the Tide of Saleh against the West. We needed you also, that is why we orchestrated the massacre at Kafee.'

Marika narrows her eyes. 'What are you talking about?'

'Those children died for you, Marika Hartmann. We killed them just so you would chase us. We shot their squirming little bodies and sent them to hell for you. Saif al-Din was very anxious that you would help to lead the chase. I surrendered so you would take me away and bring me here.'

'Bullshit.'

'Believe it, Marika Hartmann. We killed them so you would chase us.'

Dead children spread like litter. Lying alone and overlaying each other so it is hard to tell where one wound ends and another begins.

The pit opens. She rises half out of the armchair. Her words delivered with volcanic heat. 'You fucking bastard.' She takes a pace towards him before managing to stop, fighting the urge to claw his eyes from their sockets. 'I'm going to make a call. You can go back to a cell, and I will do everything in my power to make sure you rot there in payment for your crimes.'

He stands, too, towering before her, nostrils flared, seeming to metamorphose from a man playing at urbanity, until the flesh melts from his face, revealing a corpse-like thing underneath. 'Shut your mouth, you bitch. Sit down and listen to me.'

Marika sags back into the seat, and he does the same.

'The lives of a few children,' he says, 'are nothing compared to what is coming.'

'OK, but if you worked all this out in advance — if you are truly still doing this for Saif al-Din, why did you give us so much genuine information?'

'It is in our interest now for you to know the power of what we have in our hands.'

'First,' she says, 'the leak …'

'Yes, the leak. We have been provided with access to your computer database by an employee called Julian Weiss. I believe that he is a leader in the IT department. It was good while it lasted.'

Marika can picture him. A weedy little bloke. *God, so they've had the entire database at their disposal.* 'OK. What else?'

'There is a meeting tomorrow of the council of al-Muwahhidun in Morocco. Saif al-Din will not be there. I will give a time and GPS co-ordinates so that you can destroy it with your missiles.'

Marika swallows. If this is true, it is a betrayal beyond understanding. 'Why would you tell us this?'

'Because the Almohad council is made up of eleven men. Under the rules they cannot be replaced. When they are gone Saif al-Din will rule alone. That is his desire.'

Marika crosses her arms over her chest as if to ward off the truth of what he is telling her. 'Tell me about Syria and al-Hajjuf. Istikaan was in charge at both facilities. Why all the bodies?'

The informer clears his throat. 'To answer that question we must go back into history. Have you heard of Unit 731?'

'No.'

'Unit 731 was a unit of the Imperial Japanese Army. They had a facility in Harbin, Manchuria, in occupied China. The Japanese scientists killed between three thousand and fifteen thousand Chinese in their experiments with several pathogens, one of which was anthrax.'

'How do you know all this?'

'Do you think that because I am darker-skinned than you and come from a third-world country that I do not have a brain?'

'Of course not.'

'After World War Two the American general, MacArthur, did a deal with the officers and scientists of Unit 731. They would not be prosecuted for war crimes as long as they facilitated the transfer of materials and information that they gleaned through their experimentation to America.'

Marika feels sick. 'Shit. I wish that surprised me.'

'Have you heard of an American institute called Fort Detrick?'

'Yep, a US Army Medical Command research facility. Well known as a former bioweapons lab — back in the sixties and seventies.'

'Exactly. The Japanese had discovered that anthrax bacteria that have infected and killed a host become more potent towards that species — more specifically targeted, and less likely to be lethal towards other species. That's why they infected so many Chinese — collecting the improved strain from each corpse.'

'Really?'

'The technical term is "enhanced virulence after in vivo passage". The scientists at Fort Detrick did not deliberately infect anyone, but they started using a new superstrain called Vollum. They collected three new versions, taken from the bodies of workers accidentally infected and, in two of the three cases, killed at the centre.

'The bacteria strain isolated from Bernard Victor Kreh, who infected himself while scraping Vollum sludge from the inside of a fermenter, was especially virulent, nicknamed BVK-1 after his initials. When William Boyles inhaled spores and died a few days later, the pathogen taken from lung scrapings was named 1-B. This strain was considered the most lethal when the program was suspended by President Nixon in 1969.'

Marika stares, aghast. Her mind is leaping ahead. Istikaan. The Hourglass. 'Surely they didn't ...'

The informer cuts her off. 'At al-Hajjuf, over a period of three years, Istikaan deliberately infected thousands of human hosts, each time isolating the new and more powerful strain that caused death.'

Marika feels hollow, shaken. 'It was a death camp — a scientific death camp.'

'They killed criminals, POWs, dissidents, Kurds and Ma'dan, the marsh people. Did you know that anthrax bacteria will not grow in regular growth media? They require blood products in the cultures. Istikaan used human blood. It was the easiest and freshest he had available ...'

Marika swears under her breath. 'And this new strain, this thing that is now on the loose. How lethal is it?'

The prisoner shrugs his shoulders, but his eyes never leave hers. 'No one truly knows the power of what Istikaan has created but he himself. Much of his work was not just directed towards creating a higher death rate and faster lethality, but on antibiotic resistance.'

'Are there any other stocks of these spores elsewhere on earth?'

'Not that I know of. Bashar al-Assad wanted the power of this new kind of anthrax also — many times I heard him talk about killing every Jew in Israel, and he would have done so if Istikaan's work was not interrupted by the civil war. Now, within the strong protective arms of the Almohad, nothing can stop him.'

Marika squeezes the Sid in her right fist. 'Where have they taken this thing? Where is it being prepared?'

'I don't know. I was in Somalia for a short time only. I am telling you the truth. Saif al-Din kept the preparations from me.'

Her eyes blaze. 'I don't understand. Whose side are you on? You've just betrayed the organisation you apparently serve, signed the death warrant of its entire leadership. Given me valuable information, yet you will not or cannot tell me what I really need to know. Who are you?'

Looking at that grinning face, Marika begins to understand. This man is using her, has been from the beginning. 'You want the Almohad council killed because Saif al-Din will be in charge, and you think you can control the organisation through him.'

The Syrian watches her intently. 'From now on,' he says, 'think of me as an ambassador. Between you and one of the most powerful men in the world. I am your conduit, the red telephone, so to speak. In the coming days and weeks I will become the most important resource at your disposal.'

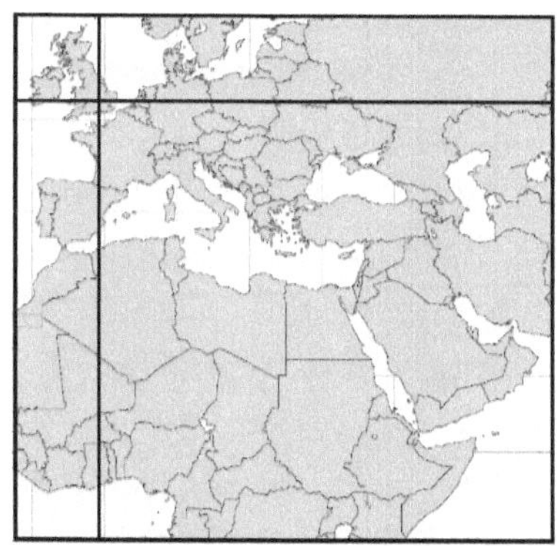

55 UNITED KINGDOM

London

All day Julian has waited for this moment. In five minutes the fortnightly system audit will be complete, and a window will open that is not available at any other time. This allows administrators with 'System Special' status, such as him, to sort out anomalies and 'clean' issues that would normally be flagged.

At this stage, Julian will create a mirror within the system of his own profile. Anyone seeing activity in that name will, in general, think nothing of it. He knows how to make the duplication, has spent most of the day planning. Since midnight the previous night he has received two MMS messages. Both had photographs of Leisel attached.

The first showed the second finger of her right hand snapped so far over that it almost rested on the back of her hand. The second ... he gags at the memory of the broken forearm, splintered bone so close to the skin that he could see it. The message said, simply: *NEXT ONE IS HER NECK.*

Staring at the screen, his eyes are bleary from days of strain. Minutes pass like bullets, and there is no future. Only today and the thought of getting Leisel freed.

A query from one of the other technicians pops up on the screen. Julian deals with it effortlessly, then begins to close applications ready for the back-up. He knows he will have only a small window in which to work, but it will have to be enough.

Bruno comes in through the door, and there is a wild look in his eye as he walks towards Julian. 'What's going on?'

Julian feels his hand start to shake. 'What do you mean?'

'There's a crowd of security in the foyer upstairs.'

'Really?'

'They're telling people not to come down here.'

Julian stands up, swallows. 'I'll go see.'

He advances part-way down the corridor, looks down with just his eyes and top of his head visible, sees the crowd of security milling up on the next floor, at the top of the stairs, silent and businesslike. Goes back to the computer workstation and finds that he has been logged off.

Frowning, he brings up the dialogue box, types in his user name and the passcode.

YOU ARE NOT AUTHORISED TO ACCESS THIS WORKSTATION.

He tries again, but the feeling of dread that began in his brain has now settled through his body. That's it. A third attempt will set off all kinds of alarms.

They know.

He picks up a yellow Post-it note and writes '23 Fawcett Lane, South Bermondsey', sticks it onto the bottom of the screen. Then stands, turns to Bruno. 'Just going for a slash. Back in a minute.'

As soon as he is out the door he turns and heads for the elevators. Punches the button, waits. Reaches the ground floor and strides out past the barriers, thankful that security is not as tight when leaving as it is arriving.

Down the stairs and along the path to the embankment, not looking at the river, the smell strong in his nostrils. He glances behind him. Five men and a woman emerge from the building. Security, fanning out along the embankment, following him. There may be more of them.

He looks ahead at Tamesis Dock and the tourists queued up to look at an ancient, rusty ship on display, some World War One relic they raised from the depths of the Channel. He starts to run, straight through the crowd and out the other side, dashing down a narrow arcade that he knows ends up at Salamanca Place, behind a block of apartments.

The phone in his pocket vibrates. He knows that they are tracking him with its signal. Knows that he must stop and turn it off, but first he opens it up, needing to know the message.

YOU HAVE FIVE MINUTES AND THEN SHE IS DEAD.

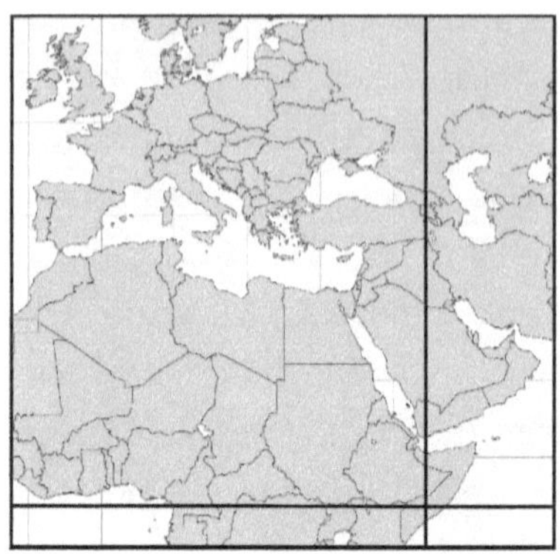

56 SOMALIA

Offshore, Badera River Mouth

The RIB makes the crossing in fifteen hours, at an offshore speed so rocky that moving on deck is almost impossible. The roar of the engines and pounding of the sea have been merciless. The journey is a nightmare in many ways, and Saif survives the pain it provokes in his temple only with help from the dark little pellets of opium, his supply now perilously low.

This is not Saif's native land, but Somalia shares some similarities in vegetation and landform to the north-eastern corner of Nigeria where he was born. Even now, at night, with the vessel powering in towards the beach, he breathes the aromatic scent of the inland. A smell that, to him, has the sweetness of sanctuary.

From up behind the beach an electric lamp blinks three, four times. Docking at Kismaayo or even Mogadishu would have been easier, of course. Saif knows that, but here, just north of the Badera River mouth, the inhabitants have almost all been driven out by starvation and thirst. Unloading can thus be effected unobserved, the shallow draft of the vessel allowing it to be pulled up high onto the sand, and there will be many hands to help.

Soon it will be midnight, the moon as yet unrisen, but Saif feels the eyes of the kufr everywhere, their breath on his shoulders, their camera drones in the sky. He knows well that delay can mean failure, that even now they hunt him with every means at their disposal. They showed in Iraq just how quickly they can converge. They are organised and ready, and it could be this moment that a missile wings its way towards them.

'Stop the engines,' Saif calls, and the deafening noise of all five outboards at high revolutions drops back to a quiet idle. The hull settles, the buoyant sponsons making the boat very stable, and Saif addresses his men.

'My brothers,' he begins, 'we are about to travel through the surf zone. It may be rough, so check again that everything is lashed into position. When I give the word you must crouch and take firm hold of a rail. We have received a signal from shore that our comrades are waiting, but take nothing for granted — look for tricks and deception at every turn. Be ready to fight.'

There is a chorus of assent, and at that moment Saif feels a love for them as deep as that of a father. They have been so good, so patient, and soon there will be a reckoning that will go far beyond even the day the towers fell in New York, the London Tube was racked by explosions, or their brothers from Jemaah Islamiyah brought death to the Australians in Bali.

'Allahu Akbar!' he shouts.

The men's voices echo his, and he knows that he has their love and loyalty. They are blooded together now; these men will carry this through to the end.

Even as he remains deep in thought the RIB drives into the back of the first of the breakers, a sheet of spray cracking over the bow, washed by a gentle offshore breeze into their faces so Saif can taste salt on his lips. He smiles, and feels the gut-swooping rush as the launch powers down the face of the wave at twenty knots, pauses as the propellers lose bite in the white water, then surges on again.

The next wave breaks as they come down the face and the vessel broaches, turning crossways, corrected by a judicious jet of power. Then they are into a gutter near the shoreline, and the hull drags as the outboard skegs hit sand. The whine of hydraulics follows as the helmsman tilts up the motors. Men rush from the sands of the dark beach and take hold of the hull while effervescent white waves drive her to the shallows.

Saif lets go of the rail, climbs from gunwale to bow, then jumps off the bowsprit. A sharp, livestock smell greets his nostrils. Camels! A line of them coming down the beach, accompanied by the gentle sound of bells.

The ancient caravan route that they will be following is, in the main, no place for motor vehicles, and so often, technology is the weak link in this kind of warfare — too easy for the kufr to trace. The old ways — the old knowledge, ancient paths and methods — offer safety.

The men who accompany the camels are older; men who grew up in the interior and treat livestock like members of the family. Many of the beasts would not feel comfortable standing this close to the sea, and with so many men moving in and around the darkness. Meanwhile dozens of hands unload the cargo from the boat and stack it while the camel masters begin to load, talking to the animals to soothe them.

It is surprising how much light can be gleaned from the stars, and Saif's Tag Heuer sunglasses are designed to enhance night vision. As time passes and no one shows a light, nor even smokes a cigarette, he finds that he can pick out the tassels on the camels and the henna-stained beards of the handlers.

Always there is the chance of discovery and Saif looks up constantly, or back out to sea towards the horizon. He picks out two satellites moving in their ungodly parabolas against the sky, and the sheer dissonance of the sight makes him curl his fists with rage.

One by one, the camels, kneeling for loading, are ready. They stagger up, yawning, moaning and spitting in the night.

'Hurry,' Saif urges again, 'we cannot be caught here at dawn.'

Even so, there are hold-ups. One of the camels throws a tantrum, rearing up, the panic spreading to others nearby until Saif orders that the beast be set free and chased away. Calm is important to him, particularly in moments when the mission might be in danger. An argument breaks out between two men — muttered threats and curses in the night.

'Save it for later,' Saif's voice stings the air. 'Shut up now or feel my knife between your ribs.'

Finally, the line of camels stand ready, and twenty men push the RIB back into the water, turning it to face the sea. One of the men, a strong swimmer, is at the helm. Behind the breakers he will open the bungs and allow the weight of the outboards to take the vessel to the bottom of the sea before swimming ashore.

The bells of the camels jingle, and their footfalls are as soft as breath on the sand. One of the handlers slaps a recalcitrant animal almost fondly on the hindquarters. It grunts in reply, then follows in single file across the sand.

Saif tucks his rifle under his arm, changing his grip so that his hand cups the magazine, the point of balance for these weapons. They are all armed, all ready, for there will be danger not just from the kufr, but from AMISOM troops, bandits and local warlords, who will suspect the caravan is carrying valuables and see it as an easy target. A display of force is always worthwhile in Somalia.

As he turns to follow the caravan, there is just one gnawing worry in Saif's mind. They have lost Istikaan. They need his knowledge, but first they need to win through to Ka Tirsan, the base they have prepared so thoroughly, with the cargo. Then they will worry about implementation.

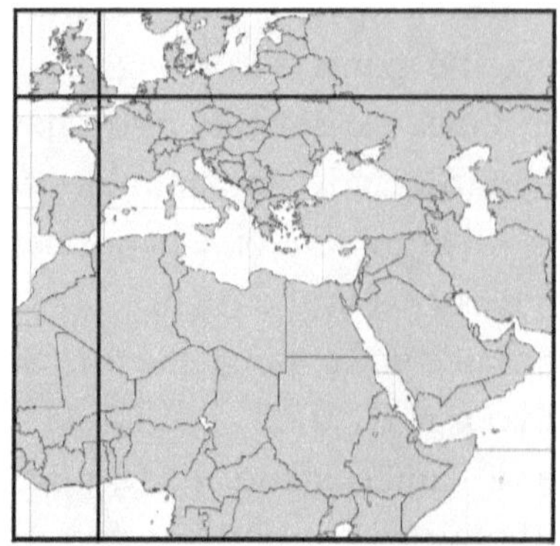

57 UNITED KINGDOM

London

Julian sees the taxi cruising along the street, one of the black TX5 fuel cell models that have taken over the fleet in recent years. His head pounds from the effort of running, fear from pursuit and worry for Leisel. At first it looks as if the driver won't stop, but Julian runs onto the road in front of it, waving his arms like a traffic cop, and the vehicle stops, traffic banking up behind.

He runs around to the side, swings open the door, clambers into the seat and drags the seatbelt across his chest.

'Bermondsey, please, and hurry.'

Someone beeps a horn from behind. Then another. The driver flicks on the meter then eases the car into motion. 'Are you alright, mate?'

'Yes, I'm OK.' Wringing his hands, turning his head to look for his pursuers, not knowing what he can do when he gets there.

'You don't look like you are.' The round face of the driver no longer looks friendly. 'You got enough money to pay for this? It'll be near enough to twenty-five quid by the time we get there.'

'I've got a credit card. Just hurry, and don't ask me anything, OK?' Julian fumbles for his phone and turns it on, needing to know if there have been more messages.

'You on drugs, mate?'

'No.' His voice breaks down into a moan. 'I just have to get there.'

'Show me the credit card.'

Julian reaches into his back pocket, slips out his wallet, but his hands are shaking so hard he can scarcely open it. Finally he manages to extract the card. Holds it up.

Please let them be there by now. Please let them get there in time to save her.

'That card in your name then?'

'Yes, Julian Weiss, that's me.'

The driver sighs. 'Well, give me a destination address, and if that card don't work I'm taking you straight to the police station, got it?'

Julian is no longer listening. The phone just beeped again. Another message. He wants to look but he is frightened.

The taxi moves too slowly. Reality is catching up swiftly. Julian recognises now that he has been in over his head from the day he agreed to betray his employer and country.

Suburbs pass by, and finally the taxi speeds past the stadium, into the narrow street. He feels the hammer blow in his chest, sees the cars still pulling up. An ambulance among them.

The taxi is stopping but Julian's already opening the door, ignoring the shouts of the driver for a fare, then men outside the house are running for him.

Uniformed paramedics are carrying something out of the house. Stretchers. Two of them. Sheets pulled right up past their heads. At first Julian doesn't understand who it might be. The truth comes like a weight from the sky.

Two men hold him down, as his world folds in like a house of cards.

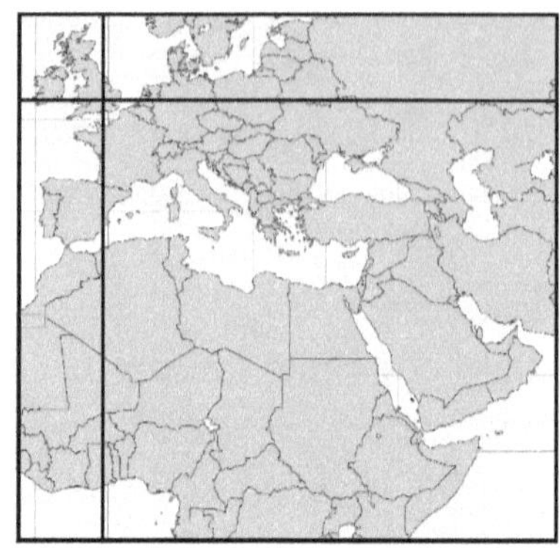

58 UNITED KINGDOM

London

Fourteen hours later, Tom Mossel stares at the screen. The video is pixellated, date-stamped some eight years earlier. Visions of violent death are not what he needs, not after a night in which one of his own has been taken into custody, having not only betrayed his country but precipitated the deaths of a father and daughter.

Putting thoughts of them aside, he concentrates on the images and sound. Five men in ragtag clothing, half-pushing, half-dragging a bearded man into a vacant lot. Slapping, kicking, hitting, jabbing him with gun barrels.

Shouting incessantly in Arabic, they push him to the ground and he lies there, trying to hold his beaten face between his hands. One of the men steps forward from the group, a handgun in his right hand, aims. Fires three, four times, and the man on the ground jerks with each impact.

The others start to call Allahu Akbar, *God is great*, over and over again as someone opens up with an AK47. Peppering the victim, each impact makes a tear in his clothes.

Despite the many, many bullets that have struck him, there is little damage visible. Mossel knows from experience that the exit wounds will be underneath. One of the killers comes forward, rolls the man's dead face backwards and forwards with his foot like a football. Only now does the dark sticky mess beneath his body start to become apparent.

The man steps back. Others open up with automatic weapons. They shoot the dead man again, over and over, hundreds of rounds, some missing and raising puffs of dust all around him. More chants. *God is great.* And the video ends.

Mossel turns to look at Marika Hartmann, sitting on the chair next to him. They both saw him with their own eyes. Large as life, wielding a gun in the Syrian civil war. The man who held the pistol in that video and committed murder is the same man now living it up in a beach house near London. Their prisoner.

'So we found him,' Mossel says. 'No name yet, but give us time.'

'He manipulated us.'

'Yes.'

'I hate the feeling that we're a step behind — every time.' She stands. 'I'd better go — I've got heaps to do.'

Silence, then Mossel clears his throat. 'There's something else I want to talk to you about,' he says.

'Yes?'

'Ronnie has submitted a report saying that you made poor decisions on several occasions. That you let the truck get away from the Red Crescent convoy. He blames you for David's wounding.'

Her face reddens. 'What? Ronnie wasn't even there. He's just getting in first.'

'In what way?'

'He's losing it, Tom. It was Ronnie who searched the truck at the rear of the Red Crescent convoy and they would have got away if I hadn't checked the numbers.'

'He's one of the best we've ever had, Marika.'

'I know that ... he was a god when I joined up here, but there is a point everyone reaches, Tom. I think he's past that point. He needs a rest.'

'You think he's suffering from CSR?' Combat Stress Reaction was uncommon in 2CG, but Ronnie had taken on some tough missions over the last twelve months.

'Yes — I think we all do, to some extent, but look at the symptoms: fatigue, indecision, focusing on the little things all the time — he might well be the best man we have in a firefight, but there's a lot more to this job than that.'

'Your observations are noted. I'll get the psych to check him out when you get back, but in the meantime he's made a complaint about you. It's on the books and I'm going to have to go through the motions. Are you prepared to make a counter-claim against him?'

'That's not my style, and you know it ... but I want him out of my team.'

Mossel shakes his head. 'If you had PJ I'd consider it, but you don't have anyone else like Ronnie. For the moment, he stays ... and you might thank me for that decision, yet.'

The door opens. Will Grace enters the room. 'Mr Mossel. The director of the CIA is on the phone for you.'

'I'm sorry,' he says, 'I have to go.'

Mossel takes the call in his office, 'Hello, Charlie, how are you?'

Mossel's American counterpart is always abrupt, but now his voice is particularly sharp and cold. 'We have assets on station in Morocco. From what I understand we have ten of the Almohad council in one place, just as your informer said. Do we take them out?'

'It seems almost too easy,' Mossel says.

'Nothing like a bit of treachery. But we'll never get another opportunity like this.'

'Yes. Do it.'

'You mean it?'

'I do. Kill them all.'

Tom Mossel feels very old as he ends the call, opens the door and walks back down the corridor.

Marika stands beside him, together watching the strike on the SITPOL screen with the others crowding around. Silent. None of them likes such images after a while. Not when they have walked among the results.

When it is over Marika goes to what Mossel has been calling the war room. A space, twenty metres by thirty, now crammed with desks and screens, men and women poring over information — doing a task that computers do not have the judgement to do. Most of the desks were not here yesterday, and most of the occupants are scrutinising detailed and constantly updated charts of what is called, in Intel parlance, the NAI. Named Area of Interest. A huge swathe of South-Western Somalia.

Finding the shipment that has passed into that country and been delivered somewhere into the interior is now the number one priority of the organisation. Occasionally someone calls out to Marika, and she will examine something, either shake her head or call for one of several experts.

'Keep at it,' she urges. They have been told to look for clues, among them the possible use of a light aircraft, necessary if air dispersal equipment is to be used. Reports of an aircraft stolen from Nairobi, Kenya have all the hallmarks of an Almohad operation, including a pilot shot five times and left slumped on the tarmac. The shipment of chemicals from Iran indicates that there will be a laboratory somewhere, most likely primitive in nature. Vehicle traffic is the key. Something new, less than six months old. Analysts compare satellite images from twelve months previously with the latest passes, looking for new tracks and paths.

Now and then something is discovered that requires further investigation, and a long-range Reaper drone is despatched from either the Seychelles or Djibouti to investigate.

'Come on, find that base,' Marika says. 'It has to be there.'

The impatience is eating away at her, and beneath it all is the burgeoning hope that PJ is still OK, that finding the Almohad base will mean finding him also.

Her team is now converging on Arba Minch airfield in Ethiopia. As soon as she has a target, Marika will join them.

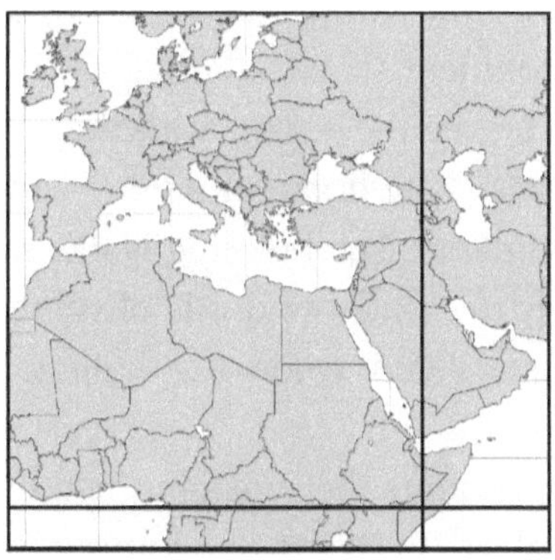

59 SOMALIA

Kal

The call to fajr sweeps across the village, the muezzin's voice laden with emotion and tradition — a people with nothing more than prayer to nourish them, living on dreams of glory a millennium past.

PJ wakes on his back, eyes flicking open, his stomach a tight drum of hunger. There will be little for him to eat: a tiny portion of ugali maize porridge, perhaps. Life is tough here. He stands up from the sleeping mat and looks out the window at the Somali village of Kal, meaning *the pestle*, so named for a rock formation of that shape on a nearby ridge. This is where the trail went cold.

The truck that carried the dhow's cargo brought him here, but the driver had delivered it to yet another carrier at the crossroads. He did not know the owner. Every day PJ goes there. Watches and waits.

PJ feels the passing of every hour and minute keenly when there is so much at stake. All he can do is wait for that one item of information that might put him back on the trail, all the time blending deeper into the background, taking on the colours and smells of his environment.

PJ dresses and leaves the room, walking down the steps and into the kitchen. This is the home of Ashkir and his wife Saamiyo, and their three daughters. The building is like many of the others, built almost entirely of stone, hundreds of years old, glowing with that unique calcium sheen when the light is kind, chalky old when it is not.

The family supplements their meagre income with the lodging of travellers. PJ plays the part — joining in prayers, meals, asking only questions that flow from a particular circumstance or conversation. The family love to talk of politics and current events, in any case, and afternoons in the shade, spent lounging with the local men, chewing qat, have provided an abundance of knowledge, both useful and otherwise.

PJ has learned, for example, that the village was founded in the Muslim year 132 by a beggar called Khajaar, who had a vision on the site, and built a shrine to God (may His name be praised), now a run-down stone plinth much defecated on by white-backed vultures and marabou storks, two of the larger and more numerous birds that call the village home.

A few days after Khajaar's arrival, so the story goes, God caused a spring to break through the earth near the shrine, thus making the area habitable and the land arable. People came from all over to settle there. The beggar protested the invasion and found himself martyred by the new mullah. He is now revered as a minor prophet. The spring is almost dry these days, a trickle gathering in an ancient stone berkaad. The population of the village has shrunk from almost a thousand in 1990 to less than fifty now.

As time passes, the villagers come to trust him more, asking him questions about the world beyond the dusty hills that mark the horizon. Just yesterday Ashkir had come to him, looking grave. 'May I speak to you?' he asked.

'Of course.'

'Not here. I need to show you.'

Ashkir is a wiry man in middle age, who wears Western jeans and a loose white thoub shirt. An embroidered kheffiyeh cap that has seen better days is a fixture atop his balding head. His sandals are made from recycled automotive tyres.

In just a few days PJ has already decided that Ashkir is worthy of respect. Without any further questions he followed the older man outside, down a series of narrow alleyways, and into the network of fields that surround the village. Ahead he recognised Ashkir's personal patch, the borders marked with a few stones.

The crop was miserable by any standard, the plants poor and stunted. Ashkir picked one ear from the plant and peeled back the husk, showing PJ the kernels inside, still white, but just beginning to yellow.

'See?'

'Yes,' PJ said, confused, 'it looks like healthy corn.'

'Yes, good, good.'

Ashkir then tugged at PJ's sleeve and led him twenty or thirty metres away to where half a dozen villagers stood around, looking at a cob. PJ, at his host's urging, peered closely. The kernels had turned to grey mush.

'It's diseased. What is it?'

'We do not know. All we know is that the good corn is from our own seeds. Not all of it, but only a few plants are affected. The bad ones are from the seeds the aid agencies gave out in Mogadishu and we purchased. They told us these were better, that they would grow taller and make us more corn. It was a trick. They are trying to starve us.'

One of the other men shook his fist and shouted. 'They want famine for us. They want our children to die and our women to become barren.'

PJ found himself sidelined until Ashkir shushed the others, stood in front of PJ and said, 'You have travelled, what do you think? Is this a trick?'

'Do you have the bag the seed came in?'

One of the men scurried away to a lean-to shed and returned with a white bag, now filled with what appeared to be animal dung. 'This one. This is what it came in.'

Much of the printing on the side of the bag had faded, but PJ could make out the words MONSANTO. GM SEED.

'I don't know. I'm sorry. But if I can find a way to find out what has happened, and a way to make it better for you ...'

One of the younger men made a sharp exclamation. 'Better? There is no way for better. This,' he said, waving a hand at the ruined crops, 'is worse than famine. We already have famine. This is death.'

Now, the gravity of those words ringing in his head, PJ stands, rolls his sleeping mat and puts it in its place, then walks outside to where the others are already gathering. He washes with them, lines up with them into rows in the prayer hall, presses his forehead to the floor.

The imam's voice is deep, magical, and despite PJ's lack of belief, has a hypnotic effect on his soul. There is something in the cadence of ritual that calls to the subconscious, tugging with the power of the moon over the sea.

PJ mutters the responses, and notices that people no longer look sideways at him. It's as if he is now part of them. The waiting irks him, but PJ is patient. Soon, he tells himself. This is the Almohad supply route, and before long they will surely reveal themselves.

When fajr prayer is over PJ walks with Ashkir back to the house, where the two men sit together on an ancient rug. Saamiyo and the girls bring them bowls containing half a handful of ugali, and a mug of steaming cha. There is so little food, yet they always press the largest portion on him.

One of Ashkir's arms was once damaged in a vehicle rollover, and it hangs withered and useless, wrapped with scar tissue. His other arm, as if in compensation, is wiry and strong, every tendon and muscle strand visible through his skin.

He fixes his eyes on PJ, addressing him by the Somali word for *stranger*, as he has ever since PJ arrived.

'Qalaad,' he begins, 'I have news that may interest you.'

'Yes?'

'While you were still sleeping I was talking to my friend Taban. It was said that a man came to our village in the night on a motorbike. He carries a bunduq ...'

Bunduq is a local word for an AK47. Carrying such a weapon is not unusual around here.

'... and it is said that he is a courier of al-Muwahhidun.'

PJ's heart jumps and he looks sideways at the older man. 'Why would this man be of concern to me?'

Ashkir strokes his short, henna-stained beard, then grins, shows a mouthful of brown and misshapen teeth, the front two as prominent as those of a mule. 'Did you think I believe that you are Somali? Heh. I know who you are and what you seek. I hate al-Muwahhidun too. They will not let aid come to us. They take any food that comes. I know you hunt them, for you walk like a hunter of men.'

PJ shakes his head. 'I don't hunt men. I hunt the truth, perhaps, but only a rogue lion hunts men.'

'In my youth, I, too, was a killer. I carried a bunduq for the leader of my clan, and I hunted men like you do now.' He holds up his withered arm. 'And then this happened, and I was no good to him any more. A warlord needs men who are whole, and can fight like animals. I was like that once.'

PJ looks down at the rug for a moment, a half-smile on his face. 'Where is this courier of al-Muwahhidun now?'

'In the home of Roble Abdikarim. You must hurry, though. He professes to be on urgent business, and will leave as soon as he has eaten.'

'Will you show me where he is?'

'No, it would attract attention.' He shouts a command, and a moment later the eldest of the three daughters, a girl of sixteen or seventeen, comes through. The hijab veil hides her hair but leaves a pleasant and appealing face open to view.

'Ayanna, take Qalaad to the home of Roble Abdikarim. Not too close. Just show him, then creep home.'

PJ studies the girl. In all his time here they have exchanged no words. Her eyes are beautiful — dark molten brown — yet a glimpse of her neck betrays just how thin she is.

Overcome by the desire to do something for these people, from an inner pocket PJ extracts a single one-hundred-dollar note, calculating that at current exchange rates, that note is worth something like a quarter of a million Somali shillings.

He folds the note and hands it to Ashkir. 'Here. This is for you, and your family.'

The man's eyes widen, and his chest rises and falls as if with sudden emotion. 'I cannot accept such a fortune. It is too much.'

'You might find this hard to believe, but it is very little to me. Take it, please.'

'Then you must be a wealthy man.'

PJ smiles, clasps the older man by the shoulders and kisses first one cheek and then the other. 'I owe you more than that.'

'Go with God,' Ashkir says softly, and PJ walks away without another word.

The home of Roble Abdikarim is at the other side of the village, and PJ walks casually, as if he is just another male on chaperone duty. Ayanna does not look at him even once, and he walks a pace behind so she can direct him.

Finally, past blocks of abandoned stone houses, they enter the village souk. Market stalls of ageing timber, vendors sitting placidly or bargaining hard with the few customers. Some sell fruit, seeds, or Western processed goods in jars. To one side is a halal goat butcher, attended by hordes of flies. Goat entrails thrown out a side window have attracted a squabbling crowd of cats, vultures, storks and crows.

Past the souk, up a rise, then ahead lies a more substantial home with hens foraging near the front door. Livestock are a sign of relative affluence here.

Ayanna gestures with one arm, her face betraying nothing. PJ wants to thank her, but she turns and starts walking away, back towards her father's home, as if he no longer exists.

Putting her from his mind PJ walks closer to the house. Parked outside the front wall he sees the dusty motorbike on its stand. A trail bike, a Yamaha XT250, with a pair of plastic jerry cans, their red polyethylene skin faded to pale pink by the sun, strapped to the rack behind the pillion.

Two men exit the house. One PJ recognises from the prayer hall, and the other is a stranger, AK47 slung over one shoulder, dressed in mismatched camo, with a handgun in a canvas holster on his belt. The older man is speaking. PJ steps into the shadows, listening, but out of sight.

'The west road is open as far as Barwaaqo. After that, I do not know.'

'But that is the quickest way?'

'Yes.'

'Then bring me food, and I'll leave now.'

After a shouted command from the older man, a woman, presumably his wife, appears with a bowl of food. The courier looks at it, sniffs disapprovingly, then smashes it out of her hands with his right fist. Somali corn porridge splatters to the ground and the bowl cracks into three or more pieces.

'Ugali, damn you woman,' the courier snarls. 'Don't bring me peasant food that will make a mess in my pack. Bring me meat.'

The woman massages her injured hand, but does not let the pain show on her face, merely backing away until she leans against the shoulder of her husband, who stands his ground, glaring balefully. It is he who speaks next, 'We have no more meat. You ate it last night.'

The courier's face is murderous, and for a moment PJ suspects that he is about to use his AK47 on the old couple, an action that would necessitate a rapid intervention.

'Go to hell, you stinking old turds. If I see you again, I'll shoot you.'

As the courier mounts the motorbike and kicks the starter, PJ knows that he has just a small window of time in which to work.

On the fringes of the village's western side, where arid winds from the interior strike first, the desert is coming back to reclaim its own. Sand piles in drifts against the walls. Eventually they will be covered over, and there will be no sign that humankind once eked out a living here.

Not a single tree, not even the meanest acacia, stands within miles of the village, all having long ago been cut for firewood, to make charcoal, or for building material. PJ walks through the dry bed of a wadi then up the other side, paralleling the track into the village until he comes level with the crossroads, where a few people, livestock, and vehicles have gathered, villagers selling what remains of their meagre produce.

Still PJ keeps his distance, stopping at the ruins of a fence, taking twenty metres of plain fencing wire. With no wire-cutting tools he grasps a short length between either hand, working at it, twisting, bending, over and over before it breaks off, hot from the movement beneath his fingers. Finally he rolls the full length into a coil and carries it with him, tabbing at least a kilometre parallel to the west road before angling in at a steady pace. The Almohad courier is the one chance yet presented to him, and he can't afford to waste it.

At the roadside itself he stands on a hillock from which he can see the crossroads. When a beaten-up old truck comes down that way he hides, and likewise when a few old men and their camels lumber up the road.

When they have passed out of sight, PJ hears the motorbike engine, approaching the crossroads, engine buzzing like a chainsaw as it does so.

Adrenalin floods into PJ's veins as he hurries down to the road. After all, he has no weapon apart from a knife he purchased in Kal, and the courier has both an AK47 and a handgun.

There are still no trees, and this site offers the advantage of high ground with its view of the crossroads, but also some Siad Barre-era road signs on either side of the road, all but ruined by bullets, age and rust.

PJ winds one end of the wire around the pole at shoulder height, using a haywire twist and a barrel roll to secure it. Then, crossing the road, relieved at having more than enough length in the wire, he stretches it tight and secures it at the same level. Finally, with the buzz of the motorbike already increasing in volume, he scrambles into a ditch just back from the verge, moulding his body and limbs to the dry ground.

The motorbike climbs through the last of the gears, the engine near redlining. Just before he strikes the wire, the helmetless rider appears to see the barrier. He ducks, but not low enough. As if in slow motion, PJ sees the wire snap the head back, bike and rider skidding off the road, stopping nearby with the front wheel spinning drunkenly.

PJ jumps up, running to the man now lying near the bike. He makes no move, his head bent to an impossible angle.

'Shit!' He wanted a machine to ride and a man to question, not a corpse and a ruined bike. He dismantles the wire trap before it kills someone else, rolling it up and throwing it away.

Then, back beside the disabled bike, he notes the badly bent front wheel, annoyed that it is no longer rideable. He manhandles the machine into a deeper section of the roadside ditch, throws earth over it, then uses his feet to scuff away the worst of the marks made by the crash.

Finally, he takes the dead man by the arms and drags him away from the road, keeping on until he is screened from view by a dune, thick with whistling thorn bushes. Here he works to get the green backpack off his shoulders, unfastening the straps and looking inside. The largest object is a box cushioned in bubble wrap. This he places on the ground, then looks again. There is a water bottle, a Mars bar and a tobacco tin. He opens the latter to find it filled with qat.

He turns back to the box, slitting the bubble wrap with his knife. Inside is a curved glass tube, purple in colour, that appears to be some kind of globe. Lab supplies? A prickle of excitement, yet regret fills his head. *If only I had taken him alive*, he thinks.

The man carries a wallet, and a government pass shows his name as Erasto Mohammed Korfa.

In a side flap of the bag he finds a folded paper map with a pencil line around a place that appears to be around one hundred and fifty kilometres distant. A remote area, circled by hills. PJ shakes his head. An amateur. The leadership would have cut his balls off, literally, for making such a simple error as marking his destination on a map.

Looking at the dead man for a moment, PJ makes a decision and starts to remove his clothes, starting with the boots, then the camo shirt, belt, trousers and cap. He strips down to his own underwear and dresses in the dead man's clothes; small and tight across the shoulders, but, leaving the top buttons undone, the fit is bearable.

Loosening the gun belt a couple of notches he checks the holster, recognising the butt of a Soviet made Makarov pistol. A smaller pouch holds a spare magazine packed with fresh rounds. He has just strapped on the backpack and picked up the AK47 when a sound from behind has him turning, thumb and forefinger pulling back the slide, a round slamming into the chamber, hand moving to the grip, finger tightening on the trigger.

There was a time when he might have mowed the figure down — but he is conscious of the trouble gunshots might bring, and this hesitation gives him time to recognise that this is an unarmed female. As he lowers the muzzle of the weapon he realises that she might have been watching while he dragged a dead man across the road, then dressed and undressed.

'What are you doing?' he asks, recognising Ashkir's daughter, Ayanna. 'I thought you went home.'

The young woman has changed clothes, he sees, into what must be her best — a striking green patterned kikoi that covers her body, head, shoulders, coupled with a hijab of the same colour. She carries a cloth bundle of possessions on her head. Not much — the size of a shoebox.

Ayanna walks towards him, pausing a pace or two away, at which point she kneels, puts down her bundle, and touches her head to his feet. This done, she stands again, all but her brown eyes covered.

'I am yours now,' she says, 'I go where you go.'

PJ feels a surge of pure panic. 'Bollocks you are,' he says in English, then switches back to Somali. 'No. Go home.'

'I can't, my father will beat me, he says that you shamed him with your generosity and that he must give me up in payment.'

PJ squats down in the dust, then points to the half-naked corpse lying on the ground. 'You saw that I killed this man. I go from here to great danger. You can't come with me.'

He reaches down for the jacket he just removed and slips out the rest of the cash, choosing another note. 'Take this back to your father, and tell him that this is your dowry. That you'll be able to marry whoever you like.'

'More money would only shame him further.'

PJ stands, knowing that he is wasting valuable time. 'I'm sorry, but you can't come with me. It's just not possible.'

Tears roll down her cheeks. 'I cannot go back.'

Swearing under his breath, PJ bends down and begins to scratch a shallow grave in a hollow for the Almohad courier before rolling him inside and covering it over. He looks up to see her still waiting. 'I'm going now, and you can't follow.' He pauses. 'I hope things improve here for you. If I can do anything for your village — later — I'll do so.'

With the AK47 looped over his shoulder and the pack settled high on his shoulders, he starts to walk away. When he looks back she is at the graveside, saying a prayer for the man he just killed, wishing him a swift road to Jannah and safe passage.

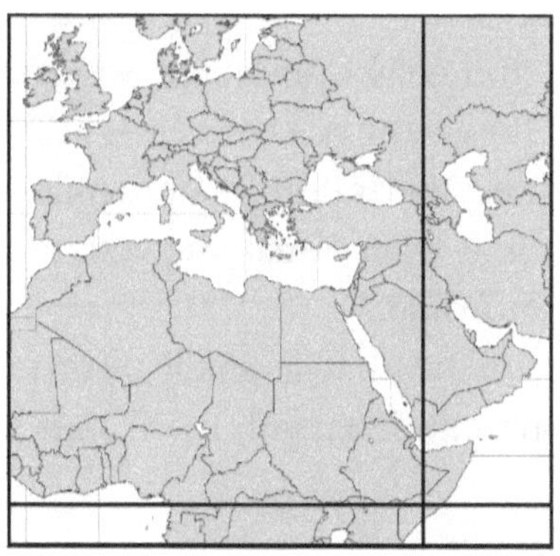

60 SOMALIA

Ka Tirsan

Istikaan's belief that he is doing God's work never falters. From Faw he flies into Saudi Arabia. From there a chartered flight takes him first to Addis Ababa, then to an uncontrolled desert airstrip at the village of Dugaag.

Finally, they arrive at what looks like a small and insignificant Somali village, surrounded by steep, stony hills. The only real difference is the airstrip they smoothed from the desert landscape. As they walk further they pass a FIM-92 Stinger SAM emplacement, so carefully screened that it is invisible from more than a few paces' distance.

Saif al-Din clasps Istikaan in a heart-warming show of brotherhood. A hundred voices shout *Allahu Akbar* together, so loud that the echoes bounce off the hills. They sit in a circle and Istikaan recounts what happened while the others listen gravely, drinking mint tea.

Istikaan meets the ten men who have been through the flight training regimen. They are competent-looking, and Saif assures him that they are devout and committed. There are faces from many different places here — allied groups such as Indonesia's Jemaah Islamiyah, and cells from major Western cities.

'Each has now flown thirty hours. It will be ten more by the time we have finished the training.' Saif smiles at Istikaan. 'Now, I imagine that you will want to eat and rest, then get started after fajr prayers in the morning.'

Istikaan shakes his head. The smell of revenge is close in his nostrils. 'If you don't mind, Sayyid, I will start now.'

Within an hour, after washing and a meal, he opens the door to the laboratory. Everything here was designed to his specifications, and the work that has been done in his absence pleases him.

The laboratory was originally a demountable shower block for an AMISOM garrison near Mogadishu, now heavily modified with some internal walls and plumbing removed, sealed as fully as is possible here. Anything less is inviting death for the operators before the work can be finished. Istikaan is proud of the facility. It is raw, but as effective as something costing a hundred times as much.

The proximity of the bacteria spores themselves is a thrill for Istikaan — the Vollum LSS-253 that is his own special work. Something that exists nowhere else in the world. They tried to replicate it in Syria, of course, but the work was cut short by the fall of al-Assad.

This strain is the culmination of a process begun in a private meeting with the Ba'athist dictator Saddam Hussein and his son Qusay, commander of Amn al-Khas. 'The work at al-Hajjuf is going well,' Istikaan had said, 'but to create the super strain you require, it is necessary to use human hosts.'

He was told to prepare the site. That living subjects would be arranged.

Istikaan used an expansive budget to build a prison within a laboratory. Waiting impatiently for the first truckloads of subjects, knowing that he was about to be given an opportunity not seen since German doctors ran experimental labs in Nazi death camps, or the Japanese cruelties in Manchuria.

The victims were, in the main, Kurdish or Ma'dan, a mix of male and female, including children and the elderly. They came in trucks, escorted by the psychopathic killers of Amn al-Khas.

After four years of watching human beings die behind glass windows in the inhalation chamber, the infection rate from aerosol spore dispersal went from 68 per cent to 93 per cent, the death rate from 72 per cent to 88 per cent and, most importantly, average time from contact to death went from just under eight days to fewer than three.

Antibiotic resistance was an important aim of the program, and considerable time and effort went into producing an antibiotic-resistant variety of the new hyper-lethal strain.

Down the far end is a tiny cubicle that serves as his office, and Istikaan spends a few minutes getting his notes in order before picking up a short-range UHF set that is used for communication at Ka Tirsan. These units have a range of less than three kilometres, and are very difficult for the kufr to detect.

'I am ready,' he says, 'to start work.'

He has trained a team of eight men — all good, respectful workers — and the first task is getting one of the flasks contained. Moving it into the sealed units where it can be opened, and a sample of spores extracted. One reason for this is to prepare cultures and begin the process of growing more LSS-253, increasing the stocks and ensuring that his life's work never dies. It will be a weapon they can use in perpetuity. Turning the cities of the kufr into uninhabited shells.

Long after midnight, two men and a woman are brought in, cuffed and bound. They are all very dark Somalis from the southern regions. They had been caught in the village of Xagar, fornicating together. The rumours had circulated and one day the local imam had reported them to al-Muwahhidun, who set the trap. The offenders would have been put to death on the spot if Istikaan had not asked for living, human subjects.

The three are a meagre sample after the glory days at al-Hajjuf, but circumstances have changed, and Istikaan is willing to adapt. Besides, this is a simple test — made for one reason only — to be certain that the spores are as virulent now as the day they were manufactured.

There is no time or facility for an inhalation test, only for the less lethal, but faster acting injection. Istikaan works with delicious excitement, injecting the serum into the upper arms of first the woman, then the two men, relishing the frightened eyes and death-sweat smell of them. The first of millions of victims of LSS-253.

As the three subjects are taken away to their makeshift cell — a shipping container next to the lab — Istikaan glories in the knowledge that only he truly knows how potent that strain has become. The knowledge that he now possesses 4.7 tonnes of spores in a Somali valley. Enough to kill more than one billion human beings. The knowledge that he has the instruments for the delivery here ready, designed to fit the stainless steel pressure flasks made in Iraq so long ago. The so-called Zubaidy machines that are able to mix the spores with Bentonite dust before spraying them out from an aircraft, well back in the slipstream, so the pilot and operator are not infected.

When it is almost dawn, just before the Muezzin's call rises and falls hauntingly across the dry air of that valley, Istikaan goes to the tiny office and reaches to a high shelf. There he finds a rusted tin. Inside, sealed in a plastic bag, is the note written from the other side all those years ago. He holds it in his hand, reading the faded handwriting on the folded top: *To the Living from the Dead.*

Tomorrow, Istikaan says to himself, *I will open it tomorrow.*

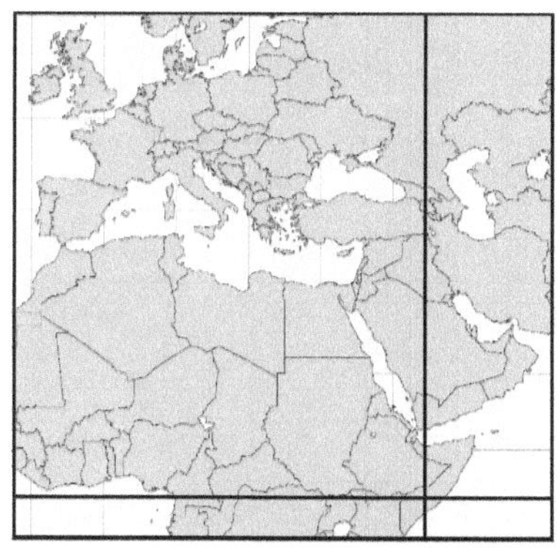

61 SOMALIA

Kal

PJ's plan is to hitchhike, paying his way north if necessary, but traffic is light, perhaps one vehicle every two hours. There are few people here now — famine and war have emptied the land. Fuel, moreover, is both expensive and scarce. By noon just two vehicles have passed. One was an ancient utility overloaded with humanity, children and adults alike, riding on the cab roof; the other a dull grey AMISOM Unimog truck, bristling with men and guns.

He makes good time over flat ground and hard-beaten road. He wishes he had his Sid — the devices make navigation so easy — but instead he has the unexpected treasure of a folded map, and an innate sense of direction that has never failed him.

By mid-afternoon, however, it is so hot that he is forced off the road to find shade, drink, and to rest, deciding to start walking again in the cool of the evening. He drinks half the water in the bottle, then sits while flies crawl across his eyelids and nostrils.

An hour passes, then another, and it seems to PJ the sun no longer burns as hot. He drinks a little more of the water, and stands, ready to move off, when he sees a green shape, sitting in the shade of an umbrella thorn tree a hundred metres away. He feels a sharp jab of annoyance and strides across.

'Ayanna. How did you get here?'

'I walked, like you did.'

'I told you. It's not possible for you to come with me.'

'I cannot go back.'

'Have you had any water?'

'No.'

He takes the bottle from his pack, unscrews the cap and hands it to her.

She refuses to take it. 'You need it more than me.'

'Drink!'

Responding to the commanding tone in his voice, she lifts the bottle to her lips, takes a bird-like sip, then hands it back.

He squats down beside her. 'What the hell am I going to do with you?'

Her eyes fix directly on his face. There is a strength in her, he can sense that, yet she is scarcely more than a child. The entire history of the famines, the wars, of this abused country of hers, is told in a few moments of looking into her eyes.

'I cannot go back,' she says again.

'What if I give you money? You could hitch a ride to the city.'

'Alone I would have no chance. Bad men do terrible things to women in Mogadishu and Kismaayo. I would be helpless.' Her chin lifts. 'I would sooner kill myself.'

PJ shakes his head, thinking ruefully that this is not the first time he has been outmanoeuvred by a woman. 'OK. I'll take you to the next village and pay the mullah to feed you — make sure you are sheltered. Understand?'

'Yes.'

'Then get up and let's go. I don't have time to waste.'

As soon as they have settled into a rhythm of walking, she a little behind and on his left side, he pauses. 'How far is the next village, and what's it called?'

'The next village is called Beraaley. I think that if we walk at this pace we will be there a little after dusk.'

PJ feels a slight easing of the tension her reappearance has caused. 'That's good. I'll make sure you're looked after there.'

They keep walking, and always she keeps to his rear. He finds this unnerving, her voice coming from behind so he cannot see her facial expressions.

'If you leave me at Beraaley, you will forget about me,' she says after a while. 'I will rot there.' PJ feels his shoulders stiffen as she goes on. 'Besides, the emir of Beraaley is a very bad man, and lecherous. He will probably rape me as soon as you are gone, and maybe his brothers will do so as well.'

PJ swears to himself in English before switching back into Somali. 'You're not making this easy for me.'

'Is everything supposed to be easy? Of course it is — you are a Westerner.'

He stops walking, turns and stares at her in disbelief, wondering at how the doe-eyed creature who would not say a word before is now arguing with him like a ... wife?

Saying nothing, he turns back and quickens his pace, yet this does not disconcert her in the slightest. She skips a few steps to catch up until she is again directly behind. 'You will stand out less in the desert with a woman at your side. People are suspicious of lone males.'

PJ has to concede that she has a point. 'OK, but the question is, what the hell do I do with you when I leave — or if I have to go into danger?' He stops, looking at her, trying to think of an argument that might convince her. 'You are a beautiful young woman, and smart too. If you come with me you might ruin your future.'

Tears form in the rounded crescent of her eyes, pooling along the bottom edge. 'My future? A future of scraping from meal to meal, of obeying my father in everything. That is, if he would take me back now. His honour is more important than my life, I can tell you.' Her voice takes on a note of incredulity. 'Why do you fret about what might happen later? We have a saying here in Somalia. "Today is the king, let tomorrow become."'

PJ says not another word, just walks away into the desert, hearing her feet behind him, knowing that short of physically restraining her, there is no way of stopping her now.

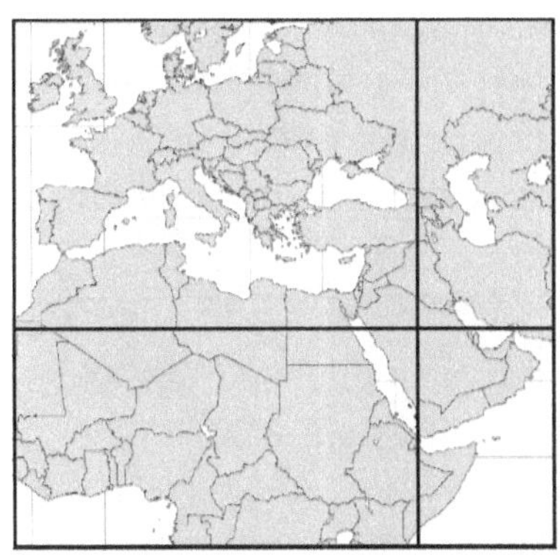

62 SAUDI ARABIA

Riyadh

Ronnie Booth feels a senseless rage against the world. Military terminals are the pits, and this one, outside of Riyadh, is one of the worst. The others are inside in the air conditioning while they wait for a flight to Arba Minch. He sits outside on a bench in the shade, ignoring the hot desert wind and locust plagues of dust that sweep across the tarmac.

The headphones in his ears deliver Megadeth at a volume that would deafen most people. He likes all the hard bands of his youth — AC/DC, Judas Priest, Iron Maiden — but Megadeth are his favourite. They understand ugliness. That life can be a bitch.

As he listens, the bass drum hammers in his mind, the lead guitar climbing ladder-like scales at dizzying speeds. He looks around, reaches into his bag. Refills the flask with Beefeater gin. Screws the bottle back up and slips it back inside. The flask goes to his lips, then into a side pocket of his combat jacket.

It pisses him off that Marika Hartmann is swanning around the world, running private informers, accusing him of not doing his job properly when she's so wet behind the ears that she …

Ronnie takes another drink. It was OK when he was with Jean. She made everything alright. Knew how to take the bad stuff out of him when he returned from a mission. Drawing it out over a couple of days so he could smile again. Now she's gone and there's nothing.

He takes out the flask, swigs again, then lets his hand creep to the packet of mints in his right-hand pocket.

'Damn them. Damn them all to hell.'

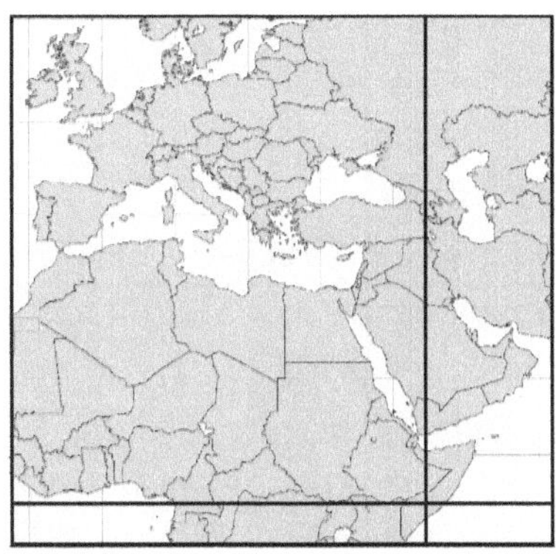

63 SOMALIA

Beraaley

By sunset Ayanna is no longer just behind PJ. Looking back, he can see her, kneeling on a prayer mat, facing roughly north with the sunset on her left side, her head pressed close to the earth. Even from here he can hear her murmuring voice. He waits for her, watching this creature of the desert communicate with her god.

The prayer is soon over, and she looks around, meets his eyes, then picks up her bundle before coming after him at that same indefatigable pace. He knows how little she has eaten in the previous days and wonders what keeps her following Qalaad, the stranger, into the unknown. Hope, perhaps, of a better life. The weight of expectation bows him, because he is on a mission that is more important than her life, or his.

They walk into the night, relying on the last glow of dusk until moon rise. The village of Beraaley is so close they can hear goats arguing in the night.

PJ stops, and they stand together. Two shadows. 'Please,' he says, 'go to the village. Seek the protection of the imam. He'll look after you.'

'Don't make me do that. I will become a slave — wash clothes, empty chamber pots and scrub from dawn to dusk each day. They will feed me scraps from the table … if I am lucky.'

'I can offer you nothing.'

'There is nothing in every direction I turn. Please let me follow.'

PJ doesn't argue, just starts to walk in tacit acceptance. For an hour or more neither one of them says a word, and then, in a small gully beside a hillock, he turns to her. 'Wait here.'

He climbs to the peak and examines the landscape in all directions, looking for lights, movement, anything that might indicate danger. Satisfied, he descends to where she waits.

'We'll rest here for a few hours,' he tells her. 'There's nothing to eat, sorry. Maybe in the morning.'

Ayanna disappears into the desert for a few minutes, returning with a bundle of sticks. Squatting on the earth, she unwraps her roll, producing a battered disposable cigarette lighter. Soon she has a hot little blaze going. Also from the roll she gets a small pot, a yellow paste and some pre-cooked rice.

The warmth, light and smell of cooking food induces a flare of pleasure in PJ. 'Well, you're a little surprise package, aren't you.' PJ settles back on his haunches. 'You seem happy enough,' he continues. 'Most girls your age would be devastated to have left home.'

She glances up. 'You can tell what my heart is feeling, can you?'

'No. Not at all.'

A minute of uncomfortable silence, then, 'I am sorry there is no spare water for cha,' she says, as if the situation is entirely her fault. She takes the tiny pan off the dying flames, removes a small portion onto another dish, then passes him the pan with nine-tenths of the food on it.

'That's way too much — you've got hardly anything.'

'That's all I want. I'm not hungry.'

He watches her eyes as she begins to eat with her hands, chewing each of those few mouthfuls twenty or thirty times at least. Using his hand, he drops a portion of his own food into her dish

'Don't argue. Eat it.'

She doesn't say a word, just lifts her eyes to indicate her displeasure at the command. They eat in silence until the food is gone.

'You're pretty smart,' PJ says finally. 'Have you ever been to school?'

'No. Will you teach me to speak English?'

'What, now?'

'Yes.'

'You can't learn something like that in five minutes.'

'But if you never start because there may not be enough time, then you will never start.'

PJ throws back his head and laughs. 'Not now,' he says, 'but thanks for the food.' He scratches a hollow for his hip in the earth and lies down with the backpack as a pillow, wondering how much of the family store of rice was sent along with Ayanna. Then he remembers the money. Perhaps they have already been able to purchase food with what he gave them. The thought makes him feel better as he watches Ayanna scrape her cooking utensils clean, pack up her bundle, and then, to his amazement, stretch herself out alongside him and snuggle back into his body.

He sits up, spluttering. 'No. I'll let you walk with me, but I'm not going to sleep with you pressed up against me. What are you trying to do, seduce me or something? Is that what your father told you to do?'

Ayanna lifts her upper body from the earth, back arching in the cobra position, eyes blazing. 'Are you so arrogant to think that I would give myself to a man without commitment and marriage?'

Raising himself on one elbow, he says, 'I'm sorry. I didn't mean it that way.'

'Well, I am not some cheap street tart of the city — obviously the kind of female you are used to.'

PJ thinks back to a day in Djibouti, when he had been tempted. 'That's not the kind of female I'm used to.'

Her voice lowers, becoming soft and wistful. 'I bet you have many wives, each of them more beautiful than the last. And twenty, thirty children — handsome boys, and beautiful girls ...'

'I don't have any wives.'

'None?'

PJ shakes his head. 'No.'

'Not even one?'

'No.'

She looks lost for a moment, eyes huge in the moonlight. Then, her face lights up, as if she has found the answer. 'Ah, then you have concubines — in all the great cities of the world. Riyadh, Cairo, Beirut, Nairobi, Mogadishu. In each of them you have a concubine. They live in fine apartments, perhaps with a view across the ocean. You bring them gifts from your travels, and ...'

'Ayanna, I'm sorry to ruin your fun, but that's not true either. I don't even have a girlfriend.'

Now her forehead furrows in deep thought. 'You are not,' she asks, 'of the persuasion of Lot?'

'No,' he says, smiling at the reference, which appears in both the Qur'an and the Bible — a euphemism for homosexuality. 'I like women.'

'Are there any, in particular, that you like?'

PJ shakes his head, unsure why he's willing to bare his soul in the wilderness to this young woman who he scarcely knows. 'Yes, there's one that I like.'

'Then I am jealous of her already. What is her name?'

'That's my secret.'

'Is she beautiful?'

'That's not the right word. She is very attractive, and strong.'

'I am still jealous.'

'If she was here she would have you under her wing in a moment. She has a heart the size of Africa.'

'She would teach me English? Right now?'

'Wouldn't surprise me. But look, I didn't say I wouldn't teach you — just that I wasn't going to start at ten o'clock at night. OK?'

When she doesn't reply, he settles back down into the bed of sand, grinding his hips and shoulders in until he is comfortable. 'Now get some sleep. We have a long walk ahead of us.'

Again she snuggles down into the sand beside him, not touching, yet close, and the depth of her trust astounds him. Within a minute or two the rhythm of her breathing becomes regular. There, with the stars in the dark sky, he feels a sense of privilege. That wonderful things can lurk in the hidden corners of life, waiting to be discovered.

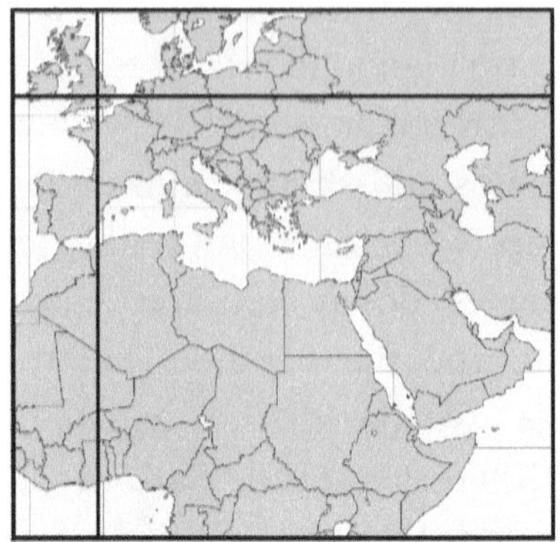

64 UNITED KINGDOM

London

With a small amount of grumbling, Will Grace, the Watcher, becomes one of those co-opted into staring at a screen all day. And it is he who Marika finds shaking her by the shoulder at ten past three in the morning.

She has been asleep at the desk, head on her hands.

'Hey, wake up.'

She looks blearily up at him. 'What do you want?'

'One of the girls has found something that looks promising.'

'Where?'

'In Sector K28. Where we thought it might be.'

Marika stands, thinks about detouring into the en suite to empty her bladder but decides against it. A quick decision might be vital.

Personnel are crowded around one screen. They look up as she enters. Of course, they should all be at their own terminals, still searching.

'OK, just give me a bit of room.'

Her eyes focus on the screen as she leans forward, studies the image: some buildings, tracks, and perhaps ... an airstrip. She turns to the trained analyst beside her.

'Is it worth a look?'

'Definitely. I'll stake my career on a light plane taking off and landing there forty-five minutes ago.'

'Good work.' She pages Tom Mossel with her Sid. He will want to be here.

Marika feels the mustard-seed burn of anticipation in her veins as she picks up the bag that has been sitting packed and ready against a wall for three days.

'Are you going there now?' Will Grace asks.

'Right this minute. And you, my friend, are driving me to the airport.'

Al-Shabaab was one of the first groups to use articulate participation in social media to disseminate their viewpoints, through their @HSMPress Twitter account — used to provoke, legitimise, explain, and correct what they see as inaccurate media reports. Infamously, they used this account to post images of dog-tags taken from Burundian prisoners they had captured and killed.

Al-Muwahhidun use Twitter, Facebook, Quora, Tumblr and half a dozen other outlets to provide interpretation, recruit, and allow interested outsiders to ask questions. Of course, a large proportion of the followers are either journalists or media outlets, giving the organisation considerable power.

Istikaan finds Saif al-Din at his desk, handling a multitude of tasks. A laptop computer is open. 'You asked for me?'

Saif finishes typing, then looks up, 'Yes. In a few minutes I will call all the brothers here together to make an announcement. I thought, however, that I might tell you first.'

'Yes?'

'Today the kufr sent a series of missiles into the heart of al-Muwahhidun.'

'Your council?'

'Yes. There are no survivors.'

'That is terrible.'

'Yes. A cataclysm.'

'I'm sorry to hear that,' Istikaan says, but he is studying Saif's eyes. *We*, Istikaan says to himself, *are brothers indeed. Your ambition knows no bounds. You reach for power with both hands.*

Saif returns his gaze. 'Have you tested the efficacy of the spores? Time has not weakened them?'

Istikaan's eyes dart hungrily. 'Come with me.'

Together they walk past the lab to the shipping container, and with three guards standing ready the doors are thrown open. Istikaan points inside. 'Bring them out, one at a time.'

The female has already been affected profoundly. On her upper arm is a massive swelling with a glowing red lesion like a burning coal at the centre. This ugly wound is surrounded by black, crusty scabs. It is these characteristics that give anthrax its English name — the same etymology as anthracite, or coal. She cannot speak, can only make weak mewing sounds from the back of her throat.

The first of the males is a little better. The wound not so developed, yet still severe.

The third victim they drag out by the ankles. Istikaan rolls back the man's eyelids so the bloodshot whites are visible. Dead.

'The spores,' Istikaan says, 'are as virulent as the day they were made.'

Saif al-Din nods. 'I can see that, but they have never been used operationally. This is a major project, with many of our resources devoted to it. The cost will be considerable.' He lowers his voice, eyes grave. The idea has been building for several days. 'A serious test would throw the enemy into disarray while our assets disperse.'

Istikaan smiles, showing two oversized brown incisors. 'That is an excellent idea, Sayyid. When and where?'

'One day from now.'

'Yes. It can be done.'

Saif thinks for a moment. 'We must move on from this place within that same timeframe. You need to prepare all the deliveries.'

'I suspect you are right.'

'They will find us soon. Maybe an hour, a day, or a week. We have a weapon beyond imagination. This situation might never arise again. We need to divide it so it cannot be destroyed in its entirety, and send out the men who will deliver the Tide of Saleh to the world.'

'I understand, Sayyid.'

'Go then. Tell the men that I will address them.'

While Istikaan goes on ahead, Saif swallows the last of his store of opium pellets before heading outside to where the mujahedin have gathered, standing in rows with their weapons, the yellow sun striking their faces. Saif waits until they are thus assembled before he leaves the building, stopping ten metres from them and shouting, using his voice like a cannon.

'Today, the enemy forces struck at our hearts. Today we are bleeding, but they have also given us even more reason to strike back. They killed our leaders in one swoop, so that I have had to take on a massive burden of responsibility. Today I assume the leadership of al-Muwahhidun across the world.' Tears coat his cheeks. 'Today we have lost men who I loved. How can I ever feel good again? Only with the blood of their murderers!

'Give me their blood. Give me their heads, and make a present of their entrails to me. Kill them all. There is no longer reason for mercy, for they have proved themselves to be beyond the pale.'

The roar in response comes from the throats of fifty men.

'Let us prepare ourselves for the final push to victory!'

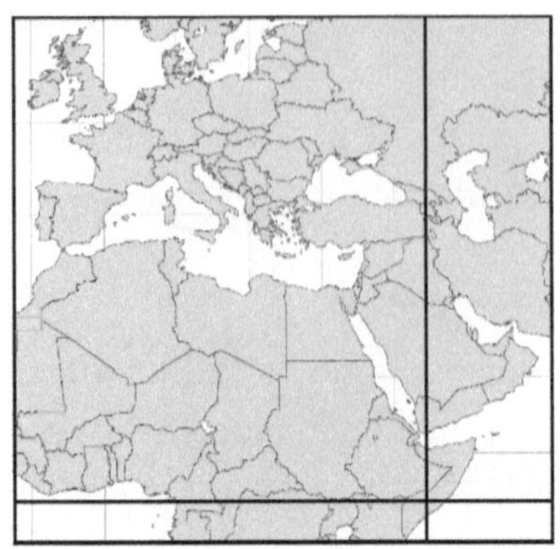

65 SOMALIA

Beraaley

Having no watch, PJ relies on the moon. When he wakes the pale crescent sits at a forty-five-degree angle in the sky, so he estimates that it is around 0400 hours. This is a good time to get moving, making the most of the cool night while it lasts.

Almost as soon as he sits up Ayanna wakes also, saying nothing, but getting up and walking well away from the camp. In the silence PJ can hear a pitiful trickle of water as she relieves herself.

He is surprised, for he has no desire to urinate. Her body, he decides, must be more efficient at utilising what she drinks than his. When she returns she looks vulnerable in the moonlight, softer than the day before. He feels an overwhelming urge to protect her.

'We might as well get going,' he says. 'Are you rested?'

'I am ready when you are.'

PJ buckles on his backpack and AK47 and waits for her to assemble her belongings. Then, without another word, he steps off towards the north. Ayanna seems to be more confident in his presence, walking alongside when there is space, following close behind when there is not. It is comforting to have her there, and even though he is a trained Special Forces point man, her senses are more acute than his.

On one occasion she taps his shoulder, signalling him to silence. Then, as he walks forward, holding the AK47 ready to fire from the hip, they hear the sound of a goat running and a man chasing it, calling to it. They stand still, and before long the stark pre-dawn world slips back into silence.

PJ slings the assault rifle back over his shoulder and continues on, conscious towards dawn that Ayanna is starting to slow. He is feeling the pace himself, which would be punishing enough for well-fed athletes. There is no water, and his mouth feels as though he has swallowed a spoonful of dry sand. He can feel his tongue swelling and a crack on his lip developing, just starting to bleed.

He cannot leave it alone, as if his tongue seeks out the moisture of the blood and the salts of his own body. Yet the moisture is an illusion; an organism cannot feed on itself and live. Salt serves only to drive his thirst.

Before long PJ stops to rest in the shade of some giant rocks. A small mammal not much bigger than a rabbit appears from nowhere, running across their path and disappearing into the brush at the base of the stone.

Ayanna starts after it, and PJ wonders why she would bother. It would be impossible to catch and would have little meat on it anyway.

He takes the opportunity to check the map, now that there is light to see. Getting a fix on their exact location is difficult without a GPS, a compass or regular landmarks, but the rising sun gives him a good approximation. The hillock they now occupy appears to be marked and named, though it is not clear from the map whether this name applies to the stretch of desert plain or the hillock. The line of hills up ahead are clearly those the courier has marked, the ridges and peaks matching the contour lines.

'A couple of hours to go,' PJ tells Ayanna. But this proximity to their destination heightens his worry at what they will do when they get there. They both need water and can hardly just roam into an Almohad camp and demand some.

Ayanna appears uninterested, casting about on the rocks, getting down on all fours and peering into crevices, even feeling down into a crack with her hand. He watches curiously for a minute, then says, 'What are you trying to do, get bitten by a mamba?'

The look she shoots back at him is that of an adult towards an unthinking child.

PJ folds the map and places it back in the pack, which he slings over his back as he stands, feeling vertigo combine with exhaustion to almost make him swoon. He feels a twinge of irritation towards her. 'Come on. Time to get moving.'

'Please,' she says, 'wait.'

Frowning with impatience, he watches her lie on a plate of shattered rock, one arm disappearing into a crevice. A smile lights her face as she rolls back to her feet, unrolls her bundle and removes an enamel mug. Then, lying at full stretch again, down goes the arm, mug in hand.

When she brings it back it is plainly heavy. 'Here,' she says, 'take it.'

When PJ takes the mug from her hands he is surprised at the weight. Even more surprised to see it half-full of discoloured water. 'How the hell did you do that?'

The pleasure in her face at the find has not diminished. 'The little hyrax showed us where the water is hidden, so we can drink too. That is his gift to us.'

'You drink first. You found the water.'

'No, there is plenty there. We can have as much as we want.'

PJ lifts the mug to his lips and drinks. The sensation is half-pleasurable, half-painful as his swollen cheeks, tongue and lips come to life. His stomach growls like stressed timber.

True to her word she removes enough water, bit by bit, so that they are both satiated. Much as he was amazed that she could manage to produce urine that morning, now he is stunned at her capacity to drink. He manages seven or eight mugs while she puts away at least fifteen. It leaves him wondering if her buttocks store water, like those of Kalahari Bushmen, but there is no visible change under her kikoi.

When they have had enough, she uses more water to wash the utensils they used the previous night.

'It's amazing,' PJ says. 'Obviously when it rains the water trickles down there and pools under the rock. But it hasn't rained for ages here.'

'It would have fallen back in the long rains, or even years ago,' Ayanna says, 'but if only the very small creatures can use it, it will stay. Lucky for us no one else found it, or they might have cracked the rock to get to it, or stuck a pipe in there and pumped it out.'

While PJ fills the water bottle she moves away twenty paces with a saucepan full of water, and there she scrubs her teeth, arms, hands, feet, ankles and face. This done, she spreads her prayer mat. From where he sits PJ can hear the low murmur of her voice as she prays, her forehead touching the earth at intervals.

Against the backdrop of the rising sun, he feels a shiver that is not entirely from the cool morning air on the skin of his arms. When she is done they will move on. Somehow he finds that he has drawn power from her — from this rake-thin young woman who should not even be here. He feels more confident, ready to face what the day will bring. They are both hungry, but hunger can be subdued, for a while.

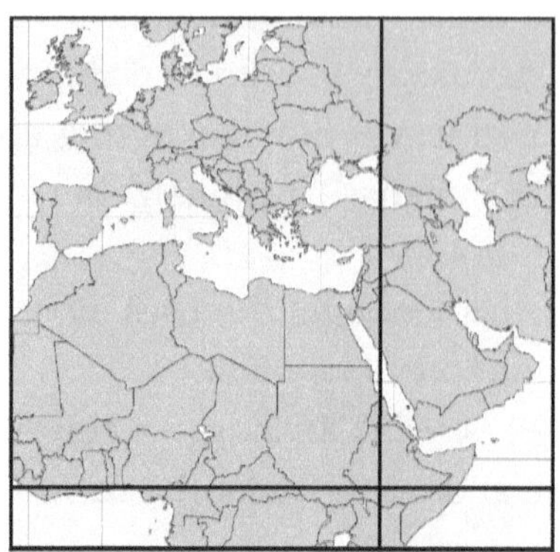

66 ETHIOPIA

Arba Minch

Nayan Dhaliwal Singh waits in the RAF flight suit just twenty metres from where the F-22 Raptor sits, dark and businesslike. The ground crew pull their refuelling and munitions trolleys back. Red Status, two-minute readiness for take-off. The tension in the dome-like hangar hangs like mist.

Nayan prepares his body for flight, hydrating with a mixture of glucose, electrolytes and water. Today he will fly his first aggressive mission, entering the airspace of a sovereign nation where he may or may not be targeted by ground-to-air ordnance.

This moment is the culmination of a lifelong dream. Nayan as a child pictured himself flying high in the air with abandon and freedom, like the angels of the Sikh religion. When Pakistan Air Force F-16 Falcon jets flew overhead he threw his head back and stared, his mouth wide with wonder.

The village of Dulmial, his home, was famous for the soldiers and warriors it produced. There is a saying that every second person from Dulmial has the heart of a soldier, and every third a poet. Even as a child, Nayan recognised elements of both in his soul.

On the main street there was a black cannon mounted on a plinth, donated to World War One veterans in the town by a grateful Queen Victoria in recognition of their service in the British Army. Nayan would run his forefinger over the marble dedication, his body racked with shivers. His own great-grandfather had died in World War Two, and an uncle had been killed fighting for the Pakistan Army's elite SSG unit in the bloody siege of Lal Masjid in 2007.

He read of great air battles. Baron Manfred von Richthofen over France. The Battle of Britain. The Lebanon War, when, in two days of dogfights, Israeli jets shot down eighty-two Syrian jets and lost just one A-4 Skyhawk in reply.

While other children fought with sticks carved into the shape of guns, Nayan ran with arms swept back like wings, making a jet-like roar with clenched teeth, strafing and bombing until his nickname was *hawai jahaj*, the airplane.

When Nayan was thirteen his father called the family together and dropped a bombshell. In his quiet way the dapper forty-two-year-old waited until they had settled, sipping his tea, his eyes serious.

'For many years,' he said, 'your mother and I have been saving, and some time ago we applied to emigrate. This morning we received a letter. May I read it to you?'

This was not a question, but merely how his father always spoke. *May I help you to sit down now and complete the homework Sardarji Tuvijat has set you? May I ask you to accompany your mother to help her carry our groceries?*

The room was silent as Nayan's father read the letter.

'... Her Majesty's Government invites you to present yourself at immigration in London ... you should bring ... it is required that you ...'

After a little while Nayan left the room and sat on his mattress, opened *Jet Aircraft of the World*, and turned to the section titled 'Great Britain'. There was a tear in his eye when he thought of the future that might one day be his.

* * *

In Year Nine at Highams Park School, London, the careers adviser told Nayan that only a tiny percentage of those who enter the RAF get to fly planes. That he was of slight build, and physical strength was important in the selection process. That in order to succeed he would be competing with the best of his generation.

But Nayan did not give up. To fulfil his dream of flying lessons he saved five hundred and eighty pounds in cash — two years of pamphlet deliveries, two years of afternoons behind the counter of Samini Raja's newsagency, selling papers and Coca-Cola and stationery, spending money only on his subscription to *AirForces Monthly*, reading and rereading it until he knew some of the articles by heart.

His first flight was at the controls of a Cessna 172. As soon as Nayan settled into the worn grey leather seats and slipped the headphones over his ears he relaxed entirely, and a new kind of excitement took hold. The rest of the world — money, job, family — ceased to exist. There was only him and this machine and the voice of the instructor.

Hurtling down the runway, propeller cutting the air like a knife, Nayan felt himself shiver from his feet to the back of his neck. When the Cessna reared into the sky he had goosebumps on his arms and legs. A prayer entered his head: the Sohila, the Sikh evening prayer, whispered every night by his father and mother at his bedside from the first memories of childhood.

One universal creator being. By the grace of the true Lord.

In that house where the praises of the creator are chanted and contemplated,

In that house, sing songs of praise; meditate and remember the creator, Lord Vaheguru.

Sing the songs of praise of my fearless lord,

I am a sacrifice to that song of praise which brings eternal peace.

It was the last line that resonated always in his mind.

I am a sacrifice to that song of praise which brings eternal peace ...

Nayan comes back to the present, his first operational sortie with RAF 47 Squadron, the Special Forces support wing, still waiting for the order.

To Nayan, his entire life has led to this moment.

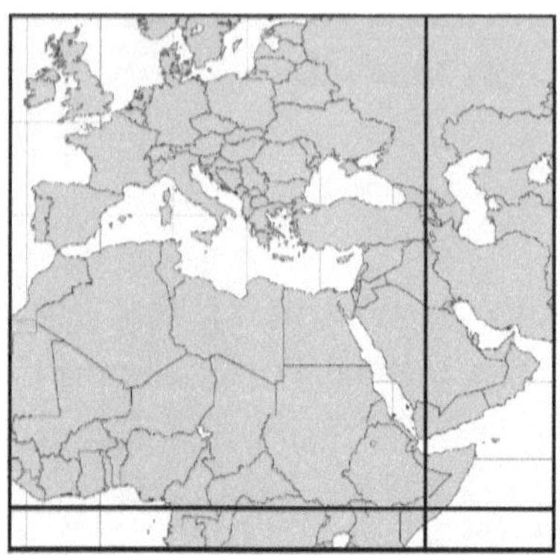

67 SOMALIA

Ka Tirsan

The hills are further away than PJ first estimated. Their pace is slow, with water sloshing audibly, at first, in PJ's belly. Drinking, also, seems to have increased his hunger.

Ayanna has become very chatty, never complaining, and PJ regrets that his mind is occupied so much with what to do with her if it becomes necessary for him to take a risk.

Still, it's nice to be able to ask her the name of a bird riding high on the developing thermals. Once or twice she suggests that a thicket of whistling thorn will get worse, and that they might deviate in another direction. Slowly, she is becoming part guide, part friend, and he reluctantly acknowledges that his chances of survival are better with her, than without her.

Eventually, however, they reach the first slopes of the hills marked on the courier's map. PJ chooses a steeply eroded stream bed as a stopping place.

'I've saved a little rice,' Ayanna says. 'Should I light a fire?'

'No. Definitely not.'

Instead, as they settle down, she passes him a handful of cold cooked rice with that aromatic yellow paste. It has the consistency of glue, but washed down with water from the bottle he feels better.

'Thank you,' he says, reflecting that without her he would not have eaten or drunk for many hours. His worry, however, is increasingly difficult to ignore. Soon he will enter the nest of the Almohad, and if they find her here alone she will be in danger.

After the meal, PJ studies the hillside, looking for the best route to climb unobserved, as well as signs of human activity. Not just sentries or posts, but worn paths made by animals or humans.

It is possible to tell the difference. Livestock and wild animals tend to follow a path made by others, so as to expend the least possible energy in travelling to and from water and grazing. Humans tend to talk as they move and like to look at each other, so often walk two or more abreast, creating wider paths.

There is one such path down that hillside, along with other signs — a Coke can, plastic bags. Foraging parties, PJ decides; firewood collectors. These would not be regular, but on an as-needed basis.

'They are not simple villagers who have been here,' Ayanna says, 'they are militia — gunmen, or even soldiers.'

PJ smiles at this assertion — he had just come to the same conclusion. 'And why is that?'

The young woman points out the glint of brass cartridge cases scattered along the path. 'Well spotted,' he says. 'What were they shooting at, I wonder?'

'Such people do not need a reason,' Ayanna says, 'they shoot because they have guns. I have seen them competing to shoot an eagle in flight, or a running cat, or even just the branch of a tree. The national anthem of Somalia is ...' She makes a noise with her tongue and teeth — a lifelike rendition of automatic fire.

'Ayanna, I need to do a close target recce on that valley. I need you to stay here.'

'A what?'

'Sorry. I have to get in there and have a look ...' *Before I call in the ordnance to vaporise it.*

Her eyes widen in fear. 'You alone cannot fight a whole camp full of men with guns. They are jackals. They do not know pity.'

'I'm not going to fight them. I want to confirm that they are the ones I'm looking for.' He searches for the words to explain. 'Then I'll call down an attack from the air. As soon as I've done so I'll come back and get you, and we'll run as fast as we can away from them.'

Ayanna looks grave. 'Will the Americans send their drones?'

'You know about drones?'

Her expression is haughty. 'Of course I do. Everyone does.'

'They might send drones, or missiles. Maybe an airstrike.'

'And then the Americans will come and get you in a helicopter and you will fly away. Don't leave me here alone. I would rather die with you. What would happen to me if you were killed?'

An awkward silence follows, then, 'If I'm not back by sunrise tomorrow you'd better assume I'm dead and go home to your father. He won't punish you if he knows that I've been killed. OK?' He passes her the water bottle, watching her fill her mug and saucepan before handing it back to him.

Ayanna's eyes widen, dark and huge. 'Please do not get killed.'

'I'll try not to.' As an afterthought he unbuckles the holster at his side and slides out the Makarov pistol he took from the courier, checks the load and hands it to her, butt first.

'Do you know how to use this?'

'Yes.'

'If anyone comes near, shoot them.'

Again a confused nod.

PJ feels a strange reluctance to leave, even after he has slung the backpack — still with the parcel of mysterious goods inside — and the AK47 over his shoulder. He stays for another full minute, saying nothing, then, with Ayanna settled into the hollow, he sets off for the nearest cover.

* * *

Having earlier picked out the route up the slope that is least likely to come under observation from a foraging party, yet also avoids the steepest slopes, PJ follows a dry erosion channel for the first part of the ascent. Stopping often, using smell, sight and hearing to check for danger, he takes no chances.

At the halfway point he stops, rests, and waits. After a few seconds he feels something in the earth, then hears it — the sound of a powerful engine.

At first he considers evasive action, worried that an all-terrain vehicle or similar is about to roll over him, but then he realises that the sound is that of a propeller-driven aircraft.

He lifts his head, then stands, screened by earth and thorn, watching as the light aircraft exits what must be an opening in the hills to the south, staying below a couple of hundred feet.

What the hell are they up to? PJ wonders.

He continues to watch as the aircraft drones on into the south, disappearing into the heat and dust. There is a new urgency to his movements as he continues to climb, still keeping to cover. He is not sure what he expected to find here, but an airstrip had not figured in those expectations.

Saif al-Din watches the Piper Pawnee roar down the dirt runway, then wobble into the air. The aircraft has scarcely been idle for days, training an initial twelve handpicked men. This number was whittled down to ten when two candidates proved to be too nervous or intellectually slow to grasp the process of flying.

The instructor, a wiry Saudi, seems to have an unquenchable appetite for the training. 'Malik,' he says, 'could be a real pilot — he is so quick to learn, his hands so sure on the controls. Mohammad is almost as good … and Djamil, the young Indonesian from Jemaah Islamiyah, will one day rule the skies.'

Saif continues to watch as the Pawnee arcs and climbs, stutters, then banks towards the massif of Mount Nabad lying darkly against the distant western horizon. Flying straight and level now, a brown cloud falls from the rear of the aircraft, continuing to do so for a minute or more before the aircraft speeds up, and turns in a lazy arc.

The cloud drifts very slowly towards the earth. Saif nods with satisfaction. The payload, in that case, was pure, harmless bentonite. When next the plane lands, it will be loaded with something far more deadly.

Approaching the top of the hill, PJ moves with caution, mindful of the flint-like stones that cut into his knees and elbows. Reaching the lip he can see a pair of sentries, both standing on the long ridge that shelters the base. One is some fifty metres away, the other the same distance further on. Prone now, he slithers on until he can see down into the valley below.

The centre is a rough bush airstrip, a windsock hanging limp at one corner. His eyes are drawn to a series of huts nearby. At one end is an aircraft hangar, with clusters of forty-four-gallon drums either upright or on their sides, stacked alongside.

There are also demountable buildings, before a camp that must house many men and possibly women. There are cooking fires burning, the smoke mingling with the ever-present dust. People are moving around, some sitting near fires, guns leaning against walls or vehicles, close to hand.

Others are guarding what must be key points. The two outer sentries become four when he notices a pair in a position dug into a low hill on the other side of the valley.

As PJ turns his attention back to the base itself, a man dressed in white exits the largest of the huts, pauses to talk with the sentry, then strides across to the other end of the camp where he appears to be remonstrating with one or more of the men.

The faint sound of voices carries, without any hope of discerning single words or sentences.

Now is the time for decisions.

The most logical and attractive option is to creep back down the slope, collect Ayanna, walk to the nearest village, beg, borrow or buy a phone and call London, get them to vaporise the place.

This is, however, not the best choice for two reasons. One is delay. Finding a village and getting a phone might take twenty-four hours or more. The other is that he has not yet confirmed that this valley holds the chemicals he first saw on the dhow from Iran. There is a humanitarian aspect to this decision. Down there are fifty or more men — with this level of organisation they must surely be Almohad, but a missile attack will leave nothing living. PJ does not want innocent souls on his conscience. He has to be sure. It is a risk, of course, but he has no choice. Using the cover of the dead courier is his best chance, on a day devoid of chances.

Even PJ's gifted eye for terrain can see no way of penetrating the valley in daylight without being seen, unless he is extraordinarily lucky. The alternative is waiting for darkness, but with an aircraft out on unknown business, time may be important, even crucial. Besides, Ayanna is waiting in the hollow. One person should not matter, but she does.

He observes for more than an hour before making a decision that he knows might mean death for him. Standing up, he feels the full force of the breeze and the dust particles borne along with it. He begins walking towards the nearest of the sentries. When he sees them turn, he waves and calls out, 'Heedheh — Hey!'

Then, as he gets closer, he sees that the man's face remains guarded, sees him cock the AK47, and PJ feels that peculiar tenseness — the expectation that his body is about to be torn apart by bullets.

'Who are you?' the sentry demands in Somali. His face is heavily bearded, shoulders broad.

'My name is Isham and I bring an important package.'

The man's eyes narrow. 'We were told to expect a man called Erasto, who I have met before. He was to arrive on a motorbike. Where is he?'

'Unfortunately there was an accident, he hit a tree, and with his dying breath he charged me to bring this for him.'

'But who are you?'

'Isham, I told you. Erasto promised that if I took this bag to a man called Saif al-Din I would be rewarded.' The presence of the Almohad leader is a guess, but an educated one.

'Why did you not walk along the road?'

'Because I lost my way in the dark — truly, I have not slept.'

Another man, from along the ridge, saunters up, and PJ waits while his story is relayed from one to the other.

'Pass me the bag.'

'I will not. I was told to give it to Saif al-Din only.'

'Put down your gun.'

'I refuse. Only a fool gives away his weapon. Take me to see this Saif al-Din, let him reward me as was promised, and then I will leave.'

'Listen to me. An ignorant stranger does not give orders around here. We are al-Muwahhidun. Turning up here and making demands will get you a bullet in the gut, do you understand?'

Even so, they make no further attempt to take the rifle from him. One of the two men gestures with a tilt of his head, then begins to lead PJ down a well-trodden track towards the floor of the valley.

PJ's arrival causes a stir, a group of men conferring near the buildings, point up at him, then stride out to the periphery of the camp to meet him. There are three of them, two very dark, one lighter. He feels a hollow knot of anxiety in his gut. They will not hesitate to kill him if he presents the slightest danger to them, or even if his demands for payment become too strident. He searches his mind for an angle — something that might make it more expedient for them to keep him alive.

As they reach the base of the hill PJ hears the airplane engine returning. Even his escort stops to watch the small craft land with a puff of dust from the landing wheels, then taxi towards the hangar. The pilot and another man step out and begin talking with some others.

PJ studies the three men waiting for him on what looks like a parade ground. Two carry AK47s, one with a bandolier of cartridges across his shoulder. The man in the centre, however, grabs his attention immediately. He wears camo trousers and shirt, black coat with the buttons long since torn away, and a hand-embroidered pale yellow kheffiyeh cap. He carries a sidearm in a green canvas holster at his hip. PJ has seen photographs of this man in briefings and on computer screens. At this moment, he is probably the most wanted man on the planet, along with Istikaan and a couple of senior AQAP and Taliban commanders.

PJ stands, one leg bent at the knee, trying to look relaxed, yet knowing that his survival hinges on the tall, dark figure who stops in front of him.

Saif al-Din's eyes are like mine entrances, tunnels hinting at shadows beneath, glancing often at the lighter skinned man beside him, a middle-aged Arab wearing Western trousers and a short coat. Grey beard. Dusty to the knees. Crooked brown teeth. PJ feels a prickle of recognition. He has only ever seen him in photographs. The reality is strangely shocking. Istikaan. The Hourglass.

PJ tries to control the fear that begins deep in his spine, sending tremors into his fingers, arms, and knees. 'I am a simple courier. A payment was promised, and when I have it I'll leave.' *Coming down here was a mistake,* he says to himself. *They will not let me leave this place alive.*

The older man bends down, sniffs like a rat as he takes the package in his hands and examines the contents. At length he says, 'These are some lab supplies we ordered many weeks ago — a replacement UV lamp and some other items.'

Saif al-Din nods, but he continues to study PJ. 'You are an unusual-looking man. Somali?'

'Yes.'

'What clan?'

The story of his appearance has been well rehearsed over several visits to this country. 'My mother was Marehan, and I was brought up in that clan, but my father was French.'

Saif sneers, 'I did not trust you before, and now I trust you even less.'

PJ opens his mouth to argue, but a shout from up on the ridge chills his heart to the core. The voice is unmistakeably female. He scans the hill, horrified by the sight of Ayanna, standing tall and brave on the peak. In one hand she carries the Makarov pistol he gave her.

'Ayanna. *No!*' he screams. 'Run.'

Oh God. You beautiful, warm, brave young woman. You can't save me, and now I can't save you ...

Many times in Ayanna's life she has been made to wait, and she has learned to pass lonely hours building imaginary castles in her mind. The castles have never been taller or more grand than today.

All of them involve the Englishman. White Mediterranean cities. Huge chestnut horses with flying manes. The best hotel she has ever seen is the al-Shekatee at Buur Hakaba, and she tries to imagine rooms even more luxurious. Each with its own white porcelain bath. She imagines herself dressed in the finest silk robes at a restaurant. The other guests at the table would be American film stars.

Part of her craves home. But she has peered through an open door of possibility, and she knows now that the village will be the death of her. She will end up third wife to Abbas the corn grinder, and she will suffocate, confined to four walls, never knowing the world outside.

Ayanna imagines herself walking on a beach with PJ. She wears a filmy white gown that opens like the wings of an angel when she spreads her arms. He wears blue American jeans and a white shirt.

She smiles, and then, a moment later, the vision changes, and she sees him lying, bleeding on the earth.

I should not have let him go alone, she thinks suddenly.

PJ is a strong man, but not very smart in many ways, with no understanding of how to find water. Sometimes he doesn't hear things that are plain to her.

I have to help him …

Heart hammering in her chest, she scrabbles for the pistol, pulls the slide back and watches it scoop a brass cartridge from the magazine and drive it into the chamber.

But I am afraid …

There is only one way she knows to banish that fear — a song that she learned at her father's knee, based on an old folk tale of a mouse and a lion. *Heedheh, libaax adiga samee maya baqo …* Hey, lion, you don't scare me …

The song, as always, banishes the fear. She loops her belongings over her shoulder and begins to walk. The pistol she carries in her right hand, her chin out-thrust with determination.

Singing aloud, in a weak and faltering voice, she sets off up the hillside, climbing slowly, choosing paths that only her eyes can see, finally reaching the summit, looking down into the valley below. Now she is truly afraid, taking one timorous step after another.

I will just look, and see if he is there …

Ayanna sees the buildings, and the airstrip. Then a group of men in a clear space. Her eyes fly wide. PJ is surrounded by a ring of men with guns, one with a bunduq pointed squarely at his back. Without conscious thought, Ayanna calls his name, then begins to run down towards him.

* * *

PJ starts to unsling the AK47, prepared to mow down anyone here who might be a threat to her, but even before his fingers curl around the grip something strikes him a colossal blow in the small of the back, sending him staggering to his knees. Then they are on him, tearing the weapon away.

One man straddles his back, grips his hair with one hand, another bores the muzzle of his gun into the side of his head. Still his eyes lift high enough to see the hillside, Ayanna running down towards him. He tries to shout to her, but the opposing pressures of the men holding him and his own efforts to rise are placing irresistible force on his spine.

His mouth opens in a soundless caw of useless emotion, seeing her closer now. One of the Almohad has his rifle raised to his shoulder, trying to hit her, using the trigger with workmanlike skill; one- and two-shot bursts that raise puffs of dust from the ground around and behind her.

Ayanna runs like a desert antelope, the dikdik of the Somali plains, her legs moving gracefully across the ground. Jinking around flying bullets with a fearless grimace.

PJ hears Saif al-Din's voice, furiously rebuking the shooter in Somali.

Then the gunman fires a long burst, and PJ sees the fall of the shot around her at thigh level. Ayanna's legs fold and she goes down.

They drag her up by her feet, one of the guards carrying the pistol PJ had given her. The lower section of her kikoi is soaked with blood, and the Almohad fighters chatter excitedly.

They dump her in a heap ten paces from PJ. Saif al-Din holds out his hands to one of his men for his AK47, checks the load, then walks up until he is standing directly over her. At the last minute Ayanna's eyes turn and fix on PJ's. A lifetime passes between them in those seconds.

The rifle stutters and her body shudders.

PJ's eyes close and he bawls out a sound that does not have a name, then fragmented sentences. One after the other. 'You bastards, you murdering bastards …'

Saif al-Din passes the rifle back to the man he borrowed it from, then looks down for ten or more seconds at Ayanna's body. His face is bloodless, lips contemptuous. He addresses the men. 'Two of you dump this …' He jabs a foot at Ayanna's body, '… in the usual place. The rest of you take this spying pig and confine him. I will interview him later.'

One of the guards swings the barrel of his assault rifle so the muzzle is trained on PJ's chest. 'What if he tries to run away?'

'Make it so he cannot run away, do you understand me?'

'Yes, Sayyid.'

'He wants a reward for bringing the package here. Make sure you give him one.'

The guard grins. 'Yes, Sayyid.' He pushes PJ hard in the back, propelling him forward. A rifle barrel drills into the middle of his back and he is forced to walk.

PJ cannot think, or react. The sky has fallen in and the sun gone dark. The act he has just witnessed, it seems to him, differs from the blackest moments of history only in scale.

God, why did she follow me … why did I let her follow me …

PJ stops walking with the ache of it, but earns a backhand blow across the left ear that snaps his head sideways and stings like a whip. He says nothing further, allowing them to push him onwards, taking the opportunity to study the area.

The base is spread out, designed to take advantage of the stony hillocks which provide cover from aerial surveillance. Twenty or so men stand around in groups, drinking from mugs and talking. Around the same number are on guard duty. A few others are part of a work party on the light aircraft that he can see through the cavernous open front of the hangar.

They push on past what must be a command centre. PJ looks desperately for an instrument of retribution. Through the door he can see some comms equipment, a couple of laptop computers open on desks. Nothing useful.

A technical is parked out the front with a Dushka hanging limp from a pintle mount. With such a weapon, PJ knows, he could decimate the camp, but getting away from the guards and up on the vehicle will take too long. Besides, as if aware of just that possibility, the guards now watch him more closely, and the rifle barrel pushes harder into his back.

PJ wonders if they will cuff or tie him, or if they have some other method of restraining him. Ahead is an open-fronted steel shed, such as might be used to store tractors, and they push him inside. His arrival causes interest, with idlers following, holding their weapons in a relaxed fashion.

PJ sees the blow coming out of the corner of his eye, the sharp pressure of the rifle barrel removed from his back and then the weapon raised, the butt landing at the juncture of his neck and skull with enough force to momentarily black out his senses. The next thing he sees is the earth floor, feels grit between his lips and teeth, being dragged by one arm so that he faces upwards.

There is growing noise from the gang of captors, a high-pitched baying for blood that PJ has seen and heard before. He lifts his head, trying to look down. Someone is slicing his boots and socks from his feet with a bilau dagger, and the razor-sharp blade cuts to the protruding bone of his ankle. He cries out in pain.

Now, he thinks, *they will kill me.*

As he lies there in his bare feet another man steps forward, takes a cell phone from his pocket and places it on the wooden cable drum that serves as a table. In his right hand he wields what appears to be a traditional Somali club. A length of shaped hardwood with a heavy knob at the end, naturally endowed with lumps and creases. Dark stains in the wood appear to be of blood.

Make it so he cannot run away ...

The first blow strikes the top of PJ's right foot just higher than his toes, shattering the tiny bones there. The pain is sharp and debilitating, and when the blow is repeated on the other foot he cannot help a long, tearing shriek.

The man with the club moves position and begins to target the soles of PJ's feet, the next blow breaking half the delicate tarsal bones of his left foot. The crowd roars.

There is no surcease, no unconsciousness that might provide relief from the pain. PJ's breath slows, becoming heavy in his chest, almost as though he can feel his body erecting defences against the pain, closing bulkhead doors like a stricken ship. The blows come one after the other, clubbing his feet into bags of blood and fractured bone.

PJ raises his head and looks down. Toes sit at odd angles. Blood has smeared and splattered as far as his knees. He tries to bring his feet up as the man with the club takes a massive two-armed swing, connecting with the point of his right ankle, pulping the bone so the pain is beyond bearing.

As he rolls to his side and hugs his knees to his chest, the crowd parts and Saif al-Din appears.

'Enough,' he shouts. 'Go back to work.'

The crowd moves away, talking among themselves. PJ lies on his side, shaking with shock, racked with waves and spasms of agony.

Saif al-Din uses a hand in each of PJ's armpits to drag him up against the wall, leaving him propped there, half-lolling, consciousness surging and receding like stage lights. 'I do not know your name,' he says, 'nor do I care, but I suspect I know where you came from.' He points out to the hangar where the light aircraft sits. 'Within hours we will begin the unleashing of a fury such as has never been seen on the earth before, yet merely a test; a sign of what is still to come.'

The truth of what the Almohad leader says is obvious from the gloating in his voice. 'If I decide to be merciful, I will have you shot. If not …'

PJ falls onto his side, and unconsciousness carries him into soft and welcoming arms.

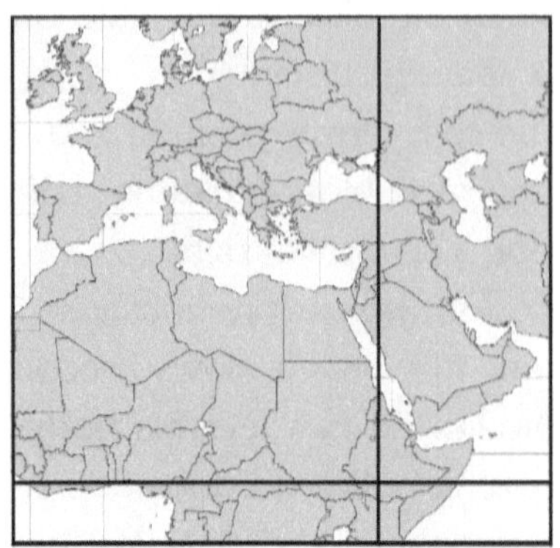

68 ETHIOPIA

Arba Minch

Not all air bases are logically organised, especially when runway space is shared with civilian traffic and several countries have assets on various sections of the apron. Marika is running almost thirty minutes behind schedule when she arrives, then faces a confused ten-minute journey while a RAF logistics officer steers the Nissan van down various one-way alleys and dead-ends.

'Where the hell are they?' she asks.

The RAF officer looks at a complete loss. He pulls over and leans down into a voice mic clipped to his shirt front. Then lifts off the handbrake, lurches back into gear. 'OK, we're in the wrong quadrant.'

This time he drives like a Dubai taxi driver, heedless of other traffic and base road signs. Marika starts to run through her orders. She can't help thinking of Ronnie. They need to talk — long past due — but there just hasn't been an opportunity.

At least David is OK. Back in Queen Elizabeth Hospital in Woolwich, London, minus about eight inches of gut, which he cheerfully tells everyone he didn't need anyway. When she visited him, what amazed her was his disappointment that he wouldn't be in on the attack on the base.

'Get a couple for me, Marika.'

'Will do, mate. Will do.'

As the van screams through a gate in the wire fence she can see a grey Hercules that looks well past its use-by date, taxiing out onto the apron.

'What the fuck?' she shouts. 'That's them, and they're going without me!' The van skids to a halt and she turns to the driver, 'Don't just sit here, follow them.' She lifts the Sid and patches through to Ronnie. 'What the hell do you think you're doing?'

'You're running late and we have a mission out there. As 2IC I made the decision to proceed.'

'You bastard! I'm here now, stop the plane.'

The sound of rubber on rough bitumen changes to a whisper as the van hits the smooth concrete of the runway.

'The plane looks like a shitheap,' the RAF driver says.

Looks, Marika knows, can be deceiving. The pilot will be a 662 Squadron hotshot, and that old bus a veteran of a thousand or more hot insertions. Scratch the paint and there will be bullet holes, patched with fibreglass filler.

Ronnie has terminated the call.

'You fucker, Ronnie,' she swears under her breath.

She tries again, no answer.

'Get in front of them,' Marika shouts. 'Make them stop.'

The RAF driver looks at her as if she is mad.

The plane, however, begins to slow of its own accord before coming to a complete stop. By the time Marika has her kit out of the van the ramp is down, and she walks across to it in the sweltering heat. Red-faced with anger, she climbs into the cavernous interior where the rest of the 2CG team are inside on the bench seats.

Ronnie is in the cockpit with the pilots. He turns to look at her, his face a mixture of defiance and ...

Marika dumps her kit on a seat and walks through, eyes blazing. 'What the hell is going on? You trying to leave me behind?'

'You were late. This mission is more fucking important than your ego, but now Air Traffic Control won't let us take off.'

Marika gives him a stare that clearly means *I'll deal with you later.* Then she addresses the pilot. 'Is this true?'

'They won't give us clearance. The Ethiopians are playing games.'

Marika removes her Sid and puts a call through to London. Mossel is unavailable, upstairs at Resources and Procurement, and won't be contactable for thirty minutes. She thinks of unloading on the duty officer, but only Mossel has the contacts, and the hubris, to sort this mess out.

Turning to the pilot, she says, 'What happens if we just go?'

His eyes widen. 'You mean, disobey Air Traffic Control?'

'Yes, that's exactly what I mean.'

'Jesus. *A*, we could crash with another aircraft. *B*, if we get in the air the Ethiopians might shoot us down, and *C*, I would lose my fucking licence. Does that sound worth it to you?'

Marika folds her arms over her chest. 'Ask them again.'

'I just did, five minutes ago.'

She points out at the main airstrip. 'I can't see a hell of a lot of planes landing, can you?'

The pilot's head wobbles. 'That doesn't matter — they're saying no, and there's nothing we can do about it.'

'Ask them again. Tell them that we demand immediate clearance for take-off, and if they refuse we'll go over their heads, through the British government. That might work.'

'OK. I'll try.'

The pilot slips on the radio headset. Talks and listens for a few minutes before removing it again. 'No dice, sorry. They say they're keeping the runways open because the president is flying somewhere in his Lear. Right now he's in his private VIP lounge, having a last-minute drink before he boards, and when President

Demeke Mekonnen wants to take off — well that's when he does. So they can't even tell us when. Might be ten minutes. Might be half an hour.'

Marika steels herself. This is not something Mossel can fix. This is local protocol, and no one is going to contradict it. She looks up at the pilot. 'So am I right in assuming that there is no air traffic at all?'

'They have incoming flights in a holding pattern until the president takes off.'

'Do you know what's going on in Somalia right now?'

The pilot shakes his head.

Marika says, 'I'm going to tell you something, and by the time I've finished you'll have realised that this is way more important than your pilot's licence.' The gist of it takes just ten sentences, and by the time she gets that far his jaw has dropped.

'But they might shoot us down …'

Marika shakes her head. 'I've been around the block a few times and I know for sure that Ethiopian assets will *not* shoot down a Royal Air Force plane, because they know that if they do they can kiss the goodwill of His Majesty's Government goodbye. Contrary to popular belief, that's still important. Not only that, but there's a very real chance that one or two of the thirty or more aircraft we have at this base might just shoot back.'

Silence for a moment. They stare at each other.

'OK,' the pilot says at last, 'let's do it. Sit down and buckle in. This is it.'

The ramp closes on its hydraulic rams, flight crew calling out orders. Marika takes a seat beside her kit in the rear-to-bulkhead seats of the cabin. There is a clack of seatbelts and hushed conversations as packs of cards disappear into Bergen packs. The PD — Parachute Despatcher — checks the stowage of the chutes.

The propellers, idling at low revolutions, start to spin in earnest, building up to a roar, one after the other. The big craft rolls down the apron, along the connecting corridor that joins the RAF sector to the long expanse of the main runway.

Patching her Sid into the aircraft comms using Bluetooth, Marika holds the unit halfway between lips and ear, listening intently. Individual words can hardly be discerned from the multilingual radio chatter, but as they reach the runway Marika can hear the traffic controllers issuing panicked ultimatums in English.

'Ignore them,' Marika calls out, 'just get this bird in the air.'

The engines build to flight speed and the C-130 hurtles down the runway. Marika has always liked the moment a plane becomes airborne, but today her body is a knot of tensed muscles as she peers out the windows, waiting for the sight of some other aircraft trying to land. Nothing appears, however, and the lightly loaded Herc leaves the ground, climbing steeply.

Marika exhales slowly as the pilot levels out at five thousand feet, hopefully well below the commercial airliners in their holding patterns. The heading is south-east towards Somalia.

A pair of Ethiopian Air Force F-15s appear to one side. Kutay is the first to extend a middle finger through the porthole, followed by Sara and a couple of the others. Marika, however, is already opening communications with London. Mossel is back in the SITPOL room.

He grasps the situation. 'Give me a minute.'

Twice that length of time passes before the two fighters peel off, climbing away and into the setting sun. Someone claps, but a moment later the aircraft race back, wingtip to wingtip, and the cheering turns to silence. The F-15s look for all the world as if they're preparing for a strafing run. The cannon ports are clearly visible on each wing as they scream in.

Marika turns to a tap on her shoulder. 'What?'

Ronnie's eyes bore into her. 'Well done,' he says, 'now you've just about started a war with freaking Ethiopia.'

A moment later, however, as if that manoeuvre was merely a final bluff, the F-15s roar overhead and disappear from sight.

* * *

Istikaan has finished directing the preparations in the aircraft. A test flight has just been performed with pure, harmless bentonite in a dummy spore tank, the Zubaidy broadcasting equipment working faultlessly. Now the spores themselves have been installed. Fifty kilograms not counting the additives. In a few minutes they will take to the skies.

Entering the demountable laboratory, he walks down to the tiny office. Reaches up to the high shelf and brings down the tin. Removes the square of paper.

To the Living from the Dead.

For the first time in many years, hand trembling with nerves, he removes the unread suicide note from the clear sachet, knowing in his heart that it is time to read it. That there might be no tomorrow.

He unfolds the sheet, the paper brown and dry from the passing years. The words, written in black ink, are as clear and easy to read as the day they were written. Istikaan stares for a number of seconds, eyes burning with fatigue.

He is at once excited and disappointed. The note consists of just two words. Nothing else.

Istikaan folds the paper, replaces it in the sachet, then the tin.

Feeling surprisingly calm, he leaves the office and closes the door behind him.

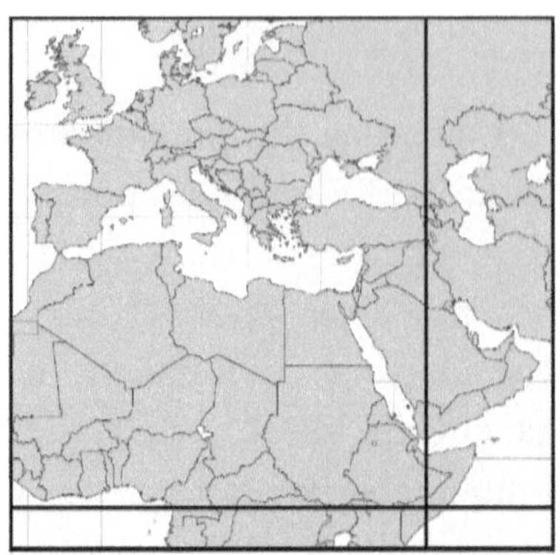

69 SOMALIA

Ka Tirsan

A dry dustbowl at the end of the universe, the end of the road and the end of reason. Rubbish on the wind. Empty cartridge cases ground like rubble into the earth.

Waves of blackness. Dark tides. A yearning to change time. To bring Ayanna back. To take away the pain.

Changing time is impossible, he knows. Retribution is the only way forward. They cannot be allowed to do what they have done and live. Nor can they bring death on the innocent from the air.

PJ remembers the cell phone on the table across the room. He can just see the outline — chunky, ancient, held together by a doubled-over rubber band. One chance to communicate. To stop this terrible thing.

PJ gathers both will and body, pushing the pain down deep. He has just one aim now, and that is to call in the missiles that will turn the air here to temperatures beyond one thousand degrees Celsius. Temperatures that will melt steel, crumble bone, and destroy the evil they have unearthed.

Rolling onto his side, he again pauses to fight the pain that throbs and twists and courses along ganglia, neurotransmitters, screaming into his brain. He tries using words to fight weakness. *You are stronger than this. Trained to fight pain. One minute of effort, then you can sleep. Forever. But first you must …*

Crawling across that floor, he feels as if a thousand hot knife blades have been inserted in the soles of his feet and hammered in with mallets. He rests against the table leg, then reaches for the phone, dropping it, watching it fall and the LCD face glow.

He cradles the handset in his palm. Sobbing with effort, he presses out the digits with his thumb. Trying to maintain consciousness through the exchange of coded signals as he passes through levels of seniority to the top.

Meanwhile, GCHQ triangulates the phone signal and calculates his precise location. In the DRFS offices a light glows red on the SITPOL screen, a set of co-ordinates now locked in place.

A delay, then a voice. Also clinical and dispassionate, because emotions waste time. 'Munitions delivery is confirmed. You have ten minutes to clear the impact zone. Is that sufficient?'

He looks down at his ruined feet. 'Yes,' he says, 'that's enough.'

'Thank you.' A pause. 'Well done.'

At the limit of his strength, PJ terminates the call and lets the phone drop from his hand. He sags to the ground. Folds himself into a ball. From outside he can hear an airplane engine spluttering, starting, spinning and warming.

He cannot be sure how fast or slow time is slipping by. Ten minutes. Then death. Pain spears up both legs and, it seems, into his heart.

For the second time in her life, Marika Hartmann finds herself deep in Somali airspace, a French-made BT80 chute on her back, wearing a Kevlar vest and battle jacket. A Glock automatic is secured in the canvas holster on her side webbing. Rather than her usual UMP, she holds a Heckler & Koch G36 assault rifle

with the 40mm grenade launcher attachment. Across her chest is
a multi-pocketed satchel with a selection of grenades including
high explosives, phosphorus and chemical markers.

The pilot has been briefed to pass fifteen kilometres south-
west of the site itself. From there they will glide as far as they
can with a LALO — low altitude, low opening — jump then
proceed on foot to the location, with a good chance of arriving
undetected. As she looks around at the others there is a knot of
tension coiling and uncoiling in her belly.

Her mind is on PJ, wondering if she will find him down there.
These thoughts, she realises, are part soldierly loyalty, part old-
fashioned mateship, and part something she is not yet ready to
name.

The team is subdued. Some listening to iPods, others talking.
One playing video games, loaded illegally onto his Sid.

Her mind can't help but flick back through the past to that other
time in Somalia, with Madoowbe at her side. Now she is a little
older. More weather-beaten. The innocence bruised out of her.

Her eyes move to Ronnie, who is sitting alone. She moves up
and takes a seat alongside. He does not look up at her.

The smell of mints is stronger than ever, and there's something
about his eyes. A lack of focus.

'You've been drinking, haven't you?'

Ronnie shakes his head. 'Just shut up, will you?'

'It's not the only way to cope, you know.'

'Don't fucking sermonise to me. You're not a priest.'

'Do you want me to go through your gear?'

'You touch it, and you're in deep shit.'

'I'm not going to let you jump with us.'

'Just try and stop me.'

She ignores him. 'OK. Gear up, everyone. Full CBRN protection.'

As they don the Dräger respirators, over-gloves and check
weapons, the PD comes down the tube, hands on either side for
balance, sheath knife huge on the side of his thigh and his voice
clear above the roar of the engines. Some of the elite para groups

love to jump to loud rock music, but 2CG teams tend not to. Marika can understand how psyching up might help when jumping into a hot zone, where sudden death might be moments away, but generally in her job they are on intelligence-gathering missions, and that kind of adrenalin-fuelled over-excitement can be dangerous.

'Two minutes, everyone,' the PD says.

Ronnie stares at Marika, helmet on his lap. 'I'm going. You need me.'

'OK, but if you fuck up ...' Her eyes stay on his until he looks away.

Marika pulls on her own CBRN gear, then makes a final check of the seals. She clips on to the static line, as do the others behind her, feeling as bulky as an astronaut. The PD walks along, checking their connections to the static line.

'One minute,' the PD says, his voice now coming through the comms system inside the Dräger. The ramp yawns open, hydraulic rams doing the work. A final surge of butterflies in Marika's belly signals the imminent jump.

Then chatter from the comms unit. Marika can scarcely believe what she is hearing. 'Target has gone live. Agent on the ground, missile strike inbound.'

The PD's face goes suddenly wild, and he shouts, 'Nine and a half minutes until the strike comes in ... we're being ordered back to base, the jump is cancelled.'

Marika's heart leaps as if connected to an electric current. The agent on the ground can only be PJ. *God, not now ...*

She slips the Sid from its padded pouch and punches in the direct line for Tom Mossel, knowing that every second that passes now will take them further away from their original destination. His voice sounds tense, strained.

'Is PJ on the ground?' she asks.

'Yes, but we've got missiles inbound — he'll have to take his chances.'

'No, we *have* to go in.'

'You don't have time.'

'We're almost on-site now. We'll jump directly onto the target at low altitude — get in and make sure PJ's safe.'

'I can't hold the strike back. Agent Johnson eyeballed the site. It's dirtier than hell itself. There's too much at stake.'

'I know that, but we can't just abandon him.'

Silence. Then, 'OK. Go for it. Nine minutes from now. That's all you've got.'

Marika does not acknowledge, just shouts instructions to the team. Feeling the plane bank, she swallows to help clear the sudden change in pressure as the aircraft dives and heads back towards the target.

'Anything lower than five hundred feet is a risk,' the PD is saying.

'For fuck's sake, we're going to have about seven minutes on the ground before the whole fucking place gets vaporised, and you're talking about dangerous.'

The PD holds up both palms, eyes wild. 'OK. I got you. Listen up everyone. This is an extreme LALO jump. Prepare for impact immediately after you exit the aircraft. You will not have time to avoid obstacles. So good luck, you crazy bastards. Get down there safe and do what you have to do.'

The plane's dive seems near vertical. The ramp opens, and the gritty desert air hits Marika full in the face, buffeting her jacket.

Through the open door she can see hills, a valley floor and muffled lights. Already she is trying to orientate herself, even as the PD is shouting and helping her through, feeling the rail half-catch her, and then she is out into open air with the luffing sail sound of the chute as it flares out, pushed the wrong way by the wind at first, before opening, holding her tight, having scarcely time to look up and see the others above and around her, feeling the air disturbed by ground fire, before the earth rushes up to meet her. She lands on the run, windmilling her feet forwards, jettisoning the chute and bringing up the G36, firing a short burst at visible muzzle flashes to cover the others still landing.

A bright light stabs through the gloom, shining through the whirr of a spinning propeller. Marika recognises a light aircraft taxiing towards them, though the pilot must have seen the gunfire and hesitated before lurching forward even faster.

The lights in the buildings go out now, leaving the valley lit only by the flash of weapons, and the aircraft. Marika turns to the others, now coming up beside her.

'Get the plane,' she calls, but the angle is awkward, and the aircraft is gathering speed. She fires a burst that takes a chunk out of the tail but does not slow it down.

As if in a deliberate ploy to draw fire away half a dozen hostiles charge out from the shadows, forcing the 2CG team to engage. This is strange fighting, but Marika knows that with just six or seven minutes left she cannot afford to let her team get pinned down.

Sensing that the plane will soon be out of range, Marika ignores the firefight, and runs towards it. Judging the critical moment she stops running, chooses a marker grenade from the selection, and loads the under-slung grenade launcher. She aims the weapon carefully, taking into account the speed of the target and distance, knowing that there's no time for more than a single shot. The round fires with a dull pop. The marker grenade bursts against the side of the plane just as it is swallowed by billowing dust clouds, disappearing down the open end of the valley, wobbling into the air.

Marika speaks into the comms unit. 'On ground, repeat, on ground. Suspicious aircraft just departed site, have marked with tracker signature Delta-Baker-five-zero-one. Aircraft crew and cargo unknown.'

'Acknowledged. Six minutes.'

Six minutes, Marika repeats to herself, running back to the rest of the team. They will need at least three to get out to a sufficient distance to survive the impending missile strike. She throws herself to the ground beside Kutay.

Behind the area where the plane emerged a number of vehicle headlights flick on, illuminating machine guns on vehicle trays. One, at least, has the unmistakeable silhouette of a Dushka. The lead vehicles start to move, then the others behind them.

'Technicals,' Kutay observes, any further words drowned out by the heavy weapons on the vehicles opening up, delivering a carpet of fire. The 2CG crew are trained not to be disconcerted by gunfire, even the heavy chatter of the Dushka, yet the fierce barrage does have the effect of forcing them to keep their heads down.

The vehicle movement throws up yet more dust, making it impossible to count them, or to see which of the vehicles are leaving or staying behind. The night becomes a confusing melange of vehicles, headlights, muzzle flashes and shouts.

Ronnie, Marika sees, is the first to return fire as the technicals' volley withers, firing in textbook, controlled bursts, muzzle flash lighting the area, the muscles in his forearms defined as he grips hard to control the weapon. For a moment she wonders if she might have misjudged him. He seems so controlled, doing everything right. Battle is second nature to him.

Marika rolls into firing position, sending a quick burst into a shape that appears momentarily through the gloom. The dust rolls in, however, and the shape is gone as fast as it appeared, with no sign of whether her bullets hit their mark.

Almost as quickly as the attack started, the technicals break off, bypassing their position in file, heading off down the road out of the valley. A wholesale withdrawal is not what Marika was expecting. It is as if they know what is coming, or — a much more terrible thought — they know their work is done.

Saif al-Din holds the Maadi AK47 rifle out the window as the driver throws the Ford truck into a tight turn. He jerks the trigger and it jumps in his hands, aiming out towards where the kufr commandos stream out of the darkness.

Even though he has learned over the years to expect them, their sudden arrival has taken him by surprise. *It doesn't matter,* he tells himself as the vehicle accelerates away, *the kufr are too late.* All is prepared and ready. The laboratory is empty.

Self-satisfaction is cut short by a sudden and massive pain in the side of his head that has him clutching the area with one hand. His mouth opens in a silent shriek of pain.

Not now, Insh'Allah. Now is not the time …

He needs medicine. Needs relief. But his supply of the dark pellets is exhausted. His need for the opium is almost as strong as the pain itself.

Tom Mossel sits with his head in his hands.

'Four T2KU missiles inbound, sir.'

There have been several times in his career when a decision might mean death for his own people. Men and women he has nurtured, grown to respect and love. This is one of the worst he can remember. The very worst had, many years earlier, resulted in the loss of his own wife.

He can picture the missiles leaving the launch pads on the USS *Obama*, offshore from Somalia in the Indian Ocean. Engulfing the area in flame. The T2KU is a serious long-range tactical missile, capable of a heavy payload. These ones will be packed with the same special mix of high explosive and super-incendiary material that was used in Iraq.

Four of them. The effect on the Impact Zone will be catastrophic.

For the first time in many years, Tom Mossel feels the desire to weep.

Marika feels torn. Harried. Desperate. Wanting to get after the fast-disappearing vehicles, needing to get out of the valley before it becomes a superheated hell. Yet what of PJ? Will she be able to live with herself if she leaves him behind to die? Without bothering to shout an order she leads the team at a run towards the structures that make up the site.

She snaps an order. 'Two to each building, see if he's here. Thirty seconds only. Watch for IEDs.' Still running, gripping her weapon so hard that the swivel where the folding stock extends from the frame digs hard into the side of her forearm. Ahead she can see fuel drums and the hangar where they must have stored the plane itself.

We have to leave now. I cannot trade these lives for PJ's, even if I ...

Sprinting so fast that she starts to sweat through the undersuit, she is almost at the hangar. The smell of avgas burns in the back of her nostrils. Almost there, her eyes catch sight of a smaller structure nearby — low-roofed like a farm machinery shed, fabricated of panels of ancient, rusting corrugated iron and patched with a variety of materials. Then she spots something trying to crawl out of the darkened entrance. Something low and dark and broken, making a deep and guttural noise.

'PJ!' Changing direction now, Marika sprints across the ground, falling to her knees beside him. 'Jesus, mate, what have they done to you?'

Just a single word, but the effort behind it is such that it escapes his lips more as a blurt than a word. 'Feet.'

Marika slips the LED flashlight from her thigh pocket, trying to make a quick assessment. It takes just a split second to see the bloody mess they have made of his feet and ankles. She feels an empathetic pain in her own chest and chokes back a sob. *My God, Pais, you poor bastard!* Walking is out of the question for him. For now, perhaps forever.

Lifting her head, she galvanises the team into action. 'For God's sake, we've got to get him out of here. Help me, quick. Ronnie, grab his legs.'

Weapon slung, Ronnie takes a grip under his knees. He is a big man, and Marika is glad of his strength as she bends, gripping PJ under the shoulders. Carrying an injured comrade is a rehearsed manoeuvre. They train for everything, even this.

PJ groans, 'I'm too heavy ...'

'You're not, you know ... my grandma could carry you.' Marika whips her head around, scanning until she has accounted for all of the others. 'Hurry,' she cries. 'Everyone. Form on me. We're out of here. Three minutes.'

PJ is conscious, head lolling as they carry him, despite what must be incredible pain. Marika remembers that he has a threshold far beyond a normal man. His test results, gained during the long IONIC training course that all of them do, are somewhat legendary in the DRFS, but this …

'Aussie,' PJ calls.

'Yes.'

'What are you doing here?'

'Came to save your arse, that's what I'm doing here.'

'You have to stop them.'

'Stop who?'

'The plane. They're going to kill … millions. They have it on board … he told me. Saif al-Din.'

Even the mention of his name is enough to bring the anger flooding through her. *He's here. The man who murdered twenty-four human beings just to get the ear of DRFS. To get a man to England who can help him call the shots — seize more and more power for his perverted cause. And now he has brutally crippled the man she —*

But there is no time for that now. No time for thoughts, only deeds, and the effort of carrying PJ is starting to tell.

Marika has no way of looking at her own Sid. Instead she turns back to Sara, making up the rearguard with Jay. 'How long to go?'

'Forty seconds.'

They have just passed through the valley entrance, but they are still too close, way too close. 'Twenty seconds.'

Marika's mind is filled with the certainty of impending cataclysm.

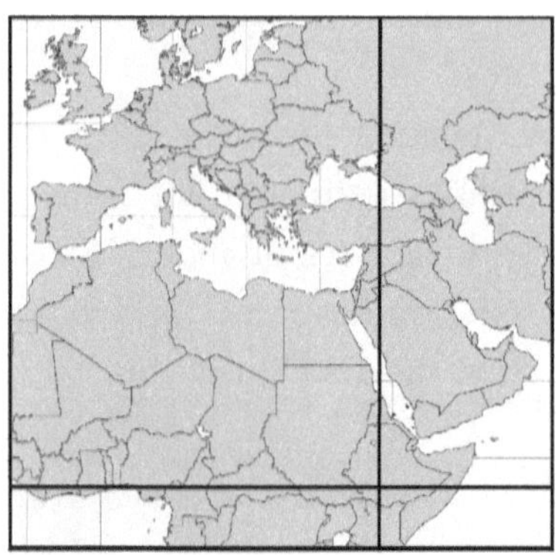

70 ETHIOPIA

Arba Minch

Nayan drops into the seat, strapping in while the Plexiglas dome closes around him, and the whine of the twin Pratt & Whitney F119-PW-100 engines begins to build, the hull shaking with restrained energy. This moment has never grown old for him, the expectation of flight, when this one-hundred-million-dollar bird prepares herself to soar.

Earphones crackling. 'Wheels up two minutes. Proceed twenty thousand feet, bearing eighty degrees south-east.'

Nayan acknowledges, and as he performs the last-minute flight checks his lips move in silent prayer.

One universal creator being. By the grace of the true Lord.

The last of the support vehicles rolls away, and the jets build to an impossible roar.

The command comes through. *'Brakes off.'*

The F-22 hurtles down the runway and climbs into the air. Banking over the vast blue expanse of Chamo Lake, past ten thousand feet, preserving fuel with a slow rate of climb, long-range fuel tanks and missiles on the wings.

Nayan's designated target is still over nine hundred kilometres away and is moving away from him. He does not start to track yet, just settles onto the vector fed into the flight computer and passes through the sound barrier, accelerating to a little over Mach 1.2. Forty minutes to target zone.

Nayan ignores the butterflies in his stomach and concentrates on making fine manual adjustments to maximise speed and range. The target aircraft, it appears, is headed for Mogadishu. The Raptor should easily be able to destroy it, then return to base with fuel to spare. The kill itself is not in doubt.

Dust will not matter, nor wind. Nayan will do his duty, then return to base.

The missiles streak over the horizon, light and fast, burning their final-stage fuel as the GPS-equipped computer makes a final fix on the target. Already Marika's every muscle, fibre and sinew is straining with the effort of racing as if for an unseen finish line, burdened with her inert comrade. Only distance will save them. The sibilant whine of multiple incoming missiles fills the air and shakes the ground. Marika opens her mouth, screaming 'Dooowwwwwn ...'

The explosion is a blinding flash. A hell of heat and noise. The combat jacket is made of fire-retardant material, yet she hears the fibres frizzle in the heat. Three more blasts follow almost simultaneously. The shockwaves hit her, combining into one enormous conflagration.

Tongues of flame from the explosion curl after them like devils' fingers. Marika knows that Jay and Sara are behind, but she can only save herself now, diving headlong, letting PJ fall as the air itself seems to catch alight. Crawling over him in some instinctive effort to protect him.

There is no longer air to breathe. Just a ringing concussion in her head. From behind she hears noises, frightening but incomprehensible in the numbness that has replaced hearing. Jay ... Sara? Yet she cannot raise her head, the heat an impassable barrier.

The worst of it passes in a matter of seconds, followed by a sudden wind. The fresh air is welcome, and Marika realises that it is occurring as the surrounding air rushes in to fill the vacuum of oxygen burned out from the valley. She plants a knee on the earth, half-rises, almost overcome by a swooning sense of vertigo.

Jay and Sara are both down. Sara has lost her helmet and her hair is flaming, burning and frizzling away. Marika unzips her jacket, going first to Sara and wrapping it over her writhing body, extinguishing the last of the flames. Jay's undersuit and jacket have provided some protection, but the heat has burned through all the layers on his back, leaving large areas stripped of flesh as if by the razor slash of a knife.

Marika looks for help. She sees Ronnie on his haunches some metres away. 'Help me, for Christ's sake.' Then, 'Kutay, you keep stag for us. Kisira, first aid kit. Hurry.'

Ronnie uses his own jacket to smother the last of the flames on Jay, talking under his breath as Kisira arrives beside them. She had been at point and was thus most protected. She is the designated unit medic and swiftly has the first aid kit out of her pack and unrolled on the ground.

Marika leaves them and goes back to check PJ. His trouser cuffs are smoking, but he is otherwise safe. Reaching out with her right hand, she touches his cheek, just above his beard, with the tips of her fingers.

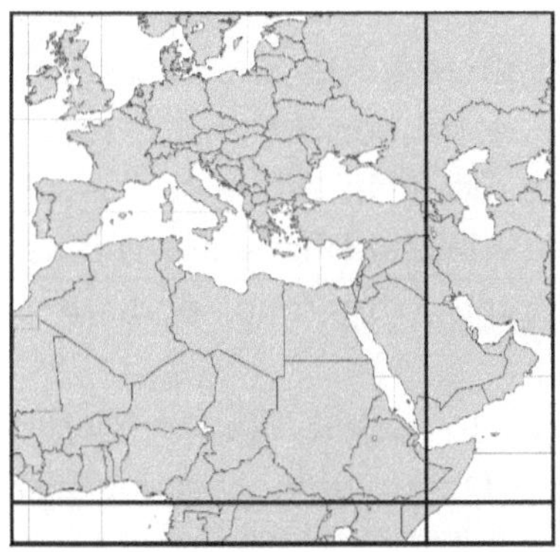

71 SOMALIA

Ka Tirsan

On one knee, Marika picks the cap off the ampoule of morphine with her teeth. Delivers it into the muscle of PJ's shoulder. Feels him stiffen.

'Sorry mate, I'm no Florence Nightingale, but I'm doing my best.' She holds a water bottle to PJ's lips to moisten them, 'I'll be back in a minute, I just want to see how the others are going.'

Face drawn with worry, she waits for an answering nod then moves up beside Kisira, who has just finished spraying a coating over Jay's burns and administering painkillers to Jay and Sara. 'Are they stable?'

'In a lot of pain, but stable, yes.'

Kutay, on watch at the top of a berm — a raised mound of earth — at the edge of their position, shouts. 'Hey, boss. I'm not sure, but I think I can see them.'

Marika, her hearing just starting to return properly, half-stands. 'Who?'

'Vehicles, a whole bunch of them.'

She walks over next to Kutay, looks through the NVG. At a range of at least three klicks she can see a bunch of regular shapes against the starry horizon that cannot be rocks or trees. They are showing no lights, but she is almost certain that Kutay is right. The Almohad have not run as far as they might have, instead stopping to regroup, perhaps even to watch the explosion.

Bastards, she says to herself. *They're not far ahead.*

Marika hates the Dräger unit, sweating inside it, feeling as if her head is being slowly boiled. She opens comms with London, her voice betraying a sense of the situation slipping out of control. 'I have three men down, I repeat, three down, two with burns, one with class three extremity injuries. Medivac required urgently. I am also confirming that the light plane we marked is carrying biological weapons to be broadcast on unknown target. We also have an enemy column just south-east of our position. Back-up urgently required.'

A long pause, then, 'Cobra gunships and medivac en route from USS *Obama*, ETA thirty-two minutes.'

Marika swears to herself, knowing that thirty-two minutes is too long. The Almohad column will be long gone by then.

Saif al-Din hears the passage of the missiles, then the ragged line of vehicles stops as if of its own volition. Even these experienced fighters are awed and shaken by the white-hot explosion that consumes the valley, sending tendrils of fire hundreds of metres into the air. Saif feels the shockwaves in the deepest recesses of his chest. His instinct was right. The kufr, as always, are just a step behind. For a moment he allows himself to be overcome with hatred, tempered by the pain in his skull.

The explosion numbs every sense. The flash is not instantaneous, as with conventional missiles, but lasts much longer. In the brightness he makes out the Special Forces troops on foot, moving out of the valley towards them. One or two look as if they are injured, but then all go to earth and it is impossible to tell.

He turns on the satellite phone and presses out a brief text message. *The seed of the Zaqqum Tree has been sown.* A reference from the Holy Qur'an that means for them to abandon target one. *They know about you. The attack will be on target two.*

Saif stares back at where he saw the kufr soldiers. If the false courier is with them he must be killed. He cannot be allowed to talk further. Besides, Saif does not like leaving an armed party in his rear — they cannot be too careful, despite the traps and subterfuges he has prepared.

The other vehicles are alongside, engines running, and Saif picks out the one that is most manoeuvrable in the sand, a big Yamaha ATV stolen from an AMISOM courier near Kismaayo. It carries two men on the pillion, with a light machine gun mounted at the rear. Saif waves the driver over once, then more urgently. The man is dazed. They all are.

That is the problem, Saif knows, with the incredible firepower of the enemy. It is awe-inspiring. God-like. It takes training to learn that behind the cataclysmic power are mere human beings with beating hearts, seeing eyes and feeling hands; human beings who can be cowed, beaten, and killed.

The driver finally responds, motoring quickly over, before kicking the machine back into neutral. 'Yes, Sayyid?'

'Did you see the kufr soldiers in the light of the explosion?'

'Yes, Sayyid.'

'They are disorganised and some are injured.' He pauses for a moment. The Yamaha ATV might not have enough firepower alone. 'Take Yasir in the Spear of Mohammed.' All the technicals have such names. 'Go back and kill them.'

The gunner on the ATV grins wickedly, teeth shining in the last glow from the strike, the fires above the valley pale orange now, tendrils teasing through the air like spirits.

'We will go back and kill them, Sayyid.'

Saif smiles back and the ATV shoots forward in a blast of sound, the gunner scarcely hanging on, swinging from side to side as it accelerates. Saif feels a grim satisfaction as it pauses next to the Spear of Mohammed. Both vehicles fly away on the mission.

'Now,' Saif shouts to the rest of the column, 'we move.'

Saif knows that the eyes of the world's intelligence communities will now converge on this area. The silent watchers in the sky will soon be out hunting them. There is no time to lose.

Marika is on her knees beside PJ when she hears a sound, a whining motorbike engine, screaming through the gears. She looks up. 'Ronnie. What the hell is that?'

'Bastards. They're fucking coming back, that's what it is.' Then she hears the click of the action on his rifle. Ronnie is one of very few men in the British armed forces who actually likes the bullpup design of the SA80, an unusual configuration that has the trigger forward of the magazine. The joke had been, in happier days, that he had shares in the factory.

Marika feels a stab of fear. 'You're kidding. How many?'

'Two of the fuckers.' There is a manic edge to his voice that worries her.

She lowers the NVG over her eyes. Studies the image. 'One ATV,' she says, 'looks like a medium MG mounted at the rear. One technical.' Then to Kutay, 'Get the Barrett over here, pronto.' The earthen berm is the only defensible bit of ground for hundreds of metres.

The enemy engines rev hard, high-pitched and angry. Moving fast towards them, the drivers change gears as they traverse higher and lower ground, showing no headlights, but visible even without NVG as they draw near.

Leaving Ronnie and Kutay at the perimeter, Marika and Kisira drag the burn victims in until the three patients are beside each other. Sara is unconscious from the morphine, and Jay close to it. Only PJ is lucid. He turns over, half-sits, takes Sara's handgun from its holster and elbow-walks his body higher up the berm.

Marika drops prone beside him, 'What are you doing, Pais? You need to stay still.'

'I don't need feet to hold a gun and fire it.'

'OK, we can do with the extra firepower if you're up to it. And everybody … hold your fire until they're closer.' This said, she loads a HE grenade into the UGL and cocks it.

As the ATV and a dark-painted vehicle come closer, the Almohad machine gunners open fire, bullets zipping through the air, punching into sand and thorn bush. Marika risks a shot with the grenade launcher, firing ahead of the technical. But the sharp-eyed driver spots the projectile and veers out of the way. The explosion is too distant to cause any damage.

The two vehicles wheel onto opposite flanks, machine guns firing. Ronnie, Marika sees, is lying prone, like the rest of them, resting his body weight on knees and elbows as if ready to spring up. One hand slaps rhythmically across the side of his stock.

'Not yet,' she warns him, attempting to reload the UGL. 'On the count of five.'

At that moment the technical finds a patch of higher ground. For ten or more devastating seconds machine gun fire rakes across the depression, once, twice, and again.

There is a particular sound that a bullet makes when it hits a human body. Marika hears it once, perhaps twice.

'Who's hit?'

Kisira's voice, drawn as tight as wire. 'Jay, I think.'

Marika forces herself not to panic, but they have lost the convoy and its deadly cargo. Now she is losing her team as well. *They've got us pinned down. They're going to circle out there and pick us off.*

Hearing movement, she turns to see that Ronnie has risen to one knee, heedless of bullets.

'Hey! Ronnie. What the hell are you doing? Get down.'

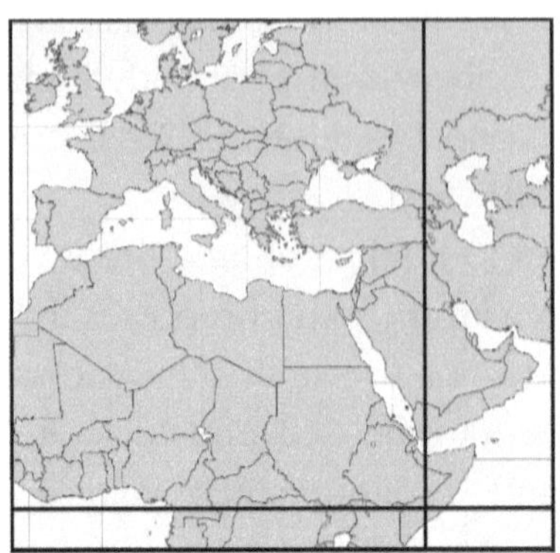

72 SOMALIA

Ka Tirsan

On the night Ronnie met Jean, he hadn't been looking for a fight. The bloke, a wiry geezer in his early twenties was in the mosh pit, gyrating his arms, rushing back and forth across the floor. He bumped Ronnie twice, the second time spilling half the pint he was holding down his shirt front.

Ronnie, in a good mood, held out a palm to fend him away. 'You owe me a beer, mate.'

'Yeah, and who the fuck are you?'

Half an hour of catcalls, shoves, and venomous stares later, they were outside on the pavement, twenty or thirty punters making up the crowd. Taxi drivers left their cabs to watch, standing with folded arms, holding cigarettes and takeaway coffee cups.

Ronnie sparred for a minute or so to put on a show, and to get his opponent's measure, then felled him with three punches. He stood alone as the spectators wandered back inside.

Only a slight woman with long henna-coloured hair, a black miniskirt and an Iron Maiden T-shirt remained, kneeling at the side of the unconscious man.

'Hey,' she called, 'you could at least help me get him into the car, since you knocked him out.'

Ronnie didn't mind, lifting him by the shoulders, helping her carry the man to a car, bundling him into the back seat.

'Is he your boyfriend?'

'No, my brother. He … can be a bit brash, I know. Thanks for not punching the absolute living shit out of him.'

Ronnie shrugged. 'What's your name?'

'Jean.'

'Maybe I should give you a call tomorrow, see how he's going?'

'Yeah, sure.'

She rifled in the glovebox, writing her mobile number on the back of an envelope.

Jean taught Ronnie how to love. Drew the ugliness out of him. Time and again she found something gentle inside him. For eight years he could wake from a nightmare and feel her arms around him, not forcing him to talk, but making him want to.

Yet his absences were too long and too frequent. Jean loved to dance, needed music. The thought of her dancing with other men made him wild, and every time he returned from a trip, he went through the house, looking for evidence of other men. He never found a thing. But the suspicion never went away.

She left, in the end. He came back from a month in Libya, and her clothes were gone from the house they were buying together.

Love left him. There was nothing and no one to take the pain away.

Gripping his SA80 in his left hand, Ronnie rises to one knee. He looks out at the circling vehicles and the guns.

The Aussie chick shouts at him. 'Hey! Ronnie. What the hell are you doing? Get down.'

He shakes his head from side to side. 'No fucking way will I let them do this.' He reaches into his side pocket, removes a hip flask that glows in the light of the muzzle flashes. Drinks deeply, silhouetted against the stars, then throws the flask away. Bullets cut the air all around him.

'Get down, you're half-pissed.'

'Don't worry, PJ, I'll pay the fuckers back. Never let it be said that Ronnie Booth let down his team.' He leans forward so his face is close to Marika's, and then he pulls a grenade from his webbing, extracts the pin with his teeth and spits it out, still holding the lever tight in his fist.

'I've got something you haven't,' he says to Marika.

'What's that?'

'Balls. You get what I mean?'

Bizarrely, he starts to sing, the chorus of a song. Out of time and out of tune. Marika has heard him play it in barracks and bases across the world. The French chorus of the Megadeth anthem to suicide. 'A Tout le Monde'.

'No, Ronnie. Don't do it.'

Then he is gone, legs moving like pistons, up and over the top.

Marika makes a last-minute effort to clutch his arm, but he is too fast for her. She leaps to her feet, after him at a sprint, sees him fire a burst, then throw the grenade in an effort worthy of a cricket outfielder, straight and low.

She hears mispronounced French over the sounds of war. The discharge of his rifle and cool, controlled bursts. '... *à tout le monde, à tous mes amis, je vous aime, je dois partir ...*'

His aim is unerring. This is the Ronnie of old. The technical becomes an unmoving pall of smoke as the grenade showers it with flame and shrapnel. The ATV, however, continues to circle around them, firing searching bursts as it does so.

Ronnie fires burst after burst at it, but the driver is clever, steering erratically and varying his speed.

Ronnie's SA80 is empty, and incredibly, he tucks it under his arm and begins a crazy air-guitar solo, screaming out the sounds, his voice a mad cackle now, he throws the SA80 aside as the Almohad vehicle opens up again, whipping his sidearm from its holster, facing the ATV and the storm of gunfire.

The song lyrics switch back to English, 'Set me free ...'

Ronnie empties the magazine ineffectually, the report from the pistol sounding all but childish against the hammer of the MG. He stands like a monolith, legs braced. 'Come on, you fuckers, I'll have you. Man to man.'

Marika stops him the only way she can, running up behind him and striking the back of his head with her rifle butt, judging the placement and strength of the blow perfectly. He drops like a stone, rolls sideways, eyes staring.

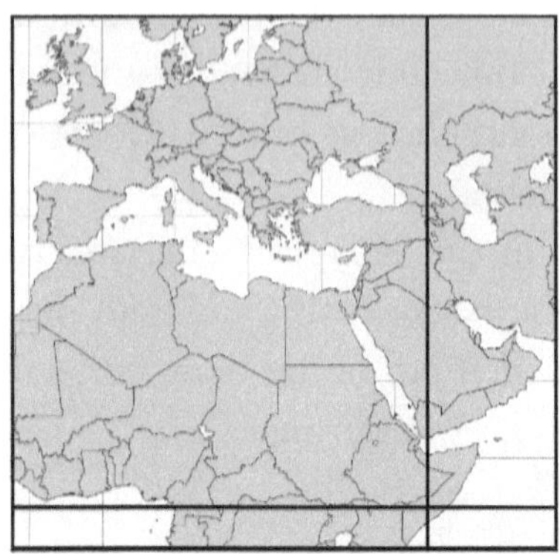

73 SOMALIA

Ka Tirsan

Kutay squeezes the trigger at the exact moment the ATV straightens out and begins to head back towards them.

Marika sees the thump of recoil from the .50 calibre rifle into his shoulder, and the accompanying muzzle flash. She knows that it is a hard thing to hold your nerve in the face of an oncoming vehicle and a steady stream of fire from an automatic weapon. Kutay fires only once, and the ATV's wheels turn sharply away so the entire machine comes close to toppling. The engine throttles wildly, then dies back to idling speed. Nothing moves.

'Come with me,' Marika shouts, and Kutay scrambles up towards her.

Marika approaches the ATV, finger on the trigger of the G36. Even from a distance, the result of the shot is visible. The driver is dead, face down on the sand, shot through the chest. The gunner half-leans against the bike, clutching a wound near his sternum.

'Straight through one and into the other,' Marika says.

It happens sometimes. Soft nose bullets are banned under the International Rules of War. The .50 cal projectiles fired by the

Barrett, originally designed for a heavy machine gun, are capable of passing through two medium-sized trees, let alone human bodies.

'Should I help him?' Kutay asks.

'We don't have time. There'll be a chopper on the scene before long.'

Marika looks down at the wounded Almohad with revulsion, then switches her attention to the ATV, painted in desert lizard camo pattern. The machine would have been looted from AMISOM troops. She places her foot on the rest and swings a leg over. The engine has stalled, and she shifts back to neutral and restarts before revving hard. There is no time for squeamishness at the blood smear on the pillion.

With Kutay riding behind her she drives the machine back to the others, stops, leaving the motor idling.

Marika sees that Kisira is bent over Jay. Their little band has been decimated by the force of the explosion and the Almohad attack. 'How is he?'

'He'll live. A bullet in the leg.'

Kutay helps her drag Ronnie's unconscious form back to the others. His breathing is strong and even, and this feels like a small victory.

You're a hero, really, you stupid, drunken bastard, Marika thinks to herself. *If you hadn't taken out that technical* ... She can't help but remember what Tom Mossel said about keeping Ronnie on the team: 'You might thank me for that decision, yet.'

The thought is a fleeting one, her mind occupied with a current course of action. They have to strike back somehow. 'Sorry PJ,' she says, 'but I'm going to have to leave you here. I need Kutay as gunner if we're going to catch up to these bastards.' Kisira, as the unit medic, needs to stay with the wounded.

PJ sits up, 'Kutay is a sniper, not a gunner. He'd be better off protecting and helping the wounded back here. I'd be useless at that, help me up on the seat — I can still shoot.'

Marika considers the idea. It could be a long time before the medivac arrives, and what if there's another roving band of Almohad, or even just opportunistic shifta? Kutay and Kisira would make a formidable force together. And besides, Ronnie might be a handful when he comes round. PJ will be unable to deal with him without mobility.

'No. You need a hospital bed as soon as we can bloody well get you one.'

'For Christ's sake listen to me. That heartless bastard Saif al-Din killed a Somali girl I got to know over the last few days. Shot her in cold blood. I couldn't live with myself if I let him get away with it. Besides, none of you are used to firing from vehicles like I am. Only Ronnie, and he's useless. That's one of the things we trained for — years of it. I'm the best chance.' He pauses, eyes fixed on hers. 'We started this together. Now let me help finish it.'

'I guess it's fitting that we hunt Saif al-Din together.' Marika lifts the Dräger respirator off her head, tosses it to Kisira. 'I've had enough of this thing, but you guys make your own choices. Someone lend PJ your NVG, he'll need them more than you will.'

'Help me up,' PJ grunts, 'I've got a score to settle.'

Me too, Marika thinks to herself. *With the man who killed those children just to get to me.*

Kutay and Kisira boost PJ up onto the gunner's seat and he fixes the NVG over his eyes. The painkiller is now surging through his veins and he feels invincible, protected by a tight cocoon of cotton wool.

'Just get the bastards for me,' Kutay calls.

'You can count on it.'

PJ focuses on the weapon on its swivel mount in front of him, a light machine gun based on the famous Belgian Minimi, manufactured illegally in China as a direct copy, chambered for the US-standard 5.56x45. This is a gun that PJ has trained on a thousand times, one of the best light quick firers in existence. He already has the breech open, checking the load, slamming it closed with a round in the chamber.

The first one is for you, Ayanna, he thinks to himself, trying not to picture her cremated body in that valley of death behind him.

Marika opens the throttle, the soft sand slowing her ascent through the gears. The weight of PJ on the back helps the wheels grip and she steers for speed, not comfort, finding the track and running the wheels along the high ground.

The world viewed through the NVG is eerie, the track itself highlighted, every pothole visible. She avoids both, in case the Almohad have had time to lay IEDs.

Half-standing on the tread plates, slipstream tearing at her eyes and whipping her hair back, she cranes her eyes ahead. The convoy of Almohad vehicles has disappeared and for a moment she wonders if she might have lost them. She glances back to see if she can discern the others, but sees only the glow of spot fires on the hills around the destroyed base. No silhouettes.

As the ground rises, however, she sees the enemy ahead, three or more kilometres. Not far at this speed, the problem being that as they approach they will have the same problem as the Almohad did a few minutes earlier. Coming from behind the vehicles, PJ will be unable to bring the Minimi to bear, while the Almohad gunners send down a fusillade of fire from the machine guns mounted on the trays of their technicals.

In those trucks there will be flasks of Vollum spores. If they get away ...

To get out alongside them they have to leave the track. Marika glances down at the fuel gauge. Full. Thankfully, they must have been prepared for this flight. 'Hold on,' she calls back, and she rears off the track, over the top of the ruts. The surface is soft, but smooth. If anything, her speed increases, the engine screaming at almost four thousand revs.

What next? One machine gun, her G36, and a few grenades against a convoy of technicals, one of which is carrying a Dushka.

Her momentary loss of concentration has caused the ATV to drop in speed. The convoy of vehicles pulls away a little. Marika flicks her wrist, drops back a gear and sends the engine almost into the redline as she accelerates.

'Jesus,' she yells. A waist-high stone wall appears ahead. Obviously some kind of animal enclosure, looking hard and ugly in the strange light. Her sudden turn to the left almost rolls the ATV, but somehow she controls it, follows the wall along before its stops, bearing off at an angle. After avoiding a thicket of acacia thorns she is back on a route roughly parallel to the track.

A section of stones forces her to slow once more, the ATV rattling and jolting so she can feel the breath *oomphing* from her lungs. Then another rise, and a plain below. The Almohad vehicles are already down there, speeding away, dust rising in twin streams from the rear tyres of each.

Marika suspects that flat ground with long visibility might provide an opportunity. She holds the throttle open as far as it will go, taking the slope so fast that the vehicle hits a drift of dust like a boat striking a wave, the NVG protecting her from the shotgun blast of grit that follows.

After being forced to change gears to climb through the slough, the way ahead is clear. Marika speeds down the slope before being swallowed by trees and scrub at the bottom. It is so dark that even the fifth-generation NVG no longer has enough natural light to amplify. It moves into infrared mode, throwing out its own beam, invisible to the naked eye. The overall picture suffers, goes from full colour to monochrome, but her vision adjusts in time for her to discern a dry creek bed, pick a crossing point, rattle over the smooth stones then up the other side, through more trees, before streaking out onto a flat plain that seems almost limitless. Marika feels the new grip on the tyres, racing up to full speed, seeing the vehicles less than a kilometre ahead now, going all out to catch them, leaning forward, head down in the classic speedster's pose.

How many minutes have passed — ten, twelve? How close will the choppers be now? No more than twenty minutes away, surely?

At the far side of the plain Marika can see broken ground, cliffs, hills, and worse, a village. If Saif al-Din and the Almohad get among people they will be much harder to stop — the missile option will then be out. It might also offer pre-arranged escape routes.

Marika is holding her breath. Now that the rest of the Almohad leadership has been killed in Morocco, Saif al-Din is the last of their leaders. The final remaining power-broker, apart, perhaps, from the mysterious Syrian prisoner who has proven to be much more than cannon fodder.

This is the chance to finish it. Finish them.

Metre by metre, Marika brings the ATV level with the convoy of vehicles, six in all. They have spread out over a kilometre to make themselves less of a missile target.

Marika turns to PJ. 'Help will be here soon. We'll try to take out the lead vehicle. That might turn the others away from the village. If they get in there we're neck deep in shit.'

'OK. Take us in. I'm ready.'

Altering the angle, Marika edges the ATV in closer. Two hundred metres. One hundred. Still no one appears to have seen them. Closer still. Fifty. So close that they can see the driver's elbow resting on the sill. Thirty metres. A shout and someone points at them from the rear of the technical, just as the Minimi opens up not far from Marika's ear.

Through the NVG she can see the bullets tear along the vehicle, shredding a tyre and causing a puff of smoke or steam from under the bonnet. Another burst and the driver falls sideways, the vehicle skidding out of control so that Marika has to swerve to avoid it.

Being able to fire accurately from a moving vehicle was no idle boast from PJ. He displays devastating fire control, and Marika doubts that he has expended more than twenty rounds of the belt-fed ammunition.

'Well done,' she shouts. There's no need for another pass on that particular technical. Disabling the vehicles is the number one priority. There was no sign of Saif al-Din, though, she tells herself, it's rare for a commander to travel in the lead, usually they're second or third in line. More worrying is that most of the technicals she has seen thus far only seem to contain one or two men. Where are the others?

Now she spins the ATV to face the oncoming vehicles. Rounds zip and sting overhead. Most are being fired from the other technicals, but some from a survivor of the stopped vehicle, now firing from a kneeling position. The Minimi hammers again and he falls, but not before Marika feels a series of thuds. Rounds slamming into the plastic and fibreglass body of the ATV.

'You OK?' she shouts.

'Yep, keep going.'

Anyone else with your injuries would be in an ICU, she thinks.

As she accelerates towards the rest of the convoy Marika sees that her aggressive attack has not made them turn. They know that the village means safety for them.

Marika steers the ATV broadside across the face of the oncoming vehicles, just in time. Again the Minimi hammers, but they are also taking fire, and she is forced to make a long, slow turn.

'Pais,' she calls, 'can you smell petrol?'

'Yes.'

'I think the tank has taken a hit.'

There is no answer, just the stutter of the gun.

Marika swings back towards the convoy but, watching them, she has a sudden uncomfortable feeling that something is wrong. These vehicles, also, are all but empty. She slows, heading away, trying to think, when PJ calls out from behind her.

'Choppers coming. Gunships.'

'The damn US cavalry,' she says, 'always in the nick of time.'

Five kilometres away, Saif al-Din stands above the stream bank, watching the Cobra gunships come out of the east. Missiles streak towards the ground, leaving phosphorescent smoke trails in the night, followed by thumping explosions. Tracer from the Dushka arcs up towards the aircraft, the distant hammer familiar to his ears, his aural memory so acute that he can recognise two dozen different weapons from their sound alone.

This place is perfect for the ruse. Thick cover. He knows the men thought he was crazy when he made the preparations — the unspoken stares telling him that they thought him overly cautious. Now, however, the respect is just as obvious.

The plan is working, but he is fighting and losing an internal battle that there seems no immediate remedy for. The pain in his head has gone from acute to extreme, and he has a shaking need for more of the opium pellets. A need that betrays his own principles, yet is undeniable.

There is a tongue of fire from one of the vehicles out on the plain as a SAM goes up. One chopper explodes into a ball of flame and falls in burning pieces, splintered rotors still turning. The other settles low and directs a devastating stream of mini-gun fire into the decoys.

A voice comes from behind Saif. 'Sayyid, we are ready.'

Saif turns away from the fight. The men in the decoy vehicles will all be killed, but they are expendable. The main body of men and all the equipment were dropped here, using the thick vegetation beside the dry stream bed as cover. Vehicles carrying the spores are already heading out in different directions. A brilliant ploy, and Saif allows himself a moment of pride as he approaches their own transport, a Toyota Troop Carrier, complete with Red Crescent medical team. One male and four female hostages occupy the rear. The roof of this one is painted with an enormous Red Crescent symbol, and the kufr would never risk firing on it.

As Saif and the two other armed men climb up into the troop carrier, five pairs of eyes look up from the rows of seats. He can smell the fear on them. One female Turkish doctor. Four nurses; one male and three females. The ceiling has been hastily insulated with twenty millimetres of foam rubber to reduce the heat signature from the occupants.

The driver starts the engine and the vehicle clunks into gear while Saif issues last-minute instructions. 'You will not leave your seat, you will do nothing but breathe unless I tell you to, do you understand?'

Silence. None of them dare to speak. Fear works. It always does. In spite of the terrible pain, Saif feels a grim satisfaction. The flasks have gone out. There are too many, by too many different routes, for them to fail.

The driver flicks on the headlights, and Saif shouts, 'Switch them off, idiot.'

'It is dark, Sayyid.'

'You have eyes, and the compass. God will guide you.'

'Yes, Sayyid.'

The driver, however, barely increases the pace at which they travel.

'Faster,' Saif shouts.

There is a groan of despair from the man, but the engine revolutions climb steadily.

'If you hit a tree I will shoot you,' Saif adds. The cold engine, he knows, will help protect them from the thermal imaging equipment of the enemy for only a minute or two. Even the body heat of the passengers, despite the insulation, might give them away.

As the Toyota begins to move faster, the pain in Saif's head surges far past any level that he has experienced before. He presses the heel of each hand into his temples. His legs and arms no longer move of their own accord, but it does not matter. There is only this terrible pain and aching need.

The driver, struggling to control the vehicle at speed across the wild terrain, looks across at him, 'What's wrong, Sayyid?'

'Nothing. Just drive!' Saif screams.

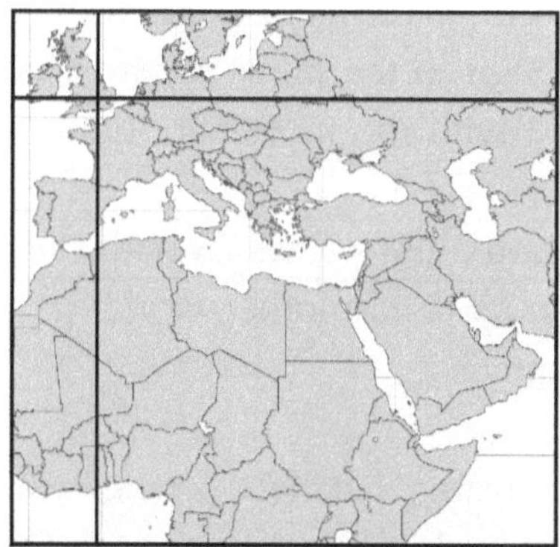

74 UNITED KINGDOM

London

'Damn them to hell,' Mossel says, pacing the Blair Room, eyes divided between the screen and the Sid in his hand. 'The Almohad aircraft has changed targets. Heading south. What's down there? It doesn't make any sense.'

The SITPOL screen scrolls as a technician searches for possible targets on that heading. 'It can't be Nairobi, sir, too far for a light plane. It must be a refugee camp — one of the larger ones. Dadaab or Chakula.'

'Jesus Christ.' Mossel covers his face with both hands. 'Chakula is the closest. That must be it. They're heading straight for it — and there's half a million people in that place.'

Tom Mossel feels like a man with one plastic cup, trying to bring it down on ten mice, all running in different directions. He has loosened his tie and even released the top button of his Pierre Cardin shirt.

Ten minutes earlier he shouted at Will Grace, and he knows that his assistant is sulking, but it doesn't matter. None of it matters. This situation is slipping through their fingers. They are too slow at every turn. Frustration burns through him as he waits to be patched through to the pilot. A man who, at this moment, has been entrusted with the most important task on the face of the earth.

Finally an ominous hiss comes over the handset. Mossel can hear the jet engine as if in another world. 'Flying Officer Singh. What's your first name?'

'Nayan.'

'Listen to me, Nayan. That light aircraft you are tracking has on board a payload of biological weapons. Their target must be one of a number of refugee camps, probably Chakula, as it is the closest. If you can't destroy it they might well kill hundreds of thousands, perhaps half a million people. Nothing matters except putting it out of action. Do you understand what I'm saying?'

'Affirmative.'

Yet, to Nayan, the target's new flight path is problematic. Each kilometre flown to the south means more fuel burned. He punches some figures into the onboard computer. 'Estimate that to engage target I must pass the point of no return. Advise.'

'Standby.'

Nayan hears nothing for one and a half minutes.

'Target too important to lose, no other aircraft in range can be equipped with suitable missiles. You have to proceed. Zomo Kenyatta airport at Nairobi is your fallback option.'

Nayan sighs in relief. If Nairobi is willing to accept him then that will be fine, and the further south the target flies the more it fits in with this plan, provided, of course, they don't start zigzagging.

'Roger, control. We have eight minutes to target area, will commence tracking in five and reduce to engagement speed.'

One chopper is down, but others are on the way and the surviving craft is more cautious, hanging back, shooting up the Almohad vehicles from a distance. Even so, Marika is nervous to be so exposed with a Cobra up there looking for targets.

'I'd give anything for Blue Force Tracker right now,' she breathes, referring to a device that emits identification to friendly assets to avoid becoming a target. She, at least, is wearing a uniform made with cenosphere technology, designed to reduce her heat signature, but PJ is not. Besides, the hot engine of the ATV itself will give them away, at least if the larger targets are all destroyed and the gunships go hunting for more.

Marika doesn't even consider leaving the ATV, at least not at this stage. Instead her eyes are focused on the Almohad vehicles, now revealed in the light of the burning technical. These vehicles were loaded down with people as they left Ka Tirsan. Now they appear to be empty apart from the drivers. Only one inference can be drawn.

'No wonder they're empty,' she tells PJ, half-turning, 'they've already offloaded the men — and the cargo.'

'Where?'

'Back further, in the trees along that dry river maybe.' Marika is furious with herself. The oldest trick in the book, and a humiliating one. She revs the engine. 'Let's go find them. Things are going to get dangerous around here when more Cobras turn up, in any case.'

Swinging the ATV into a sharp turn, she starts accelerating at the halfway point of the circle. She reaches full speed in less than twenty seconds, lowering her head against the slipstream.

They cross the tracks halfway back across the plain and Marika follows them, already with that cold feeling that it is too late. At least the lugged tyre marks are a clear and unmissable trail in the NVG, the tread patterns still embedded in the dark sands of the plain.

Her eyes focus on where the hills slope down into the banks of the dry stream. The trees there offer the only cover for miles. For the Almohad vehicles to have quickly offloaded some of their men and cargo, this would have been the place.

Into the trees: clusters of acacia, bigger bean trees, startling candelabras. The tyre tracks diverge into many. *Fuck!* These people are not stupid, and now she and PJ are in danger of being ambushed, or worse, mined. Speed is the only possible weapon, and Marika does her best to keep racing through the corners, avoiding the ruts, resisting turning on the headlights.

Something lies slumped on the middle of the track, a body, but there is no time to investigate. Marika swerves around it. Deeply rutted tracks. Her frustration builds. From here the hostiles could have taken four or five different transport options.

She feels a tap on her shoulder and slows. 'What's up?'

'Stop.'

'Why?'

'Just do it.'

Marika brakes the machine, and sits with it burbling along in idle. Again PJ's voice, whispered and urgent. 'Cut the engine.'

'What?'

'Cut the engine and listen. Charging around the place will help them, but not us.'

Marika's right hand moves to the key. The engine dies.

The silence at first seems consuming. Ticking, cooling metal parts. An explosion in the distance, the Cobra gunships still taking out the near-empty vehicles.

Taking out her Sid, Marika punches in a quick précis of the situation, then calls to Sara. 'All OK back there?'

'Medivac five minutes out apparently. All quiet. No sign of hostiles.'

'Ronnie awake yet?'

'Yep. Groggy and vomiting. Gave him a quick jab of valium.'

Marika ends the call, then scrolls through the updates. She freezes when she learns the new Almohad target. Chakula Refugee Camp. Her camp. All the faces she came to know so well.

Marika finds Kifimbo's number on the contacts file. His voice, when it comes, is quiet and subdued. Not how she remembers him.

'Hello?'

'Kifimbo, it's me.'

'Tajiri Hartmann?'

'Yes, listen carefully. Something terrible might soon happen there. Get away if you can. If you go by vehicle keep the doors and windows closed. Take as many other people as you can. OK?'

'Can you tell me what is happening? We've been summoned to the operations room. I am on my way there now.'

'I don't have time to explain. But the camp and everyone inside is in terrible danger.'

Marika ends the call. 'You OK back there Pais?'

'Yes, and if you stop talking for a moment, you'll hear an engine.'

Marika sits stock-still, focusing her senses. There is something faint. Far off to her right, into the north, the low-down, torquey churning of a diesel engine driving off-road, in soft substrate. Now it works harder, building and releasing as if climbing a drift of sand. She turns to look at PJ, his face eerie, almost unrecognisable in the darkness. 'It has to be them.'

'One of them, anyway.'

She can hear the note of pain in his voice. 'How do you feel?'

'High as a kite. Don't worry about me.'

Marika uses the Sid to take a bearing on the sound, closing her eyes for a moment to pinpoint the direction.

One last listen, the sound already growing fainter, then she slips the NVG back on and turns the key of the ATV. 'Let's go,' she warns and, gunning the engine, she steers right, racing, a low-hanging acacia branch almost striking her forehead.

Roaring across the sandy track and through a dark tunnel of vegetation, Marika sees branches like the fingers of ghosts through the IR-boosted NVG. She pushes the ATV as fast as she dares, passes tracks, camels, a motorbike. She ignores everything, keeping on in the direction shown on the Sid, just a few degrees west of north.

They rocket down into the stream bed, ploughing through gravel and sand, avoiding tree trunks strewn by some long-ago flood. Marika scans the terrain for a way up the other side, travelling almost half a klick before it becomes negotiable. 'Hold on,' she says, flicking her wrist hard on the throttle. She takes the slope at full speed, feeling the machine all but lift into the air as it strikes a bump on the lower slope, coming down accompanied by a muffled cry of pain from PJ. It has been easy to forget just how badly he is hurt. He needs medical attention, and Marika tries not to regret bringing him — she was expecting a quick foray. This is turning into a marathon.

The ATV wheels spin and churn, but gain ground on the way up. Marika's teeth grind together as she feels the strain in the gearbox. She changes down, the links of the chain stretched tight, then the machine accelerates over the last few metres of the slope, bursting out over the top into that seemingly endless African landscape of whistling thorn and scattered acacias.

Gathering speed again, she aims for the high ground, a low hillock. Gaining the crest she again cuts the engine to listen ahead. The sound of the diesel has changed bearing, and Marika adjusts the Sid accordingly.

'Head a little more easterly, and we should cross their tracks,' PJ says.

'Good idea, why didn't I think of that?'

'I was a point man on patrol. You learn these things.'

Marika glances down at the fuel gauge. The needle that had been on three-quarters five minutes earlier is now well under one-quarter. 'Looks like the fuel tank did take a hit.'

'Could be near the back, and going uphill made it spill faster.'

'Probably.' She turns the key. 'Let's go.'

The Almohad tyre tracks run beside a column of stone that rises out of the landscape as if it was placed there by the hand of a giant. On one side, curiously, grows a particular variety of moss or fungus that fluoresces in the NVG like glitter. The tracks themselves are wide-spaced as if from a truck or large SUV and Marika cannot help but feel a moment of grim excitement.

Tracks do not remain fresh for very long in these kinds of soils. This is a new trail. One vehicle alone.

Marika has hunted the predators of the world for long enough to have a highly developed sixth sense. Hers is telling her that Saif al-Din is close. That he is in this vehicle. Last to leave the site of the change-over. That's what a leader does. That's what she would have done. He will also have many of the deadly spores in his possession. Not all, perhaps, but he would want the power of possessing much of the ordnance for himself.

Hunched over the ATV, engine building to fifth gear and just over 3500 RPM, Marika pictures him. The eyes of a maniac, a fanatic and a killer. A man who put twenty children and four adults to death just so he could place his Syrian ally close to her. All in order to remove his rivals for the Almohad leadership.

Dead children spread like litter. Lying alone and overlaying each other so it is hard to tell where one wound ends and another begins.

He has been a step ahead of her all the way, and now it is her job to stop him.

The landscape here rises and falls constantly, and on one of the larger jump-ups she pauses, scanning over the three or four kilometres of horizon. Then she sees it through the NVG, a dark shape moving through the landscape.

'That's them,' she says, 'driving without lights. Going slow, too.'

PJ makes no reply.

'Are you alright?'

A grunt and groan. 'Yep. Come on. Let's get him.'

Marika glances again at the fuel gauge, then tries to put it out of her mind, twisting the throttle, the ATV surging forward. Behind her she can hear PJ working the action on the Minimi. The vehicle ahead, from what she can see, is smaller than a truck, but may well be equipped with a machine gun. This will not be easy, and much as she would like to take personal vengeance she is already thinking that the best technique will be to identify it as a target from a safe distance and call in the Cobras circling back out there on the plain.

They come up quickly on the fleeing vehicle. She recognises it as a Toyota Troop Carrier, about as big as passenger-carrying 4x4 vehicles get. The name is something of a misnomer, referring more to the people-carrying capacity of the microbus-like seats than any true martial purpose.

The crescent painted on the rear doors has not escaped her attention. At first she takes it at face value. It looks too perfect to be fake. But would a Red Crescent team be travelling at night, without lights?

It wouldn't be, but the presence of that humanitarian logo makes the idea of calling in an airstrike wishful thinking. Marika drops back. Time to think. The occupants of the vehicle have shown no sign that they have seen the ATV at this stage. She glances down at the fuel needle flicking towards empty.

PJ's mind must be working as hard as hers. 'Get me up close,' he says, 'and I'll shred the back tyres.'

Marika thinks about it. They don't want the troop carrier to crash, but deflating the tyres will more likely just immobilise them. No vehicle can travel on this kind of surface on the rims. It's their best chance.

'You'll need to duck right down so I can fire.'

Marika lowers her head as far as she can, and gives the motor some stick. The ATV surges forward in response. Stutters, another surge. Almost dies.

'Fuck, we're running out of fuel.'

'Not yet, keep it going.'

The engine catches, a final burst of power, but she can feel it faltering. She shouts at PJ to shoot, ducks down so she is out of the field of fire just as the gun belches twice. At the same time the engine of the ATV stops completely and it rolls to a halt, quickly slowed by the loose surface.

The troop carrier also lurches to a stop, rocking back on the rear wheel rims, engine running, the sound of a door opening. Voices, shouted orders.

Marika asks PJ, 'Can you lift that gun off?'

'Yes.'

'We've got to get off here, we're sitting ducks. They'll take us to pieces.'

Marika half-stands, braces herself and takes the weight of the weapon from PJ's arms. She carries it easily with one arm while helping him down with the other.

There is a rise in the earth ten or so metres away, and they crawl into cover together, PJ with his weight on his hands and knees. By the time he collapses there she can feel the cold, clammy sweat on his skin, knowing the effort he made to get there.

Giving him time to recover, Marika sets the Minimi into firing position, folding the bipod down, and the belt spread evenly beside it to help prevent jams. She is half-thinking of going back to get another belt when automatic fire rakes out from the hidden, shadowy side of the Troop Carrier, tearing the ATV to pieces, sparks and tracer ricochets burning out into the night.

Human shapes move in the darkness near the Toyota. Marika holds her fire. These people are not dressed in combat fatigues, black balaclavas or even the mishmash of clothing commonly worn by fighters in this part of the world. Marika's heart sinks.

Hostages. There really is a humanitarian team in there.

Voices are audible, and Marika has known Kutay long enough to recognise Turkish when she hears it.

A louder voice, in English, booms out across the intervening space. Patently African. Deep and commanding. 'If you try to shoot, innocent people will die. If we hear an aircraft engine, innocent people will die. We have two spare tyres and will change both. Any further attempt to hamper or hinder us, and innocent people will die.'

Again a muzzle flash, and a storm of bullets takes apart a tree stump some fifty metres away, on the other side of the bike.

Jesus, they're looking for us, Marika thinks. She tries to work out the weapon they are using; it doesn't sound like an AK47, but something with a higher cyclic rate of fire.

She sends through another update on her SID, finishing with: *Hostages in peril, do not approach area under any circumstances.*

This is something she agonises over. Bringing in a high-temperature warhead to vaporise the area would be a sacrifice she could make on her own account. But she cannot speak for the hostages. Besides, the relationship between the West and Turkey is shaky right now. Killing a team of doctors and nurses with a missile might take it over the edge.

She turns back to PJ, who has brought his knees up into his chest and has gone very quiet. Marika knows that moving from here is not an option — the effort of getting across from the ATV was almost beyond him. She is strong, yet she can't carry him. Waiting for the machine gunner to pick out their little slice of cover, however, is too fatalistic for her liking.

'I'm going to try to get around the other side. Can you man the gun, back me up?'

PJ's voice is tight with effort. 'Yeah.'

Another burst of gunfire and a small tree not far away shatters into a thousand splinters of wood and bark. Marika waits until it is over, then uses the dust and spatter of falling twigs to cover the sight and sound of her movement, sprinting up and around on an angle.

Someone, however, is watching that side, for an AK47 fires out of the cab window, bullets whipcracking over her head and through the scrub.

However, instead of stopping and risking being pinned down, she redoubles her pace, aims for a little more distance until that gun can no longer bear. She is now facing the vehicle head on, able to see the other side where they have just finished changing the first of two tyres.

Scanning the ground for a lying-up point, she spots a shallow depression. This is less obvious than the alternatives, she decides, as she drops prone and unslings the G36 from her shoulder.

The G36 has a six-power telescopic sight and, viewed through the NVG, it is almost as good as shooting in daylight. The rifle also has the stubby grenade launcher underneath, loaded, ready to fire.

Through the scope she can see two of the hostages standing against the bonnet, then a man with slung rifle wheeling the shattered tyre to the open side door. Saif al-Din himself holds what she sees now is a Russian-made PK machine gun, a heavy weapon that requires a strong man to fire from the shoulder.

It is this machine gun that has been firing the searching bursts into cover, Marika decides, watching the Almohad leader change position. He seems to know that she has moved, laying the bipod of the PK onto the hood of the Toyota, then the butt to his shoulder. Marika realises that he is searching for her with the sight.

She adjusts the crosshairs so that they centre over his chest. The head would be a quicker kill, but under these conditions she cannot be certain of that level of accuracy. The chest is a bigger target, but she has to be certain that killing him is the right course of action.

Deciding that this is too good an opportunity to miss, she starts to squeeze the trigger. But then the scope goes white as the PK opens up first. Marika has time only for the realisation that he has seen her before snapping off two rounds in return. The ground and air around her explodes with burning metal.

The G36 takes a hit, jumping in her hand as if it had been kicked, then she feels a stinging burn along her forearm as if seared with a hot knife. Dropping the weapon, she rolls away from the impact point, but the storm of gunfire has already stopped, replaced by a silence deeper and darker than a well, her senses numbed.

Regathering her wits, Marika is pretty sure that she hit him — he must have taken at least one round of the two she fired. If not, the gunfire would have continued and she would be dead.

Marika's left arm goes numb, followed by a burning sensation. She delves up inside the long sleeve of her fatigues with her right hand, finding the area sodden with blood, a long trench in the muscle of her forearm where a bullet has ploughed through. She clenches and unclenches her hand, more blood seeping from the wound.

Already she can feel the first shakiness of shock. She fights it. Reaches for the G36 with her good hand, examines it, tries to work the action, but it is stuck fast. Only the grenade launcher barrel and the scope are still operational.

Marika brings the G36 to her shoulder. Deep breath. Sights. Saif al-Din is kneeling, and one of the others is attending to a wound in his side. *If I had one more round I could kill him now. Then maybe the others.*

Marika regrets waiting so long before, wishing she had opened fire more quickly, rather than letting him set up the weapon and get the shot away. It was the hostages, of course, always that human element that makes things difficult.

At least I got the bastard, she thinks. It might not be a fatal wound, but it's something.

She watches him stand drunkenly, walk to the nearest of the Red Crescent hostages, pull a pistol from the holster, hold it to the back of the woman's head. Before she can even think through what will happen next he fires and the woman's body falls forward to the ground, one leg twitching until Saif al-Din fires again and the corpse lies still.

'That,' he calls out, 'is retribution. Every aggressive act will be met with death. Any attempt to follow us further will be met with death.'

Marika finds that her teeth are starting to chatter and she consciously forms words with her lips to keep the coming shock at bay. Pain is building in her arm, shooting through to her shoulder.

You fucking bastard, she mouths, *tonight one of us is going to die, and it ain't gonna be me.*

The last tyre they are changing is now on the hub, and she watches the vehicle sag as they release the jack and let it down. A couple of spins of a wheel brace and the engine roars to life. Saif al-Din's voice cuts through the night, ordering the hostages back into the vehicle. Marika watches them file in, helpless. Her finger is on the trigger of the grenade launcher. But she does not fire. Has no choice but to let the vehicle go. Watch it drive past, gun barrels out open windows like quills. Now she stands, working her way back to PJ and the Minimi.

When she gets there PJ is unconscious, slumped over the weapon. She decides not to try to wake him, rolls him on his side and checks his pulse, then lays the near-useless G36 beside him, peeling his fingers from the pistol grip of the Minimi. She stands with the weapon, belt of cartridges half-gathered under her arm, wondering what she should do now.

While she stands there, gripped with indecision, the churning sound of the Troop Carrier's diesel engine stops abruptly, somewhere up ahead. The hostile vehicle is now stationary, perhaps a kilometre up the track. She cocks her head to one side and hears yet another engine start up.

Another vehicle change, she thinks. *Jesus fucking Christ. This man is freakishly prepared, and that is why he is one of the world's most dangerous terrorists.*

First Marika strips off the heavy battle jacket, leaving just the Kevlar vest and CPU undersuit, the latter too time consuming to remove right now. This done, she hefts the Minimi and looks down at PJ. She does not want to leave him — there could be hyenas or anything here — but she has no choice.

'Back soon, Pais,' she says. 'I promise.' Turning, she holds the machine gun with most of the weight in her good arm and begins to run towards the sounds of converging vehicles.

Saif al-Din sees the meeting place up ahead. Three technicals are waiting there to escort him safely away — an extra layer of protection built only into his own escape route. The Troop Carrier stops and he holds the PK machine gun ready, shouting orders as both cargo and hostages are split between the vehicles.

All the time he feels fluid leak from the hole torn in his side by the kufr woman's bullet. Yet the pain is nothing compared to the need for opium; a clawing monster, talons like knives inside him. His mind wanders, impossible to control. Nightmares lurk behind the surface of calm that he must show always to the outside world.

He knows that he should be going too, but also that the woman will be coming. It is time to stop her. The bitch has dogged him enough.

'You go ahead,' he calls, 'I will catch up in the Toyota soon.'

In his tortured mind Marika Hartmann symbolises the hunters, the feeling of always being pursued. She symbolises the tracking systems, the RPAs, everything that he hates in the world. The impersonal, mechanised death spawned by the politics of asymmetrical warfare.

Now he wants to kill her. He wants that small victory. Tonight she will die. He knows that she will pursue until she has no breath. He saw her standing in the distance as they pulled away. She will be coming. He walks away, back up the track a hundred metres.

There he drops to the earth, arranges the gun to cover the road, then lies prone to wait. Soon she will be dead, and the Tide of Saleh will be unleashed upon the earth.

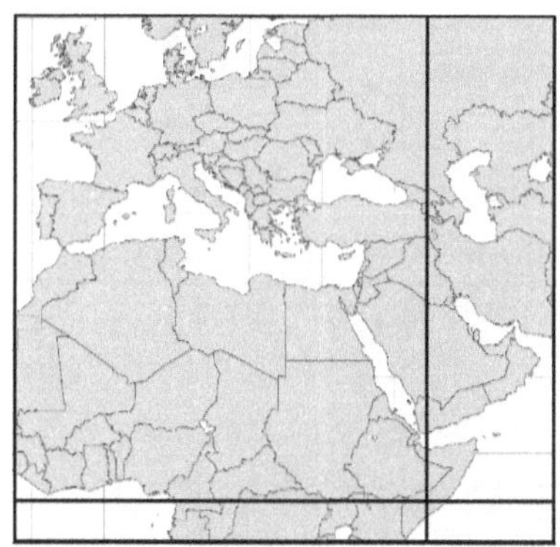

75 SOMALIA

Near Chakula Refugee Camp

Kifimbo takes one of the garrison Humvees, slips into the driver's seat, and punches in the stiff clutch with his left foot. What he has been told is a sick weight inside. Spores of a deadly killer will come from the sky. Something made by evil men long ago in Iraq, now in the hands of al-Muwahhidun.

The orphanage is no more than a kilometre away, and Kifimbo drives as fast as is safe in a place where foot, animal and cart traffic far outnumbers motor vehicles, and the old and vulnerable use the road as commonly as the younger and more mobile.

The camp is growing, the corn famine having set off a mass movement of refugees. Where before there was little to eat, now there is nothing. The Laba Quarter has become a desperate place, doubling in size in just weeks. Families stew wild grass in an effort to stave off death.

The compound itself is five hundred acres of safety, where a daily food ration means life. But now this. Death from the sky. Kifimbo's eyes fill with helpless tears as he drives. How can men

459

so randomly inflict death and pain on others? When did greed and revenge become more important than love and living?

The people in the camp are already starting to panic. News of the impending catastrophe spreads outwards like a ripple in a pool. No one is walking now, but running, and vehicles speed back towards the compound, carrying doctors and other volunteers.

The orphanage is bright with lights, including a pair of yellow floods on a pole out the front, attracting a mass of swirling insects. Kifimbo slides to a halt outside, then walks towards the entrance, opening the door and entering the lobby.

The director looks up. 'We've already heard. The staff are getting the children up now.'

'Have they told you why?'

'They said it is some kind of chemical leak.' His forehead creases in concern. 'Is that the truth?'

Kifimbo can see no point in frightening the man further. 'Close enough.'

The director moves to brush past him. 'Excuse me, but I must go.' His eyes focus on the rifle. 'We do not need soldiers with guns. We need men who will carry babies. Men to drive buses.'

'I will carry children, and I can drive a bus.'

'Then you are welcome. But hurry, please, the fuel tank is low. There are drums — can you fill it with diesel?'

'Yes,' he says, 'I can do that too.'

Kifimbo has seen the bus out and about in the camp. A Nissan minibus. Now it sits in the compound at the back, a store of fuel drums nearby. Two are empty — he can feel the lack of weight when he pushes with his palm. One, lying down, is full, and he rolls it with his foot towards the bus's filler cap, pushing it upright, before returning to the other drums for a spanner to open the filler, and the hand-drawn diesel pump, which he fits into place and begins to fuel the bus. This is a farm job he has performed many times.

The bus fills with passengers as he works, kids chattering with excitement and babies crying as they meet the cool night air.

Kifimbo cranes his neck in the hope of seeing Rajee, but the infants are well wrapped and it is impossible to identify him.

The drum is almost empty when the fuel tank spills over. Kifimbo removes the pump, replaces the lid and rolls the drum away before climbing into the driver's seat. His hands have that sweet, strong smell of diesel and he wipes them on his trousers before feeling for the key, letting the glow plug light for five full seconds before turning the key. Engine running, Kifimbo leaves the bus and helps bring in the last few children.

The director is last out of the building, carrying a ring of keys with a worried expression on his face.

'Is that everything?'

'Yes, we had better hurry.'

By the time the children have filed aboard there are more than sixty human beings in a bus made to seat thirty-eight and stand twelve. Kifimbo can feel it wallow on the springs, but when he eases her into first gear the bus grinds away down the track.

On the first corner, however, Kifimbo can feel the body of the bus swing out on its suspension. He sees the face of the orphanage director in the rear-view mirror. A deep frown belies the calm voice with which he talks to the children.

The road has choked up with vehicles of all kinds, crammed with people trying to flee the camp. Kifimbo drives patiently, hand resting on the gear knob when he is forced to wait, drawing comfort from the vibration of the engine.

For days, since the massacre of the children on the river glade, then the death of Haro, Kifimbo has been plagued by a feeling as heavy as lead and as dark as a black drawstring bag around his heart. He has tried to fend off this feeling with thoughts of his homeland. Of a village, and a lake. He has tried to think of good things. Small kindnesses and friendships that he sees in the camp every day.

Still, it is no use. Kifimbo has looked too deeply into the savage. Seen the animal things of which humans are capable. Now, fleeing in the dark bus with the singing children, the threat is a weight that he can only bear with the thought that perhaps he can save these few lives. Rajee, who has already lost two mothers, and many more who have stories no less heart-rending.

Somewhere, deep inside, Kifimbo is starting to see this night as his redemption.

The missile lock is whining now. Nayan is five minutes away from not having enough fuel to reach Nairobi.

He presses the 'arm' switch, waits until it glows green, then lifts the cover off the 'fire' switch.

The Raptor shudders as both port and starboard missiles fly off towards the target.

He watches the screen, knowing that he should already be turning away. The fuel margin is tight, yet this will be his first air-to-air kill and he wants to see it happen.

Istikaan sees the jet coming up on the radar, faster than can be believed considering their own airspeed exceeds one hundred knots.

'Preparing countermeasure flare launchers,' he says.

Over the months before the incursion into Iraq, he scarcely slept with the planning. One of the items he ordered from Iran and had shipped over by dhow was a number of these very clever Iranian missile decoys. Their main purpose is to fire high-temperature flares away from the aircraft, followed by foil chaff.

The first ploy fools heat-seeking missiles, the latter destroys any hope of radar guidance.

The flares are never one hundred per cent effective used from a jet-engined craft, with their massive heat emissions, but from a small light plane they are devastating, presenting dozens of much more attractive targets than the plane itself, throwing off an enormous heat signature for their size.

'The enemy have fired missiles,' the pilot screams.

Istikaan does not speak, but presses a switch, activating the flare launchers, firing just half the thirty tubes in case more are necessary later. He watches the screen … twenty, thirty seconds pass before the two missiles disappear from the radar, and the plane rocks gently with the distant explosions. He allows himself a smile.

Nayan watches with dismay as the twin blips of the missiles disappear and the target flies on.

'What's going on?' he shouts into the microphone.

'Stand by.' Mossel's voice again. 'We suspect that something was just shunted from the plane. Flare decoys. Strong heat signature. They must have had you on radar too. Close with the plane and destroy it with cannon fire.'

'What about the payload?'

'There is nothing but desert here, we can take it out with air-to-surface missiles once it's on the ground. Just bring the damn thing down.'

Nayan feels the cold wind of failure as he takes manual control. The Raptor responds effortlessly to stick and rudder as he races her towards the radar return of the target. Even once the small blip is almost superimposed on his own, larger image, however, he fails to get a visual sighting. 'Can't see it,' he cries into the radio. 'Dust and cloud.'

'They're dropping altitude, but they're there. Keep looking.'

Nayan grabs the stick and starts going down. Visibility remains at just a few hundred metres, however, the air tinged yellow and brown from blown dust.

'Can't see them.'

'Keep following, you're our only chance. The Kenyans have scrambled a squadron of Northrop F-5s from Laikipia Air Base, but they won't be on-site for seven minutes.'

Flying into the dust is terrifying, but almost as bad is the realisation that in a few seconds he will no longer have enough fuel to reach Nairobi. This may already be the end of the line for him. The one flight he was born to make.

Half a million people.

'You are almost over Chakula Camp,' the comms system is saying. 'It's too late …'

The shape of the Piper Pawnee appears through the gloom. His wing-mounted cannons are no longer an option.

Half a million mothers and fathers and sisters and brothers. Boys and girls with dreams that might one day …

In that microsecond he knows that there is only one course of action remaining to him. Something that will produce a fireball hot enough to kill anything organic within a wide radius — to destroy the evil weapon in that plane.

One universal creator being. By the grace of the true Lord.

In that house where the praises of the creator are chanted and contemplated,

In that house, sing songs of praise; meditate and remember the creator, Lord Vaheguru.

Sing the songs of praise of my fearless lord,

I am a sacrifice to that song of praise which brings eternal peace.

He slows almost to stalling speed, and then, consulting the radar screen, heads back into the path of the tiny plane. Every nuance of reflex and talent he can summon from all those years of wanting, all those years of waiting.

I am a sacrifice to that song of praise which brings eternal peace.

He sees an image of his fiancée, Lakshmani. Knowing her heart will break, yet also that she will understand.

The light plane appears out of the gloom. Nayan aims the jet squarely and hits the afterburners.

I am a sacrifice to that song of praise which brings eternal peace.

* * *

The ground itself is not visible, and Istikaan would have liked to ask the pilot to descend further, but he knows that only height will disseminate the spores as widely as possible.

'The device is ready,' he says quietly.

'According to the plotter we are entering the vicinity of Chakula Camp.'

Istikaan is aware of the gravity of the moment. 'I will turn on the Zubaidy broadcaster now.'

Then comes a terrible, deafening roar as a giant aircraft sweeps past them, passing into the dust in just a few seconds. Istikaan knows that the jet will circle to get back on their tail for another pass.

Reaching for the switch, Istikaan shouts *Allahu Akbar*, repeating it over again.

In his mind he hears the clamour of al-Hajjuf again, the shrieks and screams as they are herded into the cells, the angry voices and the rain of heavy clubs on human flesh. Blood hosed from the stone floor in a flood of crimson, ripe with stubborn clots and the rush of water into the drains. Women shielding babies under their shawls, sometimes delaying the effects of the bacillus so that the mother dies first and the wailing of infants pours through the glass.

Still he feels nothing. No pity.

He remembers the boys who teased him on the way to school. *Hourglass. Hourglass.*

Last of all he remembers the corpse on a rope. Perfectly still.

The words he read just a few hours ago have swirled and eddied in his mind ever since, powerful and yet inconsequential.

His final vision is of something huge and terrible through the windows as the Raptor strikes them at a combined speed of over one thousand kilometres per hour.

At that moment he sees the words on the page of that suicide note come to life before his eyes.

To the Living from the Dead

لامجلا ن ع ثبحلا

SEEK BEAUTY

The centre of the fireball reaches temperatures in excess of one thousand degrees. Nothing and no one can survive.

Marika's breath burns like fire. The Chinese gun is getting heavier with every pace, and the pain in her left arm is excruciating. Her Alt-Berg boots are too heavy for cross-country running and the NVG are so sweaty and annoying that she removes them, holding them loosely in her right hand as she runs.

More engines up ahead. Another change-over? Something is happening and she knows that the situation, held by her fingertips, is about to move beyond her grasp. The moon pokes shy of the horizon and the light is just enough to run by. She doesn't know how much further she is going to have to travel, but there is no question of stopping. She will run until all the blood has leaked from her veins. Until death itself. She can feel the sinews stretched tight across her neck and shoulders, the junctions of her arms, and in the balls of her feet.

Despite an unstoppable determination, caution does not desert her. She pauses to scan ahead, again slipping the NVG over her head in order to do so. On the third such stop she sees the Troop Carrier pulled up on the side of the road up ahead. No lights, doors ajar. She scans for more than a minute and sees no sign of life. They have changed vehicles again. They are gone.

Hostages were almost certainly on board the change-over vehicles, but that is now someone else's problem. Air assets will be used to attempt to track them, but Marika is in awe at how well thought-out this dispersal plan has been. Saif al-Din is paranoid, the intel on him shows it over and over again, but this escape was well prepared by any measure.

Marika buttons away the Sid, steadies the Minimi, flicking off the safety, cradling it in her aching arms as she starts to walk towards the Toyota. With the help of the rising moon, the view through the NVG is much brighter.

The track is the obvious site for an IED so she moves off the wheel ruts, into the scrub on one side, creeping now, minutely scanning up to ten paces ahead with her eyes, looking for trip wires or freshly disturbed earth.

Saif al-Din's eyes have always been exceptional in the dark, and he knows the techniques, using the rod receptors in the corner of his eyes. The technique allows him to spot an approaching figure — the woman, he is sure of it.

A cold tingle of anticipation breaks through even the pain and opium cravings. The woman has left the track and is moving towards his position, screened by a thick patch of thorn. He prepares himself, pushing the gun on its bipod ahead of him so it makes two furrows in the sand.

Now he settles the butt into his shoulder and lines up the sights. He waits, sees the tall figure coming closer, knowing he cannot afford to fire too early, he must make sure of his shot. She is armed, and if he misses she will have the advantage of her NVG.

He has to will himself to wait, curbing his impatience, until finally she fills the sight. An unmissable target. He smiles to himself, thanks God in a whisper, having dreamed of killing this woman.

There is no gentle squeeze — no finesse. The machine gun cannot miss. With all the indignation, hatred and anger he can summon, Saif al-Din pulls the trigger.

In that moment when the night explodes into noise and light, Marika takes two rounds across the chest, and even with the projectile vest the impacts are shocking. No Kevlar vest, even these latest variants, can fully protect against 7.62mm rounds fired at point-blank range.

The heavy slugs break ribs, slam the breath from her body and knock her from her feet. The earth seems to tilt beneath her so that she is down almost without seeming to fall, as if the ground came up to meet her.

At least one of the rounds has penetrated right through the vest and into her chest; she can feel the agony of the torn skin amid the blunt pain of sheer physical trauma. It is tempting to lie back and deal with the pain, but she knows that he will come to finish her. The knowledge takes the focus from her injuries, from the shaking, fright and fear.

Blood runs and soaks the vest, and she slides a hand underneath to feel, wincing as her hands touch damaged flesh. There is a hard, rubbery lump over her ribs, the projectile itself, and the knowledge that it did not penetrate the rib-cage steels her.

I am hit, but he did not kill me, the bastard. Not yet, anyway.

Thinking now only of defending herself, she feels for the Minimi. Nothing. It is nearby, certainly, but there is no time to search for it. Instead her hand, sticky with her own blood, moves to her Glock handgun in the holster.

Marika draws it out, holding it alongside her body, saving her strength for the moment, fighting the shaking, concentrating on getting control of herself, scanning through the NVG, knowing that this is a life or death moment. Saif al-Din was close when he fired — she remembers seeing the muzzle flash in that microsecond before the bullets struck. Of course he will come to finish her off.

Marika sees a dark shape rise from the flat landscape with a gun across his chest, extending from either side, ammo belt hanging down. He is crouching, reaching out towards her with the stealth of an animal, appearing to move over the earth with no movement of the legs. The gun barrel is like an eye, preceding him. His forefinger will be on the trigger, just above the crease of the first joint, resting with the lightest pressure, ready to send a stream of bullets towards her. As soon as he sees her he will fire, but, lying down, she makes no silhouette.

Marika flattens herself against the earth, and waits. The hunter and the hunted. Killing and the fear of being killed. Willing her arm to stop trembling, distancing herself from the terrible pain in her chest.

Extreme range for a pistol, but she brings it up in her bloodied hands, knowing they are shaking wildly. She sees the dark shape coming for her, aims roughly in the middle. Pulls the trigger three times, so close together the rounds might have been fired from a fully automatic weapon.

A tearing, terrible scream. Yet still he comes. The muzzle flashes told him where she is. Then he is on her, overwhelming all her senses. The smell and sound of his breath. His sweat. The sight of him blotting out the sky, one hand grappling for her face, pushing the NVG aside so they are half-on, half-off, his weight making her feel suffocated and crushed to such an extent that for a moment she cannot fight back. Up in the sky she sees a chopper shoot overhead, the sound of rotors whacking and thumping into the earth, a missile streaking out from the stubby fuselage, across the sky to some distant target.

Saif al-Din's right hand moves lower, over her chin and onto her neck, thumb and forefinger snapping closed with such force it is scarcely believable. Her windpipe clamps shut. Unable to breathe. Feeling her eyes bulge.

Yet there is something else, a warm, clammy stickiness, and she realises that her enemy is leaking blood from his middle, torn by bullets. Opened up as if with a jagged knife.

Marika feels herself start to convulse from the lack of air. Feels her body jump with the pain, her hand searching down his shirt for the tear, to where her bullets have ripped him open. She finds the place with her finger.

Still his grip does not slacken. Her lungs convulsing now. Legs kicking in some terrible impulse that frightens her, panics her. Now she acts from the desperate knowledge that this man is going to kill her. Her fingers stab into the tear in his abdomen, through cloth, skin and muscle, one finger, two, then more.

With his free hand he tries to drag her hand away, and his eyes bulge white with pain.

She forces her whole hand inside, into the hot, wet cave of his body, pushing with every ounce of effort to drive it in deep, through the torn diaphragm, feeling the coiled entrails. Knowing that in a few seconds more of suffocation she will have nothing left.

She gets a grip on something flat and slippery. Squeezes and pulls, feeling it tear in her hands. A noise from his face. Not a word, but something deeper. A recognition. The grip on her neck relaxes, she can feel him still trying, the shaking effort of it, but the strength ebbs from him, as if through the burst wall of a dam. Her hand remains deep inside him, grabbing and tearing, and finally he releases her completely, shaking, burbling — dying.

With a final pulse of strength Marika pushes him away so he falls beside her. She picks up the Glock from where it has fallen, then stands, spreading her feet for support, looking down on her enemy. Her throat throbs from where he almost killed her

'You chose this,' she says, and fires twice into the head of Saif al-Din.

Starting the empty Troop Carrier takes several attempts, but finally the diesel rattles away. Not risking headlights, she drives using the NVG, trembling and aching, tears fogging the lenses. Her chest feels as though she has been hit by a car. The pain is numbing, and her breath still comes hard from where he squeezed with those clamp-like fingers.

The drive back to where she left PJ seems interminable, yet soon the shattered remnants of the Yamaha ATV appear and she pulls over, spilling out the door, forcing her legs to work. Walking is an effort now, but she reaches him, using the last of her strength, ripping off the NVG and throwing them aside.

Covered in the blood of her enemy, Marika takes the unconscious body of Paisley Johnson in her arms, kisses him on the forehead and closes her eyes.

It is time to collect the good things.

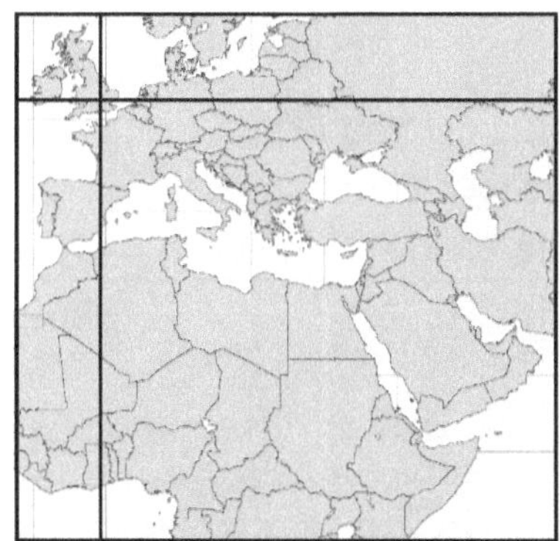

76 UNITED KINGDOM

Gatwick Airport

The white Ford van stops out on the tarmac and Julian Weiss is escorted aboard an airplane by two men in suits.

He says nothing while the plane prepares for flight. It's nothing like other flights he has taken — holidays in Greece or Ibiza. There is no talking. No fussing hostesses or safety messages.

The men sit facing him, wearing expressions of perpetual disapproval.

Julian has just endured twenty-four hours of interrogation. Hard men working in relays. Grilling him, demanding dates, times, details, when all he wanted to do was weep.

The plane climbs, and eventually the seatbelt light flicks off. One of the two men unbuckles his seatbelt.

'Am I going to be killed?' Julian asks.

'No,' one says.

The other takes over, his voice devoid of expression. 'Here's the deal. In this briefcase I have a passport in a false name. Five thousand pounds in cash. We will take you to a nominated city in any country in the world, and you will never return to the United Kingdom. Never.'

Julian stares, 'Why are you letting me go?'

'Because you are an embarrassment. You can never be brought to trial, and the director doesn't want you to disappear in a more permanent way.'

'What if I come back?'

'The director will change his mind. Something unofficial will happen to you. People died because of what you did. Our country faces a grave emergency partly because of what you did.'

Julian stares, open mouthed, thinking of Leisel. *I don't deserve to live.*

'Where do you want to go? Ottawa? Sydney? Auckland? New York?'

Julian remembers Leisel beside him in the bed one night, lying beside him, the sound of her breathing. Her smell. Her words most of all.

A Burmese mountain tribe that has existed for thousands of years in perfect harmony with their environment.

They have discovered a way of equitably sharing resources, and subduing aggression. Both genders are equal, and the tribe is governed with an amazing democratic method.

'Take me to Myanmar,' he says softly.

'Really?'

'Please, that's my choice.'

Deep in Julian's heart is the overwhelming desire not just to atone for his sins but to redeem himself.

He looks out the window.

I want to pay her back, he thinks to himself. *I want to pay the whole world back.*

As he settles back on the seat he knows that, more than anything, he wants to see Leisel smile, one last time, even if it's only in his imagination.

* * *

The country house has settled into a pattern.

Today, as has become his habit, the prisoner eats lunch on the verandah, gazing out at the distant sea with the air of one born to privilege. Then, as far as his minders are concerned, he retires back to bed for his customary nap. The housekeeper knocks with a tray of coffee and cakes at three pm and, hearing no answer, assumes that his charge is fast asleep. He leaves the tray outside the door. There are a few whispered conversations about this longer-than-usual siesta over the course of the afternoon, as well as some poring over the hidden surveillance cameras that cover most of the room. The sleeping form of the man can clearly be seen.

One of the DRFS minders sums up the general feeling. 'He wants to sleep,' he says, 'let him go.'

No action is contemplated until dinner-time when, after a conference, the three guards knock on the door for several minutes with no response from inside. Finally, the senior agent present opens the door and steps inside.

Strange, the agents think to themselves, how what looked so natural through the camera looks so fake now, spare pillows and clothing bundled up under the cover.

The tousled hair looks realistic because it is real. The prisoner must have cut most of his long hair after lunch, then glued it with hair cream to the top of a rolled-up white towel.

Blank looks, swearing. The men move out to all corners of the compound. Searching the premises, going from one room to another, most of them realise that this is a mishap of the highest order, a career-ending mistake.

Thirty minutes of searching fails to find any sign. The Syrian has taken nothing. No clothes or toiletries. They have no choice but to tell London the scarcely credible news that the man, who still has not given an official name, managed to foil a high-level security detail and has left the premises. Such a man, they suggest, will surely stand out around here. He will be found in no time.

* * *

One mile away, the Syrian closes the end cubicle door in a modern brick public toilet adjacent to a children's playground. Behind the toilet bowl is a package, tightly wrapped in plastic. He opens the parcel and drops his clothes to the floor.

Ten minutes later he emerges, dressed like a hip-hop artist: tracksuit, gold necklace, huge sunglasses. A taxi pulls up and he gets in, talks in a perfect Cockney accent to the driver, giving an address in an East London suburb.

The flat, he knows from the preparations, is modest but clean. The kitchen will be stocked with three days' supply of food. In a drawer he will find yet another passport, in another name.

The driver studies him. 'Hey, are you one of those rappers or something?'

'Not exactly.'

'Are you famous?'

'Not yet.' He smiles. 'But soon.'

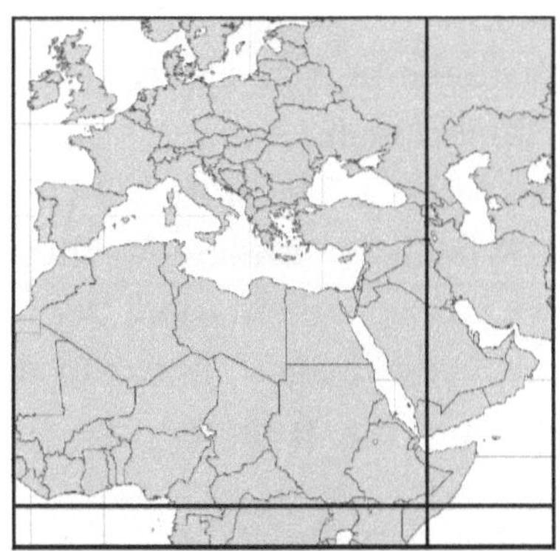

77 SOMALIA

Chakula Refugee Camp

Kifimbo brings the bus to a halt behind a hillside some twenty-five kilometres distant from the camp, near the border with Kenya. Of the coming calamity they have seen and heard nothing. The children settle down in the bus, laughing and chattering with excitement at this unexpected outing.

Opening the driver's door Kifimbo drops to the ground, stretches. He gathers sticks for a fire, lighting it away from the bus, squatting near the blaze on his haunches, letting the waving fingers and hands of flame warm his knees, his rifle propped against a forked stick nearby.

After a while the director leaves the bus, his footfalls clearly audible in the dry grass. Kifimbo looks up. 'The fire is good. Come and warm yourself.'

The director frowns, 'They told us that we are better off inside the bus, with the doors closed.'

'I would rather be here, under the sky.'

The director moves closer, holding his open palms towards the blaze. 'Thank you for helping us.'

'That's no problem.'

The two men share the heat in silence.

After a while Kifimbo realises that his jaw has begun to ache from being clenched so tight. The sound of children talking drifts over from the bus. 'What hope is there for these kids?' he asks.

'I don't know. We can give them food, but they need love.'

Kifimbo shuts his eyes. Images appear in the darkness. Hills. A lake. Mangos fresh and ripe from the tree. A thought occurs to him.

If they do not know beauty there is nothing to keep the darkness at bay.

The fire burns low, into black and orange coals that pulse with energy. The director goes back to the bus and his deep voice can be heard coaxing the children to sleep.

Kifimbo takes out his wallet. Inside is a photograph of his mother and father. He doesn't need sunlight to see them. He knows the picture intimately. Standing against the wall of a hut, his father wears an ill-fitting Western suit, his mother a yellow dress. Yellow hoop earrings hang from each ear. Her eyes are playful — a clue to her delight in living that filled his world as a child.

Kifimbo lifts the image to his lips, kisses it, then places the wallet on the earth beside him. Without knowing why, he begins to cry, racked by a shuddering reflex over which he has no control. In his mind he hears the shouting of angry men. Today people will die, others will be born. Terrible things will be done in the name of ideas.

Followers of one church will kill those of another. Fights erupt over territories and payments, and more men with guns will commit atrocities. More fanatics will roll hand grenades into crowded markets to kill and maim. Others will drop poison from the sky merely because their hatred has overwhelmed all reason.

At that moment, Kifimbo sees the world with frightening clarity. A bead of sweat runs down the slope of his cheek and onto his neck.

Standing, he picks up his rifle from where it leans against the forked stick, holding it upside down with the top of the receiver in the palm of his hand. He remembers reading that there are one billion guns, in a world obsessed with making and using them. It is time for there to be one less.

He unclips the magazine, works the action once so the round in the chamber pings away into the night. Then, his breath so loud in his ears it sounds like a sandstorm, he presses the other twenty-nine rounds from the magazine with his thumb. One at a time he flings them away.

In doing so, Kifimbo climbs back into a life that is a river and a tide, savage and beautiful. He lifts the empty weapon by the barrel and swings it against the ground three times before the stock cracks away from the barrel and chamber. Drops it to the ground, then strips the uniform from his body. Shirt, belt, then trousers.

Clad only in shorts, he walks to the door of the bus. The director meets him there, eyes wide with surprise. 'What are you doing?'

'I'm going home,' he says, 'to Kenya. I want to take Rajee with me.'

'Why?'

'He needs beauty. He will not find it here.'

The director's eyes study his for a moment, then, 'Wait.'

There is the sound of talking, protests, yet the director returns with a cloth bag packed full, and a sheet. 'There is formula in there. Diapers. Warm things for him. And a bottle. Do you know how to care for a child?'

'I am the oldest of seven brothers and sisters. Of course I do.'

The director lifts the red Nike T-shirt over his head and passes it across. Kifimbo accepts it gratefully. It is big on his slighter frame, but he has ceased to be a soldier. He will no longer wear the uniform.

One of the nurses brings Rajee, still sleeping, wrapped tightly in a blanket. Kifimbo takes the sheet from the director, ties it around his shoulders, expertly creating a pouch where Rajee will nestle.

When the sleeping child has settled comfortably, Kifimbo kisses the director on both cheeks and starts to walk away into the night. When the bus is a mere shadow in the distance behind him he stops, taking in the night sounds around him. There is nothing to be afraid of; a wart hog snuffling, a jackal's sharp cry out in the darkness. Rajee arches his back, yawns, then settles again.

At the core of his heart there is a lake, fringed by a trio of hills. The waters are caustic, seemingly lifeless, yet the mirror surface glows with living, vibrant colour.

In the shallows, one million flamingos wade. Their plumage is of a hundred shades. Pink, crimson, pale pastels. Splashes of blood-like red, patches of white. When they take to flight, their black-edged wings fill the sky. Curious, curved beaks reflect on the lake. Their cries echo from the hills.

Kifimbo stands for a moment, catching his breath, turning his face to the stars and moon as if drinking in their power. Then, Rajee asleep and warm against his body, he begins to walk. Away from the camp, away from death, towards the lake, where above the shining waters one million flamingos take to flight.

Acknowledgements

I'd like to thank:

Brian Cook, my tireless and supportive agent, Anna Valdinger my publisher (and first, insightful editor), Kathy Hassett, (my friend at court and the most organised person in the world), publicists Jane Finemore and Nicola Woods, Matt Stanton, the man behind my beautiful covers, and Shona Martyn who brings it all together. Sarah Fletcher for her caring and thorough approach to editing. I supplied the wet cement, but Sarah hammered in the formwork and the steel to reinforce it. Thanks also to Sarah Barrett, Sarah Haines, Michael White, Mark Higginson, Mark Curnow, Melanie Saward, Renee Tisdell and all the other staff at HarperCollins Australia.

Thanks to my wife Catriona. I'm so lucky to share my life with someone who loves books and literature so deeply. My sons Daly and James, the metal stuff was for you. Thanks Mum and Dad, I love how you never stop trying to convert people to my cause. To my brothers and sisters: Leanne, Maree, David and Fiona, thanks so much. The extended family: (deep breath) Brian, Cameron, Shannon, Jenny, Duncan, Suzannah, Peter, Andrew, Michelle, Chris, Adam, Dylan, Daniel, Jason, Amanda, Jess, Samantha, Courtney, Barbara, Doug, Max, Vicky, Bronte, Crawford, Elaine and Reg. You have all been incredibly supportive, and I know I'm lucky to be part of such a great crowd.

Thanks to Mark Shepherd who came up with the idea of the maps at the start of each chapter, and, along with Lisa Hall, provided valuable feedback on my first draft. Thanks to early readers Dave Barron and Rob West. Thanks to Katana, who was so hospitable and eager to share his knowledge in Kenya. To Upulie Divisekera who advised me on the ingredients of growth media for bacteria, Anne Treasure who was able to tell me what brand of gin an alcoholic would drink! Chris Martin who explained some intricacies of corporate database systems. To Laurie Whiddon of Map Illustrations in Sydney who so kindly provided the maps.

To the friends who rallied around after the release of Rotten Gods: David Hall, Sam West, Maggie and Jim Christenson, Kerryn Taylor, Bruce Swain, Michael, Claire and Tara Martin, Kylie Reavley, Steve Flockton, Phil and Fiona Grace, Steve Johns, Sarah Landers, Jenny Brownhill, Lyn Dundas, Brett and Tina Moore, Lucy Shepherd, Tony and Leanne Buckley, Ruth Buys, Nick Lambert, Bev Snook, Fiona Waddy, Ashlee Sinclair, Julie Gooch, Rowan and Jude Kallmier, Jackie Blair, Mary Bayou, Julie, Izabella, Lucia, Juanita, Ron and Margaret Martin, Ged and Di Clohesy, Mark and Paul Daffey, Steve and Nicky Russell, Lisa Heenan, Darren Doherty, Lindy Haigh, John Carroll. Thanks to John, Pat, Anne, Helen, Austin, Mary and Ian Poynten.

Thanks to everyone who has made contact on social media. It's so much fun for a writer to have direct contact with readers. It's like having thousands of friends, thank you.

Thanks to every book shop owner in Australia and New Zealand for working so hard to get my books into the hands of readers. Visiting your shops and meeting you and your customers has been one of the highlights of the last year for me.

Finally, thanks to my growing circle of writer friends; a conspiracy of devoted readers and writers who know how much we depend on each other. Happy writing!

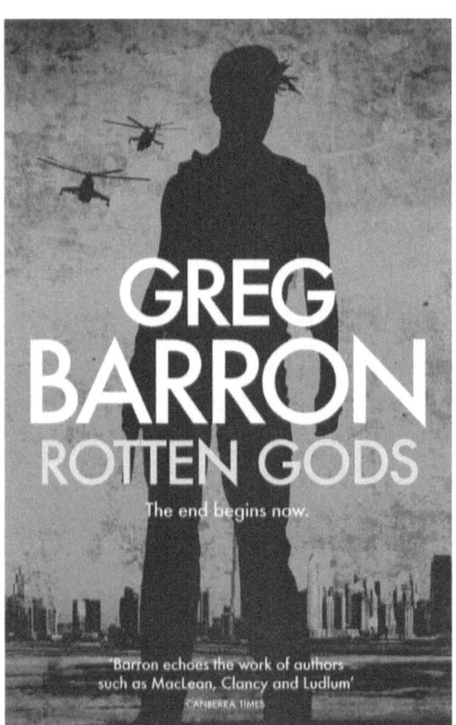

GREG BARRON
ROTTEN GODS
The end begins now.
'Barron echoes the work of authors
such as MacLean, Clancy and Ludlum'
CANBERRA TIMES

Rotten Gods

by Greg Barron

It took seven days to create the world ... now they have seven days to save it

Extremists hijack the conference centre where heads of state have gathered in an attempt to bring society back from the brink of global catastrophe, and the clock starts ticking: seven days until certain death for presidents and prime ministers alike, unless the terrorists' radical demands are met.

Marika, an Australian intelligence officer, Isabella, a treasonous British diplomat, Simon, an airline pilot searching for his missing daughters, and Madoowbe, a mysterious Somali agent, are all forced to examine their motives, faith and beliefs as they attempt to stave off disaster, hurtling towards the deadline and a shattering climax.

Rotten Gods is both an imaginative tour de force and a dire warning, holding the reader spellbound until the last breathtaking page.

'A superlative political thriller'
Rob Minshull, ABC

'Barron has written a thriller that entertains but
also for those wanting more, a thought-provoking
polemic'
Daily Telegraph